EARTH SHADOWS

EARTH SHADOWS

EARTHRISE BOOK V

DANIEL ARENSON

CHAPTER ONE

The brand sizzled.

Addy screamed.

"You sons of bitches!" she shouted, spraying saliva. "I'm going to carve open your skulls and piss in 'em!"

The creature pulled the brand back. The ugly red mark hissed on her hip.

"Prime meat. Lord Malphas will find you delicious." The alien chuckled, then shoved Addy forward. "Move along."

Addy tugged up her pants, hiding the burning brand. She snarled at the marauder, this bloated creature of claws and fangs and stench.

"I never forget a face." She pointed at the warty creature. "And your ugly mug is particularly memorable. Someday I will kill you. Painfully. Know this."

The alien lifted a crackling prod. He shoved it against Addy, and electricity raced across her. She screamed.

"Move down the line!" The marauder brandished the prod. "Or you'll taste this again."

Cursing, trembling, and sweating, Addy moved. Thousands of other humans, the survivors of Haven, stood here in a line. The colony lay in ruin around them. Skyscrapers lay toppled. Burnt homes smoldered. Rubble covered the streets. A crashed Firebird still smoked nearby, a charred skeleton in the cockpit.

All along the line, the marauders sneered, drooled, and licked their jaws. They were as big as horses, but far less pleasant. Six legs grew from their bodies, covered with spikes and tipped with claws. Their jaws could swallow men whole. The skulls of vanquished enemies, dozens of species, clattered atop their bloated abdomens, forming ritualistic armor.

They made the scum look cute.

And they were hungry. Hungry for human flesh.

We're not prisoners of war to them, Addy thought. *We're cattle.*

"Move it!" A marauder lifted a prod. "Faster!"

More electricity crackled across Addy. She yowled and moved faster. An old woman trudged ahead of her, barely keeping up. A boy wept behind Addy, calling for his mother. The line of captives stretched for kilometers. With New Earth's foggy atmosphere, Addy could not see its beginning or end.

She looked skyward, hoping to see the *Saint Brendan* swooping in to rescue her. But Captain Ben-Ari's ship was gone. The Firebirds tasked with defending Haven were gone. All she saw was ravagers covering the sky.

Had the marauders taken Marco and the other Dragons captive too? Had her friends died in the cave? Or had they escaped without her? Addy didn't know which of those three options was worse. Each possibility made her cringe.

If you're captive here, Marco, I'll find you, she thought. *If you're dead, I'll mourn you. And if you escaped without me, I'll fucking kill you.*

The line took her past the burning husk of a warship, a vessel as large as an apartment building. Marauders were spraying webs over it, dousing the flames. Two of the beasts emerged from within the ship, goading forward two bleeding soldiers, survivors of the crash. The men's hands were raised, their faces bleeding. Addy looked away, jaw clenched. She wondered if these creatures were attacking Earth too, if her planet still stood. The great Human Defense Force, the army that had defeated the scum, had been drastically downsized since that devastating and costly war. Did any humans still fight?

"Move it, meat!" a marauder grumbled, and a prod slammed into the old lady in front of Addy. The woman screamed and collapsed.

"Grandma!" Addy said, kneeling above her.

"Move it!" A marauder grabbed Addy, claws tightening around her arms, and yanked her up. "Down the line."

"She's hurt!" Addy said, glaring into the alien's four bulging eyes. "You son of a--"

The baton crackled across Addy. "Move!"

She screamed as the electricity washed over her. She lost control of her bladder. Hot piss ran down her legs. The marauder pulled back his baton and shoved her down the line. Addy tried to dodge the fallen woman, but she stumbled, crushing the woman's wrist underfoot. The other captives followed, trampling the grandmother. More bones snapped. Addy could only pray that the old lady died quickly.

The march took Addy past her old apartment building, the place where she had lived with Marco for two years. The top few stories had fallen, including their apartment. Marauder webs coated the rest, and the aliens were scuttling across them. It had been a difficult two years, living in that cage, watching Marco spiral into the depression and madness of shell shock. But Addy missed those days now.

We were alive. We were together. Tears filled her eyes. *Now I don't know if I'll see you again, Poet.*

"Move!"

The humans marched on, leaving the ruins behind. They entered a field where the rubble had been swept aside. Scattered fires burned, and metal poles rose from the ground, tall as electrical towers. Webs stretched between these jagged monoliths, and marauders crawled across them, overlooking the smoldering plain. Massive alien vessels stood ahead, rising from mist, boxes of metal the size of warehouses. Alien starships, Addy surmised. They were built from the same dark, jagged metal as ravagers but were much larger. They looked more like transport vessels than warships. The line of human prisoners stretched across the field, leading toward the cubicle ships.

Addy trudged across the field. Some people still wore their atmosuits, but Addy had lost her breathing mask during the fight. The acidic air of New Earth stung her lungs and burned her mouth. With every step now, she was coughing. Some of the homeless on New Earth survived without masks, but never for long, and Addy felt the ash fill her lungs. Her head spun from the low oxygen, and even in the shivering cold, sweat soaked her. Mud rose around her ankles. The corpse of a child lay before her, its face gone, trampled into the mud. A broken school bus smoldered nearby, human skeletons within it. Addy knelt, lifted a stuffed animal from the mud, and yowled as a marauder jabbed her back with claws. She marched on, moving toward the massive ships.

"Undress, humans!" a marauder cackled, dangling from a web between metal poles. A red triangle was painted onto his forehead, denoting his rank of command. "We burn your flea-infested clothes."

"Clothes off!" shouted another marauder, clattering toward them on six legs. "You stink of parasites."

The humans stood, staring around, hesitant. Claws reached out, grabbing clothes, ripping them off. People shouted. One man fought back, hurling stones. The marauders grabbed him, knocked him into the dirt, and ripped off his arms.

"Clothes off!" rumbled the marauder on the web.

A few humans, weeping, began to undress. Others still struggled, only for claws to shred their clothes.

Fuck this shit, Addy thought, fists clenched. *They captured me. They branded me. They destroyed my city. The clothes on my back are all I have left.*

As marauders moved across the line, ripping clothes off prisoners, Addy took a deep breath.

Here goes nothing.

She burst into a run.

She made it only twenty meters across the field before a web shot out, lassoed her legs, and knocked her down.

Addy screamed. Her face hit the mud. A marauder began reeling her back, spooling the sticky strand around his front legs. Addy dragged through the mud. She kicked, floundered, and scratched at the webbing, but she couldn't free herself. When she reached the marauder, the creature yanked her up. His jaws opened before her, bathing her with the stench of rancid meat. A human arm hung between his teeth.

"A saucy one . . ." The marauder's tongue emerged, lined with teeth like a chainsaw. He licked her cheek. She grimaced and looked away. "Delectable. I will enjoy feasting on your flesh."

"Huckshaw!" The voice boomed from behind, and another marauder advanced. "This one is branded." The alien tugged Addy's pants down her hip, revealing the brand. "She is for the table of Lord Malphas himself. Not for us to eat."

Staring at this new marauder, fury exploded through Addy. She knew him.

He was larger than the others, and a crest of black horns grew from his head. A red triangle, denoting his high rank, was painted onto his scaly forehead. But mostly Addy recognized the parasitic twin, a deformity the size of a toddler, that twitched on the marauder's side. The twisted creature stared at her, snapping tiny jaws.

You're the marauder who captured me in the cave, Addy thought, tugging her pants back up. *You're the one who stole me away from Marco. I remember.*

"But Master Orcus!" The first marauder, the one who had licked Addy, whined at his deformed superior. "Malphas has many to feed upon. Let me break this one. Let us feast on her together! We will enjoy her fear, and--"

Orcus--the marauder with the parasitic twin--lashed his claws, smacking down the smaller Huckshaw. The hungry marauder whimpered and fled. The parasitic twin growing from Orcus's side laughed.

Orcus advanced toward Addy, eyes narrowing. Intelligent eyes. Eyes filled with unending cruelty. He grabbed Addy, ripped off the webs that bound her, and shoved her back into the line.

"You are lords' meat." Orcus hissed, and his nostrils flared, inhaling her scent. The parasitic twin snapped his jaws, desperate to bite her. "I can see why, delicious one. You smell of such delectable fear. Now off with your clothes."

Growing from his side, the parasitic twin cackled. "Off, off!"

The claws reached out to tear Addy's clothes--her old security guard uniform.

"No!" she said. "I'll do it."

She undressed, eyes dry, staring blankly ahead. She was not shy. She had been naked in public while in the army, showering with dozens of soldiers. Her body was still strong, her limbs long and well-muscled. Scars, old and new, covered her--

some from the war against the scum a few years ago, others new, the work of these marauders. The ugly brand, marking her as prime meat, still sizzled on her hip, bits of cloth and mud clinging to the wound. Tattoos covered her arms: the Maple Leafs logo she had inked there in high school, the symbols of platoons she had served in, and a star for every scum she had killed. At twenty-five, battle hardened, Addy no longer had the soft, slender body she had joined the army with at eighteen. She had the body of a warrior. A survivor.

And I will survive this, she vowed. *If the others still live, I will find them. And I will fight again. Today I am a prisoner of war. But I am still a soldier.*

The marauders piled up the prisoners' clothes and burned them. The smoke stung Addy's eyes and nostrils, and sparks sizzled against her skin. The aliens shoved the naked humans farther down the line, closer toward the towering ships.

Halfway across the field, they paused again. Tall, slender marauders worked with razor-sharp claws, shearing the prisoners' hair. Addy grimaced, caught in their grip, as they shaved her head. She had always prided herself on her hair, long and smooth and the color of dawn. She had never cared much about beauty; her hips were too wide, her nose too big, and her body was now too scarred. She had always cared more about her strength than her looks. But her hair had been her one source of pride. Now the aliens burned it in the piles. They sent her onward, her head shaved, her scalp nicked and trickling blood.

The other prisoners walked with her. Children. Mothers with babies. Old men and women. Captive soldiers. All were naked. All were shaved bald, their scalps bleeding. Sheep to the slaughter. They moved into the shade of the metal cargo barges, ships the size of cathedrals.

"Now into the ship!" rumbled a marauder. "Go! In, meat! Move!"

The prods crackled. Prisoners screamed. One by one, they climbed a metal ramp, entering the jagged alien starship.

"Move!" A marauder jabbed Addy in the small of her back, and she screamed as the electricity shocked her. "Inside!"

She could not stop herself.

Naked, bald, beaten, she knelt and grabbed a stone. She hurled it against the marauder.

"Fight!" Addy shouted. "Humans, fight them! With tooth and nail, fight!"

Her stone hit a marauder in the eye. The creature roared. A few other humans raised bricks, remnants of toppled houses, and tossed them.

"Fuck the aliens!" shouted a man.

"Fight, fight, for humanity!" cried a woman, leaping toward a marauder with a shard of metal fished out from the mud.

Most people here were elders and children, but many too were veterans. With Addy, they hurled stones. They shouted. They raised sticks from the mud.

"The scum butchered us!" Addy shouted. "We will never more be butchered. Never again!"

"Never again!" they cried.

Yet even bullets could not penetrate the marauders' skin. The stones and sticks bounced harmlessly off the aliens. Claws grabbed one man, lacerated his hands, and scattered fingers into the mud. A woman screamed, leaped onto a marauder, scratched at his eyes, and died in the creature's jaws. Sticky webs lassoed Addy, pinning her arms to her sides. The aliens shoved her along the line.

"You're lucky you're prime meat," a marauder hissed into her ear. His rancid breath made her gag, and he licked her from her navel to her shaved scalp. "Otherwise I'd be feasting on your brain right now."

"Yeah, well, I was always a C student, so I'd probably give you indigestion."

The marauder struck her. She grimaced as a claw scraped her cheek.

"Still you jest. Still you don't understand. But soon you will beg, human. Soon you will beg for mercy."

The claws shoved her onto the ramp, and Addy found herself entering the dark ship.

Her breath froze. Her heart sank. Even as a hardened veteran, she shivered.

Many decks filled the ship, stacked one atop the other, rising up into shadows. A network of webs provided access between them. Each deck was just a slab of metal, wide and flat like shelves in a closet. The marauders were moving everywhere, climbing up and down shafts, herding the humans onto the decks.

Hundreds of prisoners were already here, crowding together in the shadows. The air was hot, rancid, and soupy.

A marauder with gray horns scuttled down a web, grabbed Addy's head, and sniffed her skull. He barked something at another marauder, this one burly and dark, who wrapped Addy with a web. She floundered, shouting and scratching, as the creature scuttled up the strands, carrying her to the third deck. There the alien shoved her deep into the ship.

"Stand with the others," the marauder said, saliva dripping. "At the back. Move!"

Grumbling and tugging off the cobwebs, Addy shuffled farther along the deck. The floor was raw metal, and the shadows were thick. Webs stretched along the ceiling, allowing marauders to scuttle back and forth. The skulls glued to their backs brushed Addy's head, and she grimaced at the thought of her own skull, carved open, glued onto one of these beasts.

So that Lord Malphas asshole thinks he can eat my brain, Addy thought. *Takeout all the way from Haven.* She coiled her hands into fists. *I won't let him. I'll die fighting if I must.*

The marauders goaded her to the back of the ship, where Addy joined hundreds of other prisoners. The marauders kept cramming more and more humans in. Soon people were pressing up against Addy, naked and sweaty and trembling. The heat became intolerable, and the stench of human sweat filled the air.

"We can't breathe!" shouted a woman.

"We need room!" cried a man.

The marauders laughed, spat from above, and lowered their prods. People screamed. A woman fell near Addy, crackling with electricity. Addy had no room to kneel. She reached down, grabbed the woman's hand, and tried to pull her up. The marauders kept shoving more prisoners in. Elbows and shoulders hit Addy, knocking her back. Feet trampled the fallen woman, and a bone snapped.

"A woman is down!" Addy shouted. "She has no room to stand!"

The marauders kept shoving humans in. More feet trampled the fallen woman. More bones snapped. The fallen woman screamed, then fell silent as a foot hit her neck. And still the marauders shoved captives onto the deck.

Soon they were too crammed to move at all. Damp bodies pressed against Addy from every side. A potbellied man shoved against her back. A child trembled at her side, crushed between people, struggling to breathe. A woman stood at her front, pressed against her.

"Enough!" Addy shouted. "We can't breathe!"

The marauders only laughed. And still they shoved more people in.

Addy couldn't breathe. The child beside her passed out, but prisoners pinned the boy in place, and he remained standing. New prisoners joined the deck, shoving against them. Somebody tried to fight back, managed to carve open some space, but fell and screamed underfoot, trampled by the others. The people pressed so tightly against Addy now that they were crushing her.

One woman, shorter than her, had her face crushed against a man's chest, gasping for air. Addy was thankful for her height; she was tall enough to breathe above most prisoners, but even that air was stale, putrid, hot. An old man collapsed, pinned between a few prisoners, finally falling down. The corpse soon cracked under the captives' feet.

For hours they stood here, flesh against flesh. Sweat, blood, and urine formed a foul miasma, and one prisoner vomited. Finally, it seemed, the marauders had filled the ship to capacity.

A cattle car, Addy thought. *That's all this is. We're meat in a can.*

She suddenly felt guilty for eating all that Spam.

"Where are they taking us?" whispered a girl nearby.

"To a good place," her mother answered, her arms pinned to her sides.

A graying man chuckled nearby, madness in his rheumy eyes. "To the slaughter!" He cackled. "To the slaughter, to the slaughter!"

"Silence!" rumbled a marauder that clung to the ceiling, and claws lashed down, ripping the man's lips. The prisoner kept cackling, blood spurting from his mouth.

A child by Addy collapsed, eyes rolling back. Addy managed to free an arm, grab the girl, and hoist her up. The child gasped for breath.

"Help me!" Addy whispered to those beside her. "Get her on my shoulders!"

The prisoners worked together, finally managing to squeeze the girl out from the mass of human flesh, to place her on Addy's shoulders. The child clutched Addy's head, trembling, ducking whenever the scum scuttled above. A woman nearby was swooning, and Addy wrapped her arms around her, pulling her close, forming a pocket of air--only two or three centimeters wide--for the woman to breathe.

I can't kill these marauders yet, Addy thought. *But maybe I can save a life or two. That's all I can do now.* She cringed. *Oh, Marco, where are you?*

Metallic booms sounded deep in the ship. The vessel jolted. Engines rumbled. The child on Addy's shoulders clutched her, weeping. The transport ship shook, tilted, and people fell. At the edges of the deck, some prisoners hit the wall, and others slammed into them, crushing them. Blood spilled. Another person vomited. The engines roared, louder, louder, and the deck trembled, and the air grew hotter, scorching. Sweat soaked Addy. Sitting on her shoulders, the girl lost control of her bladder, and the piss dripped across Addy's body, mingling with her sweat, sizzling against her brand.

With thrumming metal and roaring fury, the massive ship began to rise.

There were no viewports here, no portholes, no way to see the outside world. But there was no mistaking the immense pressure shoving the prisoners down. Many collapsed, others falling atop them. Addy fell to one knee, and the girl on her shoulders suddenly felt as heavy as a sumo wrestler. They struggled for air. Prisoners fell around Addy, knocked against her, and an elbow hit her teeth. Addy tasted blood.

Finally--weightlessness.

They floated up from the ground, hit the walls, hit the sticky ceiling, hovered in the cramped deck.

"We're in space," somebody said. "Where are they taking us?"

"To Earth?" somebody asked. "Are we going home?"

The old man with the lacerated lips laughed again, and his voice echoed through the ship.

"To the slaughter! To the slaughter!"

Floating upward, Addy grabbed a strand of web. Other prisoners bumped into her and one another. She narrowed her eyes and gritted her teeth.

No, she thought. *Not to the slaughter.* She sneered, struggling for air. *To war.*

CHAPTER TWO

They trundled through space, two limping ships. Inside them-- four battered refugees, the hope of humanity on their shoulders. Behind them--relentless, endlessly cruel, the enemy followed.

"Fuck me, this is boring." Lailani yawned. "I wanna fight! Captain, if I may make a suggestion? Let's turn around, charge at those bastards, and take them head on."

Marco cringed. "If I may make a suggestion--shush, Lailani."

The slender Filipina swiveled her chair toward him and placed her hands on her hips. "I was talking to the captain, not to you, *gunner*. Unless you plan a mutiny, that means Ben-Ari." Lailani furrowed her brow and tapped her cheek. "Are you planning a mutiny? Because that would totally alleviate my boredom. Yes." She nodded. "Let's mutiny! First order of the day: pizza night every night!"

Sitting in the commander's seat, Ben-Ari ignored the two sergeants. She kept checking the instruments, hitting keys, adjusting dials, and frowning at the controls. The captain still hadn't changed out of her prison jumpsuit, and the handcuffs still dangled from her left wrist. Marco had never dared asked what had happened to the prison guard on the other end.

"They're gaining on us," Ben-Ari mumbled under her breath. "How can they be gaining on us?"

The bridge of the HDFS *Saint Brendan* was small and cluttered. Here was not a large warship, not like the *Miyari* which had once transported Marco to the frontier, certainly not like the cavernous *Urchin* he had served on during Operation Neptune a few years ago. Three seats close together--one for the commander, one for the gunner, one for the navigator. An array of control panels and viewports. There was some room to get up, stretch, and pace, but not much, and not without banging into one control panel or another.

The three companions had been crammed in here for hours now, watching the enemy slowly gain on them. Marco glanced up at the monitor above Lailani's head. It showed the position of the *Saint Brendan*, a green dot, traveling through space. Smaller lights showed annotated stars streaming by. Beside the ship appeared a second dot--it symbolized the *Anansi*, the commandeered ravager that Kemi now flew. Farther back, at the edge of the monitor, Marco saw them. Twenty-two dots, clustered together--the enemy ravagers.

"Those bastards have been following us all the way from Haven," he muttered. "And I have a feeling they'll follow us to the edge of the universe."

Ben-Ari finally raised her eyes from her monitor. A loose braid hung across her shoulder, and she gave it a few nervous tugs. "Damn it! Nothing I do seems to work. The stealth engines are busted." She groaned. "I'm putting on my space suit. I'm grabbing my toolbox. And I'm going out there to fix the damn thing."

"Ma'am, taking a space walk at warp speed is highly dangerous," Marco said. "Spacetime is curved around us. It messes with your sense of dimensions, of reality itself. And if you stray too far out of the bubble, you--"

"I'm aware, Sergeant," Ben-Ari snapped, but then her voice softened. "If I'm curt, I'm sorry, but I've barely slept since busting out of prison several days ago, I'm still covered in alien blood, I still haven't had five minutes to change into a uniform, and there are twenty-two enemy ships gaining on us. They're only a light-year away now. In warped space, that's nothing. We need that stealth engine working." She rose from her seat. "Emery, de la Rosa, the bridge is yours. Call me on the comm if anything happens. I'll be out there, trying to fix the stealth cloak."

With that, for the first time since fleeing Haven, Ben-Ari stepped off the bridge.

For a moment, Marco and Lailani were silent.

Finally Lailani turned to him and whispered, "Now's our chance to mutiny!"

Marco sighed. "No."

Lailani hopped in her seat. "But I'm bored!"

"Well, load up the stealth engine manuals and learn how to fix them."

"I tried that already!" Lailani rolled her eyes. "They're busted. They're busted good. They need to be replaced. The captain won't be able to fix them."

Marco blew out his breath. "Not that they'd do us any good anyway. The *Anansi* doesn't even have a stealth cloak, and Kemi is sticking out like a sore thumb in that thing."

He turned to look out the porthole. There it flew, only meters away from the *Saint Brendan*, staying close enough to fly within their bubble of warped spacetime. The *Anansi* was twice the size of the *Saint Brendan*, a dark, jagged ravager, built by and for marauders. It had its own warp drive, but now it was sharing its funnel with the *Brendan*; left to bend spacetime on its own, a single hiccup from Kemi could send it millions of kilometers off course.

Marco hit a few buttons, hailing Kemi. Her face appeared on the monitor before him.

"Hey, Kems, how are you holding up?" Marco said.

She looked up at him, bleary-eyed. A yawn split her face. A bandanna held back her mane of black curls, and sweat glistened on her dark skin. In each hand, she held a shower curtain ring which was attached to a strand of marauder webbing. Several more shower curtain rings dangled around her. Her seat, ripped out from the *Brendan*, hung in the web. Normally, giant space-bugs with six legs piloted the *Anansi*, but with a few tweaks, they had built a human interface.

"I'm hot and tired," Kemi said, "but holding up. Wish this ship had a good air conditioner and sound system. A fridge full of cupcakes would be nice too."

Lailani leaned across Marco and peered into the monitor. She waved. "Hey, Kemi, want to help us mutiny while Ben-Ari is out on her space walk?"

Kemi's eyes widened. "The captain is out on a space walk? Marco, did you tell her it's dangerous?"

He nodded. "Yes, but you know our captain. She lives off danger like a grunt lives off Spam."

At the thought of Spam, he cringed. Addy had loved the stuff. Addy--taken captive by the marauders. Addy--his best friend, the person he loved most in the world. A prisoner of war.

Kemi seemed to see his pain. "We'll get her back, Marco. We'll find the Ghost Fleet. We'll raise that armada and defeat the marauders. And we'll get Addy back. I promise you."

Marco nodded, his throat too tight for words. His eyes stung. He hadn't stopped thinking about Addy since losing her. He kept seeing it over and over--the marauders wrapping her in a web, carrying her into their ship.

I'm sorry, Addy. I'm so sorry we left without you. I'm coming back for you--with help. I won't rest until you're back with me.

"Let me know when you're ready to switch, Kemi," Marco said. "I'll take a shift."

Kemi nodded. "Soon. I'll fly for another hour." She yawned again. "We just need to figure out the autopilot on this thing."

Marco glanced back at the monitor above Lailani's head. The enemy was closer now. He didn't know if they even had an hour.

"Fuckers," Lailani said, staring at the green dots with him.

"So this Ghost Fleet is still far, huh?" Marco said.

Lailani nodded. "Far. Very far. Farther than any human has ever flown. It'll take us months to reach the Cat's Eye Nebula where the fleet should be. And those marauders will catch us sometime today, if they keep moving this fast." She nodded. "We take 'em on. Only way. We blast 'em apart."

"Two ships against twenty?" Marco said.

Lailani shrugged. "We faced worse odds against the scum."

"I'd rather face a million scum than one marauder." Marco shuddered. "Lailani, those creatures . . . they're smart. Smarter than the scum. Maybe smarter than humans. Big and strong as bulls. The scum spent fifty years trying to defeat us and failed. The marauders conquered Earth within a few days. No." He shook his head. "We can't face them. Not without help. Not without the Ghost Fleet."

"We might not have a choice, unless Ben-Ari can fix the stealth cloak." Lailani drew her pistol. "I won't go down without a fight, though. You can be sure of that." Suddenly tears were flowing down her cheeks. "Those buggers killed Sofia, the woman I loved. They kidnapped Addy, my best friend. They destroyed Manila, my hometown, and they conquered my planet. I hate them, Marco. I fucking hate them. I will kill as many as I can before they take me down."

Marco reached across a control panel and clasped her hand. Lailani was fierce, brave, deadly, and yet her hand was so slender, so small in his.

"Not all is lost," Marco said. "I might have an idea." He winced. "Ben-Ari might not like it, but--"

"Is it mutiny?" Lailani's eyes lit up, and she wiped her tears away.

Marco smiled grimly. "Worse. Ben-Ari would prefer mutiny, I think."

A voice crackled to life from the speakers. Ben-Ari's voice. "I can hear you, you know."

A tap sounded beside him. Marco glanced outside the porthole. Ben-Ari was outside the ship now, clinging to its hull. She nodded at him through the porthole, then kept pulling herself across the hull. The starlight streamed around the captain, stretched along the curve of spacetime. A toolbox dangled from her hip. Marco switched the view on his monitor, watching her work. She held tools in one hand, a manual in the other, and her tongue stuck out in concentration.

As Ben-Ari toiled, cursing and grumbling, Marco kept considering his plan. It was crazy. Ben-Ari would hate it, but . . .

"The damn thing is busted," Ben-Ari finally said, her voice crackling through the speakers. "The hull is too dented. The light-reflector coating is all scraped off. The gears and controls are fried. We ain't getting back stealth without a visit to a shipyard, and there's no shipyard for light-years around. I'm coming back aboard. Emery, de la Rosa, meeting in the galley in ten minutes. I want to hear Emery's plan."

"See you there, ma'am," Marco said.

Like every cabin on the *Saint Brendan*, the galley--the ship's kitchen--was cramped, barely larger than a closet. Marco was wondering why Ben-Ari had called the meeting here, rather than the larger crew quarters, when he saw the captain stumble in and make a beeline to the coffee machine. During the First Galactic War, commonly known as the Scum War, Marco had often thought Einav Ben-Ari to be inhuman--remarkably calm under fire, wise, all-knowing, the exemplary officer. For the first time, perhaps, he was seeing her human frailty. Bags hung under her eyes, her cheeks were pale, and when she sipped the coffee, she let out the smallest of grateful sighs.

"They never gave me coffee in prison," she said softly. "I missed coffee."

She spent two years in a prison cell, Marco remembered. All because she had warned humanity about the marauders. And as soon as she had escaped, she landed in this mess. Marco could barely imagine the fortitude Ben-Ari needed just to keep functioning, let alone lead them to hope.

That is why she leads us, he thought. *Because she is the strongest among us.*

When everyone had their coffee, they connected the galley's monitor to the *Anansi*. Kemi's face appeared on the screen, looking even wearier than before. Sitting in the marauder web inside the ravager, she gazed at their coffee in envy.

"Anyone want to do a little space walk and bring me a mocha latte?" the pilot said.

"You mean ravagers don't come equipped with coffee bars?" Marco said. "What has the galaxy come to?"

Ben-Ari frowned. "Enough jokes." She turned to Lailani. "De la Rosa, give me your latest report."

Lailani swallowed her mouthful of coffee. "Captain, it's hard to estimate the ravagers' speed in warped space. They're traveling in a different warp than ours, and things get screwy when you bend the laws of physics. I'm no physicist, but I learned a thing or two while in the Oort Cloud. I know how to look at distant lights. One thing I know for sure: They're moving faster than we are. Not much faster, but sooner or later, they'll catch us. If we're lucky, we have five hours. If we're unlucky, we have two hours, maybe even one. Then we'll have a good ol' fashioned space battle on our hands."

Ben-Ari nodded. "And it'll be months before we can reach any help." She turned toward Marco. "Sergeant, about your plan?"

Marco suddenly felt silly. "It's . . . a bad idea." He stared into his cup of coffee. "It won't work."

"Emery, right now, unless you have a working stealth engine in your pocket, I'm open to any ideas. Even bad ones." The captain stared into his eyes, her gaze penetrating. "Talk to me."

He nodded and gulped. "All right, here goes. We have two ships here, right? The *Saint Brendan* we're in and the *Anansi* which Kemi is flying. The marauders, I imagine, are mostly interested in the *Brendan*--a human ship, *our* ship. So we all join Kemi. We climb aboard the *Anansi*. And we release the ravager into regular spacetime like a piece of junk. Meanwhile, we set the empty *Brendan* on autopilot. With any luck, the marauders will keep following the *Brendan*, thinking we're still inside. At most, they might send a couple ravagers after the *Anansi*. We can even let the *Anansi* drift like a piece of space debris, making it look abandoned. That makes our odds much better if it comes to a fight. Also, I bet anything the *Anansi* can beat the *Brendan* for speed, once we improve its rig. We already know ravagers are faster than human ships."

Both Ben-Ari and Lailani were staring at him, silent.

"Let me get this clear, Sergeant," Ben-Ari said. "Are you suggesting that we discard my ship--my beloved, beautiful ship?"

"Let me get this clear, Poet," Lailani said. "Are you suggesting that we spend months seeking the Ghost Fleet flying inside an alien deathtrap?"

Marco cleared his throat. "As I said, it's not a very good plan."

For another long moment, the two women were silent.

Finally Ben-Ari spoke. "Emery, your plan is the most reckless, stupid, and insane plan I have ever heard from any soldier. Ever." She sighed. "Unfortunately, it's also the best plan we have right now."

Lailani groaned, leaned back, and crossed her arms behind her head. "Ditch the best human spaceship still flying? Rattle around for thousands of light-years in a box of spider webs?" She sighed. "Fine! Fuck it. I'm game."

Kemi's voice emerged through the speakers, grainy. "Captain, I'm not so sure about this. I've been flying this machine for hours now, but I'm just flying visually. My portable computer here doesn't let me do much more than talk to the *Saint Brendan*. If the marauders have any computer system of their own installed here, I can't figure it out. All I can really control is the steering and thrust. Tracking, navigation, sensors, all that good stuff . . ." Kemi shook her head. "Nothing."

"Is there no way we can learn how to operate the ravager's own computers?" Ben-Ari said.

Kemi exhaled wearily, blowing back a strand of hair. "I'm not even sure this ship *has* computers, Captain. The whole thing is weird. The marauders might look like hideous zombie spiders, but they're more similar to humans than the scum were. Like us humans, they think individually rather than using hive intelligence. Like us humans, they communicate with words and facial expressions, rather than with pheromones like the scum. So in a sense, we're lucky. Their ships are a lot more similar to ours than scum pods. But they're also pretty damn alien. The screens are spherical, for one. And the controls are a network of strands I can barely figure out. Imagine playing the most complex guitar in the world, one with hundreds of strings, controlling software written in a language you don't speak. Captain, without the *Brendan* nearby for me to interface into, I'd be flying the ravager blind. In short, we can fly the *Anansi*, but not navigate." Through the monitor, she made eye contact with Marco. "I don't think your plan will work."

"Hang on." Marco paced the galley--at least, as much as the cramped room allowed. "I'm no Noodles, but after Abaddon, I spent three years as a computer technician in the army. I installed and fixed computers on starships too. Kemi, you already have one computer on the *Anansi*."

"Just this simple tablet," she said. "All it can do is talk to you. And play the odd game of Snake or Goblin Bowling."

"But we can move more computers over," Marco said. "The computers on the *Saint Brendan* are actually quite small. And every computer is redundant. The way humans have a backup lung and a backup kidney, we build our warships to have backup computers. I can uninstall half the *Brendan*'s computers and move them over. We can bring batteries to power them. And the *Anansi* must have some power generator; before the batteries die, we can figure out how to plug into it."

Ben-Ari frowned and stared around the galley. "We'll need more than computers. The *Brendan* has sensors too. Telescopes. Radio dishes. Lots of hardware. We might be able to move some of it over. The navigational systems I can probably move. We might have to duct tape them onto the *Anansi*'s hull, but . . ." She nodded. "We might just be able to navigate on that thing."

"And we'll move the oxygen tanks too," Lailani said. "And all our food and water--and coffee! And some mattresses and seats. It'll be comfy. And roomier than this dump."

"My ship is not a dump." Ben-Ari ran her hand against the bulkhead. "My first ship. I'll miss her . . ." The captain took a deep breath and stood up. "I was hoping for a shower and a proper meal, but there's no time. Let's get to work. De la Rosa, you work with me. We'll collect whatever hardware we can. Emery, you start unplugging the backup computers. We'll empty the ammo crates and pack everything in there, then take a few space walks to move it over." The captain turned to the monitor. "Lieutenant, how are you holding up? Can you keep flying for another couple hours?"

Kemi nodded. "Yes, but make sure the first crate you ship over has all the caffeine."

They got to work.

Ben-Ari and Lailani began unscrewing hardware from the *Saint Brendan*, inside and out, most of which Marco didn't recognize. They loaded sensors, lenses, and heavy navigational machines into crates. Piece by piece, they removed the *Saint Brendan*'s eyes and ears. One by one, the monitors went dark around them. As the women toiled at their task, Marco worked at the computers, moving system after system to one set of computers, then removing the idling machines and adding them to the crates. Blessedly, the critical systems on the *Saint Brendan* were redundant, allowing them to keep flying as they worked.

"All right, boys and girls," Lailani said at one point. "I'm deactivating our last sensor. We won't be able to detect our marauder friends until we reinstall everything on the *Anansi*. By my estimates, we have about an hour before they reach us, maybe less." She winced. "Better get a leg up!"

They all sped up their efforts. Marco loaded the last computer into the bin, then got to packing the food. The rations were all seal-packed in white packages: lasagna, fish and rice, chicken and peas, spaghetti bolognese, and something called Mexican fiesta. From what Marco had seen so far, they all looked the same on the inside. He dumped the rations into a crate, then began moving the water and oxygen tanks into several other crates.

As Marco was loading a crate full of cables and batteries, he glanced at Lailani. She was working nearby, unscrewing a box of navigational sensors. Tears were flowing down her cheeks, but still she toiled.

She lost so much, Marco thought. *I can't even imagine her pain.*

As he kept working, a new thought popped into his mind: *Yet right now, I myself feel no pain.*

For two years in Haven, pain had been his constant companion. Endlessly, that demon on his shoulder had whispered into his ear, spewing its venom of guilt, memory, despair. Days on end, that demon would crush him, often so heavy that Marco could only lie down, praying for death.

Yet now that demon, that creature the doctors had called shell shock, was silent.

Marco thought back to boot camp seven years ago. Despite the physical difficulties, he had rarely found time for despair at Fort Djemila. He had just been too damn *busy*. At war again, caught in another gauntlet, struggling to survive, that demon drowned.

It lives off time and silence, Marco thought. *The two things I had most in Haven. The two things I'm missing now. Time. No time!*

"How long do we have?" he called across the ship, sweat on his forehead.

"Maybe half an hour?" Lailani said from inside the engine room. "It's all just an estimate." Her head popped through a hatch, smeared with grease, and she grinned at him. "Could be five minutes!"

"All right, soldiers," Ben-Ari said, rushing down the hall. "Into your spacesuits and take everything into the airlock. Whatever we didn't have time to pack will go down with the *Brendan*. Move it, soldiers!"

They moved it.

Marco zipped up his spacesuit and took a deep breath from his oxygen tank. His eyes stung.

I will climb out of this hole. I am alive. I have purpose. I am fighting. I will be who I was.

Still piloting the *Anansi*, Kemi brought the alien starship as close to the *Brendan*'s airlock as possible. The ravager had its own airlock, operated by tugging strands of web. They stretched a jet bridge between the two airlocks, using plastic sheets to extend it around the *Anansi*'s larger opening.

"Only a few minutes until they're here!" Lailani said, checking her watch.

They began shoving crates across the jet bridge and into the *Anansi*'s cavernous hold. On the inside, the marauder ship looked like a cave draped with cobwebs. Crate by crate, they shoved in their supplies.

"Captain!" Kemi's voice emerged from the ship's bridge. "One of the glass spheres here just lit up like a crystal ball. It's showing me a visual of ravagers flying in fast!"

Marco raced across the jet bridge, heading back to the *Saint Brendan*. There was one more crate he needed, the one containing a heavy backup battery. Halfway across the jet bridge, he gazed through a small window.

His heart seemed to stop in his chest.

Light flowed around their bubble of warped spacetime like wind around a wing, but these ravagers flew directly behind them, visible now to the naked eye. Dozens of specks, moving fast, growing closer.

Marco shoved the last crate into the *Anansi*.

"All right, we're good to go!" he said.

Ben-Ari raced by him--back onto the *Saint Brendan*.

"Captain!" Marco cried after her. "We need to go--now!"

He glanced back behind them. The ravagers were even closer. Shards in the darkness, specks of fire. Twenty-two of them, far too many ships to fight.

"Isn't the captain joining us?" Lailani said, panting beside Marco in the *Anansi*'s airlock. "I'm going after her. I--"

Ben-Ari came racing back across the jet bridge. "All right, we're good!" She leaped into the *Anansi*. "Let's reel in the jet bridge!"

They worked in a fury, tugging the folding bridge into the *Anansi*. The enemy kept drawing nearer, nearer, soon only a few kilometers away.

When the last meter of bridge was folded and inside, they slammed the airlock shut, sealing everything inside the *Anansi*.

"Captain, they're right on us!" Kemi shouted.

They raced through the main hold, shoving aside webs, and onto the bridge. Kemi sat there, her chair suspended in the web, tugging on the shower curtain rings. Spheres hung around her, the size of watermelons, displaying views of the outside. In one sphere, Marco could see the ravagers closing in.

"All right," Ben-Ari said, voice tinged with sadness. "Let's send the *Saint Brendan* out on her final voyage."

She flipped open a tablet and typed commands. Through one spherical viewport, Marco could see the stealth ship--small, black, and badly scarred--change course.

The two vessels--the human *Saint Brendan* and the alien *Anansi*--parted ways.

As the *Anansi* moved out of the *Saint Brendan*'s warp bubble, they crashed into regular spacetime. The streaks of starlight slammed into points. Marco struggled to hold down his lunch.

"All right, we're back in regular spacetime," Kemi said. "If we need to, I can activate the *Anansi*'s own warp drive. At least, I think I can." She winced, patting one alien strand. "If we end up as a cloud of atoms, I pulled the wrong strand."

Still flying in a warp bubble, the *Saint Brendan* was moving away at incredible speed. It was already millions of kilometers away. Behind them, the ravagers still stormed forth as one unit, as if unable to decide which ship to pursue.

"I'm letting the *Anansi* drift like space junk," Kemi said. "With any luck, those ravagers will think we're dead in the water, and they'll all follow the empty *Brendan*." She took a deep breath. "I hope this works. We'll know in a minute."

"Captain, what did you have to fetch that was so important?" Lailani said.

Ben-Ari stared at the departing ship, eyes damp. "I set the *Brendan*'s self-destruct. It'll trigger if anyone steps aboard. Old commander's trick." She smiled sadly. "She was a good ship. *My* ship. I'll miss her."

"The ravagers are splitting up!" Kemi said. "Look!"

The crew crowded around one of the spheres. It showed two ravagers breaking off from the larger group, turning to follow the *Saint Brendan*. The other twenty continued flying together . . . following the *Anansi*.

"This can't be happening," Marco said.

Lailani rushed back into the hold. She rifled through the equipment from the *Brendan*, plugged sensors together, checked monitors, and cursed.

"My sensors confirm it--twenty of those bastards are still on our tail." Lailani groaned. "They're close too. Moving fast. Fuck! All this, and we only shook off two of them?"

Ben-Ari's mouth was a thin line. She inhaled sharply, then turned to Kemi. "Turn on this ship's warp drive. Fly as fast as you can."

Kemi nodded, pulling one shower curtain. The strand it was attached to creaked. "Engaging warp."

The *Anansi* thrummed. Marco grabbed a web for support. Lailani fell to the floor with a grunt. The stars streamed outside, their light curving. The ravager blasted forward, rattling, thrumming, bending space around them. Marco nearly gagged again.

"Damn these things can fly!" Kemi said, and wonder filled her voice. "I've never gone this fast. No human ship has. Now *this* is a warp drive."

Lailani pushed herself up and checked her instruments. "They're keeping up with us. Fuckers! How did they know to follow the *Anansi* instead of the *Brendan*? Did they see our jet bridge from afar, even in warp?"

"Impossible," Kemi said. "They were too far to see such details."

Marco stared into the sphere. He could see them there. Clawed ships, fire in their centers. Inside them, the marauders. The creatures that had destroyed humanity. That had kidnapped Addy.

"They're smart," he said.

"No shit, Sherlock," Lailani said. "They build spaceships."

Marco narrowed his eyes, watching them. "Not just tech-smart. The scum built spaceships too. But these creatures . . .

they're cunning. They saw through our deception. We can't think of them as just bugs, not like the scum were."

"They must have some way to detect our bodies," Lailani said. "Some heat sensors, maybe?"

"No." Marco shook his head. "Otherwise, why did they send two ravagers after the *Brendan*? No, they don't know for sure. They just calculated the odds, hedging their bets. They sent the bulk of their force after the best bet--that we'd be here, inside the ravager, trying to deceive them. They know how we think." He lowered his head. "I never should have suggested this."

"No, it was a good plan," said Ben-Ari. "Even if we didn't dupe the enemy, it was a worthy swap. We can move faster without the *Brendan*. Lieutenant, how long can we stay ahead of them?"

Kemi chewed her lip. "Hard to say, Captain. I can't fly as fast as they do. My piloting just isn't as smooth as theirs. They have six limbs to pull strands with, remember!"

Lailani checked her instruments. Numbers scrolled by on her tablet. "The distance is still shrinking between us, but slowly. They're still moving faster than us, but not *that* much faster anymore." She scrunched her lips, hit a few buttons, and ran calculations. "If we can keep flying the *Anansi* at this speed, we can stay ahead of them . . . for a week. Maybe eight days." She sighed. "Not enough time to reach the Ghost Fleet. Maybe enough time to come up with a new plan."

Ben-Ari nodded. "All right. That's something. Right now, we need to rest. All of us. We'll all eat a good meal, then sleep, then think more clearly. I'll take a shift flying the *Anansi*. The rest of you--eat and rest."

Marco's stomach grumbled. He had not eaten since this ordeal began, and the thought of a meal--even if it was just packaged starship food--already lifted his mood. He would choose the lasagna, maybe the--

He froze.

He felt the blood drain from his face.

"Fuck," he whispered.

Lailani turned toward him. "What's wrong, Poet? You look like you saw a ghost, and we're still thousands of light-years away from the Ghost Fleet."

His legs trembled. His head spun.

"Oh God," he said. "God. I'm sorry. I'm so sorry." He grimaced. "In the chaos, with the clock counting down, I . . ."

"What?" Lailani grabbed him. "What happened?"

"I forgot to bring the crate of food." Marco winced. "I packaged the food in the *Brendan*'s galley and I never brought it into the airlock."

They all gaped at him.

"Somebody tell me they brought over the food," Ben-Ari finally said.

One by one, they shook their heads.

If Addy were here, she'd be punching me now, Marco thought. Somehow, the silent looks the others gave him were far worse.

"My beloved lasagna," Lailani whispered.

"My salmon and rice!" Kemi said.

Lailani gasped. "You even forgot the Mexican fiesta! The *fiesta*, Marco!"

He stared at them, silent. "I'm sorry. I . . . I have some gum in my pocket." He offered it to them.

Lailani let out something halfway between a groan and a howl, then stomped off.

Ben-Ari inhaled deeply. "Lieutenant Abasi, go rest. That's an order. I'll fly the ship for an hour. Sergeant Emery, you go set up our equipment. And try to find a power source you can connect to on this ship; our batteries won't last forever. Sergeant de la Rosa will help you. And set up an alarm. I want sirens to blare if those enemy ships get within two hours of us." She stared into Marco's eyes. "It takes the human body two weeks to starve to death. By then, you better find us a space takeout."

"A Mexican takeout!" rose Lailani's voice from outside the bridge.

Marco stepped into the hold, shoulders slumped. As he worked at unpacking and assembling their supplies, he could only wonder what would kill them first: the marauders or starvation.

CHAPTER THREE

The galactic cattle car rattled on, and the thousands cried out in despair.

"I never thought I'd say this," Addy muttered. "But I miss the rush hour subway."

Thousands of prisoners were crammed onto the deck, floating in zero gravity. Thousands filled the decks above and below them. There was no room to stretch out their limbs. The naked bodies pressed together, damp with sweat, covered with filth. They had no toilets. Human waste floated with them, coated them. Sweat, piss, shit, vomit, blood, the stench of fear--all hovered in the sweltering air. Addy wasn't sure how hot it was, but it was worse than the desert, worse than the hottest day at Fort Djemila among the African dunes.

Marco, she thought, *if you left without me, I forgive you. Nobody deserves this shit. Literally.* She winced and ducked, dodging a floating blob.

Worse than all, though, were the floating dead. Several people had died back on Haven before the ship had even taken off, trampled in the chaos. Many more had perished over the past few days, succumbing to exhaustion and heat. The survivors had tried to move the corpses aside, to keep them in the corner, but whenever the ship jolted, the dead tore free. And they were starting to stink, a stench worse than any of the other fetid aromas here.

In this sea of humanity, a woman screamed, a hoarse cry of pure agony. A moment later, a baby squealed, and blood floated across the deck. Addy caught sight of the newborn, had to look away. She had dived into the mines of Corpus. She had seen millions perish on Abaddon. But she had never seen such misery, such malice.

"Sergeant!" A voice rose in the distance, barely audible beyond the weeping, the screaming, the din of brutalized human cattle. "Sergeant Linden! Is that you?"

Addy turned toward the voice. She narrowed her eyes. She could barely see in these shadows. The entire ship was a writhing mass of filth and shadows, a sea of flesh.

"Addy!"

The voice was closer now. Prisoners cried out in protest, and a one-eyed man came elbowing between them, barely squeezing through. Addy's eyes widened.

"Grant!"

The superintendent of her old apartment building, grizzled and coughing, floated toward her. Sweat coated his naked body. The bastards had even taken his eye patch, revealing his empty socket.

"I thought I heard you in here, Addy," Grant said, then hacked, shivering, feverish. "Fuckers, these spiders, aren't they? Worse than the goddamn scum, they are."

"They're not spiders," Addy said. "Spiders have eight legs. These ones have six. They're more like insects, and--oh fuck me, I sound like Poet now."

"Is Marco here?" Grant said.

Addy shook her head. "We were fighting the marauders outside the city. We had a ship. The fuckers got me. I think Poet got away."

Grant nodded. "Good. Then he's out there. Fighting for us." Suddenly the veteran's eyes were damp. "He'll save us."

Addy snorted and rolled her eyes. "Grant, I know you think Marco and I are some heroes, just because we killed the scum emperor. But we're not. We're just bozos. We're just regular people, like all the other poor suckers in here."

She sighed. Looking around her, she barely even saw people. Naked, shaved, afraid, crammed into the interstellar cattle car, they could be mistaken for animals being led to the slaughter.

"It's a sad state," Grant said, looking around. "We fought on Abaddon for pity's sake. We came in there with tanks, with jets, with cannons. Every man and woman carried a gun. And we kicked ass. Now look at us."

Addy looked around. She saw children. Babies. Elders. She also saw veterans--like her and Grant--people who had fought the scum, had killed aliens, had saved the world. She knew them by the tattoos on their arms. Some, like her and Grant, had tattooed stars, signifying that they had killed scum in combat. Others just had the tattoos of their units; they had not killed aliens, perhaps, but they had fought nonetheless.

"You're right," Addy said. "You're right, Grant. We're humans. We're soldiers. We're not lambs." She gripped his arm. "And I say we fight."

Grant looked around him, then back at Addy. "We seem to be missing the tanks, the fighter jets, the cannons, the big guns."

"We have teeth." Addy bared hers. "We have nails." She dug them into Grant's arm. "And we have human spirit. On Haven, we were caught by surprise. We know what we're dealing with now. I won't just be led to the slaughter. We're on a starship. There are only a handful of marauders here. We know their eyes are weak. We can kill them by stabbing their eyes. By God, I say we kill them and commandeer their ship."

Grant was not a young man, and crammed into this ship, naked and bruised, he seemed even older, but now his eyes flared with the fury of a young warrior. He nodded and clasped her hand.

"I will fight with you, Sergeant Linden. It will be an honor."

Addy glanced toward the back of the deck. At the edge, in the shadows, he lurked. A marauder. The alien clung to the ceiling, legs folded, hanging from his web. The creature guarded the shaft that led to the decks below and above, which Addy assumed were similar to this one, crammed full of prisoners.

She thought back to being herded into this ship.

We passed a great, rumbling room, she thought. *At the bottom floor. The engine room. That's the place we must commandeer.*

She looked back at the marauder guarding the shaft. She would have to get past him, to crawl downward to the engine room. Even in the shadows, Addy glimpsed the parasitic twin growing from the guardian's side. It was her old friend Orcus, the one who had kidnapped her, who had torn her apart from her friends.

"They weren't herding any prisoners to the lowest deck," she whispered. "That must be where the marauders are flying this ship. We need to muster whoever can fight and get down there."

"How many marauders do you think are on this ship?" Grant said.

"Not many, I'd wager," she said. "We're cattle to them, right? How many humans are in a farm truck, leading the cows to the slaughterhouse? One? Two?" A sneer touched her lips. "The marauders underestimate us. I would bet my life on it. Hell, I *am* betting my life on it."

Grant glanced around, then leaned closer. "There are a few more of us. Veterans. Some are like us, fought on Abaddon. Tough sons of bitches. I'll spread the word. We'll get a squad ready. Will you command us, Sergeant Linden?"

"Sergeant?" she said. "The HDF is dead, Grant."

He smiled thinly. "No it isn't. It's still right here." He nodded. "Commander." Suddenly his good eye was damp. "An honor!"

Addy remembered his office back in their building. It had been a shrine to the Human Defense Force, full of posters, medals, and other mementos from the war. Grant's most prized possession had been a signed photo of her, Marco, Ben-Ari, and Lailani--the team that had killed the scum emperor.

This is a nightmare for me, but it's a dream for him, she thought. *He's fighting with his heroes.*

She nodded. "Summon the squad, soldier."

Lip wobbly, chin held high, Grant wormed his way through the crowd. Addy moved in a separate direction, seeking people with veteran tattoos. It was slow progress; every meter was a struggle, a veritable game of Twister, contorting to squeeze around people, worm her way between their legs, or float over their heads. The human waste floated around her, and she had to nudge aside two corpses. Disgust grew in Addy, and soon she was shivering. She was feverish, and she hadn't eaten or drunk anything in hours, maybe days, but she refused to join the dead. Not without a fight.

There weren't many veterans here, but she found a few, war-weary souls who had found no solace on Earth, who had moved to Haven to escape their demons. Perhaps, like Marco and her, they had found that the demons came with them.

Now we will be soldiers again.

"We fight," she whispered to them. "Make your way--slowly--toward the back. Near the sleeping marauder guarding the path to the lower decks. Remember--their eyes are weak."

They all nodded. Nobody here would cower from a fight.

"For Earth," they whispered.

They collected fifteen combat veterans. In addition to Addy and Grant, three others had fought on Abaddon in

Operation Jupiter, among its few survivors. One by one, they made their way toward the edge of the deck, slowly, casually, heads lowered, silent.

Hanging from the web above, Orcus still lurked.

Addy glanced up at the marauder. A tangled black cobweb covered the ceiling, and Orcus clung to it, his six legs folded against his torso. The alien had black, blank eyes with no lids; Addy couldn't tell if he was sleeping. She kept waiting for Orcus to move, but the only movement came from the saliva dripping from his jaws.

Below the alien, a shaft led to other decks. From above and below, Addy heard the cries of prisoners. Each deck held thousands of humans, it seemed.

From where she stood, Addy could see a porthole behind Orcus. It was barely larger than her fist, but through it, she saw the stars.

For a moment, her eyes dampened and she couldn't breathe.

They were beautiful. It had been years since she had seen the stars. The atmosphere in Haven had always been too thick. Their beauty pierced her. She wasn't like Marco. She couldn't recognize what stars she was seeing. She didn't know where they were traveling. But trapped here in this hive of human misery, she wanted to be out there, floating among those lights. Such beauty, right there, just a few meters away, yet beyond her reach.

Grant hovered nearby, elbowing people aside. He met Addy's gaze across the crowd. He nodded.

Addy made eye contact with the others. Slowly, they began moving closer. The crowd parted before them.

Above, Orcus still slept, clinging to the ceiling.

But as the veterans floated nearer, the alien's parasitic twin woke. The twisted creature, no larger than a human toddler, stared down at Addy.

Addy winced and froze.

The deformed twin opened its jaws and shrieked.

Orcus's eyes blazed white, his pupils dilating. His massive jaws opened.

"For Earth!" Addy shouted.

"For Earth!" her squad answered.

Addy pushed off the ground and vaulted toward the marauder, screaming.

Orcus screeched. At once, his six legs unfurled, and his eyes burned with fury. Webs shot out. Addy pushed against another prisoner, floated sideways, kicked off another man, and hurled herself onto the marauder.

A claw grazed her arm. Another cut her leg. She ignored the pain, reached out, and grabbed one of the alien's bulging eyes.

Orcus screamed--this time in pain.

Addy squeezed the eye, and it popped in her palm like an overripe tomato.

Orcus howled, jaws opened wide.

Addy sneered, grabbed one of Orcus's teeth--it was as long as a sword--and pressed her feet against the alien's head.

She yanked mightily, and the tooth tore out with gushing blood.

A weapon, she thought. *A sword.*

Missing an eye and a tooth, Orcus shrieked and slammed a leg against her. Addy tumbled in zero gravity and plowed into other prisoners, the alien tooth still in her hand.

Above, the wounded Orcus was roaring, bleeding from his gum, his crushed eye oozing. Other humans were attacking the creature now, trying to reach his remaining three eyes.

Howling, Orcus scuttled across the ceiling. The marauder fled into the shadows, tail between his legs.

For a second or two, Addy panted in relief, holding the alien tooth like a sword.

But her victory was short-lived. From the deck below, more inhuman bellows rose.

"We're about to have company!" Addy shouted, figuring that every space warrior needed to shout that phrase at least once.

Shadows stirred in the shaft. Several more marauders leaped onto the deck. Ignoring the pain, Addy charged toward them.

She dodged a blow from one leg. Beside her, claws ripped a man apart. Above her, a woman screamed and died, chest cracked open. A clawed leg swung toward Addy, and Grant leaped up, grabbed the limb, and yanked it aside. One of the spikes slashed his side, and his blood sprayed Addy.

"Kill it, Sergeant!" Grant shouted, struggling to hold the leg back.

Addy kicked off the floor and soared. The jaws snapped toward her. She pulled back, and the teeth slammed shut a centimeter away. She thrust Orcus's fallen tooth toward the marauder. The ivory blade entered the creature's leftmost eye.

When the marauder roared in agony, Addy thrust her sword again, cutting its palate. She pulled her hand back as the jaws snapped shut, nearly losing her arm.

"More of them!" somebody shouted. "Coming from below!"

Across the deck, people were screaming, weeping, cheering. Marauders were tearing into the humans, scattering blood.

The marauder in front of Addy, one eye gone, roared and tried to bite her. She leaped back. With a battle cry, she thrust her ivory blade with all her might. She impaled another eye, this time a central one. She kept shoving, driving the tooth into the creature's brain.

The marauder mewled, then moved no more.

"I killed one!" Addy shouted. "They can be killed! Fight! Fig--"

A roar sounded. Addy spun toward the shaft.

Yet another marauder emerged.

She drove her tooth forward, trying to stab an eye, but only hit its hardened cheek. Sparks flew.

Addy tried to scamper back, but there was no room.

"For Earth!" Grant shouted, wrenching free a tooth from a dead marauder. He swung the fang.

"For Earth!" answered the survivors of the squad, yanking out more teeth.

Marauders leaped forward. Grant thrust his tooth, but he couldn't hit an eye. Claws lashed, grabbed a veteran, and tore him apart. Webs shot out, entangling veterans. One strand caught Addy's wrist. Another wrapped around her torso. She screamed, tried to kick, but strands lassoed her legs, then her throat.

She couldn't breathe.

Around her, more marauders emerged, and more webs shot out, trapping other veterans.

The strands tightened around her neck.

She gasped. No air was reaching her lungs. She couldn't move her arms.

Around Addy, the other prisoners were shouting, trying to reach her. More webs wrapped around them. Their voices grew hazy. Blackness spread around Addy's vision, closing in, until she could see only one marauder ahead. Orcus. The alien licked his lips, staring at her with cruel delight, and then he too faded into shadow.

CHAPTER FOUR

As Lailani worked in the *Anansi*, hooking up sensors and plugging in keyboards and monitors, she couldn't stop her tears from flowing.

They're gone. The children. My people. My Sofia. They're all gone.

A tear fell onto a keyboard. Lailani wiped her eyes and took a deep breath. She had to focus. She was in danger now. Her captain, her friends, her entire planet was in danger. She had to get this equipment installed on the *Anansi*, had to track their pursuers, had to find the Ghost Fleet. The cosmos was coming undone. As was her life.

She tried to plug a sensor into a battery pack, but her fingers slipped, and she snapped the connector. Damn it! Now she would have to rig a new adapter, and that could take an hour, and she had left her tools behind on the *Saint Brendan*. And she didn't even have the right rigs here, and . . .

I love you, my sweet little pea.

Sofia smiled in her memory, stroking her hair.

Lailani sniffed.

"No," she whispered. "Not now. I can't grieve now."

But the image of Sofia hovered before her, golden in the dawn, lying in bed with the sheets pulled up to her shoulders. The most beautiful sight Lailani had ever seen. She reached out to her beloved, but she couldn't grip her. Sofia was falling. Gliding down into flame. The ravager's plasma engulfed her, stripping flesh from bones, and Lailani looked away, trembling.

"I'm sorry." More tears fell. "I'm sorry, Sofia. I wanted to save you. I wanted to die with you. I'm sorry that I lived. I'm sorry that you're gone."

Two years. Two years of living with Sofia in Manila. Two years of labor, wheeling her cart of books through the shantytowns, teaching the children to read. Two years of healing after a war of killing. Two years of fixing after so long destroying.

Gone.

All gone--the children, her books, the woman she loved.

And with this fresh grief, older memories cascaded. The floodgates were open now. The horrors of her past filled Lailani. The inferno on Abaddon. The terrors on Corpus. And worst of all--that horrible night on the HDFS *Miyari*, the night the scum had hijacked her mind, had controlled her like a marionette. The night they had made her grow claws. The night she had thrust those claws into her friend's chest. The night Benny "Elvis" Ray had died, his heart in her hand, and she had laughed, had tried to kill Marco too, had become a monster, and--

No.

Lailani forced herself to take deep breaths.

That wasn't me.

She wasn't fully human. Lailani knew that. She knew that one percent of her DNA was alien. Was evil. The doctors had placed a chip in her head, caging that monster inside her. Lailani had to believe that the monster was gone for good. That she was not a sinner. And yet the guilt lingered. The grief still tore at her, as sharp as the claws she had grown.

No grief now. Now is when I redeem myself. Now is when I save the world.

She tried to plug in another cable. Again her fingers slipped. Again she snapped a connector.

"Damn it!" Lailani shouted. "This stupid fucking thing!" She tossed the cable and sensors aside. The equipment lay in a mess across the *Anansi*'s interior. "The thing is goddamn ruined! I have no tools, it's too dark in here, those fucking marauders keep chasing us, and the fucking connectors keep snapping, and I can't . . . I can't . . ."

Suddenly Lailani was sobbing, chest shaking. She lowered her head. Her bitter tears fell and her hair fell across her forehead, just long enough to cover her eyes.

Footsteps sounded behind her. She felt a hand on her shoulder.

"Lailani, can I help?"

She turned around, wiping her tears, to see Marco. Her cheeks flushed, and shame at her weakness filled her.

"I'm fine." She took a shuddering breath. "A moment of weakness. I'm fit for duty."

Marco looked at her with soft eyes. "I'm not Captain Ben-Ari. You can be human around me. Can I help? Or just listen?"

God damn it. Lailani didn't want this. She hated the kindness she saw in his eyes. Hated how she still felt about him. She wanted Marco to hate her, to scorn her. She had left him! She had broken his heart! When he had dreamed of marrying her, she had left to the Philippines, had chosen a life of charity work with Sofia over a life at his side. And after all the pain she had caused him--he would still show her kindness?

She pointed at a box of memory keys.

"You can help me install those."

He nodded, sat down, and got to work. For long moments, they worked in silence, plugging in equipment, calibrating sensors, bringing systems online. One by one, monitors came to life in the belly of the *Anansi*. The screens showed the pursuit behind them: twenty enemy ravagers, only a day or two away, moving fast, closing the gap. And the Ghost Fleet still lay months away.

"Here, let me help," Marco said as Lailani struggled to lift a bulky battery pack the size of her torso.

"I'm fine," she said.

"It's too heavy. Let me help!" He approached, took one end of the box, and helped her move it into position. "There."

Their fingers touched, then pulled away quickly. She brushed back her hair and looked at him. She bit her lip and looked away. He stared at the battery.

"Lailani," he began, "again, I'm sorry about Sofia. I--"

"Don't," she said.

He nodded. "All right."

Lailani let out something halfway between scoff and sob. "You're ridiculous."

He frowned. "Why?"

She gave a bitter laugh, looking away. "Why are you like this?"

Now some bitterness filled his own voice. "Like what?"

She reeled toward him, feeling her anger rise. "Like this. So fucking nice to me."

He took a step back, blinking. "I thought you needed help. I--"

"I don't need fucking help!" she said. "Don't you understand, Marco? You're not some knight in shining armor, and I'm not some damsel in distress, some delicate Asian flower, who needs the rich white hero to save her."

He narrowed his eyes. "I never thought that--"

"Yes you did!" She stamped a foot. "Yes you did, Marco! You always did! For fuck's sake. Back at boot camp, who was I to you? A weak, frail girl, her wrists sliced, a rose from the slums. And you thought you could protect me. Defend me. And you're still doing it!"

His eyes hardened. "If I recall correctly, you were the toughest warrior in our platoon. The first time I saw you, you were talking about how much you wanted to kill scum. That's why I fell in love with you. Because of your strength. Not because of some damsel in distress fantasy."

"Yes, you fell in love with me!" Lailani said. "And I broke your heart. I broke your fucking heart." Her tears were flowing

again. "You were so fucking nice to me. Always so fucking nice!"
She was weeping again now. "You wanted to marry me. To be
with me always. You loved me so much. And I dumped you. I
chose Sofia over you. For years in the army, we were apart, and I
didn't wait for you. I betrayed you." She was trembling now. "I
acted like a total bitch, and I hate myself for it. And I hate that
you're still so fucking nice to me. Why, Marco? Why don't you
hate me? I want you to hate me! To shout at me. I deserve it."

I'm a monster, she thought. *I killed Elvis. I'm a freak. I'm a
murderer.* But she could not bring that to her lips. That pain still
ran too deep.

Marco stared at her, silent, and sighed. It was a long
moment before he spoke. "I did hate you. For a long time. I had
two years on Haven to hate you. But that's over now. Whatever
love we had, whatever animosity that followed . . . it's over. It's a
new reality now. There's no more room for hatred."

"And love?" Lailani whispered. "Because when you look at
me, I still see it. It's still the way you used to look at me when we
were eighteen. Do you still love me, Marco? Even after what I
did?"

He hesitated as if considering his words. "How I feel is
irrelevant to this mission."

She barked a laugh. "That's Captain Ben-Ari speaking. Not
the Poet." She stepped toward him and took his hands. "Marco,
listen. I want you to understand something. I love you. I still
fucking love you with all my fucking heart, and I always will.
Always. You're the only boy I ever loved. When I left you, I . . ."

"You don't have to say anything."

"I do!" Lailani's eyes flashed. "Don't take this away from me! Because this tore at me for two fucking years, and I won't let you silence me now. When I left you, I broke your heart, I know. But I also broke my heart. My heart shattered that day. I had a terrible choice. Between a life with the man I love and a life serving my country, my church, my soul, saving those children who lived like I had lived. I could not take you with me. I could not see you wither there, see you slowly decay in the slums. I had to go with Sofia. Because Marco, after the war, I vowed something. I vowed to God. To my dead mother. To the cosmos itself. I made a vow that I could not break."

"What vow?" he whispered, eyes damp.

God damn it. Lailani had not wanted to share all this. Not here. Not now, with the enemy pursuing them. Yet, yes, the floodgates had broken. All her truths were spilling out with her tears.

"For years, we killed." She spoke softly, as if speaking to herself more than to Marco. "They trained us to be killers. They took eighteen-year-old kids, tearing us from our lives. They tossed us into a camp in a desert. They broke us, then reformed us into killers. Ben-Ari. Sergeant Singh. Corporal Diaz. All of them. They gave us guns, they made those guns become parts of us, and they sent us to kill. To destroy. To bomb. To ruin. And we did all those things. We killed the scum in their hives, and we ravaged their ships, and we bombed their home planet, and we became agents of destruction. What else could we be? We were born into such a cosmos. A cosmos at war. A cosmos where only killers survived, where the strong preyed on the meek. So we became strong. Or we died."

Marco lowered his head, perhaps remembering their fallen friends. "Or we died. Even many of the strong."

Lailani nodded, thinking of those she had lost. Of Caveman, Sheriff, Jackass, Beast, all the rest of them. Of dear, beloved Sofia, forever in her heart. Of Elvis, his blood on her hands.

"I escaped death in the war," Lailani said. "I should have died so many times. When I sliced my wrists. In the inferno of Fort Djemila. In the underground of Corpus. In the hell of Abaddon. Yet I kept escaping death. And I wondered, Marco. I wondered so many times why I lived while others died."

"Luck," Marco said. "That's what Addy always told me when I felt guilty for surviving."

"Luck? Maybe." Lailani gripped the cross she wore around her neck. "I wore this cross through the war. And I wore this in the shantytowns, places of as much misery as any battlefield. And I often doubted my faith. The priests taught me that a benevolent, all-powerful god looks out for us. And I wondered how that could be. How God could be real when teenagers died on battlefields on alien worlds. When children in slums were sold into brothels. When children lived on landfills, eating the trash, diseased and dying. How could the priests be right? How could God be good and powerful and yet allow all this pain? I asked that every day."

"Did you find an answer?" Marco said.

"Not in any church. Not from the mouth of any priest. And so I made a vow after the war. I'm not all-powerful, but I can be benevolent. I can, with what little power I have, provide some of the mercy I kept praying for, that I was always denied. If I was losing my faith in God, I would seek faith in my own soul. I vowed that I would devote my life to healing, not killing. To building, not destroying. And when I looked at you, Marco, it hurt too much. I saw the war again. I saw all those we lost. I saw my old life, the life of a killer." She sighed, smiling through her tears. "So I left. I went to follow my vow. To build and heal. And I know, Marco. I know that the inequity in the world is great. That there are so many who hurt. That I could never heal them all, never help all those who need me. But if I could help just a few, fix just a little, then I would serve a purpose in this life. That this gift of a life, almost snatched from me, would still have meaning. That I would find redemption."

He looked at her, eyes damp. "You always had meaning to me, Lailani. And you always will."

She nodded. She felt so weak. So drained. Her eyes kept watering.

"I want you to hate me," she whispered. She stepped toward him, hesitated, then embraced him. When she laid her head against his chest, and when he wrapped his arms around her, she could still feel so safe, like in the old days. "You're too damn good to me."

"No more hate," Marco said. "No more destroying. It's time for forgiveness. For healing." He touched her cheek.

"Lailani, I'm sorry for your loss. Truly. I lost somebody on Haven, somebody I loved. The pain is almost too great to bear. But what we're doing here, this journey into the darkness--this is healing. This is building. This is helping. We might just save the cosmos. Perhaps this will be the greatest thing we ever do."

She smiled, tears on her lips. "Let's focus on fixing the small things first. Like those connectors I broke. Will you help me?"

He nodded. "I will help you." And she knew he was speaking about more than connectors.

They knelt around the equipment. They kept working. As they slowly brought the systems back online, Lailani felt as if she were piecing together her soul, her cosmos.

Fixing, she thought. *Putting things together. Healing.* She looked up at Marco, smiled, then looked back at her work. *When the world is falling apart, fixing little things is all we can do. May that forever be my life--a life of fixing what is broken.*

CHAPTER FIVE

Heat.

Scuttling in the dark.

Pain--throbbing, pulsing.

Screams and clatters and grunts.

Her eyes fluttered open, saw blood and skin, and closed again.

Sharp agony on her cheek, and claws shoving her down. Addy coughed, gasping for air, struggling to reclaim consciousness. She blinked, her vision hazy, slowly coming into focus.

"Grant!" she tried to shout, but only a hoarse whisper emerged.

She tried to rub her eyes but could not. She realized her arms were bound. She wasn't sure how long she had been unconscious. Meanwhile, the marauders had moved her. She hung like a fly in a cobweb, trapped in a rusty metal room. Several other prisoners were here, sticky strands gluing them to the walls. There were no portholes here, but she was clearly still on the transport ship; she could hear the engines rumble below her, and the chamber vibrated. From above came the muffled cries of the thousands of human captives.

"Sergeant Linden?" One of the figures in the web stirred, coughed, and gazed at her with one eye. "Sergeant?"

"Grant!" she cried. He hung across the chamber. Addy struggled, tried to free herself from the web, but only entangled herself further. "I can almost free myself. We're near the engines. We can still fight. We . . ."

Shadows stirred above, and Addy's voice died.

Creatures were moving across the ceiling. Legs--serrated, clawed, rising, falling. Eyes--peering, mocking, glistening black. Jaws--smacking, drooling, fangs glistening. Abdomens--bloated, sprouting spikes, clattering with skulls. Hunters. Apex predators. Like spiders, they wove their webs, endlessly patient, hungry for their prey.

One of the marauders descended, hanging on a strand of web, and spun lazily, facing the prisoners on the walls one by one. A crown of horns grew from his head, and a parasitic twin twitched on his side, opening and closing small jaws. The marauder had only three eyes; the fourth dripped across his face, exposing a red socket. One of his teeth was missing, and the gum still bled. That missing tooth was now pinned to Addy's side, trapped in the webbing like her arms, cold and sharp against her thigh.

Dear Orcus is still alive, but we hurt him, Addy thought, chest swelling. *Good.*

The marauder's jaw unhinged, and he spoke, voice like sheets of metal scraping together. "You . . . will . . . pay . . ."

"Do you accept MasterCard or Visa?" Addy said.

The marauder spun toward her, shot out a web, and swung closer. His jaws opened, and he hissed in her face, his breath assailing her.

Addy cringed. "Lovely mouthwash you use. What flavor is this? Rotten carcass or rancid trash heap?"

"I will feast on your flesh," the creature hissed.

"Try a mint instead," Addy said.

The marauder's jaws opened wide, and he howled, blowing his breath and saliva on Addy's face.

"You are nothing but meat," Orcus said. "You rose up against us. I will make sure you can never rise again. Watch." The alien grinned. "And await your turn."

The marauder swung from Addy toward the prisoner beside her, a muscular man with several stars tattooed on his arms. The veteran thrashed in his bonds, gritting his teeth, veins rising across his neck. Orcus crept closer, dangling on strands of webs.

"The human body," Orcus said. "So weak. So frail. You may have risen to dominance on your world. But in space, you are nothing but prey." The marauder's nostrils flared, and he sniffed the veteran's head, then shuddered in delight. "Your brains--so soft, so delectable. They are not ours to eat. Not yet. Not here. They are food for my master." Orcus licked his chops. "But you don't need your hands."

The marauder placed his jaws around the veteran's left hand.

"No!" Addy shouted.

The veteran grimaced, struggling to free himself, unable to move in the web.

The jaws snapped shut.

Orcus yanked his head back, gulping down the severed hand.

"You bastard!" Addy thrashed in her web.

The alien ignored her, closed his jaws around the man's second hand, and bit again. The veteran screamed.

Blood on his teeth, Orcus worked quickly, spinning webs around the spurting stumps. The veteran gave a last scream, then lost consciousness and hung limply.

Orcus turned toward Addy and grinned. "He will never more fight marauders."

The alien crept toward the next rebel, a woman with many stars tattooed onto her arms, a veteran of the butchery on Abaddon.

When the marauder bit off her hands, the veteran screamed.

One by one, Orcus moved between the veterans, the squad that had rebelled against the marauders. Snapping his jaws. Swallowing hands. Binding the stumps with webs. Even the parasitic twin fed upon a severed finger. As he worked, Orcus chuckled.

"Nobody will miss your hands when you're butchered. But they too are delectable." The marauder licked blood off its teeth. "And once we reach Earth, I will dine with Malphas himself. I too will taste brains."

Earth, Addy thought, trembling in her web. *They're taking us to Earth.*

Even with the horror of this chamber, her mind reeled. She wasn't sure whether to be elated or horrified. They weren't taking her to their own planet; that was good. But if they were traveling to Earth, did that mean her homeworld had fallen? Did humanity still fight? Could Addy still fight?

Grant's scream shattered her thoughts. The marauder bit off his hands and gulped, and the aging veteran--among Addy's closest friends from Haven--passed out.

Finally, after mutilating all the other rebels, Orcus turned toward Addy.

"Your turn." The marauder crept closer.

Addy winced, turning her head away from the alien. She could still see fingers stuck between his teeth.

"You might want to reconsider, buddy boy," Addy said.

Orcus laughed--a sound like bubbling death. "Good. Beg. I love to hear it."

His parasitic twin cackled, blood on its little jaws. "Beg, beg!"

"Oh, I won't beg," Addy said. "But *you* might. You'll beg for mercy once your superiors hear that you mutilated me. I'm prime meat, buddy. Check out my hip." She wriggled in her bindings, revealing the brand on her skin. "See that? I'm fucking filet mignon. I'm a meal for Lord Malphas himself. How will he feel, knowing you nibbled on his feast?"

The marauder screeched so loudly Addy thought her eardrums would rip. She refused to wince.

"Lord Malphas doesn't eat the hands!" Orcus said.

Addy smiled. "I don't eat pizza crusts, but I'd be pissed if my delivery guy ate them on the way over."

The marauder screamed again, but she saw the fear in his remaining eyes.

"Very well." Orcus panted, glaring at her. "You are a feast for Lord Malphas? Then we will prepare you for the feast!" He cackled. "You will wish I had taken your hands."

The marauder turned toward a tunnel and called out in his language, voice echoing through the ship. Grumbles and clatters rose from above. Marauders laughed. Addy winced.

"Stay strong, Sergeant," Grant said, raising his head. Blood dripped from the webs around his stumps. "Whatever they do, stay strong. You are a soldier of the Human Defense Force."

A second marauder emerged from a tunnel into the chamber. The alien dragged a bloated sack tipped with a hose. Blood on his teeth, Orcus helped carry the sack. The aliens approached Addy with their burden.

"Uhm, fellas," Addy said. "You know, I'm quite delicious as I am."

Orcus shook with deep, cruel laughter. He lifted the hose. Brown, lumpy gruel spilled from it.

"We will fatten you up," the alien said. "More flesh for Malphas."

At his side, his parasitic twin laughed. "Flesh, flesh!"

Orcus brought the hose close to Addy's mouth.

Cringing, she turned her head away. "Boys, boys! Malphas enjoys the *brain*. Why don't you bring me some science books? I can get nice and smart for him."

Orcus grabbed her cheeks, forcing her jaw open. "Lord Malphas does not eat the hands, perhaps. But he will still enjoy meat for dessert." Orcus grinned. "Just pray he eats your brain before your meat."

He shoved the hose into her mouth.

"Just feed me hot dogs!" Addy said, coughing, trying to spit out the tube. "I'll eat them!"

Orcus shoved the tube deeper. Addy screamed, floundered, desperate to escape the web. She would have better luck breaking iron shackles. She gagged, tried to spit out the hose, could not. The marauder kept shoving it in--to the back of her mouth, into her throat, down her throat. Addy vomited, choked, nearly passed out.

"Fatten her up!" said Orcus and squeezed the sack.

On his side, his parasitic twin cackled. "Fat, fat!"

The gruel began flowing into Addy's stomach.

She struggled, unable to stop it. Tears flowed down her cheeks, and the marauder licked them off.

"You took my eye," Orcus said. "So now I will take all of your humanity, all that you were. You are meat. You are pain. You are misery. Nothing more. Enjoy the rest of your flight."

The aliens crawled out of the chamber, leaving the rebels dangling there--the others without hands, Addy with the feeding tube down her throat.

Earth, she kept thinking as the ship flew on, as the screams still rose, as the gruel kept flowing down her throat. *We're going to Earth. On Earth we will fight. On Earth we will rise again. On Earth we will kill them all.*

The hellish journey through space continued, and Addy closed her eyes, tears on her cheeks, and thought of home.

CHAPTER SIX

They limped on through space, trapped in an alien vessel, hungry, weary.

Before them spread the dark vastness. Behind them, twenty ravagers roared in pursuit.

"They're getting closer." Sitting on the floor of the *Anansi*'s bridge, Lailani looked up from her array of monitors, keyboards, and sensors.

"They're always getting closer," Marco snapped, recognized the harshness in his voice, and softened it. "I'm flying as fast as I can. The *Anansi* is just too slow. Or none of us are good pilots."

He had been flying the ravager for hours now. They had been taking shifts; Ben-Ari had insisted the entire crew learn to fly the alien starship. The pilot's seat dangled in the web. Before it spread the alien controls: spheres instead of screens and strands instead of keys or buttons. Shower curtain rings dangled from the alien strands, providing grips for human hands. Kemi had labeled many of the alien controls, attaching pieces of paper with their functions. A hundred notes hung before Marco: *increase thrust, decrease thrust, roll left, roll right, yaw left, yaw right, raise nose, lower nose, open claws, close claws, fire plasma.* Dozens of others.

So far, Marco only needed to reach for a handful of shower curtain rings, tugging a handful of strands. He hoped it didn't come to battle. He doubted he could defeat a single enemy ship, let alone the twenty that followed. He had used the ship's cannon once before, firing a stream of plasma into space. They all had; Ben-Ari had insisted they train for battle.

Though if those ravagers catch us, it's a battle we can't win.

He glanced again into the sphere that showed space behind them, the alien equivalent of a rear viewport. The twenty specks--the enemy ravagers--were still there. Even closer. Closer every day.

"They'll be on us in two more days at this rate," Lailani said.

"I know," Marco said.

"The Ghost Fleet is still months away."

"Lailani, I know!"

"We'll starve to death before--"

"Lailani!" Marco spun toward her, still holding two plastic rings. "Yes. I know. I forgot the food. You've been reminding me for four days now. I'm sorry, okay? I doomed us all to death. I know. But maybe we'll be lucky and those ravagers will burn us before we starve. Fine? Happy?"

"You're tilting." She pointed. "Marco, you're tilting left!"

He returned his eyes toward the controls. He adjusted his flight, traveling along their charted course again. Among the strands and spheres, they had set up human monitors, displaying their flightpath and destination. The Ghost Fleet, at least according to Lailani, still lay thousands of light-years away.

"How do we even know the Ghost Fleet is where you say?" he asked.

Lailani groaned. "I told you. You don't listen. We studied it for years in the Oort Cloud. The best scientists in the galaxy."

"And I suppose they were better than all the other scientists, human and alien, who've been searching for the Ghost Fleet for a million years."

"Maybe they were!" Lailani stood up and placed her hands on her hips. "It's not like you had a better plan."

"Your plan is ridiculous!" Marco barked. "It'll get us all killed."

She glared. "Was your plan to lose the food?"

"My plan was to save Addy!" he shouted. "Not to leave her behind! Not to--" He realized what he was saying, realized he was shouting. He took a deep breath. "I'm sorry. I'm lashing out. It's just this place, Lailani. Trapped in this metal box. The hunger. The thirst. Those fucking points of light that keep chasing us."

Lailani seemed ready to shout, then breathed deeply and nodded. "It's fucked up. I'm sorry too. It's not your fault we lost the food. We were all in a rush. We all should have checked and double-checked."

Marco's belly gave a loud growl. As if in response, Lailani's belly answered. They both looked at each other, then burst out laughing.

"They're talking!" Marco said.

"Yours is louder." She poked his belly. "And bigger."

He snorted. "Well, we can't all weigh eighty pounds."

Lailani bristled. "I'm not *that* skinny! I weigh ninety-five pounds. Fine! Ninety-three." She sighed. "I need to work out."

"How about a shift flying the ship?" Marco said. "Tugging all these strands is a good workout. And I told Ben-Ari I'd explore the crawlspace under the main hull. She still thinks I'll find the marauders' pantry. Maybe we'll dine on mummified flies tonight."

"Guh." Lailani stuck out her tongue. "I'd sooner eat my own hair."

As Marco left the bridge, some of the tension left his shoulders. That short laugh, that quick banter, had felt good. Almost normal. Almost like they were kids again back at Fort Djemila.

God, he thought. *I can hardly believe it's been only seven years. That we're the same people.*

Those kids back on that base--Tiny, Maple, Elvis, Beast, Caveman . . . It all seemed like a different life. Seven years ago, when he first met Lailani in the desert, Marco never imagined they'd end up here, stuck on an alien warship, fleeing aliens light-years away from Earth.

I'm only twenty-five, he thought. *But I feel old. I feel like I lived too much. Lost too much. Saw too much death. I feel old.*

He thought back to that last night on Haven. To standing on the roof, contemplating suicide. To that horrible night when he had fled from Anisha, had hired a prostitute, had drunk himself into a stupor, so scared of joy, so worried he could never be happy. He had never come so close to death, maybe not even during the war.

Now I must survive again, he thought. *I must find Addy. I want us all back together. Me. Addy. Lailani. All of us who still live. Maybe we'll never be innocent kids again. But maybe, if we can unite, if we can defeat these marauders, we can still find some peace, some worth to our pained lives.* He nodded, throat tight. *We'll all buy a big house on the beach, a place of peace between trees and water. We'll live together. And we'll forget. We'll all just forget.*

He stepped into the main hold of the *Anansi*, a cavernous space covered with webs. Most of their equipment from the *Saint Brendan* still stood here, sucking on battery power. Only a couple days of juice remained. Ben-Ari and Kemi sat on the floor in front of several tablets. A bed sheet was stretched out beside them, marked with arrows, dots, and numbers.

". . . and at Nightwall too, we flew it," Kemi was saying, pointing at a drawing on the sheet. "Major Verish insisted we drill the move. It might work."

Ben-Ari shook her head. "I don't know, Lieutenant. Maybe against seven ships, yes, but twenty?"

"If we adjust the tilt, and break their formation with an early Spearhead assault, we can divide and conquer. Three maneuvers, one in a row. Like this." With a marker, she scribbled new arrows on the sheet.

"Too risky," Ben-Ari said. "Let's go back to the Maelstrom Gambit. I felt it was stronger."

Kemi opened her mouth, eyes flashing, and was about to say more when she saw Marco. She turned toward him.

"Marco, tell the captain," the pilot said. "A Cabot Gambit, followed by a Spearhead to break the enemy's flight, completed with three Kummerow Maneuvers. It's how you defeat greater odds."

Marco frowned. "What are you two doing?"

Ben-Ari rose to her feet and rubbed her neck. "Figuring out a plan to defeat those twenty ravagers in a fight."

"A fight?" Marco gasped. "Ma'am, with all due respect, they're twenty, and we're just one ship, and we barely know how to fly it."

"Exactly!" Kemi said. "Which is why we need a Spearhead to break their formation first."

Ben-Ari shook her head. "In every simulation we've run, Lieutenant, we never survive the Spearhead Gambit."

Kemi snorted out her breath, blowing back a curl. "Simulators don't know what they're talking about. I've done the Spearhead a hundred times in the Scum War. It'll work."

"What works against scum pods won't work against the larger, deadlier ravagers." Ben-Ari lifted a tablet. "Let me try the Terrell Maneuver again, followed by Brooklyn Run. We'll see what the computer says."

Marco looked at the screen. It showed a small image of the *Anansi* flying against twenty enemies, blowing plasma, and quickly collapsing.

Ben-Ari cringed. "All right, maybe not the Terrell Maneuver."

Marco licked his lips. "There's got to be another way. Some way to escape them, or to negotiate with them, or to hide."

It was Kemi's turn to stand up. She stepped toward him, placed her hands on his shoulders, and stared into his eyes. "In two days, Marco, those ravagers will be on us. We're slower. We have no stealth cloak. We must fight. We must defeat them." Her eyes shone. "Remember the Scum War, Marco. We won battles against greater odds. Throughout history, there are stories of ace pilots winning against greater odds. In two days, I will sit in the pilot's seat of the *Anansi*. I will unleash our plasma. And I will destroy twenty enemy ravagers."

Marco didn't want to remind Kemi that even if they defeated those ravagers, they were still likely to starve. That even if they could destroy a thousand ravagers, it was a drop in the bucket unless they could find the Ghost Fleet, and their battery power was days--maybe only hours--away from running out. Their quest seemed hopeless.

But all Marco could do was nod. Because Kemi and Ben-Ari were right. What other choice did they have?

"All right," he said. "While the officers figure out how to save humanity, the lowly sergeant is going hunting. With all this chaos, we still haven't explored the engine room. I'll see if I can find a power source we can plug into--and some marauder grub."

"If you find mummified fly, I'll have that!" Kemi said.

"Too late, I already promised that meal to Lailani," he said. "But I'll see if I can dig you up some rancid maggots."

"Mmm, my favorite!" Kemi licked her lips.

At the back of the hold, a tunnel led into the lower level of the *Anansi*--a murky network of burrows, sticky with webs. Nobody had explored that shadowy realm yet, not with the mad dash to set up their systems. The *Anansi* was twice *Saint Brendan*'s size, and the lower deck comprised half of it. Hopefully, that basement contained hidden treasures: food, water, maybe a power source they could rig an adapter for. Marco stared down the tunnel, wincing. The shaft was thick with webs and not much wider than him; though marauders were larger than humans, they were excellent at squeezing through tight places.

Before climbing down, Marco drew his knife, a blade Addy had given him back at her apartment on Haven. On further thought, he stepped toward their stockpile of weapons and grabbed a handgun. Just in case of man-eating maggots.

He leaned over the shaft, sawed through webs, and placed his feet into the opening. It was slow going. Every meter, Marco had to pause, spend a few moments cutting through more strands, then keep descending. Marauders breathed thicker, hotter air than humans, and the stifling air aboard the *Anansi* didn't help. Soon sweat soaked Marco.

Eventually he hit bottom. The floor was soft and sticky, like walking over algae. His head grazed webs on the ceiling, the strands as thick as sausages. He lit his flashlight, and the beam illuminated a cavern that seemed organic, the belly of a living beast. The engines thrummed and grumbled ahead, and Marco had the terrible feeling that those weren't engines at all, that the entire ravager was alive, breathing and pulsing like the scum pods.

Ridiculous, he thought. *The ship has a metal hull. An airlock. A bridge. So calm down, soldier.*

He couldn't hear the others from here. The engines hummed ahead, rising, falling, a sound like breathing. The floor quivered. He swept his flashlight from side to side, seeking food stocks, hopefully something edible to humans. Many aliens in the galaxy, Marco knew from school, weren't biological beings. The more advanced ones had uploaded their minds into robots, while others had become beings of pure consciousness with no bodies at all, living in virtual worlds. But the marauders were like humans, still a new civilization, still biological, still needing to feed. Where was their pantry? Would Marco find something to stave off starvation?

I just hope it's not a fridge full of brains, he thought.

A rumble sounded ahead.

Marco froze and his hand strayed to his gun.

Just the engines, he told himself, gulping.

He kept walking, the floor softer now, the walls closer together. More webs coated the walls, yet when Marco pointed his flashlight at them, they looked more like veins. Red liquid flowed through them. He frowned.

"What the hell?"

He stepped closer to one strand. He passed his fingers over it. It pulsed.

That's blood inside, he thought.

The room quivered. The grumble rose again. Marco spun around, pointing his flashlight deeper, and froze.

Fuck me.

His beam of light illuminated a giant, pulsing heart.

He stepped closer, eyes narrowed. The heart was the size of a curled-up man, pumping blood into arteries that ran along the floor, up the wall, and into the ceiling. An airy sound caused Marco to raise his head. Above the heart, clinging to the ceiling, spread two sacks that looked like lungs.

It is *alive,* he thought. *The ship is alive. Not just built from organic material like scum pods but an actual animal.*

He had always assumed that the claws on the ravagers were merely weapons, part of the design. But they were the actual claws of a living, breathing, space-faring creature.

Red light glowed behind the heart. Carefully, Marco walked around the pulsing muscle. He passed between other organs, some as large as bean bags, others no larger than a watermelon; they seemed to have no human analogy. Forgetting his hunger and quest for food, Marco followed that red glow, seeking its secrets.

After a few more steps, he paused and stared. Again, shock filled him.

"Holy shit," he whispered.

The largest organ yet rose ahead, taller than he was. It looked like a stomach, stretched with thick membranes. But inside flowed fire. The heat bathed Marco, so intense he narrowed his eyes and dared not step closer. The flames crackled inside the organ, and a thick tube--the width of the tunnel Marco had climbed down--rose from the stomach to the ceiling.

The plasma depository, he thought. *From here, the creature spews out its flame.*

He was inside the belly of an alien--a living, space-swimming, fire-breathing alien. Even with humanity in danger, with Addy missing, with the enemy chasing them, Marco found himself smiling. The creature was amazing, and it was beautiful.

"Ravagers aren't starships," he whispered. "They're aliens." He placed his hand against the wall. "Hi there, lovely. You'll fly faster for us, won't you?"

As if in answer, the ravager grumbled.

As Marco patted it, more grumbles sounded--these ones from below.

The floor throbbed.

Marco frowned, pointed his flashlight down, and inhaled sharply.

He was standing atop another organ. A womb. And it was full.

Marco leaped back, cringing. He wanted to run, but curiosity got the better of him. He knelt, shining his light on the translucent floor. He could see the babies squirming below, grumbling, moving their clawed legs. Each was the size of Sergeant Stumpy, Marco's old Boston Terrier. They pressed against the walls, blind, squealing, as if eager to emerge.

"Marauders," Marco whispered. "Baby marauders."

He took a step back, gasping. The *Anansi* wasn't just a living starship. She was a mother. A mother to marauders.

"She's a female marauder," Marco whispered, and his eyes widened with the realization--the marvelous, beautiful, terrifying realization. "The ravagers aren't just the marauders' starships. They're the females of the species."

And this one was pregnant.

Kneeling, Marco placed his hand on the womb's translucent wall.

"Hi there, little ones," he whispered. "You're almost as ugly as your daddies, aren't you? Yes you are, yes you--"

The baby marauders leaped up, slamming against the top of the womb. Their jaws opened. They screeched. They already had teeth.

Marco gulped and stepped back.

Sooner or later, we're going to have a problem here.

He bit his lip, ready to climb back to the upper deck and rejoin his crew, when one of the juvenile marauders tore through the womb.

The creature emerged, screeching, reaching out its claws. Its jaw unhinged, full of fangs. It made a pit bull look like a poodle.

Marco took another step back.

Sooner rather than later.

Another baby marauder emerged. A third. A fourth. The womb kept spilling out its children. The creatures scuttled toward Marco, shrieking, demanding to feed.

"All right," Marco said, voice shaking the slightest, and cocked his gun. "You've been bad boys. You're in time out! I'm just going to . . . back up . . . nice and easy . . . and lock you down here forev--"

A baby marauder leaped at him, fangs gleaming.

Marco fired his gun.

His bullet slammed into the marauder. The creature fell back, mewling. Another leaped toward Marco. He fired again, missed, and the alien landed on him. The teeth sank into his shoulder, and he screamed.

"Emery!" The communicator around his wrist crackled to life, and Ben-Ari's voice emerged. "Emery, I heard gunfire! What's going on down there?"

Roaring, he ripped off the baby marauder and tossed it. It hit one of its brothers. More vaulted toward him, and Marco fired again, hit an alien, and shattered its skull.

"It's a female!" he shouted into his communicator. "And it just gave birth!"

He heard the footfalls above: Ben-Ari and Kemi racing across the deck, but he knew it was a long climb down. Another marauder grabbed his leg, clawing at him, ripping his pants, ripping his skin. He fired his gun, narrowly missing his foot. The alien shattered. Another jumped at him.

"Emery!" Ben-Ari's voice rose again from his communicator. "What is going on?"

He fired. Again. Again. He bled. Another marauder bit his shoulder, and he ripped it off, kicked it aside. He released his empty magazine, loaded another into his pistol, and raised the weapon.

Three more marauder spawn still lived, busy consuming their dead brothers. They rose together, squealing, blood on their jaws. They leaped at Marco.

He fired his gun. He hit one. He fired again, missed, again, then hit a second marauder. The third alien knocked him down, and Marco roared in pain, swung his gun, and pistol-whipped the creature, shattering its teeth. The marauder fell back, rose to its feet, and bellowed.

Marco fired, shattering its skull.

That was the last of them.

Marco lay, panting.

"Emery!" Ben-Ari came rushing toward him. "What the hell is--"

She froze.

Her voice died.

Marco leaped to his feet and stared ahead.

His heart sank to his pelvis.

"Oh fuck," he whispered.

One of his bullets had pierced the glowing, pulsing organ ahead--the repository of plasma.

Cracks were spreading across the organ, and a few tongues of flame began to leak out.

"Run!" Marco shouted, grabbing Ben-Ari.

They ran.

Behind them, fire crackled, then roared. Flames licked their backs. They sprinted, found Kemi approaching, and pulled her along. They raced back into the shaft and began climbing. Fire roared across their feet.

They were halfway up the tunnel when the ship jolted madly. The ravager bellowed, a cry of agony. The living ship, the female of the species, tilted and shook. Marco clung to the shaft's webbed walls. Kemi slipped and he caught her. They kept climbing, finally emerging back onto the main deck, singed, panting.

They crawled across the floor, moving away from the heat in the tunnel.

"What was going on down there?" Kemi whispered, wiping soot off her face.

Marco ignored her. He raced toward one of the crates from the *Saint Brendan*. He found them quickly--the fire extinguishers.

"Help me!" he said.

They returned into the *Anansi*'s lower deck, the abdomen of this living ship. They sprayed foam, extinguishing the flames.

Please let the heart keep beating, he thought.

When he reached the ravager's heart, he froze in terror. The organ was dark, enclosed with a rocky shield. But slowly, as the flames died down, the shell cracked open, revealing the heart again. The other organs too were reappearing, their own shells retracting.

"A defense mechanism," Kemi said. "Fascinating! When the plasma reservoir is punctured, shells emerge to protect the other organs. Like white blood cells defending our own bodies. The ravagers must have evolved this ability over time, along with metal skin to withstand the vacuum of space."

"Seems like the little ones aren't as immune," Marco said, pointing at the charred corpses of the baby marauders.

"Poor babies!" Kemi said.

"Poor babies who tried to eat me!" Marco said.

His communicator crackled to life. This time it was Lailani, speaking from the bridge above.

"Um, guys?" she said. "I swear I did not pull the plasma strand. But a few seconds ago, this ship belched out enough fire to burn a small solar system."

Marco raised his flashlight, pointing at the massive organ which had once contained the fire. It was cold, dark, and pierced with a bullet hole.

"Amazing!" Kemi said. "Another defense mechanism! When the plasma supply threatens to burn the ravager from within, she spews it all out into space. Like a human vomiting a meal when the body detects poison. These are truly amazing animals."

Marco winced. "Except now, twenty of these amazing animals are chasing us through space, only a day or so away. And we have no more plasma."

Both turned toward Ben-Ari. She stood beside them, very still, very silent, staring at the pierced organ. Finally she spoke, voice strained.

"Bring a medical kit."

It was almost comical, Marco thought. They stitched up the bullet hole. They placed a bandage on the wound. They hoped the plasma would return into the organ, refill it with fury. But the sack, once containing the ravager's wrath, shrank and shriveled. Finally it dangled like a wrinkled skin tag. The heart still pumped. The lungs still breathed. But the fire was gone.

They all rejoined Lailani on the bridge. They stared together at the viewport. Twenty healthy ravagers still flew in pursuit. Faster, closer than ever.

"We have a day," Lailani said. "Two at most. Then they'll reach us. And we have no more plasma to fight with."

Marco felt them all staring at him. Suddenly, he missed being just the guy who had forgotten the food.

"What do we do now?" Kemi finally whispered. "If we can't reach the Ghost Fleet . . ." She covered her face with her palms, shivering.

I didn't just doom us, Marco thought. *I doomed Addy. I doomed humanity.* He returned to the deck, and he sat in despair. The clock ticked down.

CHAPTER SEVEN

After the longest, most miserable days in Addy's life, the massive transport ship thumped down. Its engines died, and Addy knew: *We're on Earth.*

Days? Yes, perhaps only days--torturous, suffocating days in the heat, the stench. Days of the feeding tube stuffed down her throat, pumping her full of gruel. Days of her fellow rebels hanging around her, their hands severed, another one dying every few hours. Days of human waste dripping down her widening thighs, of a ship full of wretches, crying out, naked, shaved, filthy. Days of agony before the inevitable slaughter. Days? Yes, perhaps only days. Perhaps weeks. Perhaps eras of empires rising and falling. Time had no meaning here. But however long this time had stretched, it had come to an end.

They were home. And that terrified Addy more than a thousand feeding tubes.

When the cattle car stops moving, the cows are slaughtered.

As the engines fell silent, the human agony seemed so much louder. From all across the ship, the thousands cried out. Some prayed. Most screamed. A baby cried, perhaps the one born on the ship.

Marauders crept across the ceiling and walls, ripping the webs that had bound the prisoners during their journey. Half fell as corpses. Grant, still alive, thumped onto the ground. His stumps leaked fresh blood. The veteran groaned, opened his one eye, stared at Addy, then lost consciousness. Marauders laughed, lifted him, and carried him out.

Addy tried to call after him, but the feeding tube still stretched down her throat. For days now, it had been pumping her full of gruel. For days, her body had been growing, stretching the webs that held her. Finally, a marauder grabbed the tube and yanked it out. It came free like a tapeworm, flailing in protest, spurting out its gruel. Addy gagged, vomited, coughed, and nearly passed out. Every breath was a struggle.

Claws ripped her webs, and she fell to the floor. She took deep, ragged breaths, and stars floated before her eyes. Her body shivered, covered in bruises and welts where the webs had pressed against her. Her muscles and joints screamed in agony. The journey couldn't have been too long; she was not obese yet, not a quivering ball of flesh. But her limbs were wider, her belly softer, plumped for a feast.

So much for my hockey career, she thought, then burst out laughing, then wept.

"Nice and plump for the feeding," hissed Orcus. The marauder crept toward her, licking his chops. "Delectable. Soon Lord Malphas will dine. And I will feast upon the scraps." He licked Addy. "I will enjoy you."

On his side, his parasitic twin cackled, jaw snapping. "Feast, feast!"

Orcus lifted her. Addy was too weak to resist. The marauder moved on four legs, carrying her with the other two, and they left the cell. As they climbed up a shaft, the parasitic twin--Addy had nicknamed it Bitey--kept scratching her, drawing blood, and licking her leg.

Orcus carried her onto a higher deck. Thousands of humans were still here, naked, feverish, covered in their own waste. The marauders had opened the hatch, exposing the outside world, and lowered a ramp. The deck, however, was so crowded that people could barely squeeze out.

"Move!" shouted a marauder on the ceiling.

"Out, out!"

Orcus tossed Addy into the crowd. "Out and line up, maggots!"

She banged into other prisoners. With gravity restored, the deck was even more crowded. The dead lay on the floor, dozens, maybe hundreds of corpses. Elders. A baby. Some humans were pinned to the walls, still alive but crushed, crying out, suffocating. They were jammed into the ship like too many pickles in a jar. One by one, prisoners managed to trickle outside into the sunlight, but it was slow business. Limbs were tangled together. The living fell over the dead.

"Move!" the marauders screeched, grabbing prisoners and yanking them out.

Some humans had spent the entire journey pinned to the walls. Their skin had stuck to the metal with sweat, blood, and dry shit; the marauders had to rip them off with claws.

Addy took a step. Another step. Everything ached, and her thighs rubbed together; they had never rubbed together before. Covered with filth, blinking, weak, maybe dying, she shuffled through the crowd toward the sunlight.

As she walked, she placed her hand against the strands of marauder webs still wrapped around her torso. She felt it there. And even through the pain, Addy smiled.

Hidden inside the webs, pressed against her bloated body, it waited. A marauder tooth. Orcus's tooth. A blade harder than steel. It was the length of her thigh. It was a weapon. And she would use it before the end.

She trudged over corpses and out into the light. For a moment she stood, raised her head, and just breathed.

Earth. I'm home. I'm home.

Blue skies spread above her. The air stank of the aliens and prisoners, but she recognized it at once as Earth air, not the acidic, thick air of New Earth. Soil crumbled beneath her feet, and weeds rustled in the wind. This was an ugly place, a place where death dwelled, where blood and human waste soaked the ground, where humans were slaves, awaiting butchery. But it was still her home, and that gave her hope.

Standing with the thousands, she looked around. The ship loomed behind her, a massive black box, still spilling out its human cargo. The sun beat down overhead. It was noon. Farther away, Addy saw the ruins of a city. Skyscrapers rose, some smoking, some in ruins, ending with jagged crowns. Addy frowned. Could it be . . . ?

She gasped. Yes. Even in its ravaged state, there was no mistaking this skyline.

She stood outside Toronto, her hometown.

Her mind reeled. How could it be? Out of all the cities in the world, they took her home? Even after the war against the scum, there were still thousands of cities on Earth. What were the odds of the marauders bringing Addy back to her city?

Then she understood.

I'm food for Lord Malphas himself, she thought. *The marauders told me so. The ruler of the marauders. From here in Toronto, we rose. Me. Kemi. Marco. The heroes of the war against the scum, those who toppled that empire of centipedes. Of course Malphas would set his headquarters here. Where humanity had risen to defeat the scum, the marauders would see us fall.*

Once more, the marauders marched them in lines. More alien starships were thumping down in the distance, and more humans were emerging, also naked and bald. Other lines of prisoners, tens of thousands long, stretched out from Toronto's ruins, snaking for kilometers across the fields.

So Earth no longer fights, Addy thought. *We lost the war.* She kept her hand pressed against her hidden weapon. *But I will still fight.*

The marauders led their captives through the fields. Barbed wire fences stretched along each line, forming tunnels of blades, preventing escape. Some humans still tried to flee, willing to lacerate their flesh for a chance at freedom, only for the marauder webs to catch them, to drag them back into line, their skin in tatters. Addy kept walking with the others. The time to fight would come, but not here, not yet. Not with hundreds of marauders still around them.

She lost sight of Grant. She marched between the barbed wire fences, traveling with thousands. All these roads of metal and misery led through the mud toward a great complex in the wilderness. Metal fences rose high, topped with more barbed wire, and a gateway loomed ahead, bedecked with skulls.

"Go on, move it!" A marauder lashed a strand of web woven with metal spikes, ripping into prisoners' backs. "Through the gates! Into your new home."

As Addy stepped closer to the gate, she raised her eyes and gazed at the skulls. Human skulls. The tops sawed open, the brains consumed. The eye sockets gazed down at her, jaws open in silent screams. A three-headed marauder perched above this lurid gate, drool dripping, legs twisting, a guardian of this hell.

Around the gateway, the fence crackled, and the hairs rose on Addy's nape. This was an electric fence. Several human corpses clung to it, their skin seared onto the metal, their flesh blackened. Perhaps they had tried to climb, to escape what awaited Addy inside. Perhaps they had committed suicide. It reminded her of a concentration camp, the kind she had seen in history books, back from the days before space travel when humanity had faced no natural predators, instead preying upon itself.

"Go!" The marauder with the whip lashed her back. Addy kept walking, hand on her hidden weapon, and passed through the gate.

She paused, looked around, and knew at once: This was no concentration camp. It was a slaughterhouse.

They marched her down a road through the complex. Barbed wire still lined the fence, but it couldn't hide the view. The full terror of this place unfurled around her. Nausea filled Addy, and her fellow captives whimpered, wept, begged. Along the path, humans dangled upside down from hooks, moving on chains. They were still alive, squirming, pleading. As the moving chain passed over pits, marauders reached out and slit each human's throat. The blood gushed into the trench.

Addy gagged. As she walked along the line, she avoided eye contact with those being butchered. She didn't want to see any friends dying here. The whip lashed her back again.

"Keep looking," rasped the marauder with the whip. "We want you to look. See your friends squirm as they die. Let the fear flood your brain." The alien licked his chops. "Fear makes the human brain so much more delicious."

Addy kept walking, unable to hide from the terrors alongside. Farther along her path, just beyond the barbed wire, human corpses were moving on assembly lines, drained of blood. Marauder workers hunched over the moving tracks. With their claws, they carved up the corpses, then packaged them in webs. Legs. Arms. Torsos. The severed heads were cracked open, the brains removed and packed separately, the skulls then cleaned and added to crates. Some of the humans were still alive, still twitching as the claws carved them.

"Meat, sweet meat!" the marauders chanted as they worked. "Crunchy bones and soft marrow, delicious skin and blood! Brains for the rich, flesh for the poor! Meals for conquerors! Meat, sweet meat!"

They were chanting in English. Chanting for the prisoners to understand. Chanting to flood the brains with terror.

Addy wanted to resist, wanted to keep her mind strong. But she couldn't help it. The terror flooded her, soaking her with cold sweat and shaking her limbs.

I never thought it would be possible, she thought. *But I miss the scum.*

The fresh arrivals kept walking along the path, passing through the slaughter, until the marauders corralled them onto a muddy field.

A huge network of cobwebs filled the field. Addy gasped.

Metal poles soared from the earth, taller than her apartment building back in Haven. Branches shot out from the poles, forming bridges and ladders, an entire town of jagged metal rods. And between the bars hung the cobwebs, countless strands, a forest of black, sticky webbing.

In this forest hung thousands of living humans, wrapped and bound, awaiting the slaughter.

Some of the humans were silent, maybe dying. Others wept, screamed, struggled, tried to free themselves but could not.

Many cobwebs were still empty, awaiting the prisoners of Haven.

"Move! In you go. Faster!"

Mud spread between the network of webs, and blood dripped from the prisoners above. The marauders corralled the new arrivals onto the field, cramming thousands together, then lifted them one by one. The aliens carried the captives up the cobwebs, adding them to the others.

Here, in these webs, we will await our turn on the assembly lines, Addy knew. *Here we'll be kept fresh before they butcher us.*

More people kept walking down the road, entering the muddy square between the cobwebs. Most were prisoners from Haven. But some were arrivals from other colonies; Addy could see the cargo ships in the distance. And thousands were coming here from the ruins of Toronto.

Addy stood, hand pressed against her side. The webs were starting to loosen around her torso. She kept tugging them back up, hiding her marauder tooth. Her only weapon. Her only hope. Around her, the marauders were plucking prisoners and carrying them onto the webs. The aliens sang as they worked, this time singing in their language, guttural and hissing and cruel. Some prisoners tried to fight, only to lose fingers and hands to the marauder mouths, to scream as the aliens added them to the cobwebs. Addy clenched her jaw as a marauder lifted Grant--the man was barely conscious--and carried him up a web.

Are you here too somewhere, Marco? she thought. *Will I find you in this horror, or are you out there, still fighting?*

"Come on, get up, buddy." The voice rose behind her. "Come on, you're stronger than this!"

Addy frowned. She knew that voice. She spun around, seeking its source, but the crowd was too thick. The marauders were shoving more and more captives onto the field, barely keeping up with their comrades who were carrying humans onto the cobwebs.

The voice rose again. "I swear, if you just lie on your ass, I'm going to kick it up to your ears. Come on, buddy, we gotta fight this. Come on, Stooge!"

Addy's eyes widened.

Her heart burst into a gallop.

"Steve," she whispered.

It was him. It had to be him. It was his voice, and who else would be talking to a useless lump of a friend named Stooge?

"Steve!" she cried, seeking him in the crowd, but couldn't see him. "Steve, you bonehead!"

She had met Steve eight years ago, when they had both been only seventeen. They had played hockey on opposing teams, and he had body checked her into the boards. She had responded by delivering a dozen punches to his head. Later that day, she had joined him in his bed, replacing punching and body checking with hot, sweaty sex.

Marco had never liked the guy. The two could not be more different. While Marco was no taller than Addy, Steve was something of a giant, towering and strong. While Marco was studious and intelligent, Steve could hardly be called a scholar; the best thing she could say about his brain was that he was probably safe from marauders. At least he was easy on the eyes--his jaw wide, his eyes sparkling blue, his hair shining gold, his body chiseled. And Addy knew his heart was good, and she had loved him, after a fashion.

She hadn't seen Steve in two years, not since leaving for Haven with Marco. On her first day on Haven, Addy had regretted fleeing Earth, leaving Steve behind. Since then, she had missed his stinky, cluttered apartment, even missed his roommate Stooge who lived on the couch. And she missed Steve's arms around her. Missed feeling small, vulnerable, and safe in his embrace. With Marco and the others, Addy had always been the tall, strong one, the fierce warrior. Steve had always made her feel delicate and small, feel like a woman. For that she loved him.

"Steve!" she cried again. "Dumbass, where are you?"

His head popped up from the crowd twenty meters away. He gaped. "Addy?"

Across the field, the marauders were still grabbing humans, carrying them onto the webs above, and binding them there. Addy elbowed her way between the people still on the ground, approaching Steve. Bigger than almost anyone else here, he struggled to worm his way toward her. Finally they met in the crowd.

"Addy Fucking Linden!" Steve was naked, his head shaved, his body covered with scrapes and bruises. "Did they catch you too?"

"No, Steve, I'm only here for the Chinese buffet."

He looked around him, brow furrowed. "There's a buffet?"

Addy rolled her eyes. "Whichever marauder finally cracks open your skull will be deeply disappointed with his portion." She grabbed him. "Yes, they fucking caught me!"

Steve pulled her into his arms, and she leaned her head against his wide chest. He was so tall that her head barely reached his chin. For a moment, after so many days of terror, she felt safe. God damn it. Even after all this time, she still cared for the big dumb galoot.

"Hey." Steve furrowed his brow. "Did you gain a few pounds?"

She stepped back and raised her fist. "Watch it, or I'll drive a few pounds of knuckles into your teeth." She leaned in closer. "Listen, Steve. We're going to fight. I have a plan." She pulled back the webs that draped her hips, revealing the marauder tooth, then covered the weapon again. "Just stay near me."

His eyes widened. "You have a--"

"Shush!" She glared at him. "Not yet. Tonight."

He looked around, saw the marauders lifting more prisoners onto the web, then looked back at her. He leaned in close and whispered, "So let me get this straight. Are you *sure* there's no Chinese buffet?"

Addy groaned. "Where's Stooge?"

Steve's eyes darkened. "He's not himself."

"You mean he's standing upright, figured out he has opposable thumbs, that kind of thing?"

"Very funny." Steve pulled her through the crowd. "When those fucking spiders invaded, he took it hard. He hasn't said a word since."

"Steve, I've known Stooge since high school, and I've *never* heard him say a word."

"But he always spoke with his eyes," Steve insisted. "Granted, usually his eyes just said: I want more weed. Or: Got any munchies? But now they just look dead. And not the good kind of dead like after he smoked a few. The *bad* kind of dead."

The bad kind of dead, Addy thought. That seemed to be a recurring theme in this slaughterhouse.

They reached Stooge. Addy barely recognized him. She had never truly seen his face; he had sported a shaggy beard and long hair since high school. The marauders had shaved all that off. A pudgy, bald man sat in the dirt, head lowered. Thankfully, cobwebs hung across him, hiding his nakedness.

"Come on, Stooge, buddy, get up," Steve said, then looked back at Addy. "See? He's been like this for days, ever since the spiders arrived."

"Marauders," Addy said. "They're not spiders. Spiders have eight legs." She paused. "Fuck, I'm sounding like Poet."

"Whatever the fuck they are, they're vicious sons of bitches," Steve said. "I miss the scum."

"I was just thinking that," said Addy.

Steve sighed. "I missed you too, Ads. Fuck, I missed you. Why did you run off? I loved those days we had in my place. Why did you leave?"

"Steve, those hippies from Never War wanted to toss me into prison, and those Nazis from Earth Power wanted to make me their figurehead. What was I supposed to do? Stay on Earth and either become a prisoner or a skinhead?" Addy passed her hand over her bald head. "Well, I suppose that last one came true."

"You could have hidden in my apartment." Steve's eyes were suddenly red. "But you chose Marco."

She snorted. "Chose Marco? The little dude's like my little brother. I just . . . had to look after him, all right? I had to protect him."

"And did you?" Steve looked around. "Is he here? Is he . . ." He gulped.

He left without me, Addy wanted to say. *He got on a spaceship with Ben-Ari and Kemi and Lailani. And they all left without me. I'm about to be brain food, and they're off gallivanting across the galaxy. Probably eating hot dogs too.*

"He's off finding help," she said instead. "With my friends. Finding help to defeat these asshole bugs."

"And they didn't take you?" Steve's eyes hardened, and he clenched his fists. "I'll pound them all! I'll--"

"They needed me here," Addy said, pulling down his fists. "Because I have a plan. Steve, we're going to--"

"Silence!" A voice rumbled, and a marauder trundled toward them, shoving people aside. Crimson horns grew from his warty head, and blood stained his serrated teeth. "No talking, scum!"

Daniel Arenson

"Actually, we're humans," Addy said to the creature. "The scum are giant centipedes. You know, the aliens we humans killed? We're very good at killing aliens."

The marauder's eyes blazed. He snapped his jaws at her, assailing Addy with rancid breath. His claws reached out, grabbed Addy, and wrapped her in webs. She winced, keeping her hand pressed to her hip, hiding her ivory blade. She was tempted to fight now, to kill this beast, to kill them all, to die in glory. That would be a good kind of death.

But no. Her time to die was not now. Not here. She didn't just want to fight. She wanted to *win*. And that meant patience.

It took three marauders, shrieking with fury, to knock down Steve and wrap him with webs. All the while, the hulking hockey hooligan shouted, kicked, spat, even managed to dent a marauder's horn. Finally the aliens cocooned the beefy man, and all three marauders worked together, carrying up the bundle. Stooge, meanwhile, barely put up a fight as the aliens trussed him up.

The marauders climbed the poles, carrying their prisoners. They crawled over humans already in the web--mothers, fathers, children, all crying out in despair.

"Stay strong, friends," Addy whispered to those she passed. "Believe in Earth."

"Earth has fallen!" an old man said.

"We survived the scum," Addy answered, hanging in a marauder's grip. "We will survive the marauders."

"They are stronger than the scum!" cried out a woman, dangling from the web.

"Then we will be stronger than we ever were," said Addy.

The marauders took her higher, so high that the air thinned out, and she could see the entire slaughterhouse and the wilderness beyond. The lines of new arrivals were still streaming in. The assembly lines were still chugging along, the humans being butchered, then carved up, the meat and organs packaged and crated. Addy could almost sympathize with her hot dogs.

If I ever get out of here, she thought, *I swear, Great Hot Dog in the Sky, I will only eat veggie dogs.*

They climbed even higher, and she stared beyond the slaughterhouse at the distant city. Toronto lay in ruin. She wondered how many people were still there, whether anyone was still fighting, whether there was still a Human Defense Force, still a resistance to the marauders.

If the HDF fell, it's up to you, Marco. And to me.

The marauders left her at the top of the web. Steve hung at her side, still shouting curses down at the aliens. Stooge hung beside them, soon snoring. As the marauders kept carrying up prisoners from below, Addy wrapped her fingers around her hidden tooth.

"Why don't they just kill us already?" Steve said, head hanging low. Blood dripped from his lip.

"We're just here waiting our turn," Addy said. "They have only so many assembly lines and butchers. They'll get us soon. Maybe today. Maybe tomorrow. And then we're off to Marauder-

Mart's meat aisle. So do you want to turn into a steak or a sausage?"

Steve strained against the webs, unable to break them, then hung limply. "So it's come to this. We don't die at war. We die being turned into marauder Spam."

"I don't intend to die here," Addy said. "We wait until tonight, until it's dark . . . and then we'll show these assholes human pride."

CHAPTER EIGHT

"So we have no food," Ben-Ari said. "We have no fire. We're slower than the enemy. And within a day, twenty ravagers will catch us. Did I get that right?"

The crew of the *Anansi* sat on the bridge, dour and still. Kemi was piloting the wounded, living ship--a female marauder, all her fire spilled out into space. Marco and Lailani sat beside the pilot, stomachs grumbling. They had been living on whatever scraps they had found in their backpacks: a few protein bars, some candy, a box of crackers, and packets of condiments. It was all gone now, and the hunger was growing. Soon they would be reduced to eating the charred baby marauders in the bowels of the ship--not a prospect that excited anyone.

Ben-Ari paced the confined space. She had finally changed out of her prison jumpsuit into a uniform. The HDF had stripped her of her rank, and she no longer wore golden bars on her shoulders, but nobody here doubted her command. To them, she was still Captain Einav Ben-Ari, the officer who had led them to defeat the scum, who now led them on this new mission. But was this quest doomed?

"If we can still find the *Saint Brendan*," Kemi said, voice weary, "I have some new ideas for repairing the stealth cloak, and-_"

"The *Saint Brendan* is long gone," Ben-Ari said. "She's light-years away by now, and even if we *could* find her, she's set to self-destruct when the airlock opens. No. Think again. Another plan."

"We find a friendly species," Lailani said. "Other aliens must hate the marauders. They'll feed us and help us fight. We'll find help on the way."

Ben-Ari shook her head. "We're deep in marauder territory. According to every map I looked at, this is their empire. Any world we land on, we'd find them there."

Marco stood up, walked toward the wall, and lowered his head. Guilt filled him. He had forgotten the food aboard the *Saint Brendan*. He had shot this ravager in her plasma reserves, destroying any chance of battling the enemy. This was all his fault. He would have to think of a way out.

"What we need," Marco said slowly, "is another ship."

"No kidding," Lailani said. "Ideally a cargo barge, one stocked with tacos." She patted her belly and winced. "It's official now. My stomach is touching my back."

Marco paced the bridge, frowning, nodding. "Another ravager. We need to swap ravagers."

"We already tried swapping ships," Lailani said. "Remember? We hopped from the *Saint Brendan* here, and the enemy still knew to follow us."

"Because they're smart," Marco said. "They figured we'd take the *Anansi*--a faster, larger, more powerful vessel. And they've been tracking the *Anansi* since. But what if we could sneak into *another* ravager? Secretly this time. And then we'll send the *Anansi* out on her own--and let the marauders chase an empty ravager."

"But *how*?" Lailani rolled her eyes. "Do you see any other ravagers here? Oh wait! I see twenty more. Twenty chasing us, ready to kill us!"

"Wait." Ben-Ari walked up to them. "I think I know what Sergeant Emery is thinking." She turned toward Lailani. "Bring up the star maps again, the ones we were looking at earlier."

Lailani sighed. "All right, Captain, but I'm telling you. Nothing but marauder planets for light-years around."

The little sergeant pulled down a hanging monitor, hit a few buttons, and pulled up a chart of systems within a few hours' flight. The closest star had several planets, all gas giants, one with a single forested moon.

"That's the only habitable world nearby," Lailani said, tapping the screen. "And our records show the marauders conquered it a year ago."

Marco nodded. "So that's where we'll find our second ravager."

Lailani stared at him as if he had grown horns. "So let me get this straight. Facing twenty ravagers in space isn't enough for you. You want to land on an entire world full of marauders?"

Marco nodded. "A forested world, yes. A world where, under cover of trees, we'll make a swap. We just need to find another ravager on the surface, hidden in the forest. Take it over. Then send the *Anansi* back out into space. We can build a rig, a remote control to tug the right strands and fly her out--maybe not with Kemi's finesse, but enough to get her going. With any luck, our pursuers will keep chasing the *Anansi*--an empty ship."

They all turned toward Ben-Ari, waiting for her decision. She stared back, silent for long moments.

She looks older than her years, Marco thought. *She's only twenty-seven, but her eyes are ancient, tired.*

And it wasn't just the hunger, just the wounds, just the exhaustion, Marco knew. It was what they were all feeling. What had driven him to the roof on Haven. The endless anxiety, the lingering pain. The shell shock and the continuing trauma, and never a moment to catch their breath. Marco saw the same weight on Ben-Ari that he himself had been carrying since the war against the scum.

We've all been having nightmares, Marco thought. *We're all still so hurt.*

But still Ben-Ari stood tall, and still her shoulders were squared. And though Marco still fostered rage that she had left Addy behind, at that moment, he loved his captain. She was, as she had always been, his pillar of strength, his anchor in a crumbling galaxy.

Ben-Ari nodded. "We need food. We need another ship. We'll travel to this forested moon, and we'll find both. And then we'll blast off to find this Ghost Fleet and save the galaxy."

"And eat lots of tacos!" Lailani said. Her stomach growled in agreement.

"I might just be able to build us that remote control rig," Kemi said. "Do we still have the cyber-wrenches from the *Saint Brendan*? They extend and contract on command. I used them all the time as a Firebird pilot when we needed to repair things outside the ship. You can control them remotely from a tablet. I'll attach wrenches to the right strands here in the *Anansi*'s bridge. Just seven or eight should give me the functions I need, along with a camera mounted above them. I can probably set it all up within a few hours, and then I can pilot the *Anansi* from afar. Once we're safe on the moon, I can send her off into space and let our friends follow an empty ship."

"I'll work on scanning the forest moon," Lailani said. "I learned a lot about scanning for distant signatures while stationed at the Oort Cloud. I'll see if I can find us an isolated ravager down there, something hidden in the forest, and we can make the swap. Assuming we can blast whatever marauders we find inside."

Ben-Ari smiled thinly--her first smile in days. "Blasting them will be up to Marco and me." She turned toward Marco. "Sergeant Emery, you and I will form the vanguard. Into your battle fatigues. Grab your weapons. Apply your war paint. Then we'll run some simulations in the *Anansi*, practicing clearing out a ravager. Once more, we go to war."

And suddenly Marco was back there. A kid again, just a scared teenager, following a twenty-year-old ensign to battle against the scum. Once more, he was with his friends. And if his eyes dampened, it was not in fear but in memory of lost times that could never return. Of friendships that still warmed him. He saluted her--his officer, his sister-in-arms, his captain. She returned the salute, and now the smile extended to her eyes.

They changed course, heading toward the nearby star system.

Behind them, the twenty ravagers followed.

For the first time in years, Marco prepared for war. They had brought several Human Defense Force uniforms with them, and pulling on the old olive drab felt as familiar as coming home. He bloused his pants over his boots. He buttoned his shirt. He had kept his army dog tags in his wallet--he never parted from them--and slipped them back around his neck. When he was ready, he looked at his reflection in a dark monitor.

A helmet topped his head. A T57 assault rifle, the same model he had carried for years, hung across his back. War paint covered his face. He no longer saw the twenty-five-year-old veteran, shell-shocked, withering away in a cage. He saw the teenage soldier again. That both comforted and terrified him.

The hours flowed by. They drew closer to the nearby star system, and the pursuing ravagers kept following, slowly shrinking the gap. Marco spent the last hour working with Kemi, putting together a remote control rig for the *Anansi*. The cyber-wrenches were expandable, comprised of many joints, used to repair starships via remote control. It took some tweaking--adjusting lengths, fastening pieces with cable ties, removing and tightening bolts. Finally they attached wrench by wrench to the alien strands, then linked them wirelessly to a tablet control panel.

As the two worked, the tools spread out around them, Marco found himself looking up at Kemi too often, then quickly looking away. She didn't seem to notice. The young pilot's brow was furrowed with concentration, and she stuck out her tongue, screwing two hydraulic arms together. Her curly hair kept falling across her eyes, and she kept blowing it back.

Being here with Kemi again, after years apart, also felt so familiar. And once more, as when putting on his uniform, it seemed to Marco that they were teenagers again. That none of the past seven years--going to war, losing their souls--had happened. That he could go over to Kemi right now, hug her, kiss her, laugh with her, that they could cuddle in bed and watch old *Space Galaxy* episodes, make love, cook breakfast in their sweatpants and spend the day walking the city. That none of these bad things had happened, had scarred them.

But no. Kemi was different now too. Her left hand was missing, replaced with a mechanical prosthetic. She was still beautiful--devastatingly so, Marco thought--but this was no longer the beauty of an innocent girl. Kemi now shone with the beauty of a woman who had fought, loved, lost, the beauty of wisdom and courage.

"This stupid . . ." Kemi groaned and pushed back her hair. "I can't . . ." She twisted her wrench mightily, but the bolt wouldn't nudge, and she tossed down the tool. She looked up at Marco. "Thing is stuck."

"Let me try." Marco moved closer to her, took hold of the wrench, and they twisted it together. Finally the bolt loosened, and Kemi fell onto her back, then pushed herself back up, smiling thinly.

"Thank you," she said, looking up at him between her fallen curls.

Marco reached out, tucked her hair behind her ear, then quickly pulled his hand back, worried that he had gone too far. But Kemi's smile only widened.

"Too much hair," she said.

They were sitting uncomfortably close now, closer than they had been in years. Marco thought back to that day seven years ago, the first--the only--time they had made love. It had been both the best and worst day of his life. The day they had broken up. The day before going to war.

"Do you ever wonder what might have happened," he said softly, "if the scum had never invaded? If we had never been drafted? We might be back now in your apartment or mine, solving puzzles instead of building rigs."

She laughed. "When did we ever solve puzzles?"

"That one time!" Marco said. "The puzzle of Big Ben, remember? We hung it up in the library."

She gasped. "Yes! I remember that! I forgot . . . It rained that day, and we spent it indoors. The power was out again, and we lit candles everywhere . . ." Suddenly she looked away, eyes damp. "But that was a long time ago."

Marco nodded, turning his head away. A long time ago. Before he had fallen in love with Lailani. Before the girls on Haven. Before Anisha. Before the wars had taken Kemi's hand, had broken Marco's soul. Perhaps those times could never come back. Perhaps they could never be those two kids again, innocent, in love, happy. Perhaps those feelings were just ghosts, as fleeting as the Ghost Fleet they sought.

"We'll find good times again," Marco said. "We'll emerge from this shadow. We'll save Earth and fly back home. I've been thinking. Once the war is over, we can buy a house. All of us. You, me, Addy . . . Lailani and Ben-Ari too, if they want to join. A big mansion on the beach. We'll light candles at night, and build campfires on the sand, and tell old stories. Just the good, funny ones. I think after everything, we deserve that. To retire somewhere on the water." He lowered his head, his cheeks suddenly hot. "Anyway, it was just an idea."

Kemi patted his knee, smiling. "I like that idea."

Lailani burst into the room, carrying a box of equipment, and Marco instinctively moved away from Kemi.

"Are you two almost done?" Lailani said. "We're less than an hour away from the forest moon, and I need help untangling the quantum cables. Fucking things are more knotted than Christmas lights in July."

Kemi nodded. "Help her, Marco. I'm almost done here."

As Marco walked away, heading to the airlock, he felt both women watching him--Kemi and Lailani, the two loves of his life, perhaps the only two women he had ever truly loved. Perhaps both were lost to him now.

Maybe our romance is over, Marco thought as he entered the airlock. *Maybe it can never be rekindled, not with Kemi, not with Lailani. But I still love them. If anyone is up there, if anyone in the cosmos can hear . . . don't let me lose them like I lost Addy. Like I lost so many friends. Let us win. Let us put together the puzzle of our lives, navigating by candlelight in the dark.*

The star system came into view ahead. Ben-Ari, Marco, and Lailani gathered on the bridge. Kemi sat here in her seat, flying the ship by tugging on cords. Fifteen planets circled a young star--a dozen gas giants and two hellish infernos with runaway greenhouse effects. A green moon was orbiting an indigo gas giant with glistening azure rings. Toward this small verdant world they flew.

"It's remarkably Earth-like," Lailani said, reviewing readouts on her tablet. "In fact, a lot nicer than New Earth. Probably would have made an ideal human colony, if it were closer. According to my database, no human has ever set foot here. But an old scientist, seventy years ago, discovered this moon from a distance. He called it Nandaka, naming it after the god Vishnu's sword."

Marco glanced at the tablet in his hands, showing the location of their pursuers. They were close now, roaring toward the same star system.

"We won't have long down there," Marco said. "Those bastards are right on our tail."

"I'm about to turn off the warp drive," Kemi said. "At least, I think I am. I haven't pulled this strand yet. Hold on to something!"

They all clung to the webs along the walls.

The *Anansi* moaned.

It was an organic sound. The sound of a living animal. As the ship thrummed, Marco found himself stroking the wall.

Good girl, he thought. *Nice and easy.*

Since discovering the ship's secrets, Marco wondered whether the *Anansi* was sentient, or whether female marauders had simply evolved to bear the males' children, transport them across the galaxy, and have no independent thoughts. As the ship now moaned and trembled, sliding back into regular spacetime, Marco could feel her energy, her lifeforce, her pain and loneliness.

She's not evil like the males, he thought. *She's not aggressive. Not a meat-eater. She has suffered so much.*

And suddenly, as spacetime uncoiled around them, Marco found himself gazing through the ship's eyes, seeing the cosmos like an endless dark ocean. Rising from warped space, he felt like a whale breaching the water for air, thankful for a deep breath after so long in the murk.

The gas giant came into view ahead, brilliantly blue, its silvery rings catching the starlight. Before it hovered the verdant moon. The beauty filled Marco's heart with elation--no, not *his* heart but a larger heart, wounded, uplifted, pumping deep within a metal body.

Friends. Family. The thoughts flowed into Marco, not his own. *A place to rest.*

"Sergeant Emery, are you with me?"

Marco blinked, and his consciousness slipped back into his own body. Once more he stood on the bridge of the *Anansi*. He nodded at Ben-Ari.

"I'm here, Captain." He hefted his gun. "Whatever's waiting out there, we'll face it."

Lailani checked her instruments. "I'm detecting a hundred ravagers orbiting the moon. Hard to say how many are on the surface. The trees are hiding so much of what's down there, but I'm detecting heat signatures in pockets around the mountains. Probably easier for the marauders to communicate with their friends from the peaks." She bit her lip. "Meanwhile, our twenty friends are still in warped space, moving fast. They'll be here in an hour. If we're lucky."

Ben-Ari nodded. "That means we have an hour to land and send the *Anansi* back out. Until our pursuers emerge from warped space, they can't communicate with Nandaka. We fly in casually, like we're just another ravager on its business. Lieutenant Abasi, you got that?"

"Aye, Captain," Kemi said. "Taking us into orbit, nice and smooth. Lailani, send me coordinates for a good place to land."

As they approached the green moon, several ravagers detached from orbit and came flying toward the *Anansi*. Marco stiffened, gripping his rifle, as if he could fight the ships from here.

"Fuck," Lailani muttered.

"Keep us nice and easy, Lieutenant Abasi," Ben-Ari said, though her voice was strained. "They don't know we're humans aboard. We're just a bunch of marauders coming for a visit." The captain glanced at Lailani. "And mind your language on my bridge, Sergeant."

Ten or more ravagers were now racing toward them from Nandaka's orbit. Even if the *Anansi*'s plasma canon were working, they were too many to fight. Kemi's hands trembled, but she kept flying smoothly, and the forested world grew closer ahead. So did those other ravagers.

"They're hailing us, Captain," Kemi said.

"Ignore it." Ben-Ari's hand also reached toward her gun, a nervous habit. "Keep going."

"Captain, they're trying to open a communication channel," Kemi said. "The spheres are activa--"

"Shut them off," Ben-Ari said.

Kemi nodded, tugged a few strands, and the spheres across the bridge went dark.

"I don't like this," Lailani muttered. "They're suspicious. They're going to roast our asses."

"For all they know, we're just a wounded ravager returning from battle, her cannon and communication systems broken," Ben-Ari said. "Remember, our friends back there are still in warped space. They won't be able to alert anyone for another hour."

"Captain, their claws are opening!" Kemi said. "They're about to blow plasma. We have to run!"

Marco looked at a monitor; it was wirelessly connected to sensors from the *Saint Brendan* they had attached outside the *Anansi*'s hull. The enemy appeared on the screen, and Marco cringed. The ravagers had always reminded him of closed metal flowers, and now their petals were blooming open, revealing flaming innards. In seconds, that inferno would blaze across the *Anansi*.

"All right, Lieutenant," Ben-Ari said, pale. "We tried. We'll retreat and--"

"Wait," Marco said.

"Sergeant--" Ben-Ari began, voice tense.

"Wait!" Marco repeated, remembering how he had felt a connection to *Anansi*, to this living creature. He placed his hand on the wall and closed his eyes.

"Captain, their cannons are about to fire!" Kemi said.

"Defensive maneuvers!" Ben-Ari shouted.

There there, girl, Marco thought, stroking the wall. *You can hear me, can't you?*

The ship moaned. Fear pulsed through her. The walls trembled under his palm.

"They're firing!" Kemi's voice sounded distant. "We're too close to the moon to get back into warped space!"

"Dodge the assault!" Ben-Ari cried, voice muffled, echoing, as if coming from kilometers away.

Marco kept his eyes closed, kept his hand on *Anansi*'s wall.

It's all right, girl. It's all right. I'm sorry we hurt you. I want to set you free.

The ravager seemed to weep. She had suffered so much. Her memories flooded Marco--memories of the male marauders hurting her, enslaving her, driving her to war, stabbing her innards with electrical rods.

They won't hurt you again, Marco thought, passing the words into her. *But right now, I need you to talk to your sisters. Tell them to stop firing. Tell them that you come in peace. That you're coming home. Can you do that?*

The ship's fear seemed to ease. Her engines purred. Her claws began to open.

"Lieutenant Abasi, why are you exposing our cannon?"

"I'm not, Captain!" Kemi frowned. "The . . . the ship is flying itself." She gasped. "We're emitting some kind of radiation."

Lailani pointed. "The enemy ravagers are closing their claws! They're no longer attacking."

Marco breathed out in relief, pulling his consciousness back into his body. Outside the viewport, he could see it. The other ravagers were turning aside, opening a path down toward the moon.

Ben-Ari was staring at him strangely. "It seems that our dear Sergeant Emery is full of surprises."

The others turned toward him.

"Marco, what the fuck did you do?" Lailani said, one eyebrow raised.

"Put on the ole' Emery charm," he said.

Lailani rolled her eyes. "Honestly, Poet, I'm surprised you haven't fucked the ship by now, with your record."

"Language!" Ben-Ari said.

They entered the atmosphere, finding themselves in blue skies over lush forests. Alien birds fluttered over the canopy, and rivers snaked between verdant mountains. Nandaka, this large moon of a blue gas giant, rustled with life. It had been years since Marco had seen so much green. They all stood silently, watching. Kemi had tears on her cheeks.

"It looks like Earth," the pilot whispered. "Do you think Earth still has trees, still has beauty?"

"Earth might be ugly now," Marco said, "but we'll rebuild her. We'll make her good again."

And we'll find Addy.

They landed in a valley clearing, a few kilometers away from where Kemi had detected a marauder base. Before opening the airlock, Kemi and Marco installed the harness they had built, enabling them to remotely control the *Anansi* and send her back into space--hopefully with their enemies pursuing the empty vessel. But Marco knew now that the *Anansi*, even without the harness, would find her way, would find freedom and peace.

Goodbye, girl, he thought, patting the hull. *Godspeed.*

Wearing their uniforms, carrying their guns, the four Dragons opened the airlock and stepped onto the surface of Nandaka.

Trees soared around them, as tall as skyscrapers, heavy with luminous yellow flowers. Tentacled plants coiled on the forest floor like anemones, reaching out toward buzzing, translucent insects the size of sparrows, their wings purple and shimmering green. Beams of sunlight filtered through the canopy, glistening with pollen, and birds with silky blue tails fluttered above.

"It's beautiful," Kemi whispered.

Lailani licked her lips. "Those birds look delicious."

"Let's get the *Anansi* off the planet first," Ben-Ari said. "Then we'll have time to hunt for food, and just as importantly-- hunt for another ship. Lieutenant Abasi, can you boot up your tablet and--"

Shrieks from the trees interrupted the captain.

Dozens of pale creatures leaped down from the canopy. Their eyes blazed with fury, and their hands opened, revealing toothy mouths on the palms.

As his comrades raised their guns, Marco sighed.

Nothing is ever easy.

CHAPTER NINE

The sun fell, the moon was new, and Addy drew her sword.

She still hung on the web, and still the slaughter below chugged along. Still the screams, the clanking chains, and the marauder shrieks rose in a song. Still the corpses dangled on chains, moving line by line, swaying, dancing the dance macabre. Fires blazed across the camp, reflecting in the eyes of the creatures, and shadows lurched.

Through those shadows she would move. In that darkness she would creep. She, Staff Sergeant Addy Linden, who had faced the scum with fire and screaming bullets and furious raining death--she would travel through the cloak of night, armed with only the tooth of a rancid beast. And in the wilderness, she would seek life.

I was a warrior queen of fire, she thought. *Now I will be a mistress of shadows. Now I will be she who strikes from darkness, who--*

"Addy?" Steve whispered at her side. "Addy, do you have a cig?"

She blinked, her thoughts interrupted. She turned to glare at Steve, who hung on the web beside her.

"How the fuck would I have a cig?" she whispered back. "Didn't you notice that the marauders stripped us naked? Now shut up! I'm formulating my plan."

She, Steve, and thousands of other captives hung on the webs stretched between metal poles. When Addy looked down, she could see the slaughterhouse at work. The horror spread for kilometers around: hooks on chains, bearing squirming, screaming humans; pits where marauders slit their victims' throats, bleeding them out; assembly lines where the aliens butchered the corpses, packaging meat and organs; and transport vessels of jagged black metal to ship out the meat. Around the camp spread the electric fence. There was only one gate, one path to freedom, and the enemy defended it.

Yet many marauders were sleeping now. Only a handful were still manning the assembly lines, taking the night shift. A handful of others guarded the gate. If Addy wanted a time to escape, she wouldn't find a better one.

We must kill the marauders on that gate, Addy thought. *If we sneak up, enough of us, and--*

"Addy!" Steve whispered again.

"What?" She turned toward him.

"You have a marauder tooth!" he said.

She rolled her eyes. "I know, Steve. It's the cornerstone of my plan. At least, if you shut up and let me think."

Steve didn't seem to hear. "So if you have a tooth, maybe you have cigarettes too. Can you check?"

She glared at him. "How about you check that the marauders haven't removed your brain already?"

He snorted. "Yeah, Addy. Like I wouldn't know if they had done *that*." He hesitated, gingerly touched his head, then snorted again. "As if!"

Addy sighed. How had she ever wasted time on that useless lump of muscle?

"All right, listen up, Steve. You too, Stooge." She turned toward the pudgy, snoring man who hung at her other side. She nudged him until he awoke. "I'm going to cut us loose. We creep down, as quiet as can be. We make for the gate--just us. We move silently, shadow to shadow, nimble as cats in the night."

Steve cringed. "Addy, Stooge can't even walk to the bathroom without knocking over my bongs. And twice he mistook my hockey trophy for a urinal. I don't think *nimble* is his forte."

"Well, then he can be a bloody distraction and get his brains eaten while we escape!" Addy snapped. "That is, if they can find anything but bong smoke inside his skull. Now shut up and get ready for our great escape."

She slipped out her weapon--a marauder tooth, snatched during the failed mutiny on their transport ship. Orcus's tooth-- taken from the very bugger who had first captured Addy on Haven. As she sawed at the webbing, she wished she had her old comrades with her, the fellow Dragons. Lailani, tiny but fierce. Marco, bookish but noble. Kemi, intelligent, capable, calm and quick under pressure. Captain Ben-Ari, a woman Addy had grown to admire, the only authority figure she respected. Addy had fought with them in the great war, and here alone, with only Steve and Stooge, she missed them. She needed them.

And suddenly, as she was cutting the webs, she was crying. Because she missed her friends. And she didn't know if they had abandoned her, betrayed her, left her to this hell. And the thought of such a betrayal seemed worse than a thousand deaths in a slaughterhouse.

"Hey, Ads," Steve said, voice soft. "It's all right. I'll look after you. I know . . ." He cleared his throat. "I know I'm not Marco. I'm not smart like him, not with books and words and stuff. But hey, we used to beat up hockey guys together, right? We can beat up some aliens."

Addy sniffed, freed an arm, and wiped her eyes. "Steve, we used to beat up each other mostly. Well, I would beat you up."

"Only because I let you!"

"You did not!" She freed her other arm.

"I'm a big guy, Addy. I stand half a foot taller than you, and even you're a giant, and I'm probably twice your weight, and you weigh about as much as a rhinoce--"

"Watch it!" Addy said.

Steve gulped. "In any case, if I don't want to get beat up, I don't. Those marauders will learn that. I'm not smart. I know that. But I'm strong. And you have me fighting with you." Suddenly his own eyes dampened. "You've always had that, even when you didn't know it."

Addy blinked away fresh tears, reached across the web, and touched his shoulder. "I always knew, ya big galoot. Now shut up and let me cut you loose."

She reached out toward him with her tooth, then froze.

Movement below.

A marauder was climbing the web toward them.

Slowly, Addy pulled her hand back toward her, hiding the tooth behind her back. Steve inhaled sharply, pressing himself against the web. Addy had already freed his arms; he slung them back into the webs.

The marauder kept climbing toward them, gripping the webs with all six legs, grunting, snorting. In the dim light from the fires below, Addy saw the horns, the empty eye socket, the twitching conjoined twin. With flaring fury, she recognized him. Orcus. The marauder who had kidnapped her on Haven. The marauder who had bitten off Grant's hands. The marauder who had shoved a feeding tube down her throat.

Hatred flooded Addy. She had already taken one of the beast's eyes. She longed to leap down, to stab the other three, to kill this monster. He had hurt her. He had hurt her more than anyone ever had. But Addy inhaled deeply, forcing herself to calm down, to wait. Now was not her time to fight, not here, not with a hundred marauders below, ready to race up.

A few years ago, I'd have jumped onto this creature and died in battle, she thought. *Maybe Marco did teach me some prudence after all.*

Orcus reached her. The alien placed his six legs around her, three on each side, trapping her in a cage of spikes and claws.

He lowered his massive jaws, the size of a crocodile's mouth, and gazed at her with his three remaining eyes.

"Addy . . ." he hissed. "Still alive, I see . . . Still awaiting your turn . . ."

Addy nodded. "This is the longest game of Monopoly ever."

"Humor." The marauder snarled. "A human weakness. The Soul King only knows how your kind ever ventured into space." He sniffed her skull and shuddered as if savoring the scent. "Your brains, though. So full of fear, of pride, of aggression. So tender. So delectable. Only sentient species are such a delicacy. Oh, what I wouldn't give to feast upon your brain . . ."

"Have you considered switching to kale?" Addy said. "I hear it's very good for you, and it might help your complexion."

His tongue reached out, lined with small teeth like a chainsaw. He licked her, scraping her skin, and she grimaced.

"Don't worry, Addy Linden," Orcus said. "My Lord Malphas, son of the Soul King himself, knows of your presence here. He will arrive shortly to feast upon you. He enjoys his meals fresh, still wriggling, still begging."

"Great," Addy said. "Maybe he'll even leave you my hands to eat. I remember you love those. I'll be sure to flip you off as you gulp them down."

"Your mouth is big." Orcus sneered, saliva dripping. "When my lord arrives, I will enjoy hearing it scream."

"Says the guy with the crocodile jaws," Addy muttered as Orcus crawled back down the web, going to inspect other captives.

Once the marauder was far enough, Addy drew the tooth again. She continued sawing through the web, freeing herself and then Steve. They had to shake, poke, and finally slap Stooge to wake him up, then freed him too. The portly man looked around, scratched his stubbly jowls, and blinked in silent confusion.

"Whoa," was all he said.

As teenagers, Steve, Addy, and their friends would sometimes go camping at night. On one trip, they had brought Marco along. He had been miserable, bored out of his mind as the others played ball, but at night, he had taught them all to tell time by the stars. Addy had rolled her eyes then, embarrassed by her foster brother's awkward, excited nerdiness, but the knowledge had stuck. Tonight, glancing at the Big Dipper, she could tell that it was midnight. The witching hour. A good hour to escape.

"All right, the marauders are off the web," she whispered. "It's time."

She began to climb down, strand by strand, pausing every meter to gaze around, waiting for marauders to leap up. Thankfully, most of the creatures were sleeping, dangling from webs near the surface. Only one assembly line was still operating, its handful of marauders slowing down, perhaps sleepy at this late hour.

As Addy descended the web, other prisoners reached out to her, begging.

"Help . . ."

"Free us!"

"My baby is sick. Please help, please free us . . ."

Addy paused, sudden guilt filling her.

How can I just leave them here?

"Addy, hurry up," Steve whispered, climbing down at her side.

She nodded, climbed down another strand, then paused. She stared at a prisoner in the web, a young girl with black hair, with weepy dark eyes.

"I can't take you all," Addy said. "We can't all flee in the shadows."

She climbed down another strand. A meter above her, Steve and Stooge were descending too. Addy knew she had to leave the other captives here. If she freed them, if too many prisoners tried to sneak out at once, the marauders would surely notice. They would kill them all. She had to. She had to leave that girl. She had to leave them to be butchered, to be eaten.

Sometimes you have to leave comrades behind, Addy thought. *Marco understood that. Ben-Ari did too. It's why they left me.*

She climbed another strand, passing by another child. The trembling boy gazed at her.

"Oh fuck it," Addy muttered. "We're all probably dead anyway, and Ben-Ari can go suck a rotten marauder egg."

She pulled out her tooth and began cutting the boy loose.

"Now stay here," she whispered to the boy. "Pretend you're still tied up. Don't move until I give the signal."

He nodded. Addy moved to another prisoner. With her marauder tooth, she sawed at more strands.

She kept moving between the prisoners. Cutting their strands. Instructing them to wait on the web. She found Grant hanging nearby, his stumps leaking. Her dear old friend from Haven was ashen, struggling for breath. Even after losing both hands to Orcus's jaws, he was clinging to life.

"Addy," Grant whispered as she cut his bonds.

She touched his cheek. He was so cold. "Stay strong, Grant. We're getting out of here. Wait for my signal. Then run with me."

A glimmer filled his sunken eyes. "I will fight with you again, Addy Linden, my heroine." A tear ran down his cheek. "My friend."

Addy had worked for an hour, and she had freed many prisoners, when one--a teenage boy with pimply skin and a black eye--began scuttling down the web, shaking the whole structure.

"Wait!" Addy whispered to him. "Wait for my signal!"

But the boy kept descending, shaking the web. Strands creaked. A pole tilted. Two meters from the ground, the boy hopped down, thumped onto the soil, and began to run.

In the shadows, marauders woke up, raised their heads, and squealed.

The aliens cried out in their language, and a hundred more marauders rose from slumber.

"Now!" Addy shouted at the top of her lungs. "Run!"

She raced down the web as fast as she could. Around her, a hundred prisoners, freed from their bonds, scrambled down with her.

The marauders shrieked and scurried up toward them.

Addy leaped into the air, screamed, and landed on one of the creatures. She placed her feet on its snout. Howling, she drove her ivory blade down, shattering an eye, piercing a brain.

"For Earth!" Addy roared, blood splashing her, and leaped high.

She fell through open sky, kicking. She reached out, caught a web, swung through the air, and slammed her feet into a marauder. She knocked the alien to the ground, and when it leaped back up, she dived onto it. A claw grabbed her, tearing her skin, and Addy drove her tooth into another eye.

They fell together.

They tore through a web, tumbling, ripping through strands, stabbing at each other. The alien's claws moved in a fury, and Addy shouted hoarsely, bleeding, thrusting her blade until they thumped onto the ground.

The marauder lay dead, eyes pierced.

Addy rose.

Panting, wounded, covered in the blood of her enemies, she raised her ivory blade overhead. She howled in fury, tears on her cheeks, for she was a warrior again. And she hated killing. And she was scared. And she hated all this death. But this was who she was, who they had made her. All she knew how to be.

"For Earth!"

And from across the camp, the others answered her cry.

"For Earth! For Earth!"

Steve ran up to her. He kicked the dead marauder again and again, finally knocking out a tooth, and raised it alongside Addy's weapon--two swords. Two ivory blades against the endless horde.

In this camp of death, over these pits of blood, in this slaughterhouse for humans, in this fall from all their grace and vanity, their cries rose together with new pride. Here was human pride. Here was Earth at its lowest and Earth at its finest.

"For Earth! For Earth!"

The marauders leaped at them. Claws tore through flesh. Jaws ripped humans apart.

But some of the aliens died.

And more teeth rose.

And more white blades tore through webs, and more humans ran, and more added their voices to the cry. For two words that meant everything. The two most important words they knew, the most important words in human history.

"For Earth!"

Through the death, they ran. Life rising again. A phoenix from the ashes. Dozens, then hundreds, then thousands.

Addy ran at their lead, bleeding, weeping, fighting, killing. Around her, people died. Before her, marauders screamed.

And she fought. She fought until they reached the electric fence around the camp. Until they reached the marauders guarding the gate.

And here--here was humanity's greatest, noblest battle. Addy had fought at Abaddon. She had fought with a fleet of a hundred thousand starships, wonders of technological might. She had fought with millions of soldiers, armed with guns and tanks and shrieking jets of war. Here they fought naked, brutalized, weak, bald and bleeding and starved. Here they were no army, merely wretches, barely human. Yet here they were more human than ever. Here was greater courage than any Addy had seen in the great battles against the scum.

Here many died. They died between the jaws of the marauders. They died tossing themselves on the electric fence, burning. They died in mud and filth, and none would remember their names.

They died heroes.

When Grant fell, marauder claws in his chest, he gave Addy a last look, and his eyes shone.

"Goodbye, my friend," he whispered. "I die fighting alongside you. I die proud."

His eyes closed, and Addy wept for him. Grant had saved her life in Haven. She had failed to save his, and she mourned him.

She kept fighting. For him. For all humanity.

The rebels ran onward, fighting with sticks and stones, with tooth and nail. They knocked down the fence, and when it hit the mud and its power died, a great cry of triumph rose.

Roaring, Steve lashed his tooth into the eye of a marauder, slaying the beast. Even Stooge fought, howling like a berserker, swinging a tooth-sword in each hand. They raced over corpses, mostly of humans but of aliens too, and out of the slaughterhouse. They raced across the field. They raced over the good earth, the soil of their planet, as the familiar stars shone above.

The fleets around the planet perhaps had fallen. The army was perhaps no more. The city before them lay in ruins, and across the world, billions perhaps were enslaved.

But here, for one night, humanity was free.

Here, in darkness, they were victorious.

Above, fires blazed. Ravagers appeared in the sky. A hundred alien ships were descending toward them.

The captives froze, pointed, and cried out in fear.

"North!" Addy said. "Run north, to the forests! To freedom! Run!"

She ran, heading through the darkness toward the distant wilderness. Behind her, the survivors followed. Above, the fury of an alien empire rained down its fire.

CHAPTER TEN

The aliens surrounded them.

On the forest moon of Nandaka, Marco and his fellow Dragons stood, guns raised, muzzles still cold.

"Hold your fire," Ben-Ari said softly, eyes narrowed, daring not even move. "Don't antagonize them."

"What are they?" Lailani whispered.

Marco could guess. "The native Nandakis," he whispered. "And we just landed a spaceship in the middle of their forest."

Hundreds of the aliens stood on the forest floor, clung to the tree trunks, and hung from branches. They were the size of children and roughly humanoid, with two legs, a torso, and a head. But there the resemblance ended. Each Nandaki had four arms, long and slender and pale, and between the limbs stretched white skin like sails. A mouth gaped open on each palm, ringed with teeth, surrounded with clawed fingers. The aliens had no mouths on their faces, but their ears were long and pointed, and they peered with gleaming eyes the size of avocados. Their prehensile tails gripped the branches. They were intelligent enough to wear clothes and fashion jewelry: fur loincloths, feathered headdresses, and bead necklaces.

Kemi shifted uncomfortably and turned toward Ben-Ari. "Captain, we only have a few moments to send the *Anansi* back into space before the other ravagers show up."

"Wait," Ben-Ari whispered, keeping her eyes on the aliens around them. "Don't move."

The Nandakis moved closer. They chattered angrily through the mouths on their palms. A few held weapons: slingshots, bows, crossbows. Some pelted the *Anansi* with rocks. Birds hooted and fled above, and pollen rained from the flowering branches.

"Lower your weapons," Ben-Ari said to her crew, then raised her empty hands. "We come in peace, friends!"

The Nandakis shrieked. A few arrows flew, hitting the *Anansi*. The aliens hopped, swung from the trees, hooted, screamed . . . then fell silent.

Like a light switch flicking off, the sun vanished.

Darkness fell across the forest.

The flowers on the trees glowed pale blue and white. Most of the Nandakis climbed higher into the trees and disappeared. Only a few remained, watching with glowing eyes, hissing but crying out no more.

"What happened?" Marco said, glancing around. "It's like a light switch turned off. I didn't even catch a sunset."

Lailani pulled out a tablet, tapped a few buttons, and her eyes widened. "I'm reviewing the data on Nandaka from the scientist who discovered it. Amazing! The moon spins insanely quickly. Day and night only last about five minutes each. It should be light again soon."

Kemi hurried toward the *Anansi*. "A few minutes is all I need. I'm getting this ship out of here while our hosts are asleep."

The rest of the crew remained in the forest, warily watching those few Nandakis who were still awake in the branches. The aliens stared from the shadows, weapons raised, but made no further move to attack.

A few minutes later, Kemi emerged from the *Anansi*, panting. "All right, the rig is installed. I'm blasting her off!"

She hit a few buttons on her tablet. The *Anansi*'s engines rumbled, then roared.

Sunlight reappeared.

The empty *Anansi* took off with steam and smoke and rumbling fury, tearing through branches and scattering fallen leaves and flowers.

Across the sunlit forest, the Nandakis returned, screaming, firing arrows at the ascending ship. Other Nandakis pointed weapons down at the four humans. The aliens moved closer, emboldened by the *Anansi*'s departure.

"Genius plan," Lailani muttered. "We stranded ourselves on a planet full of angry alien-monkeys."

"They're angry at the marauders," Marco said. "They attacked the *Anansi*, a marauder ship, not us. They're not sure who we are." He slung his rifle across his back, then held out his empty hands. He spoke in a soothing voice. "Hello, friends. Hello. We mean you no harm."

The Nandakis all cried out in their language, each speaking with four voices from the four mouths on their four hands. One Nandaki fired a crossbow. The arrow whizzed only centimeters away from Lailani, nearly slicing her cheek.

"Assholes!" Lailani snarled and raised her rifle. "That does it. I'm going to--"

"No!" Marco pulled her gun down. "Stop. Kemi, you too. Lower your weapons." He turned back toward the Nandakis, hands held out. He knew the aliens would not understand his words, but perhaps they could understand his tone of voice. "We won't harm you. We're friends."

Kemi looked up from her tablet, which she was using to fly the *Anansi* via remote control. "We come in peace!" She smiled at Marco. "I've always wanted to say that."

"Take me to your leader!" Lailani said, then winked at Marco. "While we're speaking in clichés."

One of the Nandakis jumped out of a tree, stared at the crew, and hopped closer. He came within only a couple of meters of the humans. The alien's purple eyes were like two plums, and they sounded like camera shutters when they blinked. His pointed ears tilted. His skin was milky-white, and he wore a fur tunic. With one hand, he held a spear. He seemed smaller than the other Nandakis, perhaps only a child.

"Hello," Marco said, kneeling before the small alien.

The Nandaki hopped closer. His tail stuck out in a straight line. He raised one of his four arms and uncurled three fingers. A mouth opened on the palm.

"Hello," the alien said.

The sun vanished again.

The Nandakis retreated into the trees.

The young alien in front of Marco lay down, curled up, and snored through the mouths on his four hands.

"So we landed on a planet full of narcoleptics," Lailani said. She yawned. "I could use a nap myself, but I'd need more than five minutes."

While the aliens slept, the crew gathered around their sensors and monitors, which they had placed on the forest floor. They tracked the *Anansi*, which Kemi was still controlling remotely. The living ship had left the atmosphere of Nandaka, and it was now traveling into deep space.

Twenty other dots appeared on the tablet, moving fast-- the ravagers that had pursued them all the way from Haven.

"Come on, fellas," Marco mumbled, twisting his fingers. "Follow the *Anansi*. That's right, we only had a little pit stop here. We're still aboard. Go follow . . ."

Ben-Ari stared with narrowed eyes, her mouth a thin line. Kemi licked her lips, and Lailani twisted her fingers nervously.

"They're not falling for it," Lailani finally whispered. "They know we're on this moon. They won't follow the *Anansi*."

"Give them time," Marco said.

They all watched the monitor silently in the darkness. The *Anansi* flew out, farther, farther, heading into the blackness. Behind it, the twenty dots of light split up. Seventeen turned to pursue the *Anansi* into deep space. The last three turned toward the forested moon of Nandaka.

"Fuck!" Lailani blurted out. "It didn't work."

"It partially worked," Marco said. "We got seventeen of those bastards off our tail."

"And three more who'll be here within half an hour," Lailani said. "And they have about a million marauder friends all over this moon. Soon an army of marauders will be hunting our asses. Good luck stealing another ravager now!" The sun rose again. "And fuck this stupid sun rising and falling! And I'm fucking hungry, and if I don't eat one of these fucking aliens soon, I'm going to fucking die of starvation. We've been here for three days already, and I want to eat!"

On this third day, fewer Nandakis taunted the Dragons, perhaps bored with their presence, perhaps occupied with the marauder invasion of their world. The small, curious Nandaki, the one who had spoken to Marco, woke up and stepped closer today. Soon he was within arm's reach.

"Hello," Marco said again.

The young alien blinked, his luminous purple eyes making clicking noises. He raised one hand and opened its mouth. "Hello."

Marco pointed at himself. "Marco."

The alien tapped his chest. He spoke with one of his four mouths. "Keewaji."

Marco knelt before him. "Hello, Keewaji."

The alien tilted his head. The purple eyes blinked again. "Hello, Marco."

Keewaji reached toward the tablet Marco was holding, its monitor still showing stats of the ravagers heading toward the moon. The alien made pleading sounds, trying to snatch it.

"Cargo!" he said. "Keewaji cargo!"

"Sorry, buddy." Marco pulled the tablet back. "We need this one."

The alien whined and hopped, trying to reach it. He spoke in his language through all four mouths.

"Lailani, give him your spare tablet," Marco said. "The old one you play Goblin Bowling on."

Lailani gasped. "But I love Goblin Bowling!"

"Lailani, give him the tablet!" Marco cringed and lifted his computer higher, trying to hold off the leaping alien. "It's that, or he'll snatch valuable technology we need."

"Goblin Bowling is valuable technology, and I do need it," Lailani said.

Captain Ben-Ari looked up from a map of the planet she was surveying. "De la Rosa, give the alien your game."

Lailani let out a groan so loud the trees trembled and the flowers rustled. She fished out a small tablet, barely larger than her palm. The game was already loaded onto the screen. The words *Goblin Bowling* appeared over an illustration of several goblins standing on a bowling lane, prepared to be knocked down. Grumbling, Lailani held it out.

"Cargo!" Keewaji said, joy filling his lavender eyes. He took the tablet, then plopped down and began to play, holding the game with two hands, holding his spear with the third, and laughing with the fourth.

"Great," Lailani said. "We just rotted the minds of the natives. That's us humans, ruining civilizations."

"I think the marauders are more guilty of that," said Ben-Ari, looking up from her map. "And their three ravagers will be here any minute now. We have to move. They know we landed here. Load what you can into your backpacks."

They all had large military backpacks, nearly the size of their entire bodies. They filled them with the equipment they had taken from the *Anansi*, mostly sensors, telescopes, computers, and batteries, all seeking a new home. It took two more Nandaki days and nights, about twenty minutes, to pack up everything.

While they worked, Keewaji stayed with them. During the five-minute days, he used Lailani's tablet. He soon grew bored with Goblin Bowling and began to watch movies loaded onto the tablet, increasing their speed so that they zoomed by. He found his way into the library of books, and he flipped the pages at astonishing speed. During the five-minute nights, he slept, then returned to his tablet when the sun rose again.

By the time everything was loaded into their backpacks, they heard it.

Engines roaring above.

They all grabbed their weapons.

Across the forest, the other Nandakis--all but Keewaji-- screamed and fled.

"Here they are," Ben-Ari said. "Our marauder friends. Move! After me!"

They raced through the jungle, leaving some of the bulkier equipment behind. Marco's backpack weighed down on him, too heavy. His back ached and his shoulders bent. He forced himself to trudge on, never slowing, to follow his captain through the brush. Behind him, Kemi marched with tight lips, carrying her own supplies. Lailani brought up the rear; the little Filipina, only four-foot-ten, nearly vanished under her backpack, and sweat rolled down her cheeks.

The forest shook as ravagers landed behind them.

"Faster!" Ben-Ari whispered.

They ran between the trees. Marco remembered running with his platoon at boot camp, racing for twenty-four hours across the desert, carrying a heavy backpack. They had complained about it then. Ben-Ari had scolded the recruits, told them that someday they would run through war, run from death.

Hard in training, easy in battle, Ben-Ari had said.

That had been years ago, and it felt like a different life. Marco could barely remember Earth anymore, barely remember the kids they had been. But that lesson had stuck with him. He had followed Ben-Ari in the desert race. And he followed her today through the forest of a distant world, fleeing from a new enemy.

Behind, they heard the marauders screech, heard trees crack and fall. Birds, insects, and the native humanoids fled among the branches, crying out in fear. Keewaji hopped from branch to branch just above the Dragons, still gripping his tablet with one hand, using his tail for swinging. When two branches were too far apart, he spread out his four arms, stretching the skin between them, and glided like a flying squirrel.

"Village!" Keewaji said, making eye contact with Marco, then pointed ahead. "Secret village! Come, come!"

Marco blinked. "You speak English?"

"Hurry!" said the alien.

They ran through daylight, then darkness, then daylight again. On the third night, Keewaji began slowing down, but still the little alien plowed on, swinging from the branches above the group. During the brief days, he kept reading from the tablet, even as he swung.

"Hurry," he kept saying. "Almost at village. Warriors there."

From behind them, they heard the marauders. The aliens roared, crashing through the brush. The thuds of falling trees shook the forest. The marauders' stench filled the air, and birds kept fleeing above. Guttural voices rose in the distance.

"We smell you, humans!"

"We will drink your blood!"

"We will crush your bones!"

"We will eat your living brains as you scream!"

The four humans kept running. With their heavy backpacks, the hunger in the bellies, and the thick brush, they were moving too slowly. Every minute, the marauders sounded closer.

"How many are there?" Lailani said. "Maybe we can kill them."

Marco cringed. "There might be a hundred or more. Three ravagers landed. Each of those ships could easily carry thirty of forty of the buggers."

"Fuck!" Lailani spat. "We might have to just fight them all. No choice."

Above them, Keewaji swung down from a branch, still gripping his tablet. "No! We cannot fight them alone. They are the Night Hunters. Too strong! Come, hurry. To village! Warriors there. They don't have much cargo. But they are strong."

"Your English is improving rapidly," Marco said, running below.

The alien nodded. "I learn fast. Cargo taught me. Hurry!"

But when the sun set a third time into their run, the little alien finally fell from the branches. He lay on the floor, panting, shaking.

"Keewaji!" Marco said.

The Nandaki looked up at him, pale and shivering. "I cannot continue. I must sleep. Your kind can run for many days without rest. Will you carry me?"

Amazingly, within an hour of studying the tablet, the alien had become fluent in English.

Marco nodded and lifted him. Thankfully, the little alien didn't weigh much; Marco could barely carry all his equipment as it was. Keewaji slept in his arms as the humans ran on.

When dawn rose again, the marauders were only a hundred meters behind. When Marco looked over his shoulder, he could see them. The beasts were drooling and tearing down trees as they advanced, leaving a trail of rot and shattered wood.

"Come to us, humans!" they cried.

"Come and die between our jaws!"

The marauders laughed, racing forward. Dozens of them. Maybe hundreds.

"Keep running!" Ben-Ari said. Sweat washed her face, and her limbs trembled, and she doffed her backpack. "Leave our equipment. Just run!"

They all dropped their packs. They ran onward, keeping only their guns. Keewaji swung overhead, wailing in fear.

"Your fear marinates your flesh!" cried a marauder, only meters behind them now.

"We have your friend!" said another. "We have Addy Linden! How she screams for us!"

Marco sneered. His hands tightened around his gun. Rage and terror filled him. So Addy was still alive. But she was hurt. She needed him.

"We fattened her up like a pig!" cried a marauder. "She squealed like one."

Another marauder swung from the left, spinning around a tree. "Soon we all will eat her alive!"

A marauder leaped from ahead. "And you will feed us next!"

Lailani spat and cocked her assault rifle. "I've heard enough bullshit. Die, you fucking space shits!" She screamed, firing in automatic, emptying a magazine into one of the marauders.

A marauder swung on a web toward Kemi. The pilot shouted and fired her assault rifle, and Ben-Ari sneered as she fired her own gun.

War.

Marco loaded his gun.

War again.

He let out a wordless cry and fired his gun. His bullet shrieked, hitting a marauder, barely slowing the beast.

Once more I fight.

He hit a marauder's eyes. The alien fell. Another marauder swung toward them, and Marco fired at its strand of webs, and the alien crashed down to the ground. Kemi sprayed it with bullets. When two more marauders lunged forth, Lailani hurled a grenade, and the soldiers all knelt and covered their heads, and the forest shook.

And still more marauders advanced, circling in, a hundred or more. As Marco loaded another magazine, as he fired again, he was back there. Back in the mines of Corpus. Back on the desert world of Abaddon. Eighteen and terrified and fighting with his friends as the scum moved in.

The marauders scuttled forth. He fired. Again. Another grenade burst. And Marco was back in the subways of Haven, the trains screeching along, showering sparks. The enemies closed in, and he was in the call center, surrounded by sneers and sniggers, trapped, head spinning. He was standing on a building over a storm, moments from death.

He was with his friends.

He was following Ben-Ari through the desert, and he was holding Lailani in the tent, making love to her, laughing nervously as their teeth banged together, when their sweaty stomachs clung together, then parted with sucking noises--awkward, silly, clumsy, wonderful sex. He was with Addy again, his best friend, roasting hot dogs on a rake.

Addy.

Addy screaming on a web.

Addy bleeding, needing him.

And Marco knew he would die here. And his tears fell because he would never see her again.

He emptied another magazine, killed another marauder, but countless more were now moving in. They formed a ring around the four companions. Lailani screamed, kept firing until her gun gave a *click*, empty. Kemi too ran out of bullets. Ben-Ari panted, gun smoking. The four stood back to back, surrounded. Keewaji, their guide, had vanished into the brush.

"Fuck," Lailani whispered.

The marauders moved in slowly, grinning, savoring their victory.

"You gave good chase," hissed one, a towering creature covered with yellow boils. "You evaded us for a long time. But humanity falls."

The creatures raised their claws, prepared to pounce.

Marco inhaled sharply. He raised his empty rifle, prepared to fight with his bayonet, to die fighting.

"My friends," he said. "My sisters-in-arms." His voice choked. "It has been an honor."

Kemi nodded, tears in her eyes. "An honor. Goodbye, my friends. I love you all."

"I never thought I'd die without completing the last level in Goblin Bowling," Lailani said. "Thanks, Poet." But then she too was shedding years. "I love you, Marco. Always. You know that, right? I never stopped loving you."

Marco's tears flowed. He could only manage a whisper. "I ruv you."

Lailani laughed through her tears. "Ruv you too."

The marauders leaped in.

Howls filled the forest.

Arrows and spears flew.

With battle cries, hundreds of native Nandakis leaped from the trees. They circled above, gliding on the skin that stretched between their four arms. From above, they fired their weapons, peppering the marauders. Keewaji fought among them, firing stones from a sling.

The marauders cried out, shot webs toward the branches, and raced up in pursuit of the Nandakis. But here was not their forest, and the Nandakis had evolved here, knew every branch, every vine. The small aliens moved at incredible speed, fighting through day, through night, through day again, never resting, shouting battle cries and firing with deadly aim. Their arrows slammed into marauder eyes, and the great beasts crashed down.

When the sun rose again, hundreds of Nandaki corpses littered the ground. But among them, stinking, oozing, lay dozens of dead marauders.

Lailani shoved her bayonet into one twitching marauder and spat on the corpse. "Bastards."

Ben-Ari yanked her knife out of a marauder's eye. The alien jerked, then fell still. She looked up at Marco and nodded. "Well, Sergeant Emery, looks like your idea of coming here worked."

"Not thanks to me," Marco said. He approached Keewaji. "Thanks to this little fellow."

The young alien looked haggard. Blood splashed him-- most of it the black blood of marauders, but also green blood that seeped from his own wounds.

The alien raised one hand and spoke through its mouth. "I told you. My people are great warriors. For many days, the Night Hunters have hurt us, have destroyed our towns, have consumed our flesh. They brought evil into our pure Mother Forest."

Several other Nandakis gathered around, taller and broader than Keewaji; the largest among them stood about as tall as Lailani. Some wore patches of crude armor, and it took Marco a moment to realize the armor was formed from the hulls of spaceships, perhaps a fallen ravager. Black blood coated their spears and clubs. Seeing their dead, the Nandakis cried out in mourning, thumped their chests, fell to their knees, and seemed to pray.

Marco lowered his head. "You lost many," he said softly. "I'm sorry, Keewaji. Can we help you bury the dead?"

Keewaji took a step back, eyes wide. He raised three hands and spoke through three mouths. "Bury our dead? But they are heroes! Why would you dishonor them?"

"In our culture it's an honor," Marco said.

Keewaji frowned. "Your ways are strange. My people struggle to understand the great Night Races from the stars. We will carry our dead to the tallest mountain peaks, and carve their flesh, and let the birds feed upon them. Thus they will rise to the sky, not become the food of worms underground." He stared at a dead, foul marauder. Already insects were buzzing across it. "These things are bad. These things we will bury."

These things we will bury, Marco thought, wishing he could do the same to his nightmares, to the new trauma already breaking him here. He had emerged from the scum war in pieces. He had faced death and horror in those battles too many times. What new fractures were spreading inside him now? What new scars would still linger? *These things we will bury.* Perhaps Marco had buried too much.

He approached his companions. All had suffered wounds. Lailani knelt, a bloody bandage around her temple. She was busy stitching a cut on Ben-Ari's thigh. The captain grimaced and bit on a stick as Lailani worked, pushing the needle through the skin. Kemi sat on a fallen log, panting, wincing as she touched a scratch across her chest.

Marco approached the pilot, thankful that the HDF had taught him to always keep medical supplies in his cargo pants pockets. "Let me help."

Kemi looked up at him, and he was surprised to see that she was crying.

"I'm all right," she whispered. "Go tend to Lailani's head." She looked away. "She loves you very much."

Marco knelt beside Kemi. He wiped a glob of marauder flesh off her knee. "Kemi, whatever happened between Lailani and me, it happened a long time ago. She . . . she left me, Kemi. We're not--"

"I know, Marco," Kemi said, looking away. A tear hung off the tip of her nose. "I guess when you talked to me about puzzles, about buying that house on the beach together, about being how we were, I . . ." She wiped her eyes. "I was stupid. We were only kids then. And we're all scared. We all face death every day. So we say silly things. I understand." Kemi smiled shakily, tears on her lips. "I know those days can't come back. Go to her, Marco. Win her back."

Win Lailani back? Marco didn't want to think of such things. He had to save his species, save the whole damn galaxy for all he knew. He didn't have time for this. Thoughts of romance had perhaps seemed important on Haven, but who cared for love when the galaxy burned?

And yet, when facing death in this forest, his first instinct had been to turn to Lailani, to confess his love to her. And for that moment, near death, he had felt warmth. Now, after the battle, he found himself drawn to Kemi, and . . .

Enough, he told himself. *Focus on your mission. Focus on finding another starship. On finding the Ghost Fleet. Not on old ghosts. Because that's all this is. Old ghosts of love, as ancient as the ghosts said to haunt that mythical armada.*

As the Dragons continued walking through the forest, following Keewaji toward his village, Marco knew that a new group of ghosts would haunt him. The ghosts of this new war, of this butchery in the forest, of once more facing death and emerging into a broken life.

CHAPTER ELEVEN

When Addy had been young, her teacher had taken her class to a planetarium, a disastrous trip that had changed Addy's life.

At eleven, she had been a scrawny orphan, budding into puberty with rage and madness. Her father had just gotten out of prison again, ending his third stint behind bars, this time for getting drunk and crashing his company's truck. Still wearing an ankle bracelet, he sat at home all day, working on his motorcycle, drinking, and beating his wife. Addy's mother smothered the bruises under the haze of crystal meth, spending her days in a stupor when she wasn't beating Addy, a mimicry of how her husband treated her.

Addy never told her parents how she would steal her dad's booze, how she would smoke cigarettes behind the school, how she sometimes took some of her mom's drugs. She never spoke of letting that older boy, fifteen already, feel her budding breasts in the bathroom. How she and her friends once had found a dead cat, poked it with sticks for an hour, then tossed it into somebody's yard. How she sometimes cut her arm just to feel something. Her parents had enough worries, and whenever her dad brought another whore home, or whenever her mom sank into the murk of drugs, or whenever the fists flew, Addy ran. She ran into the alleyways and drank and smoked and stole and broke things, because she herself was broken.

They had tried to place her in a normal class with normal kids--with smart, clean kids with educated parents, with kids like Marco Emery and Kemi Abasi, and Addy had felt so stupid among them. She failed tests the others passed with ease. She heard them taunting her, calling her a whore, and she beat them, and she tossed desks, and she cut herself again.

So they stuck her in that classroom down the hall, the one with the door that locked when you closed it. Addy had heard the nicknames they gave the kids in this class. The freaks. The monsters. The science experiments. A class for those handicapped mentally, emotionally, socially. The principal called them "those who need a little extra help." Others just called them the weirdos.

So Addy sat among them. She listened to them blabber and scream and weep and slur. When the big one fought her, she fought back with all her strength, losing every fight, losing a tooth to his fist, but always fighting back. She was Addy Linden, her dad in and out of jail, her mom a strung-out junkie, and these were her kind. She was a freak. She was a monster. She was a weirdo. And every day, she hated herself, and every day, it was only the booze and cigarettes and cuts on her arm that gave her some relief, that hid the world for only a moment or two.

On that trip to the science museum, Addy had stood with her kind. With the girl who drooled and could not speak. With the big boy who hated the world and fought all those he saw. With the boy drugged out on medication and obese and barely alive.

Those who needed a little extra help. Those who had such love from teachers and parents yet such hatred from their fellow students, often such hatred for themselves. They walked together into the museum, afraid, some wailing in fear, one weeping.

"Who let the freaks in?" one student said, one of the normals, a pretty girl with pigtails.

Her friend, a boy with red hair, looked at Addy and her classmates in disgust. "It's a science museum after all. Maybe the museum wants to study them."

The pretty girl made a gagging noise. "Maybe they'll euthanize those freaks."

And there, with dinosaur skeletons and mammoth dioramas around them, Addy leaped at the girl and boy. And as she swung her fists, she screamed, and she was punching her drunk father who spent all day working on his motorcycle and bringing home girlfriends, and she was punching her mother for spending all day drugged out on the couch, she was punching the scum who kept raining down on the city. She was punching her life. She was crying by the time the teachers pulled her off.

They wanted to send her to the bus to wait out the day. They wanted to kick her out of school. They wanted to send her to juvy. They wanted to do all those things they always threatened, to hurt her, and Addy didn't care.

"Let the damn scum just kill me already!" she shouted, struggling against the teachers who held her arms. "I'll fight them too. I'll fight everyone! You can't hurt me. Nobody can hurt me anymore."

Through her tears, she saw a kid approach, another one of the normals. She wiped her eyes, refusing to let anyone see her weakness, to taunt her. She raised her chin, even as the teachers gripped her arms, and she stared at the boy. She knew his name. Marco. Marco Emery. His dad volunteered at the prison, donating used books and magazines for the prisoners, even teaching the illiterate prisoners to read.

"What do you want?" Addy said to the boy. "To gawk? I'll punch your fucking face in."

Marco hesitated, took a step back, then seemed to muster courage and stepped closer. He turned toward the teachers who were holding Addy, trying to drag her back to the bus.

"What do you want, Marco?" one teacher asked, a hulking brute who had been a drill sergeant in the army a decade ago.

Marco gulped. "Mr. Dougal, I thought that maybe Addy could still join us at the planetarium."

The burly, towering teacher frowned. His voice was like rolling thunder. "I appreciate that you care for your friends, Marco, but let me discipline Addy. She must learn the consequences of her actions."

Marco's face flushed, and his voice shook. He nervously clutched his gas mask box, but he plowed on. "Mr. Dougal, we all grew up in war. We all learned from a young age to run into bomb shelters, to put on gas masks. We all saw soldiers fight. We all learned that space is scary, that space is where the scum come from. But . . . sometimes at night, I look at the stars from my roof. And I see beauty too. And I think we all need to learn that.

That there's beauty up there, not just terror. That there's more to this universe than war."

Mr. Dougal's face softened, and amazingly--Addy couldn't believe it--it looked like he was crying. The teacher nodded silently and released Addy.

That day, Addy sat among the other students, gazing up at the stars shining on the planetarium ceiling. She was a child of the city. She had never seen more than one or two stars between the skyscrapers. Around her, kids were whispering crude jokes, passing notes, making fart noises, spitting and drawing dirty pictures on the backs of seats. Addy ignored them. She gazed up at those stars, at the Milky Way, at the planets floating just beyond her reach like Christmas ornaments, and Addy wept. Because Marco had been right. There was beauty up there. Down here was all ugliness and shit and drunk fathers and whores that reeked of cheap cigarettes and mothers lying on the couch for days on end in drugged-up stupors. But up there, beyond the skyscrapers, there was beauty. It wasn't just the scum up there. There was also wonder and light and hope.

Someday I'll fly up there, Addy thought. She would not share that hope with her teachers, her parents, her friends; she knew it would earn her only mockery. But that day Addy vowed to rise into space someday. To become a heroine who fought the scum. To become an explorer. To purify the heavens.

At the end of that day, Addy sat on a fence outside the school, smoking a cigarette, waiting for him.

"Hey!" she called when she saw Marco walk by. "Fuck-face!"

Marco turned his head. He paled, turned away, and began to walk faster.

Addy tossed down her cigarette, leaped off the fence, and chased him. "Hey, I'm sorry, all right? That's how I talk. Slow down."

Marco stopped walking and turned back toward her. Addy approached him, wearing her torn jean shorts and her Wolf Legions shirt--the loudest, scariest metal band in the world. Her eye was still puffed from her fight, her arm still scarred from her blade. Marco stood before her in corduroys and a polo shirt, holding his *Dungeons and Dragons* books under his arm.

"Look, I don't want trouble," he said. "I just thought that--"

"Listen to me, Normal," Addy said. "You stay the fuck away from me, okay? Maybe you think you can save me. Maybe you think I'll be your girlfriend. I don't know what the hell you want from me. But I'm bad news. You lie down with us freaks, you wake up with warts."

Marco's lip trembled, but he managed to square his shoulders, to stare steadily into her eyes. "I just thought you'd like the stars, all right?" He looked around, licked his lips, then looked back at her. "Did you?"

Addy looked away. Fuck her damn eyes and how quickly they grew damp. "Yeah, they were all right." She reached into her pocket, fished out a hockey puck, and gave it to him. "You can have this. Bon Gossow once signed it. Famous hockey player. My old man gave it to me, but . . . hey, fuck him."

He stood frozen before her.

Addy rolled her eyes. "Look, kid, I know you probably never watched a hockey game in your life, but this is the only valuable shit I own, and I want you to have it, all right?"

He took the puck. He pocketed it. "Thank you," he said.

"Now go." She pointed down the road. "Go back to your nice life. And never talk to me again."

Marco all but ran.

Addy promised herself that she would forget the boy. She could never be one of the normals. She could never be his friend. She could never talk to him about the stars without sounding like a retard. Addy Linden knew she was trash, but she also knew that those stars awaited her, and that Marco had given her a greater gift than any signed puck.

She kept her promise for seven months.

When the snow lay thick on the city, when the scum pods rained and killed her parents, when the monsters from space ate his mother, she spoke to Marco again.

She pulled him away from the inferno. She moved into his apartment over the library. He became the most important person in her life--but not on that night of snow and blood. It had been on a summer morning in a science museum. It had been under kinder stars.

As Addy ran through the darkness now, twenty-five years old, the stars above her and the enemy behind, that day in the planetarium returned to her. Dark trees rose before her. All around spread the ruin of the world. Once more, horrors from the darkness crawled across the earth, shrieking, stinking, killing, festering, chasing her, calling out her name. The marauders had come from space. They had come to feed.

But as Addy fled them, limping and bleeding and gasping for breath, she raised her eyes to the stars. And she knew that there was beauty there too. There was hope. Marco was out there, seeking the Ghost Fleet, and even down here in the mud and filth, Addy knew that great light shone above.

"They're catching up!" Steve said, running at her side. "We can't escape them."

Hundreds of escaped prisoners were still running across the dark field, fleeing the slaughterhouse, desperate to reach the forest a few kilometers away. Among them, Steve rose tallest and broadest, a body meant for slamming into other brutes on hockey rinks. He carried an elderly woman as he ran, and sweat soaked his face.

Addy ran at his side, a child piggybacking on her. "Shut up and keep running!"

But too many were falling behind. Hundreds had escaped the slaughterhouse, but many were too old, too young, too frail, too slow. The strong carried the weak, but their burden slowed them. The marauders bounded behind, screeching, leaping forth. A web shot out, grabbed a man, and yanked him back to the waiting jaws of a beast. Another marauder pounced off a boulder, landed on a woman, and ripped her apart, scattering globs of flesh. Every step, another human fell, another meal for the aliens.

And more marauders kept arriving.

Ravagers were rising from the ruins of Toronto behind them. The alien starships roared across the sky, came to hover over the field, and opened hatches. Marauders leaped down, jaws snapping, stingers rising, webs flying.

A strand caught a man ahead of Addy, then yanked him up to a ravager. Blood rained and severed legs thumped onto the field. Addy leaped over them, swerved, and dodged another web. She ran on, panting, eyes narrowed, desperate to reach the forest.

After so many days of privation, Addy was slower than usual, weak, her head spinning, and she still carried the extra pounds from the forced feedings. She was still naked, cut, bleeding, traumatized. Every step was agony.

Just imagine you're back at boot camp, Addy thought. *Just imagine that you're running with Ben-Ari again. Imagine that Marco is running with you, that he'll mock you forever if he wins the race.*

"Keep running!" she shouted. "We'll hide among the trees."

A child fell before her. Addy raced toward her, tried to help the girl rise, but was too slow. A marauder pounced, grabbed the girl, and leaped away, the child dying in its jaws. A ravager landed before them in the field, and a dozen marauders spilled out, racing toward the humans. More blood splashed.

Addy ran, the child bouncing on her back. Darkness around her. Blood showering her. Death everywhere. Eyes narrowed, breath burning in her lungs, she ran.

A ravager roared down to hover above her.

A sticky strand shot down, wrapped around the child Addy carried, and yanked the boy off her back.

"No!" Addy shouted.

The child screamed, reeled up toward a waiting ravager.

Addy leaped, grabbed the boy's legs, and clung.

The strand kept retracting, pulling them toward the hatch of the alien starship. Addy saw the marauders waiting there, snapping their jaws. Addy snarled, grabbed the boy, climbed higher, and lashed her marauder tooth.

The strand tore.

Addy and the child fell toward the ground.

Addy thumped down first. An instant before the boy could land, another web grabbed him, yanked him back up, and blood rained.

"You bastards!" Addy shouted. "You fucking bastards!" Tears streamed down her cheeks. "Come on! Grab me! Pull me up!" She stood in the field, weeping. "I'll kill every last one of you!"

More strands shot down from the ravager. Marauders were climbing down, sneering, reaching out to grab her. Addy stood still, naked, bloody, panting, ivory sword raised, ready to fight and die.

With a howl, Steve leaped toward her, stabbed a marauder with his own tooth-sword, and grabbed Addy. He pulled her away from the descending aliens.

"Addy, run!" he shouted. "The others need you! *Run!*"

She ran, barely able to see through her tears. The blood of the boy still coated her. With every step, she saw others die.

I hate them. I hate them. I will kill them all.

Dark shapes rose from the field ahead. At first, Addy thought them mere boulders, maybe bales of hay. As she ran closer, she realized that a battle had been fought here. A Firebird lay shattered in a burnt field, its tail reaching up to the moonlight. Armored vehicles smoldered, skeletons spilling out from their doorways. Charred corpses lay everywhere, reaching out bony hands in supplication.

The HDF fought here, Addy realized. *It lost.*

With a shriek, a marauder emerged from the crashed Firebird. Two more leaped out of a dead tank. Others appeared from within armored transport vehicles. The aliens raced toward the escaped prisoners, drooling.

"Sweet meat, sweet meat!" the beasts chanted. "Soft brains and crunchable bones!"

Hundreds of other marauders still scuttled from behind, and more flew above.

A marauder vaulted over a Jeep and came flying at Addy.

Addy knelt by a dead soldier, his eye sockets gazing through tatters in rancid skin, his belly full of worms. Cringing, she wrenched his assault rifle free from skeletal hands.

She opened fire.

Her muzzle lit the night. Bullets screamed out and tore into the marauder. The beast squealed and fell, covering its eyes. Addy riddled it with bullets, then knelt and tore off the corpse's ammunition vest. She had to shake off the maggots. She loaded another magazine.

"Steve, armor up and keep running!" Addy said, pointing at another dead soldier.

He nodded, grabbed his own rifle, and roared as he sprayed bullets.

"Die, fuckers!" he bellowed, eyes red, naked and bleeding as he emptied his magazine. Another marauder fell, its eyes shattered.

"Now keep running!" Addy cried.

The survivors ran onward, firing the guns they had grabbed, but still falling every few steps.

Barely anyone remained alive by the time they reached the forest.

The maples and elms rose around them. The ground was no longer visible, and rocks, roots, and fallen logs kept tripping Addy. She fell, bloodied her elbows, ran again, fell again, ran onward. Cries of fear filled the forest. She could not tell how many other humans ran with her: perhaps dozens, maybe fewer than ten. She saw Steve's hulking shadow in the darkness, and she grabbed his hand. They ran together.

And everywhere, the marauders scuttled. Their eyes blazed among the trees. Their webs rose and fell. Their claws reached out, snatching up fleeing humans. More and more kept filling the forest. Addy skidded to a stop in front of snapping jaws, turned, ran another way. A marauder jumped down from a tree, and she swerved again, kicking up soil and leaves. She fell. A web caught her foot, and she cried out, tore off the strands, and ran onward.

"Addy, have you seen Stooge?" Steve shouted as they raced between the trees.

"Not since the field!" Addy shouted back.

"We have to find him. We--"

Engines roared above the forest. Flames filled the sky. Ravager claws opened above the canopy.

"Run!" Addy shouted, pulling Steve along.

Plasma rained.

Trees burst into flame.

They ran through the inferno.

Curtains of coiling flame shimmered, swirled, rose higher and rained down sparks. Tongues of hellfire lashed out. Trees cracked and fell. A man ran, ablaze, a living torch, and charred people crawled, reaching out blackened fingers, then collapsing, melting away. Still more ravagers streamed above.

"The whole forest is burning!" Steve shouted. "We're toast!"

"I know a safe space!" Addy said. "Stay near me."

A marauder emerged from the trees before them, fangs shining. Addy and Steve fired in automatic, emptying magazines into its face, hitting the eyes. They ran around its corpse.

Addy glanced up. Marco had taught her to navigate by the stars, but she saw only smoke. She cursed. She didn't know where she was. The forest still burned, the fire spreading closer. Smoke filled her lungs. She had been heading north across the field. She only hoped she was still going the right way.

A dark shape loomed ahead, impervious to the flames. It rose like a demonic giant, black, peering with shimmering headlights like red eyes.

A train, Addy realized. *The train tracks. We're going the right way.*

She ran onto the tracks, and Steve followed. The trees burned alongside, and ravagers still screeched above. Addy ran along the tracks, Steve close behind, through this canyon of fire.

The forest spun around her. Her feet tripped on the rails. Her face hit the ground, and blood filled her mouth.

She floated in darkness.

"Addy!" Claws shook her. "Addy, wake up!"

Marco speaking. He knelt in the snow, the corpses of their parents around them. The boy she loved.

"You have to get up. You have to move!"

The scum rose behind him. Spaceships exploded in space, and the searing sun of Abaddon burned her.

The claws dragged her up, and Steve was pulling her along, skating across the hockey rink as burnt corpses watched from the tiers of seats. Addy ran with him, every footstep leaving blood on the ice. Her lungs burned. There were scum in her lungs. There were spiders in the forest. And still she ran.

Ahead she saw it.

It rose in the desert. It rose from ice. It rose in the ruins of her home. It rose over the corpses of her friends. A water tower. A skyscraper. A temple to cruel gods. An artifact where spiders worshiped.

Go, a voice spoke inside. *Go. This is the place you seek. A safe space. You will worship there.*

She trudged onward, leaning on Steve, toward the water tower. And its dome was a planetarium. And the stars spread above it, and they were beautiful.

"You taught me they are beautiful, Marco," she whispered. "You taught me there is hope. You taught me there is water among fire. That there is light in darkness. That there is . . ."

She felt woozy and fell. Her face hit the ground. Steve lifted her.

"Under the tower," she whispered. "Behind the stones."

He collapsed by the tower, and she saw that his leg was bleeding. She coughed. The fire was inside her chest, an alien of flame. She crawled across the burning desert, a skeleton, reaching out bony fingers.

She cleared away the dirt, and there it was. The trapdoor beneath the tower. She tried to open it. She banged against the lock. She cried out, but her voice was too hoarse. She fumbled with her gun, fired at the lock, and the kickback knocked her onto her side.

"Who the fuck is out there?" His voice came from below, echoing.

"The freak," she whispered, her tears burnt dry. "The weirdo. The girl who needs a little extra help."

She lay, panting, bleeding, burnt. The forest blazed to one side of the tracks. The water tower loomed above. And everywhere the stars spun, pulling her into their ocean with strands of light.

CHAPTER TWELVE

After so long, it should not hurt like this.

As Kemi walked through the forest of Nandaka, following the little alien toward his village, she kept glancing at Marco, then hurriedly looking away.

Why does pain so old still linger?

It had been seven years since that day, since Kemi had made that devastating mistake. Like the other monumental days in her life--the day her brother had died, her first day at Julius Military Academy, the day the Scum War had ended--the day of her mistake forever lived in her memory. A great fork in the road of her life. She had been just a child, only eighteen. She had barely understood the world. A child, that was all. Scared. Excited. Preparing for war.

And so I left you, Marco, she thought. *You were enlisted. I was to launch a military career. So I shattered our hearts.*

During the days that followed, Kemi had found herself weeping, cursing herself, and tugging her hair. She could have made it work! A long-distance relationship was not impossible, even at war, even across star systems. Their love could have given them strength during the years of war, and someday--even if, yes, years had passed--they could be together again. United, their love stronger after so long apart.

But I chose this. Kemi touched the golden bars on her shoulder straps. The insignia of an officer. Of a pilot in the Human Defense Force. *I chose to follow in my brother's footsteps. To fly for Earth. And now Earth is fallen, and Marco walks so close to me, and still it hurts when I see him.*

She looked at him walking there in this forest of alien trees, their flowers glowing. The sunlight dappled Marco's helmet, his olive uniform, and his somber face. He had always been so somber, even as a youth. He was twenty-five now, and he was no longer so soft, no longer meek. There was a new hardness to his body, his face, his eyes. But he was still so somber. He was still the boy she had loved long ago, perhaps still loved.

Walking in silence with him in the forest, it was easy to remember. Their walks through Mount Pleasant Cemetery, among the last green places in Toronto. The time they had baked a cake together, it collapsed in the oven, and they rolled it into cookies while laughing. Acting out plays together, creating silly costumes from old clothes. Secret nights of kissing, cuddling, finally making love on their last night together.

And I threw it away, Kemi thought. *And by the time I came back to him, he had found her. Lailani.*

She turned to look at Lailani. The young sergeant was walking beside Marco, telling him a story. He laughed, and jealousy--stupid, ridiculous jealousy--flared in Kemi.

Lailani was everything Kemi was not. Kemi often felt too tall, too curvy, too clumsy, while Lailani was petite and graceful. Kemi's hair had always been an untamed mess of curls that puffed up into a mane at the slightest provocation, while Lailani's hair was smooth as silk.

It was years ago that I came back to you, Marco, Kemi thought, *only to find that Lailani had taken my place. I thought that I could forgive. I thought that after so long, the wound would no longer hurt. But it still hurts me, Marco. Even now, it still hurts. Even now, I wonder what might have been.*

And Kemi knew--she knew!--that Marco still cared for her. Still loved her. She saw it in his eyes, fleeting, when he looked at her. She felt it when he touched her arm sometimes during a conversation. She knew that he and Lailani had parted. That Lailani had loved another, had lost her to the enemy.

Perhaps I can still win him back, Kemi thought. *I can still . . .*

She shook her head wildly, curls swaying. No. Foolishness! She was no longer that lovestruck teenage girl. That old Kemi had died on Abaddon. She was an adult now, an officer in the Human Defense Force, an accomplished pilot. She would not forget that. She had chosen a military career. She had chosen duty. And she would still do that duty, even here, so far from home.

I will focus only on my mission, she vowed. *To find another starship. To seek the Ghost Fleet. To save Earth. To save my parents. That's what matters now. My family. My species. Not these silly games of a lovesick girl.*

She took wide strides, passing by Marco and Lailani, leaving them behind. Ahead of them walked the woman Kemi had been following for years now. The woman who had given her new meaning. The woman she would follow into Hell itself. Captain Ben-Ari: her commanding officer, her mentor, her heroine.

"Ma'am," Kemi said, pulling out her tablet, "my scanners still detect no more ravagers nearby. According to everything I'm picking up, the marauders have a base twenty kilometers east from here. The ravagers send out distinct signals, and I can detect at least ten."

Ben-Ari turned toward her and nodded. "Excellent, Lieutenant. Keewaji says we'll be at his village within moments. We'll seek shelter and sustenance there before planning an excursion into the nearby marauder base, where we must hijack one of those ships."

There. This was good. This was comfort. Captain Ben-Ari was weary. Her shoulders slumped, her green eyes were sunken, and blood clung to the war paint on her face. But she was still a leader through and through, still speaking in confidence of their duty. This was how Kemi yearned to be. Not the lovesick girl but a capable, intelligent officer like her captain. Always a leader.

In a crumbling world, you are my pillar of strength, Kemi thought. *When everyone else hurts me, when all my life falls apart, I still follow you, Captain. Always. And that comforts me.*

"First order of business is shelter and sustenance, I agree, ma'am," Kemi said. "Once we're rested and fed, we'll plan our assault. I'm thinking a pincer move, two soldiers from each side, with the natives creating a distraction, but we'll need more intel first. I'd like a detailed map of the base if we can find one."

Ben-Ari nodded. "We can attach sensors to the local wildlife, perhaps. The birds seem large enough. If we can send them flying over the marauder base, we can obtain that map. But my father taught me something, Lieutenant. He visited many worlds in his military career. For years, he traveled the galaxy, exploring new planets, forming alliances with alien races. And he drilled this lesson into me: The locals always know best. We will obtain good intel at the nearby village, even if we must trade some of our technology." She smiled thinly. "The natives do seem to love Goblin Bowling."

Kemi laughed--too loudly, perhaps. Because this was good. This was business again. This was sanity. This was planning, not panic.

An officer, she thought. *That is what I chose to become. That is what I will still be, even with the cosmos torn apart.*

White fur flashed above, and Keewaji swung down from the canopy, holding a branch with his tail. The young Nandaki opened one of his four hands, revealing the mouth on the palm, and spoke.

"We are almost at the village, humans! We had to move when the Night Hunters first attacked, but we have built a new home. I will journey through the night, though I am weary. We will be there by dawn."

"I can carry you through the night," Kemi said.

Keewaji hopped onto the forest floor. He stood before her, as tall as her shoulders. The pale young alien looked up with his huge purple eyes, the size and shape of lemons.

"You are most generous, Lieutenant Abasi!" he said. "Not only are you humans great warriors with great cargo, you can travel for many days and nights without rest."

"What do you mean by cargo?" she asked.

His eyes shone. "Cargo is what we live for! We Nandaki greatly worship those with cargo." He pulled out Lailani's tablet from his pocket. "Cargo. It taught me much about your species. Your language, your culture, your glory."

"You mean technology?" Kemi said.

Keewaji nodded. He spoke from one of his hands. "Humans and marauders have much cargo. Great sticks that boom. Great vessels that fly. We Nandakis desire cargo too." He hugged the tablet to his chest. "Cargo is what makes one wise and strong." The sun vanished, and his four mouths--on all four hands--yawned. "Forgive me. I have spoken all day. I am weary."

As his eyelids drooped, Kemi lifted the alien and carried him in her arms. He snored through his hands. And now, as she walked through darkness, new memories rose in Kemi.

She had been late. And she was *never* late. At the time, an eighteen-year-old girl caught in a war, she had blamed it on stress. Just the nervousness messing with her body, delaying her period. Three weeks later, she had finally bled, had been regular since. During the war with the scum, who had time to worry of such things? Though over the years, Kemi's suspicion had grown into certainty.

I was pregnant with Marco's child. Her eyes stung. *I know it. I feel it. And I lost that child on my first week at Julius Military Academy.*

She looked down at Keewaji, this alien child in her arms, and Kemi wondered about what might have been. About what she had lost. About what the war had cost them.

"Well, will you look at that?" Ben-Ari said softly, and her eyes shone. "My father would have loved this."

After five minutes of darkness, the sun rose. Kemi looked up and saw it ahead.

The village.

Keewaji woke in her arms, yawned, and hopped off. He puffed out his chest with pride. "Home."

Trees soared ahead, the largest they had seen so far, trees that could put redwoods to shame. Kemi had expected to see a village on the forest floor, perhaps a collection of huts. Instead she saw a village in the air. Wooden bridges, rope ladders, and tree houses filled the branches. Water flowed through clay pipes, and gardens grew from countless hanging pots. Staircases coiled around trunks, and strings stretched between homes, ending with wooden cups--a primitive telephone network.

Hundreds of Nandakis scurried across the village, swinging from ropes, racing up and down rope ladders, and peering from windows. Mothers carried baskets on their backs, their babies peering from within. Elders hobbled across bridges on coiling canes, long white hair flowing from their heads. Young warriors perched on branches and rooftops, bedecked with feathers and beads, holding spears and bows.

"This is only a refugee village," Keewaji said. "Forgive its crudeness, please. Our true dwellings were far more marvelous. But the Night Hunters destroyed them. They burned the trees to drive us out. They raised great nets to capture us as we fled." He lowered his head. "Our great cities of wonder now lie as ashes, and so many of my kind are now farmed for their flesh." He raised his head again, and his eyes shone with tears. "But now the great humans have arrived from the Night Sea. And you are wise and bring us much cargo. You are like the Elder on the Mountain, the wise one whom we worship. You will help us defeat the Night Hunters."

"The elder?" Kemi asked, walking closer to the village. "Who is he?"

"One who is very wise!" Keewaji said, pointing at a distant mountain. "He lives upon the peak, and we worship him. But only the wisest of the Nandaki may speak with him. I am unworthy." He looked at Kemi. "But now you are here, the humans from the Night Sea, and you walk among us. It is a great honor. Come, come! You must be weary after walking for so many days and nights without food or rest."

Several Nandaki warriors ran toward the humans and saluted. Kemi's eyes widened. The little aliens--the tallest stood just under five feet--wore military insignia. They had fashioned leather shoulder straps, stitched them onto their fur tunics, and sewn golden stars onto the fabric. Each Nandaki seemed to have the rank of colonel.

I should be the one saluting them, Kemi thought with a smile.

"Cargo!" one of the aliens said, reaching for Kemi's pistol.

"Cargo, cargo!" whispered the others, gazing at the rifles, sensors, and tablets the humans carried.

Amazingly, the little aliens carried their own assault rifles--but the weapons were carved from wood. Mere mimicry.

"Forgive them," Keewaji said, turning toward his human companions. "They have never seen your kind up close before. Come now! I will take you to our elders."

They entered the village. A staircase coiled around a massive tree trunk, and Keewaji led them up the stairs. As the Dragons climbed, their stomachs growled. Since Marco had forgotten their food on the *Saint Brendan,* they had been living off scraps--a few granola bars and battle rations found in their backpacks, not nearly enough. Kemi's mouth was already watering at the thought of finding food in this village. Following their guide, they passed by tree houses, hanging gardens, bridges, rope ladders, and hundreds of Nandaki who scurried about, gaping at the newcomers.

"What the hell is that?" Lailani whispered, pointing. "Is that . . ." She frowned. "Kemi, you're a pilot. Isn't that a Firebird?"

Kemi stared in the direction Lailani pointed. Her eyes widened. A starfighter of wood, straw, and rope rested on several branches, shaped as a Firebird. It was nearly the right size, complete with a wooden pilot's seat.

"I believe it is," Kemi said.

"Cargo," said Keewaji, nodding. "We built it ourselves."

As they kept climbing, passing by more boughs, they saw more mimicry. Along two wide branches, a platoon of Nandakis was marching back and forth, holding wooden assault rifles carved into the shapes of T57s. They saluted their commander, a stern Nandaki who--like the ones below--had the insignia of a colonel. Higher up, a tree house contained several large communicators and radio dishes, except they too were made of wood and straw.

"Keewaji, what's going on here?" Kemi asked. "These look like our things."

He nodded. "They are great cargo! We have seen your kind from afar, wise beings who can travel the Night Sea, who wage great war, who have great wealth. We too desire to be as powerful someday, to have as much cargo. We have built what we could, but . . ." He lowered his head. "Still we fail."

Kemi couldn't help but smile. She wasn't surprised to hear the wooden Firebird couldn't fly or that the straw radios couldn't communicate with the stars.

"I see a great future for your kind, Keewaji," she said. "Someday you--"

The sun set again, and across the village, the Nandaki all scurried into their homes. The human companions waited on the staircase, and Keewaji slept in Kemi's arms. Several moments later, the sun rose again, and they continued their ascent.

Keewaji took them to a wooden plateau built around three tree trunks; it was easily the size of a basketball court. The foliage formed a thick canopy and walls, shielding this stage from prying eyes. Three Nandaki elders waited here, leaning on canes, wearing long blue robes woven with silver stars and moons. While the younger Nandaki were bald and smooth, these elders were wrinkled, and long white hair and beards flowed down to their feet.

Keewaji approached the elders, bowed, and began speaking with all four mouths at once. He spoke at such incredible speed that Kemi couldn't even make out individual words. The elders raised their hands, and each spoke from all four mouths. They spoke through the day, then slept through the five minutes of darkness, then rose again.

Keewaji turned toward the humans. "I've told them everything, all about your great battles and your quest. They will shelter you for as many days as you like, and we will have a feast in your honor that will last a week."

Of course, a week on this planet is just a bit over an hour, Kemi thought, but that was fine. She had never been one for long parties.

"Now bring us food!" Lailani said, and her stomach growled in agreement.

Young Nandaki females brought forth the feast. On flat leaves, they served a variety of pastes. In wooden bowls they served roasted grubs and insects. In baskets, they carried alien fruits and vegetables in all shapes and colors. Kemi had been hoping to feast upon the plump birds she had seen flying above. They weren't on the menu, but Kemi was far too hungry to complain.

Ignoring her manners, she tucked in, scarfing down the meal like a ravenous wolf.

For long moments, the four humans could not speak, could not breathe, only shovel more food into their mouths.

"This is the best damn food I ever ate," Marco said, speaking with a mouth full of fruit.

Lailani tossed roasted grubs into her mouth. "You'd say that about anything right now."

"Even roasted grubs?" he asked.

Lailani stuck her tongue out at him, revealing several grubs. "Especially roasted grubs."

Once her hunger abated, Kemi was able to appreciate the flavors. There were purple fruit shaped as stars, filled with soft beads; elongated fruit with glowing red seeds; tangy rich fruit that tasted like seasoned bread; edible flowers that dripped nectar; and many other delicacies. The pastes were just as delicious, some spicy, others sweet, some a mixture of both flavors. In clay jugs, the Nandaki served sparkling water flavored with flower petals and slices of fruit, healing and cold.

As they ate and drank, Nandaki girls giggled, raced forward, and placed glowing flowers in Kemi's hair, and they placed strings of jewels around her neck.

"Thank you," she said, but the girls only tittered, cheeks flushing, and ran off.

Night fell. In the darkness, glowing insects shone in hanging cages, casting light across the plateau. Under their glow, her belly full, Kemi raised her cup.

"To Addy!" she said. "We all wish she were here."

Ben-Ari stood up and raised her cup. "To Addy! May she be with us again soon."

"To Addy!" said Lailani. "The toughest damn soldier in the galaxy."

They all looked at Marco.

"To Addy," he said softly. "I miss her every moment." He raised his cup higher. "And to Kemi's parents, whom we hope every day we will see again."

Kemi smiled, tears in her eyes. *Thank you, Marco.*

They drank.

Several Nandaki stepped forth, demure, clad in flowing white garments embroidered with silver leaves, and necklaces of beads hung around their necks. They carried musical instruments of bone, wood, and string, and they began to play and sing. It was a song so beautiful that the humans--even Ben-Ari--shed tears. Kemi did not understand the words, but she didn't need to. Here was a song of leaves in the wind, of sunrise over mountains, of fine fare and good cheer. It was a song of innocence lost, of a longing for peace, of beauty fading under the shadow. It was a song of light. It was a song of home. And Kemi wept, because she missed her own home and her own songs, and she didn't know if the song of Earth would ever more sound in the night.

"Kemi?"

She felt a hand on her shoulder, and she looked up, blinking the tears away. Marco stood there, gazing at her softly.

"Sorry." She wiped her eyes on her sleeve. "I'm sentimental."

He reached down a hand. "Will you dance with me?"

She couldn't help but laugh. She raised an eyebrow. "Since when do you dance?"

He tapped his chin, considering. "Since finding myself on an alien world far from home, with beautiful music playing, and with a beautiful woman to dance with."

"I think you've had too much of that Nandaki juice," Kemi said, pointing at his empty cup.

"I probably have," he confessed. "But you didn't answer my question."

Kemi laughed again. She took his hand and rose. "Don't step on my toes."

She rested her hands on his shoulders, and he held the small of her back. The Nandaki musicians played on, filling the air with the soft, beautiful song of their home.

For a moment, Kemi and Marco stood still, staring into each other's eyes.

This is wrong, Kemi thought, unable to tear her eyes away. *This is wrong, Marco. This hurts too much. This is too sweet. We cannot rekindle this. It's too late.*

But they began to dance slowly, the music flowing around them. Night fell again, and the alien fireflies glided around them, joining their dance. Kemi placed her head against Marco's shoulder, and he wrapped his arms around her. They swayed, spun, a dance through darkness and dawn.

"I missed you, Marco," she whispered. "For a long time." She looked up into his eyes, blinking away tears. "Don't hurt me."

He seemed taken aback, but then he nodded. He held her close. "I'm sorry, Kemi."

She touched his cheek. "For what?"

"For everything. For how I was. You came to me on the *Miyari*. You came to find me, and I just . . . I tossed you away. I'm sorry."

She smiled shakily, and she cursed her damn tears. "That was a long time ago. In another life."

"I know," Marco said. "But I wanted you to know that. I'm sorry. I'm not who I was then. I hurt you, and I'm sorry, and I'll always love you."

Kemi laughed through her tears. "Definitely too much of that juice."

A firefly glided between them, casting its light into their eyes, and Kemi smiled and watched it fly away.

"It's beautiful," she said. "It's so beautiful."

She leaned her head back on his shoulder, letting him hold her, swaying slowly. No, they were no longer who they had been. They had both changed too much. They both hurt too much inside, both had suffered too much pain. Kemi did not know if they would find Addy again, if they could save the world, if they could ever heal themselves. But she knew that here, for this brief night, she was happy.

May the dawn never rise, she prayed silently. *May we forever be lost in this moment.*

Yet the nights here were so short. The sun rose again, and the music died. Kemi and Marco stepped apart, laughing awkwardly, the magic gone but not forgotten. She looked down at her toes, then back up at him, and she smiled and held his hand.

"There are so many bad memories," she said. "Let this be a good one. When we remember the bad times, let us remember this goodness too." And now her tears were falling again. "All the nightmares in the world cannot erase a single memory of joy."

After their feast, the Nandaki led them to hammocks that hung between leaves, large enough for human sleepers.

"We built these for you while you ate," said a young Nandaki girl, blushing and gazing down at her toes. "Keewaji told us that you can fight for many days and nights without rest, but that when you sleep, you sleep for a full month. We will guard you during your cycle of rest."

Kemi blinked at the girl. "You speak English too?"

The young Nandaki blushed a deeper crimson. "I have been studying for days now. My accent is still thick. Forgive me."

The four humans climbed into the hammocks. Kemi found herself lying between Captain Ben-Ari and Marco. In many ways, they had become the two most important people in her life. The woman she had followed through fire and darkness. The man she had loved, the man whose heart she had broken, the man whom perhaps she was starting to love again.

Kemi closed her eyes, and she thought of Noodles dying outside of Haven, and she saw a vision of her companions here dying too, of Marco and Lailani and Ben-Ari lying dead in the dirt. She winced. She knew that, like the horrors of the scum laboratory on Corpus, the images of this war would forever haunt her.

Kemi reached under her shirt, and she clasped her pendant. She did not wear a cross like Lailani nor a Star of David like Ben-Ari. Secretly, always hidden from him, Kemi still wore the pendant Marco had given her in high school: a golden pi, symbolizing her love of science. And their own love.

In this vast galaxy, I don't know if any gods are up there, Kemi thought. *But if the cosmos itself can hear my prayer, let no more of us die. Let us buy that house by the water, like Marco wants. Let us spend those evenings on the beach around the campfire. Let us solve puzzles, warmed with the joy of friendship and love as the rain falls outside. Let us return to the good, green Earth and see the evil cleansed from her seas and shores. Let only the light of stars fill the darkness.*

The sun set on Nandaka, and Kemi slept.

CHAPTER THIRTEEN

Brigadier-General James Petty stood on the bridge of his ship, hands clasped behind his back, reviewing the charred remnants of humanity's fleet.

It was not an encouraging sight.

Petty narrowed his eyes, struggling to calm that demon inside him, the demon called *horror.*

"How did it come to this?" he said in a low voice.

He remembered fighting in the First Galactic War, the great struggle against the *scolopendra titaniae,* the aliens most people called the scum. Petty had flown then with a hundred thousand starships, crossing hundreds of light-years to destroy the scum on their homeworld. The light of humanity had shone its brightest.

Now it was barely a spark.

The Scum War took everything from us, General Petty thought, staring out into space. *It took thousands of our ships. Took millions of our sons and daughters. Took my own daughter from me. My sweet Coleen.* He lowered his head and clenched his fists. *And now the marauders come to scavenge what remains.*

That old pain still hurt so much. General Petty reached into his pocket, and he felt them there. Cold. Comforting. Two metal identification tags, "dog tags" as the troops called them. His daughter's tags.

It was seven years ago that Einav Ben-Ari, then just a lieutenant, had met him in a cold, sterile chamber in the heart of a distant space station. She had given him his daughter's dog tags. Captain Coleen Petty had died in the mines of Corpus with most of her company.

"I gave everything to the military," he whispered, looking back out the viewport. "My soldiers. My daughter. Everything but the blood that still pumps through me. Do I now see humanity fall?"

From that once-proud fleet, here was all that remained. The last few starships of humanity. Here in the darkness beyond Pluto, at the very edge of the solar system, they gathered. Five warships hovered outside the viewport: The *Sphinx*, the *Cyclops*, the *Chimera*, the *Medusa*, the *Nymph*. Each carried a battalion of a thousand warriors; together these five battalions formed the revered Hydra Brigade, a force that had fought many famous battles. Among the warships flew Firebird starfighters, five squadrons belonging to each mothership, single-pilot craft able to fight in space and sky. Ten cargo ships hovered between the warships. They were massive vessels, stocked full of tanks, guns, bombs, missiles, and enough food to last a year.

The last remains of humanity's might in space. A shadow of what they had once been.

And here, General James Petty stood aboard the largest vessel in the fleet. The HDFS *Minotaur* was a starfighter carrier, the oldest and greatest of her kind. In her hangars, she carried two hundred Firebirds. In her hold served five thousand marines--the legendary Erebus Brigade, the most prestigious infantry force in the HDF. The brigade Coleen had served in, commanding the two hundred soldiers of the Latona Company.

The *Minotaur* was smaller, older, and simpler than legendary carriers like *Terra* or *Sagan*, famous flagships full of the latest technology. The *Minotaur* was a floating relic, a ship from an older era. Most of those other ships, marvels of human ingenuity, had been decommissioned after the Scum War, sold for scrap metal. The *Minotaur* had been destined to join her comrades, to be scrapped, torn apart, her pieces used to rebuild the world.

The marauders had put a stop to that.

The marauders had changed everything.

The marauders had destroyed ten thousand human starships, leaving only this. The charred, dented remains. The survivors. Here in the darkness of space. Here, hiding like cowards in the shadows.

"We must fight." Finally General Petty turned away from the view, and his fists tightened. "Madam President, I insist. The time for cowering has ended. We must fly back to battle."

Maria Katson, president of the Alliance of Nations, gave him a steely stare. Like him, she was in her sixties. Like him, she was a leader of many. Like him, she had spent her life in positions of power. But there the resemblance ended. He was fire; she was ice. He was heart; she was mind. He was a soldier, a general, wearing a navy blue uniform heavy with insignias, badges, and service ribbons. She was a civilian, the *de facto* leader of Earth, wearing a black suit. His hair was buzzed short under his cap, gray at the temples, salt-and-pepper at the top. Hers was silvery-platinum, cut to the length of her chin.

Fire and ice? he thought, gazing into her steely blue eyes. *Maybe more like water and oil. We'll never blend.*

"General Petty," the president said, "these ships, these ten thousand people aboard--we may be all that remains of humanity. And you will have us fly the last of our species into the marauder inferno?"

Petty narrowed his eyes. "With all due respect, Madam President, we are hardly the last of humanity. There are thousands of humans still alive in the colonies. There are still billions of humans alive on Earth--being fed into the meat grinders as we speak. This fleet is small. But it's all that remains of the proud Space Territorial Command, the mightiest soldiers of our species. We are humanity's last sword. And you would have us flee from battle? You would have us abandon the billions who cry out in pain?"

He had thought it impossible for her eyes to grow harder. He had been wrong.

"We cannot save them by dying ourselves, General," Katson said. "We flew to battle. We lost ten thousand ships. These few--this carrier, the five warships, the ten cargo ships, the handful of Firebirds--if we fly them to battle, we will lose them too."

"Then we will lose them!" Petty said. "Then we will die fighting. I would rather die a warrior than live a coward."

"And you would see all of humanity perish too?" Katson said. "You would see our species reduced to mere cattle, domesticated to feed the marauders? No." She shook her head. "I will not allow that. We have ships. We have enough food for a year. We'll leave the solar system." She gazed out into space. "We'll find a new home. Somewhere thousands of light-years away. Somewhere hidden. Somewhere the marauders cannot reach. And we start over."

"Start over!" Petty had always prided himself on being calm under pressure, but the words shot out from him, too loud. He took a deep breath, forced himself to regain control. "Ma'am, our planet--our homeworld--is out there. Earth is out there. Bleeding. Calling out to us. You suggest seeking a new world while our ancestral home needs us. We are soldiers. We are sworn to fight. We--"

"I am not a soldier, General Petty," Katson said. "The civilian government still commands the military, and a good thing too. Soldiers think of war. Of glorious death. Of sacrifice and honor. All noble concepts on the battlefield, perhaps. But as a civilian, my concern is more than simply victory or defeat on the field. My concern is the future of my species. Right now, there are billions of humans beyond our reach. Humans we cannot save. Humans that, yes, we must abandon--to sacrifice the many to save the few. Aboard this fleet, we have over ten thousand people. Nearly all of them are soldiers. Young. Healthy. Intelligent and emotionally stable enough to serve on elite ships. The average age is twenty years, and half are female. It's the perfect population to begin anew with. To find another world, to raise another generation. Earth is lost, Petty. That grieves me. You cannot imagine how much that hurts me to say. But I deal with facts. Earth is lost, but we're still here. And we must survive--for the future of humanity itself."

You grieve? Petty thought. *What do you know of grief? You never lost a child.*

It still hurt. Even after seven years, it still hurt so much every day. James Petty had taken a scum claw to the belly as a young man, and he had suffered a heart attack as an old man, but nothing had hurt him so much as losing Coleen.

You bring a child into the world, he thought. *You love her, raise her. You watch her struggle, try to guide her. You know she is imperfect. That she is too angry, too blunt, too hurt deep inside her. You try to heal her. You see her become an officer, a captain, a leader. You are so proud of her. Of this beautiful woman she becomes after so much struggle.* His eyes stung. *Only to lose her. Only to have a twenty-year-old lieutenant come into your office, uniform ragged, blood still under her fingernails, and tell you that your precious daughter is gone. So what do you know of loss, Maria Katson? Only a parent who has lost a child knows true loss.*

He turned away from the president, away from the fleet. He walked across the bridge toward another viewport. He stared into the void, into the space beyond Pluto, into the interstellar emptiness.

192

"There is hope for Earth," he said softly. "Captain Ben-Ari is out there. We must give her more time."

Katson snorted. In the viewport, Petty could see her reflection rolling its eyes.

"*Private* Ben-Ari is nothing but an escaped prisoner," she said. "A traitor, General. I would not put much stock in the little message she sent you."

Yes. A message. Twice Einav Ben-Ari had come to him with shattering words. Once, seven years ago, to deliver news of Coleen's death. Once, only days ago, to write of seeking hope in the darkness. Of seeking a legend.

It's true, her letter to him had read. *The legend. The Ghost Fleet. I fly to find it. Fight on, sir. I will return with hope.*

"Captain Ben-Ari defeated a scum king in Corpus," he said, gazing out into space. "She slew the scum emperor on Abaddon. She recognized the marauder threat even when you would not. She fought onward even after you placed her in a prison cell. I trust her more than any man or woman in my fleet." He turned back toward Katson. "And that includes you, Madam President."

Katson's eyes never lost their steel. "Your feelings toward me do not concern me, General. Perhaps I intimidate you. Perhaps you disagree with my commands. I don't care. You are a soldier, Petty. Just a goddamn soldier. And you will obey."

And there it was.

His rage.

That rage James Petty had fought for so many years to control, that rage he had passed down to his daughter. That rage that had gotten him in so much trouble as a young pilot. The rage that had already given him one heart attack and might kill him with the next one.

"Earth has fallen, as you said." He had to force the words past stiff lips. "Your government is fallen. Perhaps you hold no more authority here. Perhaps I will declare martial law. If we are the new society, then perhaps the military--"

"If you speak of a military coup, General, I cannot stop you," said President Katson. "Yes, you may confine me to the brig. You may have me blasted out of the airlock if you please. I have no weapons. You command ten thousand soldiers. If that is truly what you believe is best, if that is how you want the history books to remember you, go ahead." She raised her chin. "I'm ready."

They stared at each other in silence.

Do it, whispered the rage, the demon of fire. *Seize control from her. This is time for soldiers to lead.*

He looked across the bridge. His officers were busy pretending not to be listening. Fourteen men and women served here on the bridge--communications officers, engineers, pilots, a security officer. All wore pistols on their hips. Would they fight for him? If he commanded it, would they turn against Katson?

Yes, he thought. *Yes, they would. They would serve me. They would follow me into Hell and back. If I want this throne, it is mine.*

But another voice spoke deep inside him. Calmer. Softer. The voice that had always soothed the raging fire.

You are a soldier, James. Not a dictator. Not a tyrant. You serve Earth, not your own vainglory. Do not let a military uprising be your legacy.

He took a deep breath.

"Mars," he said.

Katson tilted her head. "Mars, General?"

"The Red Planet. Overtaken by the marauders. Fifty thousand humans once lived there. Perhaps they still do."

The president groaned. "Yes, General, I'm familiar with what the word Mars means. Why you speak of it is a mystery."

He turned toward a control panel. He hit buttons, and a hologram of Mars burst out. On it appeared several domes--the colony of New Carthage. Home to fifty thousand souls, now overrun by the marauders. In the hologram, Petty saw them. Two thousand ravagers, the living starships of the enemy, orbited the Red Planet.

Living ships. The discovery still shocked Petty. His scientists, studying a crashed ravager, had spread the news across the fleet. The ravagers were female marauders--their skin made of metal, their breath flaming, great huntresses who ferried the males inside their bodies. As nasty as the males were, the females were worse by far. And the females were those Petty faced here in space.

"Perhaps you're right, Madam President," Petty said. "Perhaps we cannot save billions on Earth. Hundreds of thousands of ravagers surround our world. But on Mars--only two thousand. We can defeat them, Madam President. We can liberate fifty thousand Martian colonists, or however many survived the marauder assault." He met his president's eyes again. "Let us not leave without them."

She inhaled sharply. "So you agree? You will obey me? You will seek a new world with me, a world far beyond the marauder empire?"

I must have more time, he thought. *More time! I must wait for Ben-Ari to return.*

But his time was running out.

Stiffly, he nodded. "Yes. But we take the Martians with us." His voice cracked. "We will forsake Earth. But we will not forsake Mars."

Katson gazed at the hologram of the Red Planet. "You deal with dangerous mathematics, General. Two thousand ravagers can tear through our fleet. We might all die in this assault, and humanity will perish. Even if we defeat the ravagers on Mars, at what cost? We might lose half our fleet, maybe more. Thousands of soldiers--dead. The surviving ships--if there are any--might not be able to even hold the colonists. To make room, we'd have to empty the cargo ships, to discard our tanks, our ammunition, so much of our supplies. Or perhaps, after unbearable losses, we would land on Mars to find a planet with no human survivors. Mathematics, General. And plenty of unanswered questions." She smiled thinly. "Do you see, Petty? You know how to fight. To kill. To sacrifice. But I must deal with the devastating numbers."

He stared into her eyes.

Who are you, Katson? he thought. *What pain do you hide?*

He looked back at the hologram of Mars. Numbers, yes. He might lose thousands of soldiers. He might lose much of his fleet, maybe all of it. For what? A chance. A hope to sacrifice a thousand to save tens of thousands. A risk that he might lose it all. Perhaps Katson was right. Perhaps they should flee now into the darkness. Perhaps this war was lost. Perhaps nobility dictated that he remain to fight, yet pragmatism demanded that he flee. His duty--as a soldier but also as a man. Dedication to his honor but also to his species. How did he choose while honor, duty, and the terrible mathematics clashed?

Yes, perhaps I am just a soldier, he thought. *I never asked to be the shepherd of a species.*

He thought of his father, one of the founders of the fleet. A man who had fought the first scum invasion, who had commanded the famous Evan Bryan himself. James Petty still carried a tattered photo of the man in his pocket.

What would you have me do, Father?

And he knew.

"We go to Mars," he said. "We fight. Do this with me. And then I will fly with you into the darkness."

He gazed into that darkness.

Hurry, Ben-Ari. Find your legend. Come back home. We don't have much time.

"General Petty," Katson said, "I understand your concerns. But you're still thinking like a warmongering soldier. I'm not sure you've considered the full ramifications of--"

Klaxons blared across the bridge.

Officers rushed about.

Lights flared on the control panels.

Major Hennessy, the bridge security officer, rushed up to General Petty. "The ravagers, sir! A hundred of them! They've found us."

For an instant--terror. Claws clutching him.

He shoved that terror aside.

"Battle stations, everyone," he barked. "Full red alert! All Firebird squadrons--launch at once! Move the fleet into a Briggs-Doyle defensive position."

Outside, he could see them now.

Marauder ships.

Ravagers.

They streamed across space toward the human fleet, blasting out plasma.

As officers worked, as Firebirds streamed out of the hangar bays, as the last fleet of humanity arranged itself for battle, General Petty turned toward his president.

"You did not want another battle," he said. "But that battle found us. Get down into the secure lower decks, Madam President. Let the mere soldiers handle this."

As the president left the bridge, General James Petty walked toward the main viewport. He stared outside and saw them charge toward him, closer, closer, their plasma flaring. He inhaled deeply.

He prepared to do his duty.

CHAPTER FOURTEEN

In her dreams, Addy was trapped again in the web. A marauder crept toward her, and she struggled and screamed, but she could not free herself. The alien shoved a feeding tube down her throat, deeper and deeper. As Addy struggled, she realized it wasn't a feeding tube after all; it was the alien's phallus, driving deep into her, impregnating her with its eggs, and she wept as her belly bloated, as the aliens hatched inside her, as they clawed their way out, and--

She freed herself from the web. She jolted up and her eyes snapped open. She was lying on a bed, drenched in sweat.

She gazed around, panting. She saw rusted metal walls, pipes, figures in the shadows. Her heart raced.

I'm back in the trap, she thought. *I'm back in the cattle car. I'm--*

"Addy!" A shadowy marauder rose from the darkness and lumbered forward, reaching out claws. "It's all right."

Addy lurched backward, ready to fight, and then the figure stepped into the flickering light of a fluorescent bulb.

Addy breathed out in relief.

"Steve," she said. "I thought you were a marauder."

He nodded. "I certainly stink like one. The water is out in the showers. Can you believe it?"

Addy's memory returned in bits and pieces. Fleeing the marauders' net. Racing through the burning forest. Making her way along the train tracks to the water tower, pounding on the hatch . . . After that she remembered nothing.

But she was here. In the bunker. In the safe space.

As her heart slowly calmed down, Addy looked around, getting a better view. She was in an infirmary. The old crazy bastard had actually built an infirmary. The room was formed from the hollowed husk of a school bus, its seats removed. Through the windows, she could see the soil they were buried in. The other cots were empty.

When Addy glanced down at her body, she winced. She wore a hospital gown, and bandages covered wounds on her limbs. An oxygen tank stood beside her, its mask lying by her head.

"We both inhaled too much smoke," Steve said. "We both got burns and cuts and look like two raw steaks. We got here just in the nick of time, Ads. How the hell did you know about this place?" He leaned closer, glanced around, then whispered, "The guy who runs this show isn't quite right in the head, is he?"

Addy let out a weak laugh. "So you met Jethro. Oh, he's a total loon. But he also saved our lives. And he's also an old friend." She clasped his hand. "You saved my life too, Steve. Thank you."

He let out a weak, shaky laugh. "Me? I did nothing. It's you who saved *my* ass. *And* the asses of seven other captives who found their way here, following our tracks."

Addy lay back down. Her. Steve. Seven others. Were they truly the only survivors among the thousands?

The infirmary door rattled open, and Addy saw him there.

"Jethro," she said.

He stepped into the infirmary, the buckles clanking on his heavy boots. He wore camouflage pants and a tactical vest, though Addy knew he had never served in the Human Defense Force. She remembered him ranting years ago, back when she would spend time on his farm, about the bastards not letting him in. Since then, Jethro's hair had grown even shaggier and whiter, and his beard hung halfway down his chest. But even in his fifties, his tattooed arms were still wide and strong, and his eyes were chips of flint.

"Addy Fucking Linden," he said, staring at her. "The same girl who'd run up to my farm, shoot tin cans with my rifles, and spend days sleeping in my barn."

Addy snorted. "Don't give me that look. You loved it when I came over. Only time you had somebody to talk to other than your pigs."

Finally a grin cracked Jethro's weathered face. He sat by her bed, clasped her hand, and squeezed it. "Fuck me. You've grown. Last I heard, you were a war hero. Come a long way from shooting cans off a fence on my farm. Heard you killed about a million scum."

"And only half a million marauders so far. Still need to catch up." Addy looked around her and gave a whistle. "So you did it, Jethro. You built it. You actually built your little bunker. I still remember you buying the old school buses and leaving them to rust in the rain, talking about how you'd bury them some day."

His grin grew. "Forty-two school buses, all buried sixteen feet underground. Welcome, Linden, to the Ark! Ten thousand square feet of comfort and safety. All powered by redundant diesel generators, with air filtration, stockpiles of food, and--once my guys get it working again--running water. And you used to call me crazy."

"You're still fucking crazy," Addy said.

"A crazy man who saved your ass." Jethro sucked his teeth. "Yeah, lots of folks called me crazy. The government. The fucking HDF when they kicked me out of the enlistment camp. The lying media buzzards when they came to film me digging. All said I was nuts to think the world was gonna end." He barked a laugh. "But my old Pa lived through the Cataclysm. He saw the world burn. I knew it would happen again someday, and, well . . . not much left aboveground now. All those guys who laughed at me? Dead. And old Jethro and his friends are still here."

Addy slung her legs off the bed. "Give me the grand tour." She stood up, swayed, fell back down.

"Ads, maybe you should rest," Steve said.

"I'll rest when I'm dead. Steve, help me walk, will ya? I gotta see this place."

Jethro led the way, and Addy followed, limping, leaning on Steve.

He did it, she thought, gazing around. *The crazy old bastard actually did it.*

The forty-two school buses had been rusty, dented, and dilapidated even before Jethro had buried them sixteen feet underground; they looked even worse now. The seats had all been removed, leaving scratched, dusty floors. The fluorescent lights flickered, and mold grew in corners. But God damn it, Jethro had pulled it off, had managed to survive the apocalypse. Two school buses served as kitchens; old sinks were attached to their walls, and canned goods stood on rough wooden shelves. One bus served as a decontamination room; Jethro had installed handheld shower heads and drilled drains in the floor. There were buses filled with wooden bunks, even a nursery where Jethro had stashed secondhand baby toys between cardboard boxes. There was an armory where a handful of rifles--the same ones Addy would come fire with Jethro a decade ago--stood on shelves.

Every piece of equipment here--from the dishes to the toilets--was old, cracked, falling apart, bought from garage sales or fished out of landfills. Rust and mold and dust covered everything. Half the lights didn't work, and the water still wasn't flowing.

It looks less like a cozy refuge to wait out the apocalypse, more like a serial killer clown's torture dungeon of horrors, Addy thought. *And it's beautiful. Right now, it's fucking beautiful.*

"I built this place for five hundred souls," Jethro said. "For years, I drove across the farms and villages handing out flyers, offering tours of the Ark. Barely anyone listened. This place could have kept five hundred humans alive. Only seventy-two showed up, and that includes you and Steve."

Even with seventy-two people, the place was crowded. Most of the people seemed to be farmers, judging by the amount of overalls, flannel, and straw hats Addy saw. About half were children. They crowded in the dingy buses, eyes darting. In one room sat four women, one about fifty years old and the others in their twenties. Jethro introduced them as his lovely wives.

"The rules are different now," he explained. "With the world population decimated, it'll be up to us men to breed as much as possible. Every man in the Ark must marry four wives."

"*Really*," said Steve, perking up.

Addy glowered. "It all comes down to sex fantasies with you men, doesn't it? Even the end of the world." She grabbed Steve's arm. "This one has me, and I'm worth more than four hundred women. You got that, Steve?" She twisted his arm. "*You got that?*"

Steve winced. "Ow, ow, yes!"

Addy spun toward Jethro. "And you listen to me, mister. You talk like we're the last humans alive. But there are millions still up there, I wager. The marauders didn't come to exterminate us. Not like the scum wanted. The marauders want to eat us. They'll place us in pens, breed us, butcher us, and--"

"Breed us?" Steve asked, perking up again.

Addy silenced him with a punch to the chest. "The next thing you breed with will be my foot as I kick your groin." She turned back toward Jethro. "How long can we last down here?"

"We have enough power, food, and water for a year," he said.

"I won't wait that long to die," Addy said. "I'm going back up there."

Steve cringed, rubbing his chest. "Ads, we saw what's up there. Toronto is gone. The whole world might be gone. We should lie low for a while, try again in a year, and maybe--"

"And maybe millions more will have died by then," Addy said. "Steve, what did you do in the army? Did you fight the scum?"

Steve bristled. "You know I wanted to. And you know I'm deaf in one ear. They wouldn't let me fight. Stuck me to fix antennae on the mountains. But goddamn it, the signals we picked up saved lives. I did my part. Even if I didn't kill any scum."

Addy turned toward Jethro. "And you, Jethro. What did you do in the war?"

The bearded survivalist grumbled. "I tried to join. Those kids in the HDF kicked me out. Said I'm mentally unstable." He snorted. "I'm saner than all of them. Who's laughing now?"

Addy gave them a crooked smile. "Well, boys, I'm giving you two a new chance. The HDF may have shoved you aside. But you both may join the HR."

"And what," Steve said, "is the HR?"

"My new army." Addy raised her chin. "The Human Resistance."

CHAPTER FIFTEEN

Even among the beauty of the Nandaki village, Ben-Ari could not stop her bitterness from rising.

This is what you withheld from me for so long, Father. These are the adventures you had while I wasted away.

The village spread around Ben-Ari across the trees, a jungle of tree houses, bridges, rope ladders, and wooden pipes that grew like mushrooms, nearly vanishing into the foliage. At first, she had thought the Nandaki frightening, what with their four arms, the mouths on their hands, and the massive eyes in their pale round heads. But she had come to admire them. They were a peaceful, intelligent race with a deep love of nature, art, and music. A race that someday could join the alliance of Milky Way civilizations.

She closed her eyes, and she was a child again. No longer Captain Ben-Ari, a leader of soldiers, but just little Einav, a girl, the daughter of a great colonel. She ran across the military base, passing between tanks and cannons. Fighter jets soared above and soldiers marched ahead. She raced into the building, and she leaped onto her father.

"Papa, take me with you!"

The tall, slender man pulled her into his arms and kissed her cheek, his mustache so bristly. Einav had inherited Colonel Ben-Ari's green eyes, pale skin, and dark blond hair, rare colors among her people. Everyone said that Einav looked like him, not like her dark, demure mother, and that saddened Einav. Her mother had died so long ago, killed by a bee sting, and Einav could barely remember the woman's face, only what she saw in photographs.

"Einavi, you know it's dangerous out there." Papa placed her down.

"But I want to go into space!" she said. "I'll help you find aliens. I'm good at making friends."

Papa only laughed--his deep laugh, head tossed back. He mussed her hair. "Someday, Einavi, you'll be an officer like me. An explorer. And you'll travel the galaxy. But today there is a war in space. Today I need you to stay here. My sergeants will take care of you."

"I don't want them!" Einav shouted, tears in her eyes. "I want my mother to take care of me. But she's dead. She's dead, and now you're leaving again!"

Across the base, soldiers turned toward her, then quickly looked away.

"Einav Ben-Ari!" Papa rumbled. "You will not speak to me like that."

"I'll say whatever I want, because I hate you! I miss Mama!"

With that, tears on her cheeks, Einav fled her father. And with that, only an hour later, smoke blazed and fire roared as Colonel Yoram Ben-Ari took off in his rocket, flying into the sky until he disappeared, leaving her alone again. In a few months, he would return, as he always did. He would bring her some gift, often just purchased at the base's spaceport. And in a few months, he would leave again.

Einav sniffed, tears in her eyes, and ran into her quarters. Every few months, they switched bases, had a new little room for a home. She sat on her bed, and through her tears, she read books of space adventures, fictional stories about imaginary places. Because true space was forbidden to her.

"Someday I'll fly out there," she whispered, staring out the window. The trail of smoke from the rocket was already fading away. "Someday I'll find my own worlds."

Ben-Ari sighed, looking around her at the Nandaki village. That had been twenty years ago. She was twenty-seven now, a grown woman. She had taken no husband, had no children, had chosen a career as an officer. The career she had been groomed for since childhood, the daughter of a colonel, born to a people with no nation. The scum had destroyed Israel, her tiny homeland, long ago. Her parents had died. All Ben-Ari had now was her career, and even that lay in shreds, her commission stripped away. Perhaps all of humanity now lay in ruins. Perhaps all she had left was her crew on this distant world. Marco. Lailani. Kemi.

They are my family, she thought. *Truer family than my father ever was.*

The colonel had died a few years ago--right after she had graduated from Officer Candidate School. He hadn't even been there for the ceremony, had died alone on some distant world, off on another adventure. She had visited his grave on Nightwall only once. She had left no flowers.

Ben-Ari gave a quick laugh and wiped her eyes. *I'm a captain, an explorer, a warrior, a survivor, but I still have daddy issues.*

She looked at her new family, at her soldiers. They sat before her on the wooden platform here high in the trees. Marco and Lailani sat cross-legged, their rifles slung across their backs. Kemi was kneeling by a diorama showing the Nandaki village in the trees, mountains and cliffs, and an alien base full of miniature ravagers. The pilot had built the entire diorama--it was as large as a dining table--from wood, straw, and stone.

"I got the scale wrong on the ravagers," Kemi said, biting her lip. "They look as large as warships here, and I didn't give them enough claws. And I think the eastern mountainside is too steep." She looked up at Captain Ben-Ari. "I'm sorry, ma'am. If you'd like to postpone the meeting, I can--"

"It's all right, Lieutenant." Ben-Ari smiled thinly. "This'll serve nicely. You did good work."

Kemi thrust out her tongue and began adjusting the slope. "If I could just--"

"Lieutenant, sit down." Ben-Ari had to stifle a wider smile. "It's fine."

Kemi dutifully sat down, joining Marco and Lailani. Ben-Ari did not miss how the pilot purposefully sat between the two, keeping them separate.

Even here, across the galaxy, with Earth burning, we find our little problems, our little dramas, Ben-Ari thought. *Even here, matters of the heart--dead fathers, bitter childhoods, lost loves--they still haunt us, as surely as the monsters do.*

"All right, soldiers," Ben-Ari said. "We've rested here on Nandaki for too long. We must continue our quest to the Cat's Eye Nebula. We must find the Ghost Fleet, bring it back to Earth, and save everyone there--including Addy. For that, we'll need another ship. According to our scanners and intelligence from Nandaki spies, there are seventeen ravagers at the nearby marauder base, only fifty kilometers away. Lieutenant Abasi has prepared us an accurate diorama of the terrain. Moving fast through the brush, it'll take us two Earth days to travel there, three if the vegetation is thicker than we expect. Once at the enemy base, we'll storm the nearest ravager, all guns blazing. We know how to fly them. We'll commandeer one, take flight, and blast the others from the air before they can take off. We don't want another chase on our hands."

Marco frowned at the diorama. "It'll be tough. That eastern mountainside is pretty steep."

Kemi punched him.

Ben-Ari stared at her soldiers. "Yes, it will be tough. War is tough. There are many marauders there. We'll have to move quickly. We'll have to face sixteen of their ships in battle--more if they call for reinforcements before we win. The odds of success are small. But it's our only way. As much as the idea is tempting, we will not retire on this planet. We have a war to fight."

"Forgive me," rose a small voice from above. "But there is another way."

Ben-Ari leaped to her feet and raised her eyes. Little Keewaji emerged from the foliage above, hanging from a branch with his tail. Only he wasn't that little anymore. Over the past couple Earth days here, the young Nandaki had sprouted up. When he landed by Ben-Ari, he stood as tall as her shoulders. When she had first met him, he had stood barely taller than her bellybutton.

"Do Nandakis often eavesdrop?" Ben-Ari asked, trying to sound stern, and she cursed the smile that tickled her lips.

Keewaji bowed his head. "Apologies, ma'am." He glanced up at her. "Is that the right term?"

She nodded. "That is what my soldiers call me."

His eyes filled with pride. "I would gladly be a soldier fighting for you, ma'am! But fighting at that base across the mountains . . . that is suicide." He lowered his head. "Many of my people have attacked the marauders there. They all died. The Night Hunters patrol their base on every side. They set many electronic eyes in the forest, many fences and traps, with holes to fall into and metal jaws that snap. Please, ma'am." Keewaji tugged her sleeve. "Do not die there like my brothers and father died. There is another way."

Ben-Ari placed her hand on the alien's shoulder. "I'm sorry to hear about your father and brothers, Keewaji."

"They were brave warriors," the alien said. "And they died too young. I want to fight too, but not to die young. There is another ship on this planet, ma'am. A great piece of cargo, mightier even than the clawed monsters the Night Hunters fly. The Night Hunters do not know of it. But the Nandaki know all the secrets of the forest."

"Another ship . . ." Ben-Ari whispered.

Nandaki nodded. "It is very old. It has existed in our forest for many generations, an ancient artifact of legend."

"So it's been here for about an hour now, yes?" Marco said, earning a glare from Ben-Ari.

Keewaji approached the diorama, then glanced up at Ben-Ari. "If I may adjust the map, ma'am?"

She nodded.

"Fix the mountainside while you're at it!" Marco said, then groaned as Kemi punched him again, harder this time.

Keewaji took clumps of soil and wood, and he fashioned a second mountain, this one north of the village. On the mountain, he placed the tablet Lailani had given him.

"Here." He tapped the tablet. "This tablet represents the ancient ship."

"Hey!" Lailani leaped up and gaped at the tablet. "You beat my Goblin Bowling high score!"

"So we'll fly in one ancient ship to find a fleet of them,"
Ben-Ari mused softly. "That is, if this old ship can even fly.
Keewaji, is this distance to scale?"

The Nandaki nodded. "Yes, ma'am. It lies thirty of your
kilometers away. But the way is treacherous, and the canopy is
thick, making the mountain difficult to see from the ground. I will
gladly guide you there, though the voyage will take many days."

Many days for only thirty kilometers? Ben-Ari wondered, then
understood. Of course. With day and night only lasting several
minutes here, the Nandaki had a different concept of time.

"Very well," Ben-Ari said. "We'll examine this other
starship before taking the risk of attacking a marauder base. Pack
quickly for the journey. I want to leave within moments." She
glanced at Keewaji. "That is, within days."

They headed north through the forest: four humans and
one Nandaki guide.

If Ben-Ari felt a tinge of sadness at leaving this peaceful
village, she drowned it under her duty. She would not hide from
this war, no matter how beautiful the village was, how much she
had loved her time here. The marauders mustered only a few
kilometers away, and their malice was spreading across the galaxy.

I am a soldier, she thought, walking through the brush.
*That's all I ever was, all I know how to be. And I will continue fighting. I
will not leave Addy and all of Earth to slow death.* She glanced back at
the village and felt a twinge in her heart. *But I'll still miss that place.*

Keewaji led the expedition, swinging from branches
during the day. At night, he slept on a litter the humans carried.

Every few days, they paused to rest, to eat and drink, then carried on. They had found their abandoned backpacks in the forest, and it was slow going with the weight. Ben-Ari refused to show weakness to her soldiers. She trudged on, drawing comfort from the beauty around her. The trees rose the height of skyscrapers, their leaves rustling. Flowers bloomed in the day, white and pink and deep purple, and at night they glowed and lit their path. The plants were unlike any Ben-Ari had seen on Earth; some sent forth wriggling tentacles like anemones, others had feathered leaves and flowers rich with beads, while some seemed like animals that peered with shining eyes.

The journey took an entire Earth day--and many Nandaki days and nights. Keewaji had been right. They did not see the mountain until they were nearly upon it. It soared ahead, its slopes rich with greenery, its peak capped with snow. Countless birds flew above it, and a waterfall cascaded near its base, filling a river.

"This is a holy mountain to our people," Keewaji whispered, staring with awe. "Here the Old One has lived for many eras. He is powerful and wise, and his ship is mighty." He trembled. "I fear his wisdom. He is the Lord of Cargo."

They rested, ate, then climbed the mountainside. Thankfully, it wasn't steep. But the vegetation was so thick that every step was a struggle. The alien plants rose around their feet, vines dangled from above, and the canopy hid the sky. Finally, when Ben-Ari was wondering if they'd ever reach the crest, Keewaji pointed.

"There!" he whispered, tears on his cheeks. "The alien ship!"

They all stared ahead, silent.

Several Nandaki females were there, wearing silvery dresses and bead necklaces. They were bowing before a hillock of wood and straw and leaves; it was roughly the shape of a starship. Baskets of fruits and nuts were laid out like offerings to a god. One Nandaki was playing a harp, swaying as if in prayer.

Ben-Ari sighed.

It was another fake ship, just made of wood and straw. Just like the ones back at the village.

"Great," Lailani muttered. "We came all this way for nothing."

Kemi nodded. "They're a cargo cult. Like cargo cults on Earth. Back in the Second World War, tribes in Earth's jungles saw American and Japanese planes flying overhead. Seeking such power, the tribesmen would build planes from straw and wood, believing them magical artifacts. They thought that with such so-called cargo, they too could become mighty nations. They never realized they needed more than straw." Kemi gazed at the pile of greenery ahead in the shape of a ship. "The Nandakis too seek cargo, so they built a giant starship to worship."

Ben-Ari approached Keewaji and touched his shoulder. "Keewaji, thank you for leading us here. We'll return to the village now."

The Nandaki shook his head. He pointed at the starship of leaf and wood. "A ship! A ship you can fly! Don't you like it?"

Ben-Ari knelt before the little alien. "Keewaji, I love it. But we seek a ship built of metal, not one of wood and leaf. A real ship."

"This is real!" He pointed again. "Real ship! Ancient ship of powerful cargo!"

Lailani stepped closer, frowning. She held a sensor, pointing it at the leafy starship. "Uhm, Captain? This makes no sense, but . . . my sensor is detecting a starship ahead."

They all looked back at the starship-shaped mound of greenery.

Ben-Ari stepped forward, frowning. She pulled back several vines, revealing a metal hull.

Her eyes widened.

"A ship," she whispered. "A ship hidden in the vegetation."

She pulled back more vines. Her crew cleared away leaves and branches. More of the hull was revealed, letters upon it.

Ben-Ari gasped.

English letters. *The ESS Marilyn.*

Ben-Ari stumbled back.

"No," she whispered. "No, no, it's impossible. How can this be?"

Kemi walked up to her. She placed a hand on Ben-Ari's shoulder. "Captain, are you all right? Do you recognize this ship?"

Ben-Ari nodded. Her voice shook. "It belonged to somebody I knew. Years ago."

A hatch opened on the ship's roof. A man popped out, his wild yellow hair streaked with white, his mustache bristly.

"The years go by quickly on Nandaka, Einav! I've been waiting for you."

Ben-Ari stared.

Her heart seemed to shatter.

Her lungs seemed to collapse.

"You died," she whispered. "You died. I was at your grave."

Her father smiled down at her. "In that case, dear daughter, we must be in heaven."

CHAPTER SIXTEEN

A hundred ravagers.

Living starships. The female marauders, evolved to fly through space, to tear enemies apart. Great huntresses of the darkness.

They flew toward the last human fleet, blasting out their plasma.

"Fire all your guns!" Petty boomed. "Fire everything!"

And across the fleet, they fired.

The missiles flew out, and Brigadier-General James Petty clenched his fists.

You took our homeworld, he thought. *You slaughtered millions of our sons and daughters. But there are still humans who stand. Humanity still fights!*

And the wrath of humanity slammed into the attacking ravagers with blasting fire and furious vengeance.

"For Earth," Petty whispered through clenched teeth, staring from the bridge of the *Minotaur.*

It was an onslaught that could have taken down armadas of warships. An assault that could have destroyed a thousand invading scum ships.

Perhaps three ravagers collapsed.

The rest kept streaming forth, barely even scarred.

And their fury followed.

Streams of plasma blasted out. The flames roared over Firebirds, and the starfighters spun madly, melting, ejecting their pilots into the void. A cargo ship listed, hull blasted open, spilling precious reserves of water.

"Defensive maneuvers!" Petty shouted. "More power to the shiel--"

A blast hit them.

The starfighter carrier, the largest ship left in the human fleet, jolted and tilted. Klaxons blared. Smoke filled the ship. The lights shut down, then returned as the backup power kicked in.

"Keep those missiles flying!" Petty said.

"Systems booting up on backup power!" cried an officer.

"Turn our starboard shields toward the enemy!" Petty shouted. "Divert all power to our starboard!"

They swerved in space. But they were an old ship. Large. Clunky. Slow. A ship from a different era, showing her age. Some called her a living museum. And the ravager fire slammed into their side with enough force to capsize them.

The artificial gravity system died again.

Pens, tablets, and officers flew through the bridge.

And through the viewport, Petty saw them. By God, they were everywhere. Only a hundred ravagers, but terrifying. They moved with incredible speed. They were bred to kill. They were the galaxy's apex predators.

And we are their prey.

Petty clenched his jaw.

But we will not go down easily.

He grabbed a control panel. He barked orders into his communicator.

"Firebirds, rally around the *Minotaur*!" he said. "Our ship will charge through their lines, breaking their formations, front cannons firing. We can still take a few hits. Fly above and below us and tear the ravagers apart."

His squad commanders answered, one by one.

Those that remained, at least. They had begun the battle with hundreds of Firebirds. Petty wasn't sure how many had survived this long, but he saw far too many floating in pieces through space. At least the five warships, massive vessels, still flew, and--

The ravagers regrouped. They charged. Their plasma blazed.

The HDFS *Nymph*, a warship with a thousand marines aboard, tore open.

Petty stared, breath dying.

Explosions rocked the legendary warship. Missiles flew like fireworks. Hundreds of soldiers spilled out from the breached hull, some still flailing, most already dead.

The *Nymph*. Gone. Petty knew those officers. They were his friends. They--

Not now, he told himself. *Mourn later. Fight now!*

"Helms officer, charge forth with thruster engines!" Petty shouted. "Full speed ahead, and keep those cannons firing. Take their plasma on our prow. We can resist a bit more." He spoke into his communicator to his warships. "*Sphinx, Cyclops*--fly above us! *Chimera, Medusa*--cover our belly! Attack formations, go!"

The fleet charged.

They were like buffaloes storming through a cloud of enraged wasps.

The ravagers scattered, then swooped in. Their metal claws tore into human vessels, ripping open hulls. Their plasma spurted out, melting Firebirds. One Firebird pilot flew upward, spun, then plunged, firing a missile into the open maw of a ravager. The alien vessel shattered. The *Minotaur* slammed into another ravager, crumpling the smaller ship. Blasts from the *Minotaur*'s cannon finished the job. Marauders--twisted creatures, flailing their legs and snapping their jaws--tumbled out from their ships, only for the Firebirds to shatter them with hailstorms of bullets.

They can be hurt, Petty thought. *They can be destroyed.*

Yet it came at a horrible cost.

For every ravager ship destroyed, the humans were suffering devastating losses.

And we need our soldiers more than they need theirs.

"All ships, hear me!" Petty said into his communicator. "Firebirds, move close to us. All ships, lock onto our beacon. Engage your azoth engines in ten, nine, eight . . ."

Osiris turned toward him. The android had been serving in the fleet for years, but she looked barely older than twenty. If you asked Petty, it was damn foolishness. Her engineers had shaped her as a beautiful woman, her skin pale, her pageboy hair platinum, her eyes lavender. Petty would have preferred a damn box. Boxes didn't talk back either.

"Sir?" Osiris said. "We're still too close to Pluto, sir. The forces of bending spacetime in a gravity field can--"

"That's an order, android," Petty said. "Three. Two. One. Azoth engines--engage!"

Across the battle, the human ships glowed blue.

The warp engines weren't primed. They wouldn't get very far. But it might just be enough.

A move you invented, Einav Ben-Ari, he thought. *A move you used when escaping from prison. A move that might just save humanity right now.*

They sucked spacetime through their engines, refracting it through their azoth crystals like a diamond scattering light.

Spacetime curved around them.

Two Firebirds were too slow. The bubble of bending spacetime crushed them. The other starfighters had moved close enough to the larger warships, were sucked into the tunnel like boats sucked into the wake of a steamship. As spacetime itself curved around them, propelling them forth at several times the speed of light, it crushed everything in its perimeter.

Including the ravagers.

Petty glimpsed scattering, severed claws and explosions of fire before they blasted into the distance.

With Pluto's gravity so close, the *Minotaur* groaned in protest. Its hull dented. Smoke blasted from its instruments.

Alarms blared and engineers howled in protest from the engine room. One bridge officer vomited, another man fainted, and Petty struggled to cling to consciousness.

"Azoth engines off!" he barked. "All ships, return to regular spacetime and regroup around the *Minotaur.*"

They sealed off their azoth crystals. Spacetime straightened around them.

They had traveled, within only a few moments, millions of kilometers. Pluto was now invisible in the distance.

Five ravagers emerged from warped space behind them. It was all that remained of the alien raid. With missiles, laser beams, and the loss of three more Firebirds, the human fleet defeated the enemy.

The battle was won.

For a long time--shouting, running, spraying fire extinguishers, emergency repairs, and medical bays full to bursting.

A thousand men and women--dead.

An entire warship and seventeen Firebirds--gone.

General Petty floated on the bridge of his flagship, its gravity still not restored. He gazed out at his army.

A hundred ravagers nearly destroyed us, the last human ships, he thought. *And a hundred thousand of them still fly around Earth.* He inhaled deeply. His chest felt too tight. His heart--that weak muscle in his chest, still recovering from nearly shattering two years ago--ached and twisted. *By God, Ben-Ari. Come back soon.*

From the speakers came frantic reports--mechanics sealing the breaches on the hull, power sources lost, the starboard engine sputtering.

Petty turned toward his android.

"Osiris, chart a course to the coordinates I give you. Have all other ships lock onto our beacon. We head out now."

The android stared at him. She tilted her head, and mechanical clicks rose from inside her.

"Sir, these coordinates lead to . . ." The android's eyes widened. Was her shock real or simulated? "The Ship Graveyard. Sir, why would we go to such a place?"

Across the bridge, other officers glanced at one another. He could practically hear their thoughts racing: *The Ship Graveyard? The place is cursed. Haunted. What madness could drive him there?*

But Petty needed something there.

He needed a treasure buried in that graveyard.

If they were to ever fly to Mars, ever liberate the Red Planet from the marauders, they needed to make a pit stop where all other starships feared to fly.

Petty frowned at Osiris. He spoke loud enough for his entire bridge crew to hear. "It's not your job to question my orders, Osiris. Chart the course to the graveyard."

The discipline of Space Territorial Command--coded into the android--kicked in.

"Yes, sir!" Osiris said. "It'll be a few moments until our azoth engines are primed again, but the instant they are, we'll take off."

Petty nodded. "Good."

Osiris smiled. "In the meantime, sir, would you like to hear a joke?"

"No," he said.

The android ignored him. "Why are ghosts banned from the liquor store? Because they would steal all the boos! It's funny because ghosts don't need to eat or drink."

Petty sighed.

A voice rose behind them. "What is the meaning of this?"

Petty turned to see President Katson walking toward him, wearing the magnetic boots they kept in case of gravity failures.

"Madam President, the enemy might return any moment," Petty said. "You should be in the ship's bunker."

"The battle is over for now," she said. "And we need to get the hell out of here, not fly to the most dangerous place in the solar system."

Petty gave her a steely stare, the kind of stare that could cow even the most battle-hardened soldier.

"Madam President, the marauders know where we are. We destroyed their sortie, but you can bet the house they sent out a signal before that. The enemy now knows there are still surviving human ships. They'll hunt us across the solar system. They'll send thousands of ships to every planet orbiting Sol to seek and destroy us. If we still want that chance of saving the Martian colonists, we need to do some grave robbing first."

Katson paled. Unlike his officers, she had no reservations about speaking her mind.

"General Petty, we suffered serious damage in the ravagers' assault. We lost a thousand lives! How many more will you sacrifice? We saw what only a hundred ravagers can do. Now might be our last chance to flee into exile. To start over." She trembled, then steeled herself. "It's not too late to flee. There is no dishonor in that." She squared her shoulders. "That is my order. You will obey it."

Petty froze.

His officers all turned to stare at him.

She's right, whispered a voice inside him. *This is why civilians rule the military. Because the instincts of a soldier--honor, duty, sacrifice--can, without prudence, lead to ruin.*

But another voice, deeper, more tempting, spoke too.

Yet what is life without honor, duty, and sacrifice? We are not machines. We are human! We are noble. How would we live if we, the last soldiers of our species, fled and let the weak among us perish?

Two voices. Two paths.

And Petty knew--he *knew*--his officers would follow him whether he led them to paradise on another world or to the hellfire of Mars.

"Human Defense Force Code of Conduct," he found himself saying, reciting the rulebook from memory. "Core Values, Article Seven: Space Territorial Command must defend the existence of humanity's colonies, their freedom from alien oppression, and the security of their civilians. Core Values, Article Eight: HDF servicemen and women will fight courageously in the face of all dangers and obstacles. They will persevere in their missions even to the point of endangering or sacrificing their lives."

Katson narrowed her eyes. "I'm well familiar with the document, General Petty."

Petty squared his shoulders. "Then you'll know, Madam President, that I swore on this document when I became an officer. That I cannot be asked to disobey it. That its laws are above the commands of any officer or government official. I am beholden to the core values of the Human Defense Force, and I will not break their rules. We head to Mars."

She stepped closer to him. She whispered harshly for only his ears, a sound more like a hiss. "It will be on your head, General. If humanity perishes, if this is our extinction--it will be on your head!"

"I am ready to bear that burden, Madam President. Now I ask of you: Return to your bunker. This ride will get bumpy."

As she stormed off the bridge, Petty reached into his pocket. He felt her tags there. His daughter's tags.

I wish you were with me, Coleen. I miss you every day.

His wife--gone. His daughter--gone. Perhaps all of Earth-- gone.

And the fate of humanity itself, this young, ambitious, confused species--all in his hands. Victory or the total extinction of human civilization--all resting on his shoulders.

No, not only mine.

He gazed out into the darkness.

On yours too, friends.

He whispered their names like a prayer. "Captain Einav Ben-Ari. Lieutenant Kemi Abasi. Staff Sergeant Lailani de la Rosa. Staff Sergeant Marco Emery. You must succeed on your mission. You must find help. Or humanity falls."

Osiris approached him. "Sir, we're ready to make the jump to warp."

"Wait," Petty said.

The android tilted her head. "Sir?"

Major Hennessy, his security officer, rushed toward them. "Sir! We're detecting another flight of ravagers! They'll be here within moments!"

The fate of humanity. Here we stand or here we fall.

He inhaled deeply through his nostrils. He spoke into his communicator.

"HDFS *Sphinx*, do you read me?"

The voice of the *Sphinx*'s commander came through. "Aye, sir! We're ready to deploy to battle."

"Negative," Petty said. "You're not fighting today, *Sphinx*. I want you to break off from the formation. Chart a course to the following coordinates." He read them out.

"Sir?" came the commander's voice. "That would lead us into uncharted territory. Sir, might I ask why--"

"You're leaving," Petty said. "You and a thousand young men and women aboard. We're hedging our bets, Colonel. If we lose this war, your orders are to find a new habitable world. To start over. To rebuild the human race. Over and out." He hung up.

"Sir, the ravagers are coming in fast," said his security officer. "We only have seconds."

Petty nodded. He broadcast his orders across the fleet. "All ships other than the *Sphinx*, lock onto our beacon. We're making a jump in three, two, one . . . engage."

The stars streaked into glowing lines.

They blasted through space, charging faster than light, heading into the darkness.

To the Ship Graveyard.

To the haunting ghosts of warriors.

To find a treasure that could save humanity . . . or doom them all to extinction.

CHAPTER SEVENTEEN

She faced the wall, arms crossed, eyes stinging.

"Einavi." He spoke behind her, voice soft. "You have to talk to me eventually."

Ben-Ari clenched her fists. She grimaced, struggling not to weep. Standing inside the *Marilyn*, she kept staring at the wall. Her chest was an inferno of raging fury.

"Daughter." He placed a hand on her shoulder.

She spun around, shoving him off. Her father took a step back, eyes soft with concern.

He had aged. She had not seen him in eight years, and more white filled his hair and mustache, and more wrinkles surrounded his eyes. He was still tall, still thin--even thinner than before. He no longer wore his military uniform. Instead, the famous Colonel Yoram Ben-Ari wore Bermuda shorts and a Hawaiian shirt, the most casual clothes she had ever seen him wear, this man who used to wear his uniform even off duty.

However, some of the old soldier obviously remained. Father still kept a tight ship. The *Marilyn*, though covered in brush on the outside, was spotless on the inside. The ship was a good twenty years old, Ben-Ari knew from the model, but sparkling clean as if fresh out of the shipyard. Father had always taken so much pride in a clean ship, a clean home, a clean life.

"Why?" she finally whispered, eyes damp. Her voice shook. "Why did you lie to me?"

His face evinced his grief. He was a good actor. Ben-Ari gave him that, had always known it.

"I wanted to contact you many times," he said. "I didn't know how to. Not without the risk of somebody intercepting. They had to believe I was dead. That the *Marilyn* had crashed and disintegrated on a distant world beyond our borders."

"For what?" Ben-Ari said, raising her voice. "So that you could live here among the natives, with Nandakis to worship you, to serve your every need?" She gave a bitter laugh, gesturing at the back of the room. "For this?"

Three Nandaki females knelt there, holding out baskets of fruit.

Father's cheeks flushed. He spoke to the three. "You may leave, darlings."

They backed away, bowing, leaving the fruit in the chamber.

Ben-Ari barked a laugh. "So they worship you as a god. But I know you. You are no god. You're just a man. A weak, pathetic, lying excuse for a man."

Father winced. "Those words wound me. But I deserve them. I know."

She couldn't stop her tears from falling now. "I visited your grave! I thought I was an orphan! You left me alone in the world, alone to fight a war, while you were here, having these aliens serve you!" She was shouting now. "Did you fuck them too? Is that what you're into? Some kind of weird alien fetish?"

She was being hysterical now. Ben-Ari knew that. She was being the bitter teenage girl again, ranting against the world, ranting against her life on military bases. She was too old to be an "orphan." She was too old to have tantrums. But still, after all these years, he could make her feel this way. Still he could hurt her. She was an adult now, a leader, a war heroine, but he still hurt her so much.

Father stared at her in silence for a long moment, eyes still soft. "You're angry," he finally said. "I know. What I did to you is horrible. But you have to understand, Einavi. You have to see my side." He heaved a sigh. "I was tired. I fought for so many years. But with the war flaring, I knew they'd never let me retire. When I found this place, I knew it was my home. That I could rest here. After years of serving my species, I deserved rest."

"And what of me?" Ben-Ari whispered hoarsely, able to shout no more. "You just abandoned me, like that, without a word? Letting me believe you're dead?"

His eyes hardened. He squared his shoulders. "You didn't need me. You were already twenty years old. A grown woman. An officer in the Human Defense Force."

"A cadet," she said. "You never even showed up at my graduation. I was the daughter of a famous colonel. Everybody there knew my name, waited to meet you. And you never showed up. By then, you were already here, weren't you?" Her voice rose louder. "Do you know what happened then? Did you hear about Corpus? About Abaddon? About the war with the scum? About what I had to do, how many I saw die?"

He winced. "Is the war . . ."

"Over," Ben-Ari said. "We beat the scum. Only for the marauders to arrive, to reach Earth too, to carry on where the scum stopped." Bitterness twisted her voice. "I assume you know about *them*."

He nodded, face pale. He stepped toward a counter. With shaky hands, he poured himself a drink, then sat in a chair.

"Yes," he said softly, gazing at nothing. Suddenly he looked even older than before. "Yes, I know of the marauders. I know what they did here. I did *not* know they reached Earth." He shuddered. "They're a nasty lot."

Ben-Ari stepped toward him. She grabbed his glass from him and tossed it. It shattered against a wall.

"Einav!" He leaped up. "That is rare Earth rye! From my last bottle."

"You goddamn deadbeat loser!" She shoved him against the wall. "You lying piece of filth!" Her tears kept flowing. "Most of my platoon died! Millions died! We fought the scum on Abaddon. We fought the marauders in space. I needed you! Humanity needed you! And you were here all the time. I thought you were dead. You lied to me. You hurt me, like you always did." She could barely speak now. "Like you always did when I was a child. You never cared . . . Never cared . . ."

She fell to her knees, shaking, sobbing. Father tried to wrap his arms around her, and she shoved him away.

He sat down again, and he placed his head in his hands.

"I was never a good father," he said softly. "I know it. Your mother, now . . . she was a wonderful parent. We both loved you so much, but I never knew how to take care of you. I never knew how to be a dad. She was a natural at being a mother." He laughed softly. "She could always make you laugh with her silly faces. How your eyes lit up when you saw her come home! Even if she was only away for a few moments. You look like her, do you know?"

"I look like you," Einav said hoarsely, refusing to look at him, still kneeling, staring at the floor. "I have your hair and your eyes."

"But you have her face," Father said. "And her wisdom. And her kind heart. When she died, I . . . didn't know what to do with you. I admit it. Suddenly I found myself a colonel in a war, my duty to travel the galaxy, to seek alliances with alien nations. All with a little girl, a precious child I loved so much, would have done anything to protect."

She snorted. "You never cared for me. You just went off on your adventures, leaving me with some sergeant on some military base."

"Adventures?" Father scratched his chin. "Yes, I suppose some were. There was the exotic waterworld of Gourami, quite lovely. And the forested world of the Silvans was rather nice. But for every nice adventure, there were ten worlds that tried to kill my crew and me. With fire. With radiation. With acid rain. Mostly with vicious local life that saw us as monsters, that tried to kill the invading aliens, that refused to believe we came in peace. Sometimes half my crew would die on missions. One time, only I escaped, leaving thirty dead corpses below for the natives to murder, rape, and finally eat. I'm pretty sure I got the order right." He cringed. "I know some of those sergeants were a little gruff, but surely they weren't that bad."

"Nobody tried to brutalize my corpse," she confessed. "Not until I faced the scum, at least."

"Einav, I know that saying sorry won't help." Father took a broom and dustbin and began sweeping up the broken glass. He paused and looked at her. "But I'm sorry. Truly."

"You were right," she said. "It didn't help."

Father sat back down. "Tell me, then. Tell me about the cosmos. About your life. About the war. Tell me what I can do now to help." His shoulders slumped. "I'm old now, and I'm tired, but I want to help."

Ben-Ari turned away from him. Her fists clenched again. With a tight voice, she spoke.

She spoke of fighting a battle at Fort Djemila, a larger battle in the mines of Corpus, and finally invading Abaddon with an army of millions. She spoke of rising to captain, of commanding her own ship, the *Saint Brendan*. She spoke of discovering a conspiracy to hide the marauders, of spending two years in prison after leaking the information. She spoke of Addy being captured, of Haven burning. She spoke of the marauders conquering Earth. She spoke of the legend of the Ghost Fleet, of her quest to find that mythical armada, of fleeing the marauders here to this world.

But some things she did not share.

She did not tell Father of the nightmares that filled her sleep. Of her guilt over so many soldiers dying while she lived on. Of the faces of those she lost--Caveman, Sheriff, Elvis, Diaz, St-Pierre, Webb, so many others--and how she thought of them daily. How she would never forget them. Perhaps she did not need to tell him. Perhaps Father already understood. And perhaps he never would.

"Well now," Father said, standing up and dusting his shorts. "Can I give you a tour of the ship?"

"Father, I'm not interested in--"

"Come on, take the tour." A sparkle filled his eyes. "She's a classic Orion model Space Territorial Command explorer, built by Asmotic Institute in 2125. Same year you were born."

"I was born in 2123," Ben-Ari said.

He gave her a sidelong stare. "Are you sure?"

"Quite."

He cleared his throat. "Well, in any case, the grand tour! Come now. Trust me. You'll love this."

When he speaks of his starship, he's excited, she thought. *I wish he ever showed half that much enthusiasm about me.*

Reluctantly, she followed him through the ship. The *Marilyn* was a small vessel, about the size of her own lost *Saint Brendan*. The *Marilyn* didn't have the latest stealth technology, and she was quite different from any other starship Ben-Ari had been on. Ben-Ari had only ever flown in the highly militarized vessels built by Chrysopoeia Corporation, the main contractor for the Human Defense Force. The Asmotic starships were more elegant, fluid, whimsical, like something out of a mid-twentieth century comic book. There were red barstools in the galley rather than simple folding benches, an actual jukebox, and a milkshake machine. Gleaming blue handrails ran along the walls, and the lamps were shaped as planets. A poster of Marilyn Monroe hung on a bulkhead, presumably the ship's namesake, alongside framed portraits of Buddy Holly, Elvis Presley, Audrey Hepburn, and other old icons, most of whom Ben-Ari didn't recognize. The symbol of Asmotic Institute--a cartoonish rocket, leaf-shaped, with two fins--was engraved on every door.

"She might look whimsical, but she's surprisingly good in a fight," Father was saying. "Armed to the teeth! A whole bunch of heat-seeking missiles, still functioning, and a photon cannon. Machine guns too. Purely for self-defense. She wasn't built for war. She was built for exploration . . . and for fun." He gazed around at Ben-Ari, eyes sparkling. "So, what do you think?"

"I think somebody attached wings to a 1950s diner and launched her into space," Ben-Ari said.

"It's the ice cream parlor, isn't it?" He laughed. "I installed that part myself. A little nostalgia for the long days in space. Do you like her? Come on, be honest! What do you think?"

Ben-Ari heaved a sigh. "She's a good ship," she confessed.

"Good!" Father said. "Because she's yours."

She spun toward him, her rage flaring anew. "Father. No." She gave a bitter laugh. "I should have known. Just more tricks with you. Do you really think that after all these years, I'll let you back into my life? That you can fly with us to find the Ghost Fleet, just another adventure for you?"

His shoulder slumped. His eyelids drooped. And suddenly he seemed so old. "Is the thought of traveling with your old man so horrible to contemplate?"

Ben-Ari closed her eyes, breathed deeply, and had to count to five. She looked at him again. "Don't you think of guilt-tripping me. I know all about Jewish guilt."

"No guilt," Father said. "I don't mean to come with you. No." He looked out a porthole at the rustling trees. "This planet is my home now. I've come to deeply love Nandaka--its pristine wilderness and its gentle people. I even got used to the rapid days and nights. I don't intend to leave. I will grow old here. Perhaps I will die here, surrounded by my new friends. But I think it's time for me to leave my old ship. To live among the natives. They need help, Einav. The marauders destroyed so much. The Nandaki need a soldier to help them defend themselves. They need somebody to help them rebuild. I can no longer hide away in my ship, letting them think I'm some ancient mystic." He clasped her shoulder. "And you need this ship. Take it, you and your crew. Chase your dream, Einav. Save the world again."

She looked at him, eyes damp. "Why are you like this?" she whispered. "Why, even now, does it seem you care more about the world than about me?"

And suddenly her father was crying. She had never seen him cry before. Not him, Colonel Yoram Ben-Ari, the famous explorer, a man so stern, so proud. But now the tears flowed down his cheeks, and he pulled her into an embrace. She resisted at first, then let him hold her.

"I love you, Einav," he said. "I know I never told you that before. I know I was a bad father. I didn't know how to show you my love. I knew how to be an officer, even at home, never a father. I'm sorry. But know this: Since the moment you were born, I loved you deeply. Perhaps I have lived for Earth. Perhaps, throughout your life, I have loved my career, my duty, and my homeworld more than my own family. I cannot atone for that now. But know that I will always love you. And I will always be very, very proud of you, of the woman you've become."

In the darkness of the brief Nandaki night, the ESS *Marilyn* took flight.

A meteor shower was raining on the forested moon that night, hiding their glow from the marauders below. The ship was old, and she had not flown for years, but she soared fast and true, breaching the atmosphere and shooting between the falling stars. Aboard her flew the last hope, the last heroes of humanity. Captain Einav Ben-Ari, leading the quest. Her pilot, Lieutenant Kemi Abasi, flying the ship. Her navigator and her eyes in the darkness, Staff Sergeant Lailani de la Rosa. Her computer systems analyst, her trusted warrior, and more importantly--her friend-- Staff Sergeant Marco Emery. And with them flew a young

Nandaki, loyal Keewaji, who had chosen adventure with a foreign race.

One among them was sorely missed. Addy was still a captive of the marauders, never forgotten.

Perhaps in the future, nobody would remember their names. Perhaps the world would fall and all memory of humankind would vanish. Perhaps they would save the world but their names would fade into obscurity. Ben-Ari knew that none of them flew here for glory, for fame; they knew what fame cost. They flew for a memory of loved ones, of green hills and blue skies. They flew for a dream--a house by the ocean, campfires on the beach. A dream of peace.

May we know peace someday, Ben-Ari thought, gazing off the bridge at the stars. *May future generations look at these stars and see not terror, not monsters, but beauty and wonder.*

"Azoth engine is primed, Captain," Kemi said.

Ben-Ari nodded. "Excellent, Lieutenant. Send us out there."

"Aye, Captain."

The stars stretched into lines. They shot out into the darkness.

CHAPTER EIGHTEEN

Addy arched her back and moaned, wrapping her legs around him. Steve moved atop her, sweaty, thrusting into her, and Addy gripped him so hard, closed her eyes, and bit his shoulder until he cried out.

"Harder," she whispered into his ear, grabbing fistfuls of his hair. "Harder, damn it."

Dutifully, he fucked her harder. It had been too long. Too long without this, without a man inside her, without the smell of his sweat and musk, without the abandon of sex, without quenching that thirst inside her. She scratched her fingers down his back, tearing his skin, and he moaned with pleasure and pain.

"Jesus," he said.

"Think of me, not Jesus. Harder. Oh God. God!"

"Think of me, not God," he said.

"Faster," she moaned into his neck. "*Faster.*"

She placed her hands on the mattress, and he gripped them, pinning her down as he moved atop her, and Addy surrendered to the feeling. The bed banged against the wall, and she didn't care if the whole bunker heard. She was beyond caring about anything but him, but this. Too long. Too long without this. Their naked bodies moved, damp, hot, slapping together.

Addy had always been too tall, too strong, had always felt too . . . *beefy* by boys like Marco, especially with the petite Lailani hanging around. But she felt so fragile with Steve. This felt so good, so right. The bed rocked, and the ship kept flying through the darkness, and she tried to move her hands but could not. He pinned her down. The webs wrapped around her. The spiders were moving.

"Addy . . ."

The voice of Orcus. The marauder with the missing eye. He licked her. He hissed into her ear. He mounted her, fucked her on the web, shoved a feeding tube down her throat.

"No," she whispered. "No. No!" Her voice grew louder. "No!"

She pushed the marauder off, scurried back, and hissed, teeth bared.

Steve sat before her on the bed, naked and sweaty. Concern filled his eyes. "Addy?"

She panted, trembling, and hugged herself. "I'm fine. It's just . . ." She shook her head wildly, clearing it of memories. "Lie down. On your back."

She straddled him, and he cupped her breasts in his big hands, and she rode him, eyes closed, head tossed back. She was in control now, safer now, safer from the spiders, from all those who would hurt her. When she closed her eyes, the creatures grinned at her, licked their teeth after slurping the brains. So she kept her eyes open, staring down at Steve, letting the fire grow inside her, slowly, then erupt across her.

She lay beside him, curled up in his arms. In the old days, after sex, she would lay sprawled out, smoke a couple of cigarettes, and yammer on about hockey or wrestling. Today she just wanted him to hold her. To feel safe against his wide chest. To feel small, protected. To never leave this bunker. To never face the world outside. She had sex sometimes before a hockey game, thought that it gave her strength, but it gave her no courage for the battle today, only a taste of what she was so afraid to lose.

"I don't want to leave," she whispered, held in his arms. "I never want to go back out there."

Marco would have stroked her hair, kissed her forehead, spoken of soft love and comfort. Steve gave her a smack on the ass.

"Come on, Ads." He mussed her hair. "You're a warrior."

She shoved his hand away. "A warrior? To everyone else." She closed her eyes. "Out there, yes. I was a warrior on the ice. I was a warrior in the army. I was a warrior in the underground of Haven. And when I step out of this room, I'll be a warrior again. I'll be Addy Linden, ruler of the Resistance, tall and strong and full of fire." A tear fled her eye. "But I don't want to be a warrior today. I want to be soft. Afraid. Safe. Just for one day."

Steve's body loosened. He blew out his breath slowly. "It was terrible out there, wasn't it? In space. Fighting the scum."

Addy nodded, eyes still closed, tears burning. Her throat felt too tight. "Yeah," she said, voice hoarse.

"Man." Steve blew out his breath slowly, then shuddered. "Fuck that shit, man. Fucking sucks."

Eloquent as always, my dear boyfriend, Addy thought. That was another thing she loved about dear old Steve--he was the only man who could make her feel like an intellectual. Sometimes Addy had felt dumb around Marco and Ben-Ari and Kemi. There was no danger of that happening here.

She rose from bed, naked, drenched with sweat. She thought of showering, but she remembered that mold grew in the Ark's shower room, and she decided against it; she was pretty sure the tiles were evolving sentience. The whole damn world stank now. Nobody would notice if Addy did too.

"Come on, Steve." She pulled on boy shorts and a tank top. "It's time to fuck up some aliens."

Steve pulled on boxers, and they walked down the Ark's central corridor. It was a shadowy tunnel, the walls made of raw concrete. A few old lamps flickered on the ceiling, moths flying around them. Doorways peered into the buried school buses that formed the Ark's forty-two rooms. Bunks for families. A nursery. A kitchen. Storehouses. All filled with clutter, rust, dust, and rundown equipment from a thousand garage sales, black markets, and landfills.

The marauders have their hives, Addy thought. *We have Jethro's Ark.*

She and Steve entered the armory. It was the largest room in the Ark, formed from three school buses stretched in a row. The seats had been removed, and shelves full of weapons rose here, enough to supply a small army. Addy saw assault rifles, handguns, boxes and boxes full of bullets, even grenades and grenade launchers.

"My life's work," said Jethro, walking toward her from the shadowy back of the armory. "Took me thirty years to collect all these weapons." He looked around at the shelves, stroking his long gray beard. "Sold my house and most of my land. Sold all my tractors. Used all the money my old pa left me. Here are the fruits of my labor, the sum of my worth."

"I can't believe the HDF thought you were too crazy to serve," Addy said.

"Look who's crazy now," Jethro said. "The HDF are skeletons on my farmlands, and we're alive underground with enough ammo to blast the marauders apart."

Addy wanted to remind Jethro that the marauders had destroyed thousands of human warships, had killed thousands, maybe millions of trained soldiers, and that even three school buses full of old weapons was nothing compared to their might. But she kept her reservations to herself. Right now, they all needed hope.

A dozen other men and women stood farther back in the armory, pulling on fatigues and grabbing weapons. They saw Addy and saluted.

"Our squad leader--Addy Fucking Linden!" shouted a young man. "Heroine of the war!"

A young woman with flaming red hair hooted. "Time to kill some aliens with goddamn Addy Linden!"

A burly, bald man attached a grenade to his belt. "That's right, boys and girls, we got the famous Addy the Alien Killer fighting with us today!"

Addy stared at them. Farmers. Maybe a few veterans who had only seen combat from afar. The world knew the stories of her, Marco, Lailani, and Ben-Ari killing the scum emperor. People worshiped them as heroes or loathed them as war criminals. But this squad, these dozen people buried in the Ark, what did they truly know of war? They knew nothing of the horror, the blood, the fear that froze the muscles, the nightmares that haunted.

They would learn.

"All right, you perverts," she said to them. "Stop looking at me in my undies. I'm getting dressed for war."

Jethro had perhaps never served in the military, but he had stocked his bunker full of military uniforms bought on the black market, a mix of pilfered HDF fatigues and the cammies of various militias. Once more, as she had so many times, Addy dressed for war. Olive green trousers with tattered pockets. A breastplate of Kevlar, and above it a tactical vest. Heavy boots. A bandoleer of bullets. A helmet, the words *Hell Patrol* scrawled across the front with a permanent marker. She slung her assault rifle across her back, and she stuffed her pouches and pockets full of ammo, as much as would fit.

She looked at herself in the mirror, prepared to apply war paint, and paused.

She stared at herself.

She didn't know who she saw.

On the surface, she looked the same as always. Blue eyes. A nose that she had always thought too big. Under her helmet-- blond hair, slowly growing back. She was something of a mutt, and her face betrayed that. In her features, she saw the broad honesty of her English and Scottish blood, the cold nobility of her Danish roots, and the fierceness of her First Nation ancestors. A bruise marred her cheek and a scrape lined her chin; she had always worn bruises and scratches as her makeup. The same face as always, not much changed since her teenage years.

But the eyes were different. Less fire burned in them. So much more ice. So many more ghosts.

Don't join those ghosts, Marco, she thought. *Or when I die, I'm going to catch your soul and kick its astral ass. Be safe, Marco. Be alive. Come back to me.*

She smeared the paint on her face. War paint. A mask. Perhaps she had always worn masks. Perhaps her uniform had always been just a costume.

Addy Fucking Linden, the heroine of the Scum War, she thought. *If only they knew how terrified I am.*

The squad was ready. Steve, wearing fatigues, grenades on his belt and an assault rifle slung across his back. Jethro, wearing a bandanna instead of a helmet, his white beard hanging over his tactical vest, his boots clattering with buckles. Thirteen men and women of the Ark, ranging from the teenage girl with red hair to white-haired men.

And me, Addy thought. *Commander of the squad. Famous warrior. Survivor. A scared girl who only wants to hide again in her boyfriend's arms.* She inhaled deeply. *Put the girl aside, Addy. Put her aside for one more war. Let the warrior roar again.*

"All right, boys and girls," she said. "Gather here and listen up."

They stepped closer. She reviewed her squad. None of them were experienced warriors. She missed fighting with Marco, Lailani, Ben-Ari, with soldiers she knew she could count on. Here were a bunch of farmers, preppers, eccentric survivors. But it was the only army she had.

"You all probably want some inspiring speech," Addy said. "I have none to give you. War is hell. I won't try to rile you up with talk of victory, or honor, or any of that shit. Some of you will die today. Maybe all of you. You'll die in pain, your guts spilling out. You'll die shitting your pants and shouting for your mommy. Those who come back will never forget, never stop having nightmares. I know. I still wake up screaming most nights."

They all stared at her, somber. Their faces grew pale.

Addy spat right on the floor. "Ah, fuck this shit. This is why I'm not an officer. Ben-Ari would know how to inspire you. I just know the truth. We're going out into Hell today. And I want you all to know this in advance. Because if anyone wants to back out, do it fucking now. I would rather you stay behind than chicken out on the battlefield when the screams rise and the guts spill and the monsters roar."

They all still stared, silent. Nervous now. But nobody backed down.

"I see how it is." Addy nodded. "You're not scared enough yet. That will change. But I want you all to know something. Whatever hell awaits us out there today, that is nothing compared to the hell in the marauders' slaughterhouses. And every day, the marauders are leading thousands of humans to the slaughter. We can't save them all. But we can save a few. We can bring a few more back here. We can't defeat the marauders, but we can hurt them, if only a little. So long as we can do that, we'll keep fighting. We are the Resistance!" She raised her fist. "We fight!"

They all raised their fists together. "We fight!"

Jethro opened a crate, revealing animal horns and a bottle of hooch.

"Mead," he said, handing out horns to the squad. "Fermented honey. In the days of old, Vikings would drink of this holy elixir before battle."

"No beer?" Addy said. Beer and sweaty sex; she would always partake of both before a big hockey game.

"No beer." Jethro poured the golden liquid into the horns. "Today we are the new Vikings. Today we are the last warriors of humanity. Let us drink--for Earth!"

"For Earth!" they all cried out, raising their horns.

They drank the mead. It was sweet and strong, and Addy thought about her ancestors. The fierce First Nations warriors, raising hell across the plains of ancient Ontario. The proud Anglo-Saxons, building castles, forging steel. The noble Danes, sailing the seas, fighting for their gods. As a mutt, Addy had always been envious of thoroughbreds, as she sometimes called them. Of warriors who had one ancestry, one culture to guide them. Warriors like Ben-Ari, an Israeli, descended of great leaders like King David and Moses; like Lailani, a Filipino, heir to a people who had defended their islands from conqueror after conqueror; like Sergeant Singh, a Sikh, who had proudly worn his turban and gone to battle with his ceremonial *kirpan* dagger; like Kemi, her family from Nigeria, an ancient land of beauty and nobility. They were all descended of but one nation each, finding strength in its customs and gods, something Addy had never been able to do. Yet now, standing here underground, drinking this mead, Addy realized that only one thing mattered here. She was human. She was from Earth. And all of humankind now fought as one nation.

Addy tossed down her empty horn. "Let's rock and roll."

They left the armory. They walked through the Ark, weapons in hand. From the other buried buses, survivors watched them, whispered prayers, cried out encouragements. A little girl ran out from a bunk, handed Addy a teddy bear, then fled and hid behind her mother. A frail veteran, well into his eighties, saluted as they passed, still wearing his old uniform and medals.

This is why I fight, Addy thought. *For all our faults, we humans can be noble. For all the shit we do, we can be kind. This is my species. We are not perfect. We are, maybe, deeply flawed. But when we're pushed into a corner, we can be wonderful. And that makes me proud.*

She led the squad down the corridor. The way led into an underground garage with concrete walls. An armored delivery truck stood here, its walls and windows bulletproof. Beside it stood seven motorcycles.

"The Human Resistance's armored division," Addy said. "All aboard!"

Jethro climbed into the truck. The rest chose motorcycles, two riders per bike. Steve climbed onto one motorcycle, patted the seat behind him, and Addy hopped on. She wrapped her arms around Steve and pressed her knees against his sides. The garage door opened, and they all rumbled up the slope. One truck. Seven motorcycles. Fifteen warriors. They emerged into the world.

Outside in the sunlight, they lined up and idled, engines purring.

"Fuck," Addy whispered.

Devastation sprawled around them.

Addy had not stepped aboveground since fleeing the slaughterhouse. She had fled here through a blazing forest. Before her now, she saw a wasteland.

The forest was gone. All was ash, charred chunks of wood, and skeletons.

She lowered her head. Memories filled her: herself as a youth, hiking here alone, fishing in the streams with rods she made from wood and string, climbing onto hilltops and howling at the moon like a wild animal. Sneaking into farmers' fields to steal fruit and tip cows, then running and laughing as they chased her. Shooting here with Jethro, knocking tin cans off fences, preparing for the war ahead. She had come here a few times with Steve and their friends, smoked pot in the forest, swam naked in the rivers, made love under the stars. It was here that Marco had taught her the names of the constellations, how to tell north from south and the time of night, like the planetarium in her childhood but a million times larger.

So many memories of these good woods, running with skinned knees, hunting, laughing, weeping when she needed to weep without anyone to hear. All of that--gone, burnt like the rest of this world.

"Fuckers." Steve spat.

Addy nodded. "Fucking assholes." She lit a cigarette, took a puff, then raised her voice. "All right, you filthy alien killers! Roll out! To war!"

"To war!" they cried out. "For Earth!"

Addy tightened her grip on Steve's waist. "Giddy up."

He pushed down on the throttle, and the motorcycle roared forth.

Behind her, the armored truck and the other bikes followed.

They rumbled along the train tracks. Riding through the forest was too risky; their wheels would leave a trail in the ash. The motorcycle rattled madly over the tracks, shaking every tooth in Addy's jaw and every bone in her body. Her rifle kept banging against her back, and her grenades kept slapping against her thighs. Behind her, the others followed, raising an unholy racket.

"They'll hear us!" Steve shouted over the din.

Addy patted her rifle. "Put on your earmuffs!"

"What?" Steve glanced over his shoulder at her.

"Your earmuffs!" She saw them dangling from his belt, put them on his ears, then raised her rifle. "This is going to get even louder."

They increased speed, roaring south along the tracks through the burnt forest. Soon Addy saw it ahead, and she bared her teeth.

The slaughterhouse.

"Fuck," she muttered. "The bastards have been busy."

Since Addy had fled that place, the marauders had fortified the slaughterhouse. Once an electric fence had surrounded the complex. Within only weeks, the marauders had raised stone walls, ten stories tall. Atop the walls, hundreds of marauders clung to webs that rose between iron poles like guard turrets. Beyond the walls, Addy saw several chimneys pumping out smoke--perhaps crematories burning whatever remained of the corpses. The smell of burnt flesh filled the air.

It'll take more than our squad to destroy that place, she thought. *We'd need a squad of tanks to tear down those stone walls. No more prisoners will be escaping from there again anytime soon.*

Addy watched a massive ship, a great cube of metal, rise from within the slaughterhouse, belching out smoke, roaring with fury. It was larger than her old apartment building. The dark vessel tore across the sky, finally vanishing above.

A meat delivery, she thought. *Bringing the flesh of humanity back to the marauders' homeworld.*

A single gateway broke the slaughterhouse wall. A line of humans--tens of thousands of them--still stretched across the plains, moving from the ruins of Toronto into the slaughterhouse. Hundreds of marauders surrounded the line, prodding the humans onward. Barbed wire surrounded the line of captives, further limiting the chance of escape. The captives were, essentially, traveling through a tunnel of barbed wire between Toronto's ruins and the slaughterhouse.

We cannot break into the slaughterhouse, Addy thought. *But we can tear through that line.*

She raised her rifle overhead. "Resistance, follow! For Earth!"

"For Earth!" they shouted behind her.

Steve yanked the handlebars, and their motorcycle veered off the train tracks and onto the dusty field. They stormed forth. Behind, the others followed. Clouds of dust roared around them, and their battle cries nearly drowned under the roar of the engines. They stormed toward the barbed wire road.

Ahead, the marauders saw them.

The aliens screeched. They leaped forth. They abandoned the line of prisoners. They raced toward the humans, moving at incredible speed, their claws kicking up dirt.

The two forces charged toward each other. An armored truck with seven motorcycles roaring around it. Before them-- dozens of marauders racing across the plains.

As Steve pushed down on the throttle, Addy aimed her rifle across his shoulder. Around her, the other riders raised their own guns.

"Fire!" Addy shouted and pulled the trigger.

Her bullets blasted out. The kickback slammed into her shoulder, nearly knocking her off the bike. She tightened her knees around Steve, and she kept firing until she emptied her magazine. Her bullets tore into a marauder ahead, sparking off its metallic body, doing it no harm. Around her, the other riders fired their own bullets, but they hit no eyes.

"Scatter!" Addy shouted, loading another magazine. "Meet up at the line!"

The motorcycles spread out. They charged onward. The marauders ran closer, then leaped toward them.

Addy fired again.

She caught a marauder in midair. Her bullets entered its roaring jaws and one hit an eye. The creature crashed down, and the motorcycle nearly hit it. They veered aside, raising a cloud of dust, and rode around the corpse.

"Addy, to your left!" Steve shouted, steering the bike downhill toward the slaughterhouse.

She spun.

A marauder raced toward them.

She fired, knocking it back. It fell, rose, leaped forward again. The motorcycle roared past it, and the marauder ran close behind.

"Steve, as fast as you can!" she shouted, pulled the pin off a grenade, and lobbed it behind her.

Steve glanced over his shoulder. "Fuck!" He shoved down the throttle as far as it would go.

The grenade burst behind them.

Addy screamed as the shock wave blasted against her, nearly knocking the motorcycle over.

They had moved just far enough to avoid the shock wave shattering their bodies. Addy was still thankful for her body armor; that blast had felt like a piano slamming against her. The marauder hadn't fared as well. The creature crumpled behind them, its severed legs twitching in the mud.

"To the line!" Addy shouted. "Break through the line!"

They roared onward. Another marauder leaped their way. Addy fired, knocked it back, and Steve swerved around it. The tires raised clouds of dirt. The line of human prisoners was close now, less than a kilometer away, but more marauders kept racing toward them. Dozens. Hundreds. One of the aliens leaped from an electrical pole and slammed into a motorcycle at Addy's side. Its riders hit the ground, limbs snapping, and the marauder tore them apart, laughing as the blood splashed. Another motorcycle leaped over a ditch, only for a marauder to slam into it in midair. Both fell, and the motorcycle spun madly in the dirt, tearing its riders apart.

"Steve, the truck!" she shouted.

Marauders were racing toward the armored vehicle, slamming against it, clawing at its walls. One alien managed to leap onto the roof.

"Hold on!" Steve said, tugging the handlebars. They raced toward the truck, and Addy fired. Again. Again. She hit some marauders, knocking them off, and the armored truck rumbled over them, crushing the aliens beneath its wheels. Addy loaded another magazine, fired again, and hit the marauder on the roof. Four other motorcycles remained. They roared back toward the truck, firing their own guns, knocking off the creatures.

They kept plowing their way through the aliens. A marauder cast a web, caught one of the motorcycles, and sent it flying. Still on their bike, Steve and Addy knelt, and the webbed motorcycle flew over their heads. Addy tossed another grenade, knocking back another marauder. Serrated legs flew, and a shard sliced Addy's shoulder, and other shards dug into her thigh. She bellowed in pain but kept firing.

"Jethro, now!" she shouted. "Here!"

Driving the armored truck, Jethro nodded at her. They were only a hundred meters from the fenced pathway that snaked across the plains, delivering thousands of humans from Toronto into the slaughterhouse. Jethro wheeled the truck forth, then slammed down hard on the brakes. The truck smashed through the fence. Human prisoners scurried back, and the truck spun around, knocking down more barbed wire, clearing an opening. Dirt flew. Barbed wire scattered.

As marauders swarmed, Addy and the others fired, knocking them back.

"Into the truck!" Jethro shouted. He leaped out from the driver's seat, opened the back hatch, and fired at a leaping marauder. "Climb in! Now!"

Naked, bleeding prisoners began leaping into the back of the truck. Marauders scuttled everywhere, tearing people apart, scattering limbs.

"Addy and Steve, cover me, damn it!" Jethro shouted, firing a gun with each hand.

Steve pushed down on the throttle, and they roared forward, circling the truck on their motorcycle. The other motorcycles followed, roaring around the truck, scattering dirt and firing bullets. Addy kept shooting, tossing grenades, and holding the marauders back as more prisoners entered the truck.

"Enough, enough, we're full!" Jethro shouted, trying to shove people back. "We're out of room!"

"Let us in!" shouted a man.

"Please, my child!" cried a mother.

Addy shouted as she fired. "Load more into the front seat! Let them cling to the side. We can take a few more."

Jethro nodded, gathered the mother and her child, and all but shoved them into the front seat. A marauder raced toward him, and Jethro gritted his teeth, pulled the trigger of his rifle, but the gun jammed.

The marauder leaped onto him, jaws snapping.

His gun useless, Jethro kicked.

The marauder bit down hard, severing Jethro's leg.

The bearded survivalist fell, leg gone above the knee, spurting blood. He writhed in the mud.

Addy stared in terror.

"Steve, let me off!" she shouted. He slowed down, and Addy leaped off the motorcycle and ran toward Jethro.

The marauder reared before her, blocking her way. Jethro's severed leg still dangled between the creature's teeth.

Addy recognized the alien. The three eyes. The crest of horns. The parasitic twin growing from his side.

The marauder gulped down Jethro's leg and grinned at her. "Addy . . ." he hissed.

Addy sneered. "Orcus."

The memories flashed before her in a split second. The marauder mutilating Grant, shoving the tube down Addy's throat, and brutalizing her in the slaughterhouse. Among the marauders, he was the nastiest--and that, Addy knew, was saying something.

Orcus licked his jaws. On his side, his conjoined twin--no larger than a toddler--licked its own small jaws.

"I knew you'd return to me, Addy," Orcus said, his voice like slithering serpents.

With a shriek, the creature charged toward her.

Addy raised her rifle. She fired again and again. Orcus wouldn't slow down. None of her bullets hit his eyes. He leaped toward her, and Addy cringed, and--

Steve reared on his motorcycle, flew through the air, and slammed into the marauder.

Steve, his motorcycle, and Orcus hit the ground.

"Steve!" she shouted, running toward him. The bike, human, and marauder lay in a tangled mess.

Orcus reared from the wreckage, howling, prepared to feed.

Screaming, Addy fired, hitting his face, hitting his parasitic twin, ignoring the shards of bullets that ricocheted back onto her.

The deformed twin squealed, riddled with bullets.

"Pain, pain!" the little creature cried.

Orcus howled and scuttled behind the armored truck, hissing, drooling, screeching with fury.

Addy panted. She wasn't sure if she had killed the parasite. She hoped that the little creature rotted. She wanted to chase Orcus, but she could barely stay standing.

Only three motorcycles were still driving, circling the idling truck. Hundreds of marauders were racing toward them. Steve was pinned under the motorcycle. Jethro was still writhing in the dirt, clutching the stump of his leg. Corpses of prisoners lay around them, and they had no truck driver. Addy was dizzy, losing blood fast.

She fell to one knee.

Stay standing.

She pushed herself up.

Fight.

With trembling hands, she loaded another magazine.

For Earth.

She fired, knocking back the nearest marauder. Letting her gun hang across her back, she knelt and grabbed the fallen motorcycle. It burned her hands. She howled in agony, digging her heels into the dirt, and pulled it off Steve.

He moaned on the ground, his leg broken.

"Up, you idiot!" She grabbed him, and he screamed. "Up! Into the truck!"

She shoved Steve into the passenger seat, where he crowded with the mother and her child.

A marauder raced toward her.

Addy cursed and lobbed a grenade.

She leaped behind the fallen motorcycle, flattened herself on the ground, and covered her head.

The grenade exploded. Dirt, shrapnel, and shards of marauder flew, pattering against her body armor.

Addy rose again. She yanked up Jethro. He was still alive, but barely, and his stump still bled. She applied a tourniquet and pulled him up. She shoved him into the passenger seat too, cramming them in. Firing with one hand, she leaped into the driver's seat. She shoved down on the gas pedal.

"We're going home!" she shouted out the window at the three remaining motorcycles.

They stormed across the field, a hundred people in the back of their truck, more clinging to the roof. She slammed into marauders, plowing through them, crushing their bodies beneath the wheels. Another motorcycle went down, and only two now rose around the truck, providing some protection.

We lost nearly the entire squad, Addy thought, gripping the steering wheel. *But we saved a hundred prisoners. We saved more than we lost.* Her eyes burned. *It has to be worth it. It has to.*

She was a kilometer from the train tracks when the creature rose before her.

Addy felt the blood drain from her face.

Around her, the bikers screamed and fired their guns.

The marauder ahead was huge. It was the size of the truck. Addy had never seen one this large. Five bloated faces grew from its abdomen, snapping jaws the size of cars. Its claws tore through the earth. It raced toward the truck, howling. One of its claws swiped, hitting a motorcycle, tossing it aside as easily as a child tossing a toy.

Addy grabbed Jethro's grenade launcher.

Holding the wheel with one hand, she leaned out the window.

The massive alien roared ahead, thundering toward the truck, roaring from five mouths.

Addy fired.

The grenade flew and entered one of the snapping jaws.

Addy yanked the steering wheel, pulling hard to the left, as the grenade exploded.

Shards of metal and globs of flesh peppered the truck. In the rear view mirror, she saw the giant alien crumble, one of its legs gone. Mewling, it limped back toward the slaughterhouse.

The lone surviving motorcycle rode alongside the truck; the redheaded girl rode on it. They reached the train tracks, and they began to drive along the rails, rattling, heading north through the burnt forest.

We're going to make it back to the Ark, Addy thought, daring to hope.

"Addy!" The roar rose from behind, guttural, inhumanly deep. "Addy Linden, my friend!"

She saw him in the rear view mirror, racing along the tracks on six legs. Blood covered him, and human flesh draped across the skulls on his back. His parasitic twin squealed, riddled with bullets but still alive.

"Fucking Orcus," she muttered. "He's like a goddamn Energizer Bunny with claws."

"You cannot hide from me, Addy!" Orcus cried, leaping along the tracks, gaining on them. "Your skull will be mine!"

Addy grabbed a grenade. She hurled it out the window. It exploded behind them. Another grenade. Another. Orcus kept leaping over the explosions, racing forward, gaining on her, soon only meters away from the truck. Several other marauders emerged from the forest, joining Orcus, bounding forward.

"Come on, come on, where are you?" Addy muttered, staring ahead, seeking the landmark.

There!

She saw it. The old railroad station.

"Addy!" Orcus cried, laughing, and leaped through the air. His claws reached out, about to grab the truck.

Addy hit the remote control mounted on the dashboard.

As the truck roared through the station, the explosives-- planted along the tracks and station yesterday--burst with deafening sound and heat and the fury of a supernova.

Blinding light filled the truck. The shock wave slammed into them, nearly tossing them off the track. Stones, dirt, and chunks of marauders peppered the roof of the truck. Addy clung to the steering wheel, just barely managing to keep driving. Beside her, the lone motorcycle roared out of the fire, racing alongside.

Addy released a shaky breath.

Behind her, the railroad station was gone, and piles of concrete and stone covered the tracks.

Shards of marauders--several legs, broken jaws, seared flesh--covered the forest.

There was no sign of Orcus.

Addy kept driving.

Finally, no aliens were pursuing.

They reached the water tower. They rolled the truck and motorcycle into the garage, slammed the door shut, and vanished underground.

They limped, crawled, were carried into the infirmary.

They lay on the cots, screaming, passing out. Dying.

As the medics fished shrapnel out from Addy, she screwed her eyes shut, gritted her teeth, and felt tears burn down her cheeks.

What are more scars? she thought. *What is more pain? I'm already broken beyond repair. I'm already barely human.* She bit down on a scream as a medic pulled out a chunk of claw. *So let me become the monster.*

She opened her eyes, saw the wounded around her, saw Steve writhing in bed, his leg in a splint. Saw Jethro passed out, his skin sallow, a medic transfusing blood into him. Most of their squad--gone. All but one of their motorcycles--gone. A hundred humans saved, mostly women and children, more mouths to feed when they needed more warriors.

The Human Resistance? An army to fight the marauders? They were living on borrowed time, all of them. How long until the marauders found this place, until the aliens burrowed underground and killed them all?

And Addy knew--knew it in her bones--that Orcus had survived. That he was still out there. Waiting for her.

"If you're alive, Marco, come back," Addy whispered. "Find that Ghost Fleet of yours and come back. I can't do this without you. I need you. I miss you."

"This will help with the pain," said the medic, sticking her with a needle. Addy tried to rise, tried to reach Steve, but she fell back on the cot. Her eyes closed and dreamless slumber rolled across her, tugging her into blackness like marauder webs.

CHAPTER NINETEEN

"It's as if the set of *Happy Days* blasted off into space." Marco looked around him at the ESS *Marilyn*. "I keep waiting for the Fonz to show up."

Outside the portholes, the stars streamed as the ship flew, heading across the Milky Way. Inside the lounge, history had come to life. Asmotic Institute, the builder of the *Marilyn*, was obviously big on nostalgia. The floor was a checkerboard of black and white tiles, and red barstools lined a gleaming counter. Milkshake glasses sparkled by ice cream dispensers. A jukebox stood by a vintage Coca-Cola vending machine. Framed photographs of Little Richard, Elizabeth Taylor, James Dean, and some historical entertainers Marco didn't recognize hung on the walls. The centerpiece was the bumper of a historical automobile that hung above the bar; its license plate read *Route 66*.

"It's heaven." Kemi walked into the lounge, eyes damp, a smile trembling on her lips. "It's absolutely heaven."

Marco's eyes widened. His jaw hung loose, and it was a moment before he could speak. "Where did you find that?"

Kemi had removed her military uniform. She now wore a red poodle skirt, a fleecy white sweater, and a headband. If not for her metal hand, she could have stepped out from an Elvis movie. She grinned at Marco.

"I found them in the storeroom! There's a whole closet of vintage clothes here." She brushed her hands across the skirt. "I don't think they're actually two hundred years old, but they're a good imitation." Her eyes shone. "There are some boy clothes too. Jeans and leather jackets. You should get dressed up with me! You can be a greasy."

"You mean a greaser?" he said.

Kemi nodded. "I think so." She tapped her chin. "Yes, better not be greasy."

Marco couldn't take his eyes off her. It had been years since he had seen Kemi wear anything but her uniform. And there she was again--the girl he had fallen in love with a decade ago. His old Kemi. And she was beautiful. She was so damn beautiful that it hurt.

Finally he found his tongue again. "I'm not sure Captain Ben-Ari would want us in civvies."

Kemi skipped toward the jukebox, and old rockabilly music filled the lounge. "I think we need to dance again. A happy dance this time."

Marco cringed. "I don't do happy dances."

She grabbed his hands and hopped around. "Sure you do!"

They stood in still silence for a moment as the music played. Kemi lowered her head, her smile fading. They held hands. Her one hand was warm and soft, the other cool and metallic. Dancing? Happiness? The innocence of music and ice cream and youth?

Those things were taken from us, Marco thought. *We lost them in the snow of Canada, in the mines of Corpus, in the searing desert of Abaddon.*

And he knew that even should this war end, even should they find peace and a home on the beach and music and friends around them, there would be no dancing. There would be no laughter of abandon. There would be no true joy.

Those things will never more be ours, he thought, still holding Kemi's hands. *Aside from a glimpse soon fading like a rainbow under quick rain.*

Carl Perkins's "Blue Suede Shoes" played through the lounge. Kemi glanced up at Marco, her head still lowered, and Marco knew that she understood--deeply, fully, in a way their words could never express. But her smile returned, hesitant, and she bit her lip.

"Some milkshakes at least?" she said.

He smiled. "Milkshakes would be nice."

As they were stepping toward the barstools, a voice rose behind them.

"I would like one too."

They turned around, and Marco's jaw unhinged for the second time.

For a moment, he didn't recognize her. But it was her. Captain Ben-Ari stepped into the lounge, and she too wore a poodle skirt and sweater.

My God, she's human, Marco thought.

His captain's dark blond hair flowed freely, no longer in its usual ponytail. She had even applied a touch of makeup. It was only a skirt, a sweater, a dab of eyeliner, but it seemed almost like a costume to Marco. He was so used to seeing his commander in her uniform, holding her weapons, an officer ready for war. He had never imagined she even had a civilian life.

"I guess this means you're okay with civvies on the ship," Marco said.

For the first time in years, maybe ever, Marco saw his captain grin. Not just a tight smile but an actual grin--a huge grin that showed her teeth, that lit up the room.

"It's Sunday," she said. "Our day off. And I want that milkshake."

Marco thought back to Nandaka. He had stood with Kemi and Lailani outside the ship, trying not to eavesdrop. Yet they had all overheard Ben-Ari arguing with her father, shouting, weeping. The two had spoken in Hebrew, and Marco had not understood the words, but he understood enough from the tone. He understood the tears he later saw drying on Ben-Ari's cheeks.

Yes, she's human, he thought. *And she too needs to just be a girl sometimes.*

"Three milkshakes coming right up," Marco said.

"Strawberry flavor for me!" Ben-Ari said.

They sat on the barstools, sipping from straws as the music played. "C'mon Everybody" by Eddie Cochran filled the lounge.

"Ow, brain freeze!" Kemi winced and touched her temples.

"Slow down!" Ben-Ari laughed. "The ship is well stocked. We have enough to last until the Cat's Eye Nebula and back-- which should take at least six months." She took a quick sip, and a sigh ran through her. "Damn. I missed ice cream. One of the things I missed most in prison, I think."

Marco swallowed his sip. He looked at his captain. "Ma'am, I never told you, but I'm sorry for what happened. That you had to spend so long behind bars. I should have been with you."

Ben-Ari raised an eyebrow. "In prison?"

"Well, no." Marco shook his head. "But when you and Kemi were fighting for truth, trying to warn the world about the marauders, I should have been there. Fighting with you." The milkshake turned bitter. "I ran. I ran away from Earth, from my duty, from myself. I fought a war on Haven. A war that I lost. Meanwhile, the real war was somewhere else. The war you were fighting, ma'am."

Ben-Ari smiled, reached across the counter, and patted his hand. "You're fighting it now. With us. Whatever you suffered on Haven, whatever horror I endured in prison--it's over now. We're free. We're strong. And we have a plan. And we will win."

"We'll see Earth again," Kemi said softly. "Green hills and blue oceans. We'll find my parents."

"And we'll find Addy," Marco said, voice choked. "And we'll chain her up so she can never get lost again."

Ben-Ari laughed, eyes damp. "What was it that you wanted, Marco? A house on the beach?"

He nodded. "A big house for all of us. You too, ma'am, if you'd like to join us. A house with many rooms. A house between sea and forest. You, me, Kemi, Lailani, Addy . . . all of us broken people. All of us survivors. All of us who understand without words." He wiped his eyes. "Because nobody else would ever understand, would they? What we saw. What we lived through."

Kemi and Ben-Ari both lowered their heads.

"Nobody else would," Ben-Ari whispered.

For a long moment, they were all silent, staring at their glasses. The only sound came from Little Richard singing about Miss Molly. Then Kemi grinned.

"And we'll have campfires on the beach, right?" she said. "And roast marshmallows?"

"And hot dogs," Marco said. "Addy loves them."

"And baked potatoes wrapped in tin foil," Ben-Ari said. "My father taught me how to build a campfire and bake potatoes."

"And we better have a jukebox and milkshake-maker in that house!" Kemi shook her fist. "We better!"

Marco laughed. "We'll park the *Marilyn* next door. If Captain Ben-Ari allows it, at least."

She nodded. "I do. Though by then, when we retire, I'll just be Einav."

"It would be strange to call you that, ma'am," Marco said. "But I would like that. For us to retire. To just be friends. To be a family."

His captain's hand was still touching his. Kemi placed her hand atop of their hands.

"A family," she whispered.

They sat in silence, hands touching, and Marco loved them--deeply, fully, as much as he had ever loved anyone.

And you'll be with us soon, Addy. You--

"Ravagers!" Keewaji barged into the room, waving a tablet in one of his four hands, speaking through the three others. Warnings blared on the monitor. "Ravagers approaching!"

They leaped off the barstools. They ran.

They burst onto the *Marilyn*'s bridge. Three white seats rose here before an array of gleaming panels and viewports. Lailani was sitting at the pilot's station, still wearing her military uniform.

"Fuckers showed up out of nowhere!" she said, yanking the ship's joystick to the left.

They tilted. Through the viewport, Marco saw them-- several ravagers charging toward them, flying through warped space. The alien ships opened their claws, and fire gathered, and plasma roared, and--

Lailani screamed and yanked back the joystick.

The *Marilyn* banked hard. Plasma roared over them and under one wing. A blast hit their side, and they jolted. Keewaji cried out and grabbed a rail with his tail. Marco hit the wall hard.

"Emery, man the missiles!" Ben-Ari shouted, leaping into a seat. "De la Rosa, move to the machine guns! Abasi, take over the helm from her. Defensive maneuvers!"

They had all trained for this. They had spent hours just yesterday learning these controls. Yet Marco still shook, still felt close to passing out.

Fire.

Blood.

Screaming faces.

Gritting his teeth, he ignored the flashbacks. He leaped into the elevated gunner's station, a turret that rose above the rest of the bridge. He grabbed the controls and turned on the missile systems.

The ravagers spun back toward them. They roared forward from all directions.

"Fire!" Ben-Ari shouted.

Kemi grabbed the controls from Lailani and yanked madly, and the ship barrel-rolled. More plasma hit them. Smoke filled the ship. Marco's control panel wouldn't come on. The display belched out sparks. He cursed, got a visual through a viewport, and released a missile.

The missile flew from its bay, swerved in space, sought the heat in the center of the ravager, and shot into its plasma cannon.

The ravager exploded.

Metal claws flew through space, spinning toward them.

"Kemi, incoming!" Marco shouted.

"Damn it!" Kemi yanked the controls madly, spinning, rising higher. She dodged several careening claws. One slammed into the bottom of the ship, metal screeched, fire roared, and the stars slammed into points around them.

"We lost our warp engine!" Lailani shouted. "Hold on!"

Spacetime straightened around them. Immense pressure shoved against them. Keewaji wailed and fell. The ship spun madly. Marco couldn't help it. He vomited, losing his milkshake onto his shirt.

Alarms blared and smoke filled the bridge.

"Status report!" Ben-Ari barked.

"We're back in regular spacetime," Lailani said. "Azoth drive is down. One wing is cracked. Our heat sensors are down. Everything else is functional, and--fuck, here they come!"

Marco saw them. His scanners no longer worked, but he saw the ravagers just outside. They came streaming out of warped space toward them. Three remained.

"Fire!" Ben-Ari shouted.

Both Marco and Lailani hit buttons on their control panels. A hailstorm of bullets and two more missiles flew toward the enemy.

Kemi soared as another ravager exploded, showering shards.

"Damn this ship is fast!" the pilot cried.

"Keep firing!" Ben-Ari said.

Kemi rose higher, looped behind the ravagers, and Marco fired two more missiles. The missiles flew over the ravagers, spun around, then drove into the living ships' gaping maws of plasma.

The alien vessels exploded, and more shards flew. Plasma sprayed upward, catching the *Marilyn*. The controls ripped out of Kemi's hands. They tumbled through space, spinning madly.

One of the ravagers still flew, badly wounded but roaring more fire. The flames hit the *Marilyn*, and the bridge heated up, and a control panel shattered.

Blindly, Marco fired the last two missiles.

The cosmos seemed to explode.

The *Marilyn* spun like a top.

Smoke filled the bridge. Warnings beeped. Klaxons blared. Sparks flew across Marco.

For a moment--nothing but smoke, the *beep beep beep* of an alarm, and coughing. Lailani pulled herself up from the floor. Ben-Ari clutched her bleeding temple.

Marco stared through the viewports, seeking more enemies, waving aside smoke.

Outside in space, he saw nothing but the husks of ships.

"We beat them," Marco whispered. "The ravagers are dead. They--"

Kemi screamed and pointed. "Marauders!"

Several of the aliens had spilled out from a ravager. They tumbled through the vacuum of space, still alive, casting out webs, flying toward the *Marilyn*.

Marco fired the ship's Gatling guns. Bullets tore through the aliens, ripping them apart. Only corpses slammed into the *Marilyn*'s hull.

The crew sat in silence, just breathing. Marco bled from a gash on his elbow, and sparks had seared his side. Ben-Ari held her hand pressed to the cut on her head. Keewaji was trembling in the corner, scratches and bruises covering his pale body.

"All enemies are gone," Lailani finally said, checking the controls. She sighed. "So is our azoth engine."

Marco stared at her, the horror seeping in. "How far out are we? Can we make it back to Nandaka using our regular nuclear engines?"

Lailani met his gaze. "We're several light-years from the nearest star. Without our azoth engine, reaching the nearest world would take ten thousand years. Reaching the Cat's Eye Nebula, where we hope to find the Ghost Fleet . . . Well, we better have enough ice cream to last a million years for that."

"So we fix the azoth drive," Marco said, struggling to hide the tremble in his voice. "Easy! We patch it up, and--"

"Marco. Marco! You don't understand." Lailani took his hand in hers. "The azoth crystal in the heart of our warp engine shattered. We can't fix it." She turned toward the others, and she spoke in a whisper. "Guys, we're stuck here."

They all sat in silence. Even the alarms died.

I'm sorry, Addy, Marco thought. *I'm sorry, Earth.*

He lowered his head. The ship floated on through space, ten thousand years away from salvation.

CHAPTER TWENTY

He lay in shadows.

He lay in shame.

His twin twitched on his side, whimpering, snapping his jaws.

The rocks crushed him, and the fury burned through Orcus like the bombs that had burned his body.

He reached out a claw, hissing with pain. On his side, his brother cackled. Orcus reached out another claw. The rocks shifted above him. A skull on his back, one of his trophies, cracked.

With fury, Orcus roared and thrashed and shoved against the stones, casting back the darkness. His jaws snapped, ripping through rock. Like a hatchling crawling out from a ravager, he emerged from the rubble into searing moonlight.

He looked around him.

The explosion had leveled the concrete building and buried the train tracks. Trees crackled and dust still swirled. The humans and their vehicles were gone. His fellow marauders were gone. Addy was gone.

Orcus tossed back his head and howled at the moon. On his side, his beloved twin opened his small jaws and added his cry.

"She escaped us, little one," Orcus hissed. "The one who took our eye."

On his side, his twin mewled.

"Yes, it still hurts," Orcus said, blinking his three remaining eyes. He still remembered Addy grabbing the fourth eye, squeezing, popping it, the goo flowing between her fingers.

His twin whimpered as if feeling the pain himself.

"Yes, I know you can feel it too," Orcus said. "You think my thoughts. You feel my pain. And I promise you, my beloved. We will find Addy. We will hurt her so much. She will beg for death."

His twin clacked his jaws, struggling to speak. He could form few true words, but Orcus had always understood his beloved.

"No, my little one," Orcus said. "We will not follow the tracks tonight. Not alone."

His twin squealed.

"Lord Malphas wants our report before dawn," said Orcus. "We must speak to him."

His twin screamed, thrashed, trembled. He seemed to cry, "No, no! Hurt, hurt!"

Orcus shuddered. "Yes, beloved, he will hurt us."

He dreaded this. He dreaded this more than battle. Yet what choice did Orcus have? Meat did not satisfy his hunger. To be a mere drone, a soldier like the millions of others, did not satisfy his ambition. No. Orcus had vowed, even as a deformed hatchling, that he would rise. That he would join the alphas, the leaders of the great swarm of hunters. That, with the alphas, he would crawl into the warm, moist innards of the ravagers, the females of their species, would spill his seed upon their eggs. That his sons would fill the galaxy, great warriors. That, with his fellow lords, he would feast not upon meat but upon the brains of his enemies. There was no meal more satisfying than the brain of a sentient creature, lush with fear.

And so Orcus served his master.

And so Orcus bowed before Lord Malphas.

And so he had risen in the ranks, becoming a leader of warriors, inching ever closer to true lordship.

And so, even now, he would not run . . . no matter how much his lord hurt him.

Burnt and dented, Orcus traveled south along the tracks.

He walked through the charred forest, and when he gazed up, he could not see his home star. His world was too far to see. A world of deep, misty forests, of trees lush with webs, of cold, thick air. He had lived there among the bottom boughs, near the soil where things rotted, where the excrement of those above fell upon him, where he could not see the light of stars. But as Orcus limped here, one of his six legs twisted, he vowed: *I will go home an alpha, and I will live in the treetops in the light of our blessed red moons of war.*

He walked past the slaughterhouse and kept going, moving toward the ruins of the human city. Toronto, the humans called it. A festering hive of concrete and filth. The humans had no respect for nature, for growing things. They cut down their trees and raised monstrosities of stone. They flew in ships of metal, for their females were small and weak. Orcus loathed them. With every fiber in his body, he loathed the hairless apes.

"Look at their city, my beloved," he said to his twin. "Look at the evil they raise. These creatures defeated the centipedes, the great empire that once sprawled across a hundred stars. They sent their tentacles into every corner of the galaxy. But we crushed them, my beloved. Yes. We grind them down, and we feast upon their flesh, for we are the true masters. We are the apex predators of the galaxy. The evil of humanity will never rise again, and their fearful brains will satisfy our cravings."

His twin squirmed and snapped his jaws, his hunger running deep.

"Yes, my beloved," Orcus said. "You will feed upon the humans with me. You will taste their brains."

His twin nodded excitedly. "Brains, brains!"

They entered the city. Orcus walked between the skyscrapers that still stood. Thousands of marauders lived here now, scurrying between the buildings, weaving more and more webs, coating the city with their silk. Thousands of ravagers, precious females, hovered above. Orcus ached at the sight of them, ached to crawl into their moist cavities, to find their precious eggs, to fertilize them as he shuddered with pleasure. Yet he was not an alpha. Not yet. He was allowed to fly in a ravager, but never to breed with one.

"But soon," he said, raising a claw to caress his twin. "Soon, once we have proven our worth to Lord Malphas, we will have a great harem of ravagers. Soon we will feast upon brains."

His twin shuddered with anticipation. "Feast, feast!"

As Orcus walked through the city, he gazed around him at the webs that rose between the buildings. Countless humans hung from them, trussed up, squirming, screaming. Prey animals. Precious food. Their brains so soft, so juicy, the flavor of their terror so sweet. They hung everywhere. Orcus gazed at them, his hunger rumbling in his belly and the belly of his twin. On one web, marauders were lashing whips, forcing the male humans to impregnate the females, to create another generation of meals. On another web, human offspring hung, wailing, newly born. On yet another web, marauders were shoving feeding tubes into human mouths, shattering the teeth of those who resisted, fattening up the captives. Their brains would feed the alphas; their meat would fill the marauder warriors with vigor. Between two buildings hung a great web, many female humans upon it, screaming as the marauders milked them, harvesting the precious milk for the marauders' young.

But Orcus cared not for human milk nor flesh. He desired the meals of the alphas. He desired brains, the most precious of foods. He licked his jaws.

He rounded a corner, and he saw it ahead.

He hissed, fear flooding him.

There it rose. A tower woven of metal, stone, and webs.

The lord's hive. The domain of Malphas, King of the Night.

On his side, Orcus's twin whimpered.

"We must see him, my beloved," Orcus said. "He demands it. We must obey."

"Run, run!" the twin seemed to say, but Orcus knew that there could be no running from Lord Malphas. Only servitude. Only love.

He stepped toward the hive. Imperial guards stood here, towering marauders painted crimson and white, and upon their backs writhed living serpents that hissed, snapped their jaws, and spat at Orcus. His twin snarled.

"I have come to bow before Lord Malphas." Orcus sneered at the guards. "Step aside and allow me passage."

Saliva dripped down the guards' fangs. Their hot breath blew against Orcus, and he could smell it there. The smell of human flesh and blood. It had been so long since Orcus had fed. A human corpse lay at the guards' feet, half-consumed, the smell intoxicating.

"We will enjoy hearing your screams, Orcus," said a guard, his jaws twisting into a grin.

The second guard tore a piece off the human corpse. He fed the morsel to the snakes on his back. "Perhaps our pets will feed upon your flesh next."

Orcus snapped his jaws at them. "Silence, guards! When I am an alpha I will wear the skulls of your serpents on my back."

The guards laughed. "You will never rise, Orcus. You are weak and Lord Malphas is wroth. Speak to him." They stepped aside, sniffing. "You already stink with fear."

Gnashing his teeth, Orcus walked between the guards. The living serpents snapped at him, bit his skin, ripped into him as he walked between them. Bleeding, Orcus entered the darkness.

Back on their homeworld, in the holy forest of mist and starlight, Lord Malphas lived upon the highest trees, gazing upon the cosmos. Here he had chosen not a skyscraper, one of the human monstrosities of metal, but a simple hive of webs and stone on the ground. A ring of fire burned here, illuminating a great web. Several humans were dying on this web, skulls carved open, brains exposed. The smell of their terror filled the hive. The web rose tall, fading into shadows above.

Orcus stepped forward. He knelt and lowered his head.

"My Lord Malphas!" He shuddered. "I have come to serve you, as you requested."

The web trembled.

A marauder descended from the shadows above, dangling on strands.

Orcus tried to control his shivering, and his twin twitched as if trying to tear free.

Lord Malphas was not the largest marauder in the horde. He was not one of the giants who came from the deep caves. But he was still twice Orcus's size. And there was terrible, burning power in his four black eyes. There was horrible wisdom. There was knowledge as deep as the cosmos. There was cruelty as dark and deep as a black hole. Looking upon him, there could be no doubt--here lurked the lord of all marauders.

For a long time, Malphas stared at his servant, silent. Finally, slowly, the lord's jaw opened. His tongue slithered out. His voice emerged, deep and ancient as the darkest forests, rumbling like a storm.

"Orcus."

I must run, Orcus thought. *I must hide.* Yet he could not move.

"Master," he hissed, kneeling lower, pressing his head against the floor.

Malphas crept off his web. Slowly, leg by leg, he walked closer. He loomed above Orcus.

"Orcus . . . where . . . is . . . the girl?"

Orcus swallowed the bile that filled his throat.

"My lord, I slew many of her warriors. Addy Linden has managed to escape, but I believe I know her location, and--"

Malphas grabbed him, digging in his claws, and Orcus screamed.

Pure evil flowed from those claws into Orcus. Starlight burned him. Spacetime cracked around him. The might of the cosmos itself twisted his innards. His beloved twin squealed. Above him, Malphas glared with those horrible four eyes, four black orbs, four universes of malice. A god of vengeance, of terror, of unending cruelty.

"You let her escape again?" Malphas let out a rumble, a roar. "You let Addy Linden flee your claws?"

Orcus trembled and wept. "I will find her for you, master! I swear it. I am close. I--" He screamed again as his master's grip tightened.

"I want her, Orcus." Malphas gripped him with a second claw, squeezing his head. "I want Addy Linden. She is one of them. One of the humans who slew the scum emperor. One of the great heroines of humanity, their legendary warrior. I want to feed upon her."

He released his claws, and Orcus fell to the floor, convulsing. Smoke rose from him. His twin wept.

"Yes, master!" Orcus said. "I promise you. I will bring her to you!"

"Promise, promise!" his beloved twin said.

Malphas growled. "Twice already you have failed me, Orcus. I sent you to grab the humans in their colony of Haven. Yet you let the others escape. Marco Emery. Einav Ben-Ari. Kemi Abasi. Lailani de la Rosa. They all fled from you. You caught only Addy Linden, and she too escaped you." The marauder lord circled him, his claws crushing skulls. "I want them, Orcus. All of them. I dream of them. I yearn to feed upon them, to carve open their skulls, to swallow the sweet feasts within. Do you know why I built my hive here, Orcus? Why I lurk here on the ground rather than on a mighty tower?"

"No, master." Orcus cowered on the floor.

"Because here was their home." Malphas sniffed the air. "Here, upon this very ground, did Marco Emery and Addy Linden live. Here they began their quest to defeat the scum, that cruel empire of centipedes. Humanity is weak, frail, pathetic . . . yet these ones are strong. And these ones I must consume."

"You will consume them, master, I vow it!" Orcus said. "Addy Linden lurks just outside this city, hiding in the wilderness. I will find her. The others will return for her. They will not abandon their world. I will bring them all before you, Lord Malphas!"

Malphas sneered at him, looming above him. His saliva dripped onto Orcus, sizzling in his wounds.

"I should tear you apart and let my guards feast upon you!"

Orcus trembled, his death near. As he cowered, he remembered himself as a hatchling, his bigger brothers striking him, cutting him, laughing as they consumed pieces of him.

I vowed to rise, he thought. *I vowed to be an alpha, to never more be weak.*

He forced himself to raise his three remaining eyes. To stare at his master.

"Addy Linden took one of my eyes, Lord Malphas," he said, keeping his voice steady. "I will pursue her and her friends with the vengeance of a storm, with the fury of a supernova, with the determination of all the forces of the cosmos. I will not fail you again."

Malphas stared at him in silence for a long time. Slowly, his jaws curled up in a grin.

"Very well, Orcus."

Relief flooded him. His master forgave him! His master loved him! He wept. On his side, his twin wept with relief too.

"Thank you, my lord!" Orcus said. "I thank you deeply, I--"

"But first," said Malphas, "you must be punished for your failures."

Orcus froze. He bowed low. "Of course, master. Punish me! Hurt me! I will gladly endure."

"No, my slave." Malphas shook his head. "You do not understand. I don't desire to hurt you. I desire for you to hurt yourself." He pointed at the parasitic twin that grew from Orcus. "That abomination that sprouts like a boil from your body. It is dear to you?"

Orcus nodded. "He is my twin. He is my beloved."

"Good." Malphas nodded. "Rip him off. With your jaws. Then eat him alive."

Orcus froze. He took a step back. "Master! Anything but--"

"Do this now!" Malphas roared. "Feed upon him as I watch! Do this or leave my presence, go into exile, and never more return."

Tears flowed down Orcus's hardened skin.

My beloved . . .

His twin whimpered.

Orcus shut his eyes.

I'm sorry. I'm sorry . . .

He closed his jaws around his twin. His beloved wailed. Shivering, Orcus snapped his jaws shut.

Orcus screamed with pain, but he did his duty. He fed.

Malphas grinned.

As Orcus stumbled outside, bleeding, nearly collapsing, he shed tears of joy. His master had forgiven him. Orcus would still climb the great web. He limped back into the wilderness. For the first time in many days, he was not hungry.

CHAPTER TWENTY-ONE

They sat in the *Marilyn*'s lounge, silent. This time there were no milkshakes, there was no music. They were lost in darkness. They had failed.

"All right, I want plans," Captain Ben-Ari said. She had switched back into her olive drab uniform, and her hair was in a ponytail again. "Any idea, no matter how stupid you think it sounds. What do we do?"

They all stared at the shattered azoth crystal on the counter. It lay in hundreds of pieces, some no larger than grains of sand.

Marco tried to control his fear. Terror would not help now. He was not afraid to die; he had cheated death enough times already, felt lucky to have lived this long. But the thought of never saving Addy, of never finding the Ghost Fleet, of leaving Earth to the marauders--it was almost intolerable. To have come so far, only to fail here . . .

"We fix it," Marco said. "We glue it together."

Ben-Ari shook her head. "Impossible. My father once took me to see a gemcutter who specialized in azoth crystals. The man spent months on each crystal, working for hours a day with microscopes and the finest of atomic tools, calibrating the crystal down to the last molecule. A single atom off, and it won't work. I remember the gemcutter telling me that if he ever shattered a single crystal, he would lose his career. We just don't have the tools, skills, or time."

Lailani looked around her. "Well, there's got to be a spare then. Hell, cars have spare tires. Humans have spare kidneys. You'd want a spare of the only thing that lets you fly faster than light."

Again Ben-Ari shook her head. "You'd sooner find a safe full of diamonds. It would cost about as much as a single azoth crystal. No. This crystal was worth a hundred times more than the ship itself. Every ship gets only one."

Kemi rose to her feet and clenched her metal fist. "So why was it so vulnerable? I remember when we crashed the *Miyari* on Corpus. Its azoth crystal was kept inside a massive tank of steel. If a saboteur hadn't gotten inside . . ." She glanced at Lailani and bit her lip. "Sorry, Lailani."

Lailani grumbled something under her breath.

"Remember," Ben-Ari said, "this ship wasn't built by Chrysopoeia Corp like most military vessels. The *Marilyn* was built by Asmotic Institute, a boutique company that normally builds android replicas of celebrities from Hollywood's golden age. Their biggest clients are nostalgia buffs, rich men who want android companions who look like Jayne Mansfield or Raquel Welch. This ship is bespoke. My father must have thought it quaint." She sighed. "Clearly, it wasn't built to last in war. I think the missiles were more for show."

Marco bristled. "With all due respect, ma'am, I used those missiles to destroy four ravagers. Well . . . it was less my aim, more their heat-seeking technology. Thankfully, I don't think they were built by Asmotic Institute like the rest of this ship."

"And yet it was a hollow victory," Kemi said, gazing out the porthole. "The ship's regular engines are fast. They could take us from Earth to the moon within hours. But out here, so far from everything . . ." The pilot winced. "Anyone up for a ten thousand year flight back to Nandaka?"

Lailani sighed. "I knew it. I always knew that someday I'd die of milkshake overdose in a 1950s diner. People thought I was crazy. They said I was being far too specific, but I knew it would happen."

"We're not dead yet," Marco said. "We just need to find a solution. Maybe another azoth source nearby."

"There's nothing but empty space for light-years around!" Lailani said.

"So we send out a signal--"

"It would take years to reach anyone," Lailani said. "Years! Not unless you know how to open a wormhole by rigging the jukebox and milkshake maker. Captain, your dad's ship came stocked with lots of food, but it'll only last a few months. Maybe if we still had battle rations, we could last a year or two, but--"

Kemi glared at the shorter woman. "You don't have to keep reminding Marco he forgot the battle rations. You've been talking about that for weeks."

"I did not!" Lailani said, spinning toward Kemi. "I said nothing about that."

"You hinted it!" Kemi placed her hands on her hips. "You keep trying to harass Marco over one mistake."

"One mistake?" Lailani scoffed. "Maybe if you flew better--"

"Maybe if you detected the ravagers earlier!" Kemi said.

"I wasn't the one dancing and drinking milkshakes." Lailani pointed at Kemi. "I was on the bridge, working, keeping us safe."

"And how safe are we now, Lailani?" Kemi's voice was rising.

"Girls, enough--" Marco began.

"Don't call us girls!" they both said together, spinning toward him.

"What did I do now?" Marco took a step back.

"Soldiers, enough!" Ben-Ari barked.

"I didn't do anything!" Lailani said.

Kemi stomped her foot. "Yes you did!"

"Girls--I mean, women, will you--"

"Marco, shut up!"

Everybody was yelling at once now. Lailani and Kemi were still at each other's throats, turning on Marco whenever he spoke, and Ben-Ari was shouting at everyone to calm down, and accusations flew and soon tears were falling.

A small voice rose between the shouts, barely audible.

Marco turned toward its source.

Keewaji stood nearby, speaking softly through one hand, impossible to hear.

"And it's not my fault the sensors on this damn ship are pieces of shit!" Lailani was saying.

"As if it's my fault the joystick leans to the left!" Kemi said, staring down at Lailani.

Lailani laughed bitterly. "You'd know how to fly the ship if you--"

"Quiet!" Marco roared, surprised at the anger inside him.

They all fell silent. They all stared at him.

"My God," Lailani said. "I've never seen Marco this angry before."

Marco exhaled slowly. His legs shook. He didn't need this. It was bad enough having Lailani and Kemi--the two great loves of his past--here on the same ship. He didn't need them to become enemies. And he certainly didn't need them fighting now when they should be finding solutions.

"I'm sorry for yelling," Marco said. "Keewaji was trying to say something. I couldn't hear him."

He turned back toward the young Nandaki, who had fallen silent and trembled.

Except he no longer looks young, Marco thought. When they had first met him, Keewaji had been the size of a human toddler. He now rose four-and-a-half feet tall, nearly as tall as Lailani. A thin plume of white hair grew on his head, the mark of Nandaki puberty. Only a few weeks had passed, but he seemed to have grown by years. His old clothes no longer fit, and he had taken to wearing human clothing. Like all Nandakis, he had four arms, and he had cut extra arm holes into his shirt.

"What were you saying, Keewaji?" Lailani said, her voice soft now, all its anger gone. She stepped toward the alien and placed a hand on his shoulder.

The Nandaki raised one arm, opened the mouth on his palm, and spoke hesitantly. "You said we could use a wormhole."

Lailani sighed and smiled thinly. "Yes, I said that if Marco could build a wormhole generator using the jukebox and milkshake maker. I was angry. I told a bad, mean joke." She looked back at the others. "I'm sorry, Marco and Kemi. I get mean when I'm scared. I'm sorry."

Kemi nodded and stepped closer. She touched Lailani's arm. "I'm sorry too. I acted like an ass."

Lailani nodded. "You did."

"Hey!" Kemi bristled. "You're supposed to deny that!"

Marco cleared his throat and felt it best to steer the conversation back to Keewaji. "Was there anything else, Keewaji? About wormholes?"

The alien nodded. "They appear in the lore of my people. In ancient stories, tales from ten thousand generations ago, wormholes are great bridges through the sky. All Nandaki children know of them. I heard their tales many times as a child. The ancient ones, the beings of light, built many bridges of starlight. They flew through them to visit many worlds, including Nandaka when our planet was very young, and they gave my ancestors many gifts. An ancient boulder still rises in our forest, brought to us by the sky gods, engraved with a map of the stars and the bridges that pass between them. The sky gods gave the holy map to our hero, the wise Yesawi, and blessed him. Someday, the sky gods told him, we Nandakis would build great ships and sail the skies, and we would need this map of the heavens."

Ben-Ari stepped closer. She narrowed her eyes. "The sky gods? What species are they? I'm unaware of any intelligent civilizations--other than the Nandakis--in this galactic sector."

"Hunters slew them long ago," said Keewaji. "There was a great war in the sky. My ancestors witnessed it. Great empires with much cargo fought among the stars. The centipedes, the great predators of darkness, emerged the victors. The sky gods faded away. All that remains of them are my people's songs, our tales, our stone with its map. And perhaps . . . perhaps their bridges of starlight." His eyes gleamed. "Their wormholes."

Marco looked at the others. He could see the doubt in their eyes. Old legends from thousands of generations ago? On Earth, legends from just a hundred generations ago were full of inaccuracies, their grains of truth drowning in seas of myth.

"Keewaji," Marco said, keeping his voice soft. "In our world, we have old legends too, but they're just stories."

"True stories!" said Keewaji. "My ancestors would not lie. Stories are holy to us Nandakis, as holy as cargo. We are not mighty like the great sky gods, the Night Hunters, or the humans. We are small, weak, and lack cargo. Our lives are short, our cargo made of but straw and wood and stone. Our stories give us strength. I myself have worshiped often at the Sky Boulder, studying the map of the stars. Often I have climbed the tallest trees, gazed upon those distant stars, and imagined the bridges of light flowing between them. The wormholes." His lavender eyes shone, as large as lemons. "We are near one. That white star outside the porthole, and the blue one ahead of us. A bridge of light passes between them, and beyond it, we can travel many bridges to many distant stars. The ancient bridges of the sky gods. They are real."

Again Marco glanced at his peers. They looked as doubtful as he felt.

"Even if the wormholes were real," Ben-Ari said, "they would take enormous energy to maintain. If an ancient civilization built and powered them, the wormholes would be long gone now."

Marco hated the hope that was springing inside him. A fool's hope. Hope based on an old legend. Hope that would still shatter. Ben-Ari was right. This could not work.

"His story . . . might have some merit," Lailani said. She chewed her lip and tapped her chin. "Maybe."

Ben-Ari turned toward her. "Explain."

"For three years, I served in the Oort Cloud, stuck in a little research station on the outskirts of our solar system. Our task was to study, well . . . galactic myths. Primarily the Ghost Fleet, the greatest myth there is. But we studied other myths as well. Observing. Seeking clues. One myth we called the Tree of Light. According to the myth, an ancient civilization built a network of wormholes across the galaxy, portals letting their ships hop from star to star. The network was shaped like a great tree, giving the legend its name. Inexplicably, about a thousand years ago, the civilization vanished. We found no recent signals from them." She glanced at Keewaji. "This little one might be telling the truth."

Keewaji nodded. "Our stories are truth."

Lailani looked back at the others. "We detected what we thought were good signs of the Tree of Light, this branching network of wormholes. But are the wormholes still around? Who knows? Any signals from that far are ancient by the time they reach the Oort Cloud. I don't want to get my hopes up, but . . . Hell, it's worth checking out." She pulled out her tablet and ran some quick calculations. "I can dig up my old notes, and . . . yes. According to our theory, there should be a portal nearby. A wormhole."

"How close?" Ben-Ari said. "Assuming it's still there."

Lailani ran a few more calculations. Her eyes brightened. "Close! Of course, with an azoth engine, we could be there within minutes. But even with our conventional engine, the one we use for flying at sub-light speed, we can get there soon enough. If we fly at top speed--and I mean giving our engines every last bit of juice on this ship, and plugging in the milkshake maker and jukebox for an extra boost--we can be there in two months. It's a fighting chance. And it's hella closer than the ten thousand year journey back to Nandaka."

They all glanced at one another.

There it was, a warmth inside of Marco. Hope.

Can you hang on for another two months, Addy? he thought. *Can you stay strong for me?*

Ben-Ari nodded. "All right. Lieutenant Abasi, return to the bridge and set a course. De la Rosa will give you the coordinates."

Kemi nodded. "Yes, ma'am! But . . . I'm not getting rid of my jukebox and milkshake maker. Even if it adds an extra month to our journey. I need my Elvis, and I need my ice cream."

They all laughed--a shaky laughter of relief, of new light.

"Find us that wormhole," Ben-Ari said, "and I'll buy you an ice cream factory."

Kemi saluted, then raced onto the bridge. Lailani joined her, shouting out coordinates.

For the next few hours, Marco wore a space suit, helping Ben-Ari repair the ship's damaged hull. He had done space walks before during his integration into Space Territorial Command, but it was still a dizzying experience, hanging here in the middle of so much emptiness. The ship was moving at incredible speed, as fast as her conventional engines would take her, but without any point of reference she might as well have been still.

By the time Marco returned into the ship, the lights were dim, mimicking the natural cycle of day and night back on Earth. The engines purred, and the others were asleep, the ship coasting on autopilot.

The *Marilyn* came with a decently-sized shower, its water cycling through a filtration system, purifying itself with each round. Marco stood under the hot stream for a long time. He leaned against the tiled wall and lowered his head.

The images still danced. The subways screeching under Haven. His walk through the labyrinth of desks at work, hearing them whisper, call him a war criminal, a freak. Dinner with Anisha, fleeing from her home, hiring the prostitute, leaving Anisha, running from her, so afraid of healing, so afraid of living. Feeling so unworthy. So hurt. So scarred. Standing on the roof of a skyscraper, ready to jump into the storm, to end his life. The marauders reaching out, grabbing Addy, taking her from him.

Marco grimaced and his tears flowed with the water.

He forced himself to think of the good things. Of roasting hot dogs on a rake with Addy, laughing, sharing their secret joke. That day at the planetarium long ago, the first time he had spoken to Addy, watching the stars with her. Kissing Kemi for the first time. Making love to Lailani in the tent at basic training.

There will be more good times, he thought. *We'll make it out of here. We'll save the world. We'll buy that house on the beach.*

"And you'll be with us again, Addy," he whispered. "I promise."

It was late, and Marco was tired, but he couldn't bear the thought of lying in his bed, of staring up at the darkness, of remembering. Wearing only boxer shorts and a T-shirt, he returned to the lounge, sat at the bar, and made himself a cup of tea. He opened a book--an old paperback about knights, princesses, and fiery dragons--and prepared to spend an hour vanishing into an older, simpler world.

Feet padded behind him.

"Oh, sorry! I didn't mean to disturb your reading."

He turned to see Kemi standing there in her pajamas.

"Couldn't sleep?" he asked her, closing the book.

"I was waiting for you in the bunk," she said. "And Keewaji snores anyway. Through four mouths!"

Marco laughed. "He just needs to curl up his fists when he sleeps."

"The poor thing would suffocate!" Kemi joined him at the bar, climbing onto a stool beside him. "Well, also . . ." She looked down at her hands. "We never finished our milkshake. Ben-Ari interrupted our date earlier."

Marco raised an eyebrow. "It was a date, was it?"

Kemi twisted her fingers--both the real and metal ones-- still not looking up. "No." She shrugged. "I dunno. Maybe?" She looked at him, then looked away. "I know, I know. I'm being an idiot. Same old Kemi . . ."

"You're very intelligent," Marco said.

She laughed awkwardly. "When it comes to books maybe. To numbers." She pulled out her pendant--the pi pendant. "Like this."

His eyes widened. "You kept it! I gave you that . . . Damn, how long ago was it?"

"We were seventeen. Eight years ago. I never stopped wearing it. Even after . . ." Kemi sighed. "My tongue feels all twisty." She touched his hand and looked into his eyes. "I know you still love Lailani. I see it when you look at her. She's sweet.

She's pretty. She's kind. You're right to love her, especially after what I did, how I left you. And she loves you too. Oh, she still misses Sofia. And she's confused. But she loves you, Marco, and she'll realize that before the end." Kemi's eyes filled with tears. "And I don't want to come between you two. I don't want to force you to choose. But I do want us to finish our date." She smiled, wiping her eyes. "So can I buy you a milkshake?"

He smiled, and his heart seemed to melt with sweet sadness. He touched her hair. "I'll never turn down a milkshake."

She poured a milkshake, got two straws, and they shared it. A moment of nostalgia. Of a little peace. Of a little return to their youth. They stared into each other's eyes, and they didn't need to say anything. They spoke without words, as they always could.

I still love you, Kemi. Always.

"Ow, ow!" She pulled back and touched her forehead. "Brain freeze!"

Marco laughed. The *Marilyn* flew on.

CHAPTER TWENTY-TWO

Ben-Ari was weary.

She was not merely tired. Not merely exhausted from the chase. She was weary to her bones, a deep destruction inside her.

She had been hiding it from her crew. The headaches. The blurred thinking. The dizziness that sometimes hit her, the despair that clawed inside. She was their captain. She was more than just their commander; she was their leader, their beacon, their source of strength and inspiration, of comfort in the dark. How could she reveal her weariness to them?

And so she was weary in silence, in secret, in quiet despair.

She was weary after two years in prison, struggling to maintain her sanity in a cell. She was weary after fleeing her career, abandoning all that she held dear for the sake of truth. She was weary after the great battles on Abaddon, on Corpus, in the deserts of North Africa, of the nightmares that never ended.

She was weary of war.

And so are they, she knew. *Kemi. Lailani. Marco. My soldiers. So I will be strong for them, even if I'm crumbling inside.*

Kemi and Marco were both on the bridge; they were taking the night shift, Kemi at the helm, Marco at navigation. Ben-Ari had not slept last night. She had sat up in the bridge, calculating, thinking, worrying, remembering. Tonight, with nothing but empty space around them for millions of kilometers, she walked toward the crew quarters. She needed to sleep. For a few hours, she needed to forget.

Ben-Ari entered the bunk where four cots stood. Three were empty. Lailani sat on the fourth, knees pulled to her chest. She was crying.

"Sergeant?" Ben-Ari sat on the bed beside Lailani. "Are you all right? How can I help you?"

Lailani rubbed her eyes and looked away. "I'm sorry, ma'am. I'm fine."

"Sergeant de la Rosa." Ben-Ari stared at her. "You are my soldier. I will do anything I can for you. Tell me how I can help."

I'm weary, she thought. *I'm weary to the bone. But my soldiers come first. Always.*

Lailani let out something halfway between sob and laugh. "It just hurts. Losing people. Being confused. Feeling guilty." She lowered her head. "I'm sorry. I feel awkward. I need to be a good soldier, and you're my commander, not my therapist."

"Lailani." Ben-Ari placed her hand on the young woman's shoulder. "You're my soldier, and I'm here for you. A commander's job is to listen to her soldiers. To help them find strength. There's no need to feel awkward. All good soldiers cry at night."

"Even you?" Lailani asked, raising red-rimmed eyes.

Ben-Ari smiled. "Sometimes. Secretly." She winked. "Don't tell Emery."

Lailani laughed and dabbed her eyes, but her smile soon faded. "I . . . I feel like a monster."

Ben-Ari grew solemn. "Lailani. You are not a--"

"I know, I know." Lailani sniffed. "I'm 99% human, and the chip in my head stops the 1% monster from manifesting. But I can't forget, Captain. I can't." She met Ben-Ari's eyes. "It was seven years ago, but I can't forget how I killed him. How I killed Elvis. My friend. How I grew claws, tore into his chest, and ripped out his heart." She looked at her slender hand. "How that monster is still inside me."

Ben-Ari clasped Lailani's hand. "You did not kill Elvis." She stared into Lailani's eyes and spoke forcefully. "The scum were controlling you. You were nothing but their puppet. You are not guilty of his death. Do you understand that, Lailani?"

Lailani wiped her eyes. "I know. But it still hurts. I miss Elvis." She gave a weak laugh. "And he would have loved this ship. There's even a statue of the real Elvis in the bathroom!" She sighed. "I miss all my friends from boot camp. Caveman and Beast and all the others. And more than anyone, I miss Sofia. I let her go. When Kemi was airlifting us, I just couldn't hold on, and Sofia fell into the fire, and . . ." Lailani's tears fell, overpowering her words.

Ben-Ari embraced the little soldier. "I've known you for almost eight years. And I know you to be noble, kind, and righteous. In war, we face horrible choices. In war, sometimes we must watch our friends die, even leave our friends behind. Your hands are clean."

Lailani cried softly against Ben-Ari's chest. "Maybe I just need a good cry," she said between her sobs.

"We all need to cry sometimes," Ben-Ari whispered, stroking the sergeant's short black hair. "We all sometimes shatter. We all suffered so much loss. I cannot even imagine the grief you're feeling. To lose a loved one is a terrible pain."

Lailani mumbled into Ben-Ari's shirt. "What if I lose Marco too? What if he chooses Kemi? What if I want him to choose Kemi, because I know that I can't commit to him, can't be the woman he deserves? Even though I still love him? Oh, I sound like a stupid teenager! I'm an NCO in the military, and now I'm acting like a lovesick girl."

"You're acting like a human." Ben-Ari brushed back strands of Lailani's hair; it was just long enough to cover her eyes. "These feelings are normal. It's normal to be scared, confused, hurt."

"Even for you?" Lailani said. "You're strong, though. And smart. Stronger and smarter than I am. I wish I could be like you."

Ben-Ari smiled softly. *If only you knew the pain and fear inside me, Lailani. But perhaps those are feelings I must keep hidden, feelings a captain cannot reveal to her crew. It's my job to guide you. To give you strength. To lead you through the grief and terror.*

She wrapped her arms around her soldier. "You are strong, Sergeant de la Rosa. And you are wise. And you are decent. You make me proud."

"I feel safe like this," Lailani whispered. "When you hold me. I never had an older sister. But I imagine that it feels like this." She looked up at Ben-Ari, eyes still damp, and smiled. "I love that you're my commander. I always tell Marco and Kemi that I love them--even Kemi, with all those times she annoys me. And I love you too, ma'am. I know it's stupid and not professional. But I do. You're my heroine."

This is why I do what I do. Ben-Ari had taken no husband, no lover. She had borne no children. She had no home waiting outside of the military, no people to love her, no pets. Nothing but this ship in the darkness. Nothing but this crew to stave off the horrible loneliness.

But this is enough, Ben-Ari thought. *This is my family. This is my home.*

"Get some sleep, Lailani. We have a long day of building probes tomorrow."

Lailani hesitated, then kissed Ben-Ari's cheek. She curled up on the bed. "Goodnight, Einav."

Ben-Ari lay down on the cot next to Lailani. It was a crowded ship, and the beds were only a meter apart, but tonight, being close to Lailani comforted her.

You draw your comfort from my strength, she thought. *But my comfort has always been in protecting people. In keeping others safe. And I will keep you safe, Lailani, Kemi, Marco. And I will find you, Addy. This is my life--it is yours. You will never know how proud and happy you all make me.*

Ben-Ari closed her eyes, and she let her weariness drag her into the deep.

CHAPTER TWENTY-THREE

The snow fell as they hiked up the mountain. Addy shivered and cursed.

"You did this for five years in the army?" she muttered. "And you didn't go insane?"

"Oh, I went insane all right." Steve hiked ahead of her, clearing a path through the snow. "Everyone who survived this long has to be crazy."

They were a hundred kilometers north of the Ark, and their bicycles lay hidden under branches at the foothills. For an hour now, they had been climbing, trudging up snowy slopes. The ruins of Toronto lay beyond the southern horizon, and the stench of death no longer filled the air. For all the cold, exhaustion, and fear, Addy found herself sometimes pausing, looking around at the wilderness, and inhaling deeply.

There you are, she thought. *Earth.*

"Almost there," Steve said, hefting the antennae across his back. "Damn, my leg is still fucked up. Doc says the bone is healed, but goddamn the thing still hurts like a son of a bitch."

Addy snorted. "Wuss. No worse than a hockey injury. I once got both legs broken and fought the scum the very next day."

"Bullshit." Steve looked back at her. He frowned. "Really?"

Addy nodded, climbing behind him, carrying the other half of the heavy antennae. "For real. Another time I got my arm chopped off. A scum bit it. I grabbed it from him and beat him to death with it."

Steve snorted. "Well, that's nothing. A marauder sliced open my belly once. I used my own guts to strangle the alien to death, then stuffed them back into me, stitched myself up with his cobwebs, and kept fighting."

"Luxury," Addy said. "A marauder once cut my head off. I bit its ankles until it died, hopped back onto my own body, stitched my head back on using my own hair, and still managed to kill ten more aliens."

"Oh yeah?" Steve said. "Well, a marauder once killed me. I rose as a zombie, ate its brains, caught my own ghost, wrestled it back into my body, and never even broke a sweat."

"Oh yeah?" Addy said. "Oh *yeah*? Well, I--"

I once had a feeding tube shoved down my throat, she wanted to say.

I once watched almost all my friends die underground at Corpus, she wanted to say.

I once watched millions of lives snuffed out on Abaddon, she wanted to say.

I once watched Marco wither with shell shock until he was a ghost of himself, fading away, dying, she wanted to say.

I once watched my friends return to life as scum hybrids, and I killed them myself. I shot my friends, and I can't stop seeing them over and over, she wanted to say.

But none of those words came to her lips.

"You win," she said instead.

Steve began to whoop in victory, then seemed to notice the expression on her face. His grin vanished.

"Well, we'll call it a draw," he said. "Now come, Ads. I'm freezing my ass off. Let's get this over with."

They climbed higher, finally emerging onto the mountaintop. A frozen lake sprawled to the north. In the south, they could see snowy fields, a deserted town, and icy trees. They began setting up the antennae.

"Used to do this all the time in the army," Steve said. "Thought it was finally behind me. Thought I'd spend the rest of my days in my apartment, watching *Robot Wrestling* with Stooge." He attached two rods and twisted a bolt. "You think Stooge is still alive?"

"I'm not sure he was ever alive," Addy said.

"Very funny. I miss the guy, all right? He was my friend. He was--Son of a bitch!" Steve wrestled with the antennae, and two pieces finally snapped together. "There. Good. I think we're rolling now. If there are other human pockets of resistance in Ontario, this'll find 'em. It might take a while, though." He pulled out two folding chairs, like those Hollywood directors sat on, and a thermos. "Coffee?"

"No beer?" Addy said.

"No beer." A twinkle filled his eyes. "But I might just have some brandy." He opened his pack, revealing a bottle. "For later."

"Brandy!" Addy whistled and affected an English accent. "Well, look at Sir Steven Throttlebottom, Esquire. How genteel. Shall we swirl the drink while adjusting our monocles?"

"Fuck you. It keeps you warmer than beer. Trust me, I spent five years on snowy mountaintops. Coffee and brandy-- better than a campfire."

They sat on the small folding chairs.

"Fuck, my ass is so big now I can barely fit." Addy wriggled to squeeze in.

"I should have brought you a sofa," said Steve, earning a punch.

They sat, wrapped in their coats, drinking hot coffee. Steve had chosen some horrid hazelnut flavor, adding far too much sugar and cream, but Addy was willing to forgive him when the warm liquid filled her belly. The antenna thrust out, its sensors below ticked away, and Steve kept turning dials.

"How long does it usually take?" Addy said.

Steve shrugged. "A minute or so. Two if I'm tired." He waggled his eyebrows.

She rolled her eyes. "Oh, you're being generous. You know what I mean."

"I don't know, Ads. I never had to look up signals after an apocalypse. I'm used to searching for scum in space, not humans on the ground." He adjusted the dials. "Nothing so far. It might be a long day. Pass me more of that coffee."

She took a swig and passed it to him. "Drink up. The sooner we're done with the coffee the sooner we crack open the booze."

He adjusted the dials again, again picked up nothing. He filled his little cup with more coffee. They sat for a while in silence, gazing at the winter wilderness. A hawk glided above.

"Hey, Ads?" Steve finally said.

"Yeah?"

Steve cleared his throat and scratched his cheek. He had been growing a beard these past couple weeks. It suited him, Addy thought.

"Sorry again," he said. "For not being there with you guys. When you were kicking scum ass. I lied before. I didn't kill any scum. I was just doing this for five years. Sitting around, raising antennae, drinking coffee and booze. I hear the stories you tell, and I wish I could have been there. You know, just to help you. So you wouldn't be alone with your memories now."

She gasped, eyes wide. "You mean you never strangled an alien with your own guts?"

"Shut up." He drank again. "Look, I'm no good with words like your little buddy Marco. But I'm sorry, all right? I see how you sometimes seem to remember things. How you sometimes scream in your sleep. How you're hurt." He looked at her. "It hurts to see you dealing with all this by yourself. I wish I could understand."

"Nobody will understand," Addy said softly. "Nobody but those who were there. I doubt Marco and I will ever talk about it, even if we meet again. But we'll understand."

Steve nodded. He lowered his head, staring at his lap, and twisted his hands around his thermos. "So it's true, isn't it? That you love Marco. That you'll probably marry him."

"What?" Addy barked a laugh. "What the fuck are you talking about?"

"You and Marco. You love him, right?"

"With all my heart," Addy said.

Steve looked devastated. "Maybe it's time for that brandy now."

"Steve!" Addy punched him. "You big dumb galoot! I love him like a brother. For fuck's sake, he practically *is* my brother. I lived with him since I was eleven. I don't love him all sexy like. First of all, he's the same height as me, and I like taller guys. Second, he's too book smart for me. I like big dumb idiots like you."

"Really?" Steve's eyes lit up. "I mean--hey!"

She leaned over, kissed his cheek, and mussed his hair. "My big dumb abominable snowman."

He gave a mock roar. "That's me." He leaned back and stared at the wilderness. "It's beautiful, isn't it? Forests. Frozen rivers and lakes. The sky. Earth as it should be. There's still some good on this planet. Something to fight for."

Addy nodded. "Something to fight for." She watched another hawk glide.

Steve held her hand. "After all this shit is over--after we win--we should shack up again. Not that old apartment that stank of weed and beer. I'll build you a real house. With my own hands. I'm good with my hands. A house somewhere up here, in nature. Somewhere beautiful. Maybe we can even get back together, you know? Like a couple or . . . a husband and wife or something."

She raised an eyebrow. "What the fuck, dude? Why aren't you getting on one knee and giving me a diamond the size of my eyeball?"

"I don't kneel before nobody." Steve groaned. "Fine, fine!" He rose from his chair, knelt, and lifted an ice crystal. "Addy Elizabeth Linden, will you--"

"Get up, you idiot. I was kidding." She stood up and yanked him to his feet. "I fucking hate boys who kneel and cry and shit. Wusses. That's like Marco shit right there. Just be a man and fucking kiss me."

He pulled her into his arms, and he kissed her. The snow swirled around them. And it was safety. And it was warmth. And it was some comfort from the pain. And it was love.

The radio crackled behind them.

Through the static, a voice emerged.

"This is K107.7, voice of the Human Rebellion, broadcasting every . . ." Static crackled. ". . . reports of marauders making their way along the Oak Ridges Moraine, all survivors advised to . . ."

Steve leaped toward the radio. He adjusted the dials. Some of the static cleared.

"... and remember, folks, keep off the main roads and stay out of the main cities. Try to stay in groups smaller than fifty. Melt snow to drink, and remember--never eat snow. All right, folks? Never eat snow, even if you're thirsty--melt it first. You can still find lots of farms up north with living cattle, and small towns still have grocery stores. Take what you need. But stay out of the big cities. Stay out of big groups. Stay off the main roads. Stay safe. Thanks for listening to K107.7, voice of the Human Rebellion."

"This is bullshit!" Addy said. "*We're* the Human Rebellion!"

Steve frowned. "I thought we were the Resistance."

"Same fucking thing!" Addy groaned. "Who the fuck are those bozos?"

The voice on the radio continued speaking. "And remember, folks, the Human Defense Force is still around, just splintered into bits and pieces. Based on our last reports, there are still divisions out there, infantry and armor, all ready to fight. We can't tell you everything we know, but there's somebody looking after you. And as we like to remind you here every day, the heroes of the Scum War are still fighting. Captain Einav Ben-Ari. Lieutenant Kemi Abasi. Staff Sergeant Marco Emery. Staff Sergeant Lailani de la Rosa. Staff Sergeant Addison Linden. We all know their names. We all remember them from the war. We all know they're still fighting. Say a little prayer today for our heroes. And now, we leave you with the golden notes of Bootstrap and the Shoeshine Kid. Some soothing music from K107.7, music and news on the hour, every hour."

Electric guitar and bass played.

"Other survivors," Addy whispered. "We're not alone."

Steve frowned. "Wait a minute. Your real name is *Addison?*"

Addy lifted her fist. "Your real name will be Toothless Smashed-face if you *ever* say that name again."

Steve paled and grabbed the microphone. He twisted a few dials. "Hello out there! This is Ice Tiger, broadcasting from the Human Resistance. We--"

"Ice Tiger?" Addy said. "Really?"

"Shush, Snow Pigeon!"

"I'm not--"

"Addy!" he mouthed. "We can't use our real names!" He returned to the microphone. "This is Ice Tiger, voice of the Human Resistance. Not the Rebellion, mind you, the Resistance. My partner Snow Pigeon informs me that they're quite different. If you need assistance, we have food, we have weapons, we have medicine. Broadcast back on the following frequency."

He repeated the call a few times, then placed down the mic.

Addy rolled her eyes. "So you're the tiger and I'm the pigeon."

"Hey, it was pigeon or snail, and I figured you'd prefer pigeon."

"Dragon." She nodded. "I'm the Snow Dragon. It was the name of my old platoon."

Steve nodded and clasped her hand. "Snow Dragon."

The radio crackled. "Ice Tiger, do you copy? This is White Lion."

Addy grabbed the mic. "Snow Dragon here! We read you loud and clear, White Lion."

For a moment there was only static, and Addy cursed. Steve adjusted the dials, and Addy's heart pounded, sure the transmission was lost. But finally the voice emerged again.

". . . holed up for a while here. Marauders are on the hills all around. We're holding out, though."

"Repeat please," Addy said. "Where are you holed up? Do you need assistance?"

Again static. Then the voice returned. "We only report that information in code. I'll send you a key to interpret it. The marauders can't break it without knowing human keywords. Do you prefer actors, cartoon characters, or hockey players?"

"Hit me with that hockey puck, dude," Addy said. "Unless the marauders have been watching Leaf games, they won't crack your code."

During the Scum War, soldiers had often used "keys" for their codes--short phrases, often just two or three words long, that acted as passwords to scrambled messages. White Lion's scrambled code came in over the radio, along with the team and jersey number of a hockey player. Addy was able to recall the player's name from memory, which gave them the key. Addy couldn't make odds or ends of code-breaking, but surprisingly, Steve was able to quickly decode the encrypted message.

I never knew you had it in you, she thought.

A hundred and forty men. A mix of military and survivor types. They were holed up in a base nearby, with weapons galore, according to them. Marauders on the hills around them.

"Let's take this back to the Ark," Steve said.

Addy nodded. "Hopefully climbing downhill is easier than up."

By the time they reached the foothills, the stars shone above. They rode their bicycles through the night, rifles slung across their backs. Steve had wanted to take the truck up here, but Addy had refused. Trucks rumbled, beamed out headlights, and would alert every marauder for kilometers around. On their bicycles, they traveled quietly, off road, the stars guiding them. Only once, about ten kilometers south, did a marauder leap toward them. Addy and Steve raised their rifles, silencers on the barrels. It took two full magazines of bullets to finally hit one eye, knocking the marauder down, and another two magazines to finish the job.

It was dawn before they reached the Ark and returned underground. They shared the news with Jethro and the others.

"Another group of rebels," Addy said. "Nearby. And they need help. We ride out tomorrow. And we grow stronger."

Yet as she lay down to sleep that night, Addy couldn't shake her anxiety. There had been something about that voice on the radio, that White Lion. Something familiar. Something disturbing. She couldn't place it. When she finally fell asleep, the voice haunted her, calling her name over and over as she tried to flee.

CHAPTER TWENTY-FOUR

Time flowed strangely in space.

According to myth, the nearest wormhole--built by that ancient civilization of light--was two months away. As the ESS *Marilyn* sailed through the darkness at sub-light speed, its azoth crystal broken, some days seemed agonizingly slow to Marco. They were long days of silence, of contemplation, of memory. Days of pacing, gazing out of the portholes, praying to finally see the wormhole. Days when Marco found himself going mad with grief. Every day here, he knew, Addy was suffering in captivity, if she was even still alive. Every day here, all of Earth cried out under the yoke of the marauders, penned and slaughtered like cattle. Every day here, more guilt filled Marco--that he had survived while Anisha had burned, while so many suffered. Every day was an eternity.

Yet time also seemed so fast.

During the flight, Marco had time to read. To work on a second draft of *Le Kill,* writing more about Tomiko, his fierce heroine with the kabuki mask and katana. To meditate. Most importantly, he spent these days with those dearest to him.

Many days on this journey, Marco spent time with his captain. He and Ben-Ari passed hours in the lounge, speaking of literature and theater, of history, of science and art. They found comfort in the cerebral, an escape from this cosmos of nightmares and pulsing emotions. Marco had known his commander for years, but only now did she reveal her extensive knowledge, and he marveled at how well-read, how educated she was, as easily fluent in Victorian literature as she was in biology and physics. One day, she showed him her watercolor paintings, and another day, she played her favorite operas for him, and she cried during "Che gelida manina" from *La bohème*. Marco let her read *Loggerhead*, and they talked about the book, and he learned that Ben-Ari wrote too, had spent two years in prison writing poems and her memoirs.

Often, on Sundays or evenings, she wore her civilian clothes. Sometimes Marco called her Einav. For years, he had admired her, had seen her as a great leader. Now he saw the woman beneath the uniform--kind, intelligent, a woman whose eyes sparkled when she spoke of art and music, who marveled at the secrets of the cosmos. She spoke little of her personal life. Perhaps she wasn't ready. But somehow, his long conversations with Ben-Ari about science and art and history felt more intimate than any conversation he'd ever had.

On other days, Marco spent hours listening to music with Kemi, going over album after album in the jukebox, everything from Little Richard to Elvis to Buddy Holly. Kemi would dance, smile, and finally--after so much suffering, after so many years of nightmares--she was laughing again. She was happy. Marco never forgot finding Kemi captive in the mines of Corpus, the scum experimenting on her, how a part of her had died that day. Seeing the old Kemi, twirling around to music, her smile and eyes shining, made Marco happier than she'd ever know. Here was the old Kemi again, the girl he had fallen in love with years ago. And with his anxiousness to return to Earth, to save Addy, Marco never wanted to leave this ship.

Other days on this journey, Marco spent time with Lailani. They reminisced about boot camp, laughing at the old stories: how they had pissed into milk cartons and bottles while stuck in their tent on high alert, how Caveman had tried to plant a flower grove one Sunday in the desert, how they would pilfer packets of jam from the cafeteria and use them as currency, and how Addy had once paid two entire cans of stolen Spam--a treasure for her-- for three cigarettes.

Sometimes during this long flight, Marco and Lailani would play cards--gin rummy was their favorite--smack talking each other all the while, the winner mercilessly teasing the loser until they almost came to blows, but always collapsed laughing at the end. Some days, they just lay on a cot together--Lailani was small enough to lie beside him--and watched movies, hours and hours of movies. They spent one full day watching all three *Lord of the Rings* movies, crying during the last half hour. For a whole week, they had a marathon of *All Systems Go!*, watching every episode in the anime series. Sometimes their fingertips would touch, and a faint smile would raise Lailani's lips. Sometimes her hand slipped into his, as if by chance, and she let him hold it. Sometimes Marco caught her looking at him, her eyes soft, but then Lailani would quickly look away, her cheeks flushing. Perhaps she was remembering Sofia--sometimes she still wept at nights--and perhaps she was thinking of Kemi.

She still loves you, Kemi had said, and when Marco spent those days with Lailani, he knew that it was true. And he knew that he himself still had feelings for Lailani. He felt torn between them, the two great stars in his night. Kemi and Lailani. The two women he had loved most in his life, had lost. But even should he let his love bloom with one again, he would wait. Not here. Not in this darkness. There was another woman who needed him. There was Addy. And Marco would focus on no one else until he saved her.

Time. Time that felt too rushed, the moments of peace too brief. Time that seemed agonizingly slow, every moment full of concern for Addy. But nobody seemed to feel the passage of time more than Keewaji.

"Poet," Lailani said to him one day, "does Keewaji look . . . different to you lately?"

The young Nandaki lay curled up in a hammock he had fashioned from sheets and ropes, mimicking the nests his kind slept in back on their forested world. His four arms were crossed, the palms open, the mouths snoring softly. White hair flowed from his head, and his skin had begun to sag, wrinkles forming around his eyes.

"He looks weak," Marco confessed. "He no longer leaps about like he used to. Remember how he used to jump all over the ship, swinging from his tail? Now he walks. Slowly."

"Maybe we're not feeding him the right food," Lailani said. "We have frozen meals of lasagna, spaghetti and meatballs, chicken curry, salmon and rice, and thankfully tacos. But what if he needs to eat grubs and all those fruits back from his home world?" She winced. "Look at him, Marco. His skin is gray and loose."

The young alien opened his eyes, stretched, and rose from his bed. His joints creaked. Like all Nandaki, he was used to days and nights that lasted only several moments. Throughout the journey, he retired to his bed every five minutes, only to awake refreshed and ready to spend another five minutes talking, reading, and playing Goblin Bowling.

"Good morning, master and mistress!" the young alien said, speaking through one hand and waving the other three.

Marco and Lailani glanced at each other, then back at him.

"Keewaji," Marco said, "how are you?"

"I am well, master," the alien said. "We are close now to the Tree of Life, the mythical bridges between the stars! I yearn for the day I travel the paths of the gods."

Lailani placed her hand on the Nandaki's shoulder. "Little one, how are you feeling? Physically? Are you getting enough rest here? The food you need? Is there anything we can do for you?"

He blinked his large eyes at her. Their lavender glow had faded to a dull indigo these past few days, and the eyes had sunken among wrinkles. "You are most kind, mistress. I am blessed every day that I get to spend among the mighty humans and their cargo." He lowered his head. "Though I do miss home."

Marco decided to be a little less diplomatic. "Keewaji, lately you seem slower on your feet. You don't leap around as much. Are you ill? You look a little ashen, and . . . we want to be sure you're fine."

Keewaji bristled. "Master! I am at the pinnacle of health for a Nandaki my age! Many Nandakis in their middle age spend all day in their hammock, but I still run about, learn, and explore. Though I do miss climbing trees . . ."

Marco tilted his head. He blew out his breath slowly.

Of course.

"You were just a child when we met you a few weeks ago," Marco said softly.

Keewaji nodded. "You are beings of great lifespans, master! Humans live for many generations. I am but a humble Nandaki, a mere mortal. I age faster than you, master. Many generations of Nandaki come and go within a single human life. How ephemeral we must seem to you! To wise and powerful beings like you, it might seem so recent that you were on Nandaka. To me it was half a lifetime ago."

Lailani gasped. "You should have said something! We could have left you in Nandaka! We didn't know . . ." Her eyes dampened. "We took half your life from you."

"Mistress!" He wiped away her tears. "Do not cry for little Keewaji! For I am blessed. I could never imagine a greater honor than to spend so many years with beings as wise, beautiful, and strong as humans." He laughed. "Look at me, talking half the day away! I will go eat now before bed. I look forward to another day tomorrow in the company of heroes!"

Within a moment, he was sleeping again, another day gone.

As the journey toward the wormhole continued, Marco's concern for Keewaji grew. Marco watched the little alien age before his eyes. Within a few more human days--a long time for a Nandaki--a white beard grew from Keewaji's cheeks, soon hanging halfway down his chest. The alien developed a paunch and stoop. His wrinkles deepened, his claws turned brittle, and his voice became raspy.

They were two months into their journey, nearly at the wormhole, when Keewaji fell for the first time. He had attempted to swing from a beam by his tail, fell, and bruised his hip. After that, he walked with a cane. Their friend, young and eager so recently, now hobbled around the ship, cane tapping, beard flowing to his knees, his face a nest of wrinkles.

And yet, whenever Marco felt pity, Keewaji would smile and wink. A sparkle still filled the old alien's eyes.

"We are near now!" Keewaji said when they were only a day--an Earth day--away from the coordinates they sought. "After so long, we will reach the Tree of Light!" His eyes watered. "I have waited for so long. I am so blessed."

As they flew onward, concern grew in Marco that they would find nothing. That Keewaji had waited so long, growing old here, only to find empty space. That they would never be able to return the alien to his homeworld, that he would die of old age on this ship. If they found no wormhole here, they would *all* die on the *Marilyn*, Marco supposed. They would never reach the Ghost Fleet, never save Addy, never save Earth.

As the *Marilyn* came within a million kilometers of the coordinates, Marco found himself on the bridge, clutching his chair's armrests, chewing his lip, staring through the viewport.

"Anything?" he asked.

Lailani sat beside him, checking instruments and running scans. "Patience, Poet! Let me work."

Kemi sat the helm, gently guiding the ship forward. "Beginning our deceleration." She chewed her lip. "Ready to guide the ship into whatever portal I see."

Ben-Ari stood at the front of the bridge, hands held behind her back, staring out the largest viewport into the darkness. She wore her uniform and her beret, and her hair was pulled into a no-nonsense ponytail. She said nothing, and the starlight flowed around her.

Marco licked his lips, staring out there. Seeking something. Anything.

Come on, he thought. *Come on, Wormy . . .*

Lailani stiffened. She hit buttons in a fury.

"Do you see something?" Marco said.

Lailani scrunched up her lips, typing, adjusting knobs. "An anomaly." She stuck out her tongue in concentration. "Kemi, can you adjust our left yaw by three degrees? I see . . ." She gasped. "Something is out there. Let me send out a blast of photons. Kemi, that adjustment?"

Kemi nodded. "Here we go."

The ship turned slightly. Lailani flipped some switches, then leaped from her seat.

"Something is ahead! Definitely!"

Keewaji leaned against a viewport, eyes wide. "We are nearing the Tree of Light! Like in the legends."

"We might just be able to get a visual soon," Lailani said. "There's enough light and space dust that . . ." She exhaled slowly. "Well, will you look at that?"

Marco saw it.

He lost his breath.

"There are more things in heaven and earth, Horatio, than are dreamt of in your philosophy," he whispered, eyes dampening.

Lailani nodded. "I have no idea what you just said, Poet, but . . . yep, that's a wormhole all right."

A luminous ring shone ahead, shimmering, bending the starlight around it. Within it, a tunnel of light flowed into the distance, visible only when viewed through the ring.

"A branch on the great Tree of Light." Keewaji fell to his knees, weeping, shaking. "The stories are true." He placed his hand against the viewport. "I always believed."

Lailani hopped toward the elderly alien, embraced him, and kissed his head. "You were right, Keewaji. I always knew you were right. You led us to hope."

Finally, for the first time, Ben-Ari turned toward them and spoke. "Send the probe in first. De la Rosa, that's your job."

Lailani nodded and returned to her seat. Over the past couple months, they had constructed probes from old sensors and pipes, then loaded them into the missile bays. Lailani hit a few buttons, and a probe flew out from the ship, heading toward the wormhole.

They all watched with bated breath.

The probe flew closer, closer, entered the wormhole . . . then vanished down the tunnel.

"All readings are gone!" Lailani said. "I'm not picking up anything." She looked up at her captain. "If the probe is still out there, it's . . . Wait a minute." She frowned. "Bloody hell. A signal is coming at me--through the wormhole! It's . . . it's impossible, ma'am. These coordinates . . ."

"Report them, Sergeant," the captain said.

Lailani blew out her breath and laughed. "According to this, the probe is a hundred light-years away. Normally, it would take this signal a century to reach us. The probe must be speaking to us through the wormhole." She shook her head in wonder. "As I said. Yep, it's a wormhole."

Kemi raised her eyes from her controls. "Captain?"

Ben-Ari raised her chin and took a deep breath. "Very well. Fly us in, Lieutenant."

"We began as wanderers, and we are wanderers still," Marco whispered in awe, quoting Sagan, as they flew toward the ring.

"Oh, and can somebody shut up the poet?" Lailani said.

Marco wanted to give her a dirty look, but he couldn't tear his eyes away from the wonder ahead. Kemi guided the ship closer. The portal's true size became apparent as they drew closer. They were like a bumblebee approaching a hula hoop. Humans had only recently developed wormholes, but they were only a few atoms wide, big enough to send information but not ships, and even those took enormous amounts of energy. Whatever civilization had built this wormhole--large enough for fleets to fly through--would make humans seem as simple as chimps.

"Here we go," Kemi said. "Hold onto your butts!"

She pushed down on the throttle.

They flew into the wormhole.

Beams flowed through the viewports, casting dapples of gold and silver across the crew. Luminous beads shimmered. They zoomed forward, flowing through a tunnel of purest light. It was so beautiful Marco could not breathe. So beautiful that all his pain seemed to fade away, all his memories, his nightmares, his anxiety, all peeling away under the light of this wonder. He gazed upon beauty, upon purity.

With a thud and clatter, they burst out into cold dark space.

They floated above a sea of distant stars.

Marco blinked and leaned back in his seat.

Lailani turned toward Marco. "Any more inspirational quotes?"

He exhaled slowly. "Whoa," he said, suddenly feeling a lot like Stooge.

Lailani returned to her instruments. "Amazing." She whistled softly. "I can barely believe it. According to my sensors, we're a hundred light-years from where we started."

Kemi's eyes widened. "Even the fastest ship in the galaxy, flying with the best azoth warp engines, would need days--hell, weeks--to cross such a distance."

"And we crossed it within moments," Lailani said. "And guess what? I'm picking up three more wormhole portals ahead. They're only half a million kilometers away. A quick flight, even with conventional engines. I'm passing you their coordinates, Kemi."

"Which wormhole do I take?" Kemi said.

They all looked at one another, silent, lost for ideas.

"Keewaji will know," Marco said softly.

The elderly Nandaki hobbled forth, leaning on his cane. Tears were flowing down his wrinkly cheeks. He placed a tablet on the floor, hit a button, and a holographic image bloomed upward, the height of a man, showing a field of stars.

"I have seen the Tree of Light so many times in my childhood," Keewaji whispered, voice raspy. "For many days, I worshiped at the Boulder of the Sky Gods, tracing the map they had engraved into the stone." His voice shook. "I have traveled in their path, and I can still see the paths ahead."

Keewaji placed a finger on the holographic map, touching one star, then traced his finger toward another star, drawing a luminous line. He worked silently, line by line, drawing many paths flowing between the stars. Slowly, he formed a luminous tree that grew from the tablet below, branching out, shining with light.

Knees creaking, he knelt before the holographic drawing.

"The Tree of Light," Keewaji whispered. "The paths of the heavens. Here is their glory. And here are we." He pointed at one intersection where four branches met, and a point of light shone. "And here are the paths we must take."

Kemi gazed in wonder, the light in her eyes, and nodded. "Here we go."

She led them toward another wormhole.

They flowed through another tunnel of light. Within seconds, they emerged at another location in the galaxy, hundreds of light-years away.

Keewaji touched the three-dimensional map again, updating their location on the tree.

They flew for days, hopping from wormhole to wormhole. They took shifts at the helm. Even Marco, who had never trained as a pilot, took one shift, and guiding the *Marilyn* through a wormhole, traveling a hundred light-years within seconds, was among the most wonderful moments of his life.

And they were not alone.

"Look!" Kemi leaped from her seat as they were flying through a particularly long wormhole. She pointed out a viewport. "Look, everyone!"

They all raced toward portholes, and Marco's heart hammered, sure that the marauders had found them.

Instead he saw something he could not explain.

It looked like a massive, shimmering plankton, gliding forth, a ring of luminous beads spinning around a central stalk crowned with ribbons.

"What is it?" Lailani whispered. "It's huge. It's ten times the size of our ship."

"It's a starship," Marco whispered.

"Bullshit." Lailani shook her head. "It's not made of metal."

"It's beautiful." Marco placed his hand against the porthole as it glided by. "It's so beautiful."

As the two ships crossed paths in the wormhole, Marco thought he could see figures--tall and dark and slender--that stood within the beads of light like fireflies in amber.

Then they flowed apart, and the *Marilyn* emerged into space, and they saw the alien ship no more.

On other days, they saw other ships. One massive ship, nearly the width of the entire wormhole, was made of a flowing sail held between four points, a great glider of the cosmos. Another ship was a flying terrarium, and an alien forest grew within, home to colorful birds. One ship looked like a dragonfly, its four wings coated with solar panels. Other ships were giant bubbles full of water, and swirling aliens with no physical forms, merely swirls of liquid, lived within. One ship looked like a giant conch, spiked and shimmering. It reminded Marco of the conch the ghostly, masked girl had given him on Haven, which he still kept among his possessions.

"I wish we could talk to them," Ben-Ari said wistfully, sitting at the bar as they traveled toward the next wormhole. "These are unknown species. Humanity has never ventured this far. Our galaxy, once thought to be mostly just emptiness, is teeming with life." She sighed. "My father would have loved to be here."

"I wish Addy were here too," Marco said. "She'd have loved this." He wiped a tear from his eye. "When we save her, I'm bringing her back here. Our little vacation among the stars."

Ben-Ari smiled--a smile of such sadness and warmth that Marco nearly cried. She placed her hand on his.

"I will do everything I can to bring her back, Marco. I will not rest until we find Addy. I promise you."

He nodded. He found himself unable to speak. They entered another wormhole, shooting forward through streams of light.

Three months after fleeing the devastation on Haven, the ESS Marilyn emerged from the last wormhole.

They reached the end of the Tree of Light.

They floated through space, three thousand light-years from Earth. They had crossed just a small fraction of the Milky Way galaxy, barely even leaving their galactic neighborhood. But it was the farthest any human had ever traveled.

The crew gathered on the bridge, stared forward, and tears filled their eyes.

"It's beautiful," Marco whispered. "Look at it. And I think it's looking at us too!"

It rose before them, as large as a full moon as seen from Earth. The Cat's Eye Nebula. A great eye in the sky, blue and silver, shimmering with light.

"This is the landmark," Lailani said, though her voice sounded strangely flat. "According to what we studied in the Oort Cloud, the Ghost Fleet should be behind it."

Excitement grew in Marco. "So let's go! We're almost there! We'll find the fleet. We'll find help for Earth. Come on! Kemi, what are you waiting for?"

They were all staring at him, silent. Kemi bit her lip.

"What?" Marco said.

Kemi looked back at the Cat's Eye and sighed. "Marco, it's still a light-year away."

"That's . . ." Marco winced. "That's still very far without a working azoth engine, isn't it?"

"It would take centuries," Kemi said.

"But . . . the wormholes!" Marco pointed at the glowing tree Keewaji had drawn. "The Tree of Light! Can't we--"

"We've reached the end of the line, buddy boy," Lailani said. "This is the last stop. It took us three thousand light-years within days. An azoth engine would have required months to cross the same distance. The Tree of Light took us almost the entire way there." She leaned back in her seat. "And we're stuck on the last light-year. Without an azoth engine, we ain't going nowhere."

"So what do we do?" Kemi said.

Lailani raised her eyebrows. "Play poker and drink milkshakes until we die?"

"No," Marco said. He rose from his seat, stared at the nebula ahead, and nodded. "We hitchhike."

CHAPTER TWENTY-FIVE

The convoy rolled out: an armored truck, five motorcycles, and three vans. Fifty rebels, armed with rifles, handguns, and grenades. They left the Ark behind, rattling into the snowy wilderness.

We'll find the others, Addy thought. *We'll find White Lion and his rebels. We'll build an army.*

She rode at the lead on her motorcycle, her rifle slung across her back, her handgun on her thigh. The cold wind whipped her face, flapped her hockey jersey, and ruffled her short blond hair--whatever had grown back after the marauders had shaved it off. Steve rode at her side on another motorcycle, wearing an old leather jacket and bandanna. Jethro drove the armored truck. The gruff old graybeard wore a homemade peg leg engraved with dragons, and he still wore his tactical vest and camouflage pants, one of the pant legs cut off.

We don't look like much of an army, Addy thought. *But the HDF shattered. We, the rebels, the misfits--we're still fighting.*

The sun was high and bright but the day was cold. The forest swayed alongside the road, branches coated with ice. Cars lay dead on the highway and along the roadsides, and they navigated around them. Several times, they had to stop and shove cars off the road before they could keep going. Fifty kilometers north of the Ark, they reached a massive cobweb that rose ahead, blocking the road, and ten marauders leaped down and scuttled toward them.

"Fire!" Addy shouted, sending forth a hailstorm of bullets.

The other rebels needed no encouragement. Bullets and grenades flew. Three marauders made it past the inferno. One lashed out a web, caught a man, and yanked him off his motorcycle; he died between the beast's jaws. Another marauder vaulted toward the armored truck and cracked its windshield. Jethro knocked it off with bullets, then crushed the alien under the tires.

One marauder came racing across the road toward Addy, and all her bullets could not stop him. She roared forward on her motorcycle, skirted around the alien, then spun back toward it. They charged back at each other like ancient jousters. As the marauder leaped, Addy raised her rifle, piercing an eye with her bayonet. The creature knocked her off her bike as it died. She tore her hockey jersey, but her body armor absorbed most of the impact, and she emerged without broken bones. A few bullets into the remaining eyes finished the job.

They burned the cobweb. They buried three dead rebels. They rode on.

Three dead, Addy thought as she raced down the highway on her motorcycle. *Three lives. Three entire worlds. You better be worth it, White Lion.*

Still that call on the radio bugged her. The voice of White Lion, familiar and troubling, taunting her in her dreams. The man had claimed to have over a hundred fighters holed up in a military base, that they had more weapons than hands to wield them. They had agreed to join forces, but as Addy rode onward, her anxiety rose.

Three dead. Maybe more along the way. And I can't shake that bad feeling.

They rolled along the hills, and they saw more webs on the trees. Five more marauders leaped toward them. It took a dozen grenades to knock them back. The encounters grew more frequent the closer they got to their destination, the military base where White Lion and his rebels waited. Soon, marauders were attacking along every kilometer of road, and bullets rang across the countryside.

Finally Addy saw it in the distance. A concrete complex, engulfed in barbed wire. Once an HDF base, it now housed White Lion's Rebellion. Addy could see guards patrolling its fence and manning its towers.

Let my Resistance and their Rebellion unite, Addy thought. *I'll find every militia, every surviving HDF unit, every survivalist in the wild, and I will lead the greatest uprising the world has known.*

They were almost at the base when shrieks rose, and a hundred marauders leaped from the trees toward the convoy.

For an instant her heart stopped.

Fuck.

Then Addy shouted.

"Onward!" She raised her rifle, roaring forward on her bike. "Break through them! To the base!"

Bullets flew. Grenades exploded. The marauders leaped everywhere. A stray bullet ricocheted off the asphalt and hit Addy's motorcycle, and she careened off the road, flew from the bike, and fell into the snow. Her helmet banged against an oak root.

She leaped up with her assault rifle firing. A marauder squealed before her. The creatures were everywhere. Addy kept shooting, couldn't kill the marauder before her. The beast reared, exposing its hardened belly, and lashed a claw toward her. Addy parried with her barrel. She fell back. It lurched toward her, jaws snapping. She pulled her leg back an instant before it could bite it off.

"Addy . . ." the creature hissed. "We know your name. My master much desires to eat you . . ."

"Eat this," Addy said, lobbing a grenade into its mouth.

Not her cleverest quip, perhaps, but it did the job. She ran, leaped downhill, and covered her head. The explosion raised fountains of snow, rock, and shattered marauder.

Addy rose, ears ringing, and stumbled back onto the road. A hundred marauders were still there, surrounding the convoy.

Fuck, fuck, fuck, Addy thought. Every instinct in her body screamed to flee, to vanish into the forest.

But Steve was still fighting. Jethro was still fighting. The whole damn world was fighting, and Addy wouldn't run. She had never run from a fight. Not in the army. Not in the tunnels of Haven. And not now.

She raised her rifle. She fired. She shouted.

That is all I am now. Tears flowed down her frozen cheeks as hot casings flew around her. *A warrior. A killer. A machine. That's what they made me. That is how I will die. At least I will die on my homeworld.*

She was almost out of bullets, prepared to go down fighting with her bayonet, when the helicopter roared above.

Wind blasted her. Bullets stormed down from the helicopter, tearing marauders apart. A second, then a third helicopter joined it. Marauders shrieked and died in the hailstorm. Twenty Grizzly-class armored vehicles charged up from the military base ahead, and men stood in their turrets, firing machine guns. More marauders fell. The surviving aliens turned tail, only for the helicopters to chase them and slay them on the hills.

Addy stood panting, bleeding in the snow, her ears ringing. Steve walked up to her, coated in sweat and marauder blood.

"Well, I'd say we found White Lion's Rebellion," he said, grinning. "Fuck yeah!"

But Addy only stared. A chill ran down her spine. Her heart sank.

No. Oh God, no.

For the first time, she saw the symbols painted onto the armored vehicles and helicopters, the flags fluttering from the base ahead.

"Iron crosses," she whispered.

Steve frowned. "What's that mean?"

Addy took a deep breath. "It means we're fucked."

One of the armored vehicles rolled to a halt before her. The door opened, and a beefy man emerged, his head shaved. He carried a riot shield with a white lion emblazoned across it. An iron cross was tattooed onto his forehead, and a swastika was stitched onto his leather overcoat.

"I knew your voice was familiar!" he boomed, a grin splitting his face. He stretched out his hand in a Nazi salute. "Addy Linden! Hail to the heroes!"

She remembered him now. Of course she did. He and his goons had rallied to her cause outside the library two years ago. She could still hear their voices from that memory. *Hail to the heroes! Earth Power! Hail Hunt!*

"The White Lion," she said to him, unable to hide her disgust. "Hunt."

CHAPTER TWENTY-SIX

"Hitchhike?" Lailani gave him a sidelong glare. "Are you mental?"

Marco shrugged. "Why not? We're parked next to the last station of a galactic subway network, aren't we? We've seen other ships traveling the tubes. So we just wait. Somebody will show up--with a working warp drive, ideally--who's traveling to the Cat's Eye Nebula."

"And what, we just stick our thumbs out the porthole?" Lailani said.

"I was thinking more along the lines of a sexy leg in a fishnet stocking," Marco said.

"Well, then you better shave that leg of yours," Lailani said, "because the only thing I'm doing with mine is kicking you."

They waited.

A day passed. Another day.

Nobody else emerged from the wormhole behind them.

Marco spent his time reading, but he found himself unable to focus. He tried to work on *Le Kill*, to delve into the cyberpunk world of neon lights and graffiti, of evil corporations in decaying cities, and of the heroine Tomiko with her magical kabuki mask and her quick katana. But his thoughts kept returning to Earth so far away. As they had dinner one day--packages of meatloaf, peas, and lima beans--he tried not to think about their dwindling food and water, how the frozen burritos and pizzas were already gone, how they'd soon be forced to tighten their belts.

If we can't reach the Ghost Fleet, it won't matter, he thought. *Nothing will.*

On the third day, Kemi sighed. "I'm ready to wear that fishnet stocking if it'll help."

"It won't," Marco said, "though I'd love to see it anyway."

"Get us home alive," Kemi said, "and I'll dress up as Slave Leia for you."

"I'll get out and push," Marco said.

It was another day before a ship finally emerged from the wormhole. At least, they thought it was a ship. It was formed from a dozen white disks, each engraved with a red rune, that spun around one another, casting beams of light back and forth. Lailani tried signaling the alien vessel, but it vanished into warped space without a word. The next day, yet another ship emerged, a gleaming rocket lined with portholes, its wings denoting atmospheric capabilities. It seemed promising until it flew nearby, and they realized it was the size of a cigar. A third ship emitted so much radiation that they had to blast away as fast as they could; it was like flying near a miniature star.

"What are the odds we'll find a flying Taco Shack?" Lailani said.

"Not good," said Marco.

"Hey, this is a flying ice cream parlor, so it's possible!"

After a week of floating here, eating meatloaf after meatloaf--the only meals still left--they began debating going back into the wormholes.

"All right, how's this?" Marco said on the eighth day of hovering uselessly. "We don't have much fuel or food left. Soon we'll be down to eating the condiments, then the cushions. So we backtrack. We return into the Tree of Light. When I first arrived on Haven, I didn't know the city. So I took the subway and stepped out at each stop, rose to the surface, and looked around. We do the same thing here. We hop between the wormholes until we find a friendly planet--somewhere to land, gather food, maybe find a civilization that can lend us a starship with a working warp drive. The odds of finding such a civilization are small, but they might be better than waiting here, failing to hitchhike, until we starve."

Lailani shook her head. "It won't work. The wormholes never exit too close to a star. They'll hop five hundred light-years at a time, but then stop a light-year away from any world. Probably they can't work with a star's gravitation field nearby. Anywhere we emerge, we'll face the same problem--that last light-year to cross, impossible without an azoth engine. It's like taking a subway in a wheelchair, and every station has a staircase and no ramp."

Frustrated, Marco turned toward Keewaji. The little alien, over the past week, had aged beyond recognition. He could now barely walk, even with his cane, and his limbs were twisted. His beard flowed to the floor.

The poor guy will die of old age before we reach our destination, Marco thought.

"Keewaji, any old legends in your land?" he said. "Any ideas?"

The Nandaki shook his hoary head. He spoke in a hoarse whisper. "I am sorry, master. I have failed you. I did not think that I would lead you to this dead end." He wept. "I am so sorry."

They all looked at one another.

"Are we going to die here?" Kemi whispered.

They were all silent. They all knew the answer. They dared not speak it.

That night, Marco lay on his cot in silent despair. The others slept around him in their bunks, but Marco could find no rest.

Yes, we're going to die here, he thought. *We're going to starve to death, so close to the end of our journey.*

Claws seemed to clutch at his chest. The old pain returned, the pain that had driven him to doctors again and again on Haven. The pain that hadn't left him since Corpus seven years ago. The pain that even now brought cold sweat to his skin and spun his head.

And as bad as starving to death was, he knew that Addy was suffering far worse. He thought back to their times together.

To their first meeting at the planetarium. To taking her into his library after her parents had died. To their good times at boot camp, to their hard times on Haven, to how they would argue and fight but always remain best friends. He knew that they would forever love each other, forever be there for each other.

But how can I be there for you now, Addy? How can I help you when I'm stuck halfway across the galaxy?

He thought back to their two years in Haven. How he had descended into a pit of addictions and trauma. How he had hurt Addy, had almost driven her away. How, in his spiral of self-destruction, he had nearly lost his best friend--had nearly lost his own life.

"I'm sorry, Addy," he whispered. "I'm sorry for those years. For how I treated you. And I'm sorry, Anisha. I'm sorry for what I did to you. I'm sorry, Terri. I'm sorry, Liz. I'm sorry, Ria." The women in Haven, women he had loved, some for a night, some eternally. Anisha. Terri. Liz. Ria. He didn't know how many others. "I'm sorry, all those I hurt because I was so hurt."

And here on this ship, deep in the darkness, Marco felt lost again. Lost like he had been on Haven. Trapped like he had felt trapped in his old apartment, the storm all around him. Again, as he had on the rooftop, he faced death. And this time not his death alone but the death of his friends too, of his species, and the pain seemed too great to bear.

I was lost then in darkness, he thought. *I stood above a storm, the shadows all around me, my death looming below. And she came to me.*

His mind returned to that night. To the figure emerging from the mist on the rooftop, clad in a tattered, ashy dress, her black hair flowing in the wind, blown back from her kabuki mask. To the clawed hand, a hand with three large fingers, that held out the shimmering conch.

A gift from the cosmic ocean, she had said. *May it shine in your deepest darkness.*

She had saved him that night, whoever she had been. She had given him a beautiful, glowing gift, and he had stepped back from the abyss. Now Marco faced an abyss again. Now again he faced death, and the darkness again wrapped all around him, endless, enveloping.

He did not like to think of that time on the rooftop, that time he had almost jumped, the way he did not like thinking about Corpus and Abaddon and the inferno at Fort Djemila. He had placed that conch aside, had not looked at it since, for it was a memento of the darkest hour of his life. Yet now, in this new shadow, Marco rose from his bunk, stepped toward his closet, and rummaged through his belongings.

He found it there, wrapped in an old shirt.

He left the bunk where his companions slept, entered the lounge, and stood by a porthole. The stars hung outside, frozen in place. Their azoth engine--dead. Their fuel and batteries--nearly gone. Their food--down to scraps. Trapped. Floating here in a coffin, so close to the end. And in his mind, it seemed to Marco that he stood again on that rooftop, that outside he didn't view space but the storms that forever whipped Haven.

A gift from the cosmic ocean. May it shine in your deepest darkness.

He unwrapped the bundle of cloth, and he pulled out the conch. It was the size of his fist, silvery and gleaming, lavender where it caught the light. Smooth and cool to the touch.

"But how can this help?" Marco said, speaking to the emptiness outside. "It's beautiful. But now I, my friends, and my species all face death. Is this conch just a trifle? A beautiful object to inspire me, to comfort me?"

He turned it over and over in his hands, feeling its smoothness, admiring its grace. Yes, it soothed him. It was a piece of beauty, a memory of life. It would not save him. But perhaps he would not die surrounded by ugliness, not like he had almost died on Haven, had almost died on Corpus.

I will die in beauty, he thought. *With music and light and friends. With a gift from the cosmic ocean.*

He placed the conch against his ear, and he heard a deep, soothing echo, white noise, a pulse. The conch, though empty, seemed almost alive, perhaps harboring the ghost of life that had once filled it, still singing its song. A thing of beauty, yes, but of music too. Marco placed the conch against his lips, and he blew softly into it. A pale, quivering note emerged, like the song of an ocarina.

He returned to the crew quarters.

He stood for a moment in the shadows, looking at his sleeping friends. In such a small ship, they all shared a room. Captain Ben-Ari lay on her side, her hair in a ponytail, the woman who had taken in a scared librarian, who had turned Marco into a soldier, into a man, who had taught him honor, dedication, duty, leading by example. The woman he admired more than anyone in the cosmos, a true leader he had followed across the galaxy.

Beside her, Kemi lay on her own bunk, her curly black hair spreading around her, peaceful and beautiful in slumber. Yet then her mouth twisted, and a frown touched her brow, and Marco knew she was remembering her old pain. She was his first love, the girl he had seen become a woman, an officer, a pilot, intelligent and brave and forever kind.

Marco turned to look at Lailani next, and his heart twisted in sudden pain. Looking at her sleep, it was so easy to remember. Holding her in his arms, making love to her at Fort Djemila, wanting to marry her . . . then losing her, only to have her return to him, to still see the love in her eyes when she looked at him. Lailani--broken and strong, ephemeral and constant, angel and demon, the breaker and healer of his heart.

I love you all, Marco thought. *You are the dearest people to me. I can't stand the thought of losing you all here. And I can think of no better people to die with. I love you all so much.*

Light glowed, and dapples of silver and lavender danced against his sleeping companions. A rain of luminescence fell upon them, and Marco wondered if this was the light of death, shining from that great wormhole to life beyond.

Wait a minute.

He frowned. He blinked. That light was real. It was shining through the portholes.

He stepped between the bunks, gazed out a porthole, and lost his breath.

"Fucking hell," he whispered. Not his most eloquent quote perhaps, but right now, amazement washed over him. His eyes watered. "It's a whale."

It was a dream. It had to be a dream. Perhaps a hallucination. A massive whale, large enough to swallow the *Marilyn* whole, glided outside through space. Its body was fluid, deep indigo tinged with purple, and its eyes shone gold. A finned tail flowed behind the alien, barbels flowed around its mouth like whiskers on a catfish, and pulsing organs glowed on its temples like eardrums the size of bathtubs. The whale swam toward the starship, curious, gazing at it. Gazing at Marco.

"Hey, turn off the lights!" Lailani said, tossing a pillow at Marco. "Trying to sleep here."

Marco blinked. He ran toward Lailani and grabbed her hands. "Come see this! Can you see it?" He hopped toward Kemi. "Kemi, Kemi, wake up! Come see!"

She groaned, blinking. "What?"

"Captain, Captain!" He raced toward Ben-Ari. "Do you see it too? Keewaji, you too, wake up! Do you see it?"

They all rose from their beds and approached the portholes.

Their jaws all unhinged.

"What is it?" Kemi whispered, the light in her eyes. "A whale? A whale in space?"

Lailani nodded, smiling tremulously, tears on her cheeks. "It's a starwhale."

Kemi laughed, rubbed her eyes, and stared outside again, then at Lailani. "Let me guess. You studied them in the Oort Cloud.

Tears still flowed down Lailani's cheeks, and her smile widened. Outside, the whale was circling the ship, gazing at them curiously, its tendrils and tail flowing like streamers. Its eyes glowed, filling the ship with light.

"Not this time," Lailani said. "My people tell stories of them. In the Philippines we would look up at the sky as children, and we would speak of the starwhales. On bad nights, after a scum attack or a flood, we would imagine that the starwhales would visit Earth someday, would carry us poor, hungry children to their world. It's said that they can travel at great speed between the stars." She pointed. "See those glowing things on its cheeks? Maybe those organs let them bend spacetime like azoth engines."

The starwhale passed by the portholes, gazing inside. Marco thought he saw wisdom in that eye.

"It's beautiful," Ben-Ari said, and a sad smile touched her lips. "I too have heard tales of starwhales. My people told similar stories. I always thought they were legends. Like the Golem of Prague, just legends we told, imagining that a great beast out there could save us."

"We told the same stories in our land," Keewaji said, gazing with damp eyes outside the porthole. "The starwhales fly in many of our old tales. Some of our ancient heroes were able to summon them using mystical conches, then ride them to distant worlds."

Marco lost his breath. His fingers trembling, he raised his conch, his gift from the mysterious girl on a distant world.

"Conches like this?" he whispered.

Keewaji gasped. He touched the conch, then pulled back his fingers. He looked up at Marco with awe. "Where did you find this?"

Marco smiled softly. "A friend gave it to me. Long ago."

"You are truly a mighty hero!" Keewaji knelt before him. "Like the blessed whale-riders of old!"

The whale flew even closer, bringing its snout up to the ship, sniffing. The whale circled around, and its eye gazed through another porthole--right at the crew, it seemed. Marco placed his palm against the porthole. The whale stretched out one of its barbels. The ship rocked as the tendril hit the opposite side of the porthole.

"We're holding hands." Marco laughed and his eyes watered. "I wish Addy could see this."

A sound pulsed through the ship. A deep voice like a whale's song.

"It's speaking to us!" Kemi whispered.

"Then let us speak back." Marco blew into the conch again. The soft song filled the ship, and the whale's eyes shone. It sang in return, a whale song, answering the conch. The music of the cosmos. A song of stars.

"What did you just tell him?" Lailani said, looking at the conch.

"I'm not sure," Marco said. "I think I just said hello." He looked at the others. "Your old tales speak of heroes riding the starwhale. Maybe today we will be heroes." He laughed. "Kemi, you're a good pilot. Ever tried landing on a whale?"

Kemi, who was gazing with wonder through the porthole, turned toward him. She frowned. "You can't be serious. You can't truly suggest we ride a whale through space."

Marco shrugged. "It worked in the old stories, right? Even I heard the tales. I had a book as a kid. *Selene and the Starwhale*. A girl rode one through the galaxy."

"Children's stories!" Kemi said. "Old legends!"

Marco pointed out the porthole. "I see a real one just out there."

Kemi looked out the porthole again. The whale reached out to her with a whisker. Kemi looked back at the crew. She laughed. Her eyes watered, and she laughed and laughed.

"This is ridiculous," she said. "And this is beautiful. And this is wonderful." She was half sobbing, half laughing now. "All right. It's time to be heroes." Kemi raced out of the bunk, heading toward the bridge. "Marco, keep playing that conch! Let's ride the whale!"

Marco looked out the porthole again. He placed his hand against it, and the whisker reached out to make contact.

"Can you take us there, friend?" Marco said. He raised a tablet, displaying an image of the coordinates beyond the Cat's Eye Nebula. "Can you take us beyond the great eye?"

Beads of light glowed on the whisker. A rumble passed through the ship, moving from the whale into the hull. The whale gazed into his eyes.

He understands, Marco thought. *He will help.*

As Kemi guided the ship above the whale's back, Lailani pointed out the porthole, eyes wide.

"Look!" she whispered. "There's more!"

Keewaji pressed his face against a porthole, his voice filled with awe. "Like in the old stories. The great gods of the sky. The dancers of light."

They all stared outside, and they laughed with joy. Through space they glided, a whole pod of them, mighty starwhales. The largest were the size of starfighter carriers. The juveniles were no larger than the *Marilyn*, quick and playful. Gently, Kemi lowered the ship onto the whale's back. The pod moved closer together, and the round organs on their temples expanded, pulsed with light, and thrummed. Around the pod, the light of stars stretched out.

"They're forming a bubble of spacetime." Marco rubbed his eyes. "They evolved organs for it. Amazing."

Lailani shrugged, smiling. "Hey, it works for the ravagers. Why not the starwhales?"

The whales reached out their flowing barbels, interweaving them, and streams of light ran across the elongated organs. The whales bugled, the sound passing through the tendrils, into one another, into the ship. A whale's song. A song of joy, of exploration, of family. The song of the cosmic ocean. They swam onward toward the distant, glowing eye.

CHAPTER TWENTY-SEVEN

Addy stood in the compound, staring at the skinheads.

"I'd prefer fighting alongside the marauders," she said.

The skinheads snickered and muttered. They were an ugly bunch, ranging from muscular brutes to scrawny men with missing teeth. All had shaved their heads. All wore iron cross armbands with the slogan *Earth Power* written underneath. Over a hundred of them lived here in this abandoned military base.

"Now now, Linden." Hunt--the White Lion--stood before his men. He wore steel-tipped boots, a leather trench coat, and a bandoleer of bullets. "These are good folk here. Most are HDF soldiers. Others are just farmers and survivalists who joined us. But they all fight for me now. For the Rebellion."

Addy scoffed. "For the Rebellion or for Earth Power? I remember your rallies, Hunt. Don't think I forgot. Are you truly organizing an uprising against the marauders or just building up your little Nazi brigade?"

"We were always fighting aliens, Linden," Hunt said. "Even back before this war. We knew it was coming. We tried to warn the world. They called us xenophobes. White supremacists. Neo-Nazis. All for speaking about the danger in space. They didn't listen. Now the aliens are here. Now all those voices are silenced. Where is Never War, that group of hippies who attacked you? Dead. But Earth Power is still here, strong, brave, eager for the fight. We are the Rebellion."

Behind him, his men voiced their agreement. Hands rose in Nazi salutes.

"Earth Power!" they chanted. "Hail to the heroes!"

Addy looked over her shoulder at her men. At Steve. At Jethro. At the forty others she had brought here. The Resistance.

"They're a bunch of lunatics," Addy said to her people. "We wasted our time coming here. We, the Resistance, will continue the fight on our own. It's time to go home to the Ark."

But her people glanced at one another, then back at her, hesitant.

Jethro limped toward her on his prosthetic leg. "Addy, beggars can't be choosers."

She leaned toward the bearded man and whispered harshly, "They can when it's fucking Nazis!"

Steve joined the huddle. "Hey, Nazis are those fuckers from the history books, right? The real nasty bad guys?"

"Yeah, Steve." Addy rolled her eyes. "The real nasty ones."

The hockey player glanced toward the skinheads, then looked back at Addy and Jethro. "I don't like this. If Addy says they stink, these guys stink. They got a bad look to them. We'll fight without them."

Jethro inhaled deeply and narrowed his eyes. "Look, I don't like these assholes either. But I hate the marauders more. These guys have helicopters. Armored vehicles. They say they even got a bomber, an actual plane. How long can we last on our own? We need more people."

"We'll get more people," Addy said. "But these are not people. These are monsters, just as bad as the marauders." Her fury rose in her. "Fuck this shit. My friend Ben-Ari is Jewish. My friend Kemi is black. My friend Lailani is Asian. I won't tolerate no goddamn fucking white supremacists."

Boots thudded and belt buckles clanked. Addy turned to see Hunt approaching the group.

"Sergeant Linden," the skinhead said, "hear me out. Those were the old ways. Yes, I admit--there was a time when we cared for racial purity, for the pride of the Aryan race. There was a time when we called for the Jew, the black, the inferior races to be exterminated along with the scum. But today, all humans have a common enemy. Today we fight alongside all races against the only threat that matters: the marauders. In other times, perhaps we would be enemies. Today we must fight together." He raised his chin. "For humanity."

Addy glared at Hunt. "You don't represent humanity. You represent our lowest, most vile instincts. You represent what we outgrew. If you are what humanity is, then let the marauders wipe us out. Then we don't deserve to exist on this planet."

A flicker of anger crossed Hunt's eyes. Behind him, his men grumbled and reached for their weapons. But Hunt raised a hand, holding them back.

"Sleep on it, Linden," Hunt said. "You're tired, you're hungry, you're wounded. Shower, eat, tend to your wounds, sleep.

Tomorrow we'll speak again. And I hope you choose to unite our forces." He gave her another salute, this time a military one. "I will gladly accept you as my commander. This will be your army, and it will be my honor to serve the great Addy Linden, she who defeated the scum. Your army, not mine. So sleep on it, Addy Linden, heroine of Earth."

That night, Addy lay in a bedroom on the Rebellion base. The cot was comfortable enough, and the room was warm, but she found no rest.

"This is fucked," she said to Steve, who lay beside her.

He bit his bottom lip. "I dunno, Ads. He said he's changed. He said he'd serve you."

"I don't want his kind in my army," she said. "He's a fascist, Steve. Even you know what that means. How are we any better than the scum, than the marauders, than any of those space bugs if we fight with guys like Hunt? They're the predators of humanity. We should be nobler than that."

"We are!" Steve said. "I am. You are. Your friends are. Hunt is just a tool. We use him, then toss him out."

Addy fumed, and she punched the mattress. "I hate this. I fucking hate this! If Ben-Ari were here, she'd never agree to it. Marco wouldn't either. I fucking hate that you make me even consider this."

Steve sat up in bed, naked, the sheet pulled over his lap. The moonlight poured through a window, limning his form and shining on his hair. Thin scars crawled across one shoulder and arm, but they could not mar his beauty.

I've always thought him beautiful, Addy thought. *He doesn't even realize how beautiful he is, the big dummy.*

"Have I ever told you about my dad?" he said.

"Just a bit," said Addy. "He owned a bar, right?"

Steve nodded. "Yeah. We all worked there as kids. My mom, me, my brothers--we worked in the kitchen, at the door, at the taps, the cash register. One time, when I was fifteen, I remember how Big Joe and his boys showed up at our bar."

Addy cocked her head. "Big Joe?"

"And his boys," said Steve. "Gangsters from the lower west side. Real slimeballs. Racketeering. Shark loans. Assassins for hire. They pimped prostitutes all over town. They drove nice cars, wore nice clothes, had money to spare. They came into our bar, ordered a feast, lots of drinks, lots of food, racked up a massive bill. Then left without paying."

"Fuckers," Addy said.

"Yeah. I was pissed. My dad was too. But who wants to get in trouble with Big Joe and the boys? They came back a few nights later. Same deal. Drank and ate and left without paying. Well, maybe we could have tolerated that. Better than getting in trouble with the gang. But see, other patrons started ditching us. They got scared. Joe's boys would slap girls on the ass, pick fights with their boyfriends, break glasses . . . They even stabbed somebody once. Pretty soon we were losing loyal customers."

"Fuck," Addy said.

Steve nodded. "So my old man tore open a mattress and pulled out all his savings. Big musty wads of cash. And he hired security guards--tough veteran dudes--to man the door and bar. Next time Joe and his boys showed up, we sent them home."

"And I imagine they didn't like that," Addy said.

"Oh, Joe and the boys left quietly that night," Steve said. "But the next morning, somebody slashed the tires of our car. The morning after that, we found a severed pig's head in our yard. The third day, somebody shot our dog. Drive-by dog shooting."

"Jesus Fucking Christ," Addy said.

Steve nodded. "We knew that next time, Big Joe would be shooting at *us*. And our security guards mysteriously stopped working for us. Probably threatened. We thought we'd have to close down the bar."

"Yikes. So what did you do?"

Steve sighed. "We did something I'm not proud of. But it had to be done. My dad went and talked to Red Chiyo."

"Another gangster?" Addy said.

"A ruthless one. Chiyo and his gang were notorious. Big drug money, lots of meth. They smuggle firearms too. They mostly operated in the Pacific, but their tentacles reached everywhere."

"They seem nice."

"Oh, very nice," Steve said. "Cost a fortune, but they solved the problem for us. I'm still not sure *what* Red Chiyo did. But Big Joe and his boys stayed the hell away from us after that."

Addy sighed. "So let me guess. Big Joe and the boys are the marauders. Red Chiyo is Hunt."

"The enemy of my enemy is my friend," Steve said.

"Hunt will never be my friend."

"Then think of it as fighting fire with fire," Steve said.

"I prefer using water.

"Well, baby, it's a drought."

Addy turned away from him. "Fuck, fuck, fuck. I hate this. I don't want to sell my soul to win."

Steve placed a hand on her shoulder. "You're not selling your soul. Maybe you're just . . . lending it out for a while."

She closed her eyes and gritted her jaw. Could she do this? Could she truly make a deal with the devil? Even if they survived, how would she then live with herself? Steve hugged her from behind, and Addy held his hands, silent, eyes closed. They made love--silent but hard, eager yet so weary. When she climaxed, she shouted into his palm, and she fell asleep in his arms. She never wanted to leave his embrace.

In the morning, she walked through the military base. She wore no uniform, just jeans and a hockey jersey. She carried her rifle across her back, a bandoleer of bullets hung around her waist, and a cigarette dangled from her lips. Her helmet hung askew, scrawled with the words *Hell Patrol*. Her people walked behind her, just as ragged. She looked like a haggard survivor, bruised, scratched, her eyes sunken. But the fire burned inside her. And she would tame it.

Fire with fire, she thought. *And I will be its mistress.*

She met Hunt in the courtyard. He stood in his leather coat and steel-tipped boots, his goons around him. The iron crosses shone on their armbands and the flags above. Addy stood across the courtyard from him. A gust of cold wind scattered snow across the concrete ground.

She spat out her cigarette and stepped on the stub.

"Hunt!" she called.

He stared at her across the distance. "Linden."

She took a step forward. He took a step in turn. They walked, meeting in the middle of the courtyard. Her people stood behind her; his stood behind him. Here, in the center of the snowy yard, they stood alone.

"Here are my terms, Hunt," she said. "You take down your flags. You take off your armbands. You burn them. Any Nazi tattoo you have--whether it's an iron cross, a swastika, or Sig runes--you keep them covered at all times, or you grab a cheese grater and you scrape those fuckers off. You want to fight with me, the heroine who defeated the scum? Then you serve me. You play on my terms. You forget about Earth Power. That group is dead now. You will not fight *with* me. You will join the Resistance, my group, and fight *for* me."

Hunt stiffened. "These symbols are our identity. Our pride."

"Fuck your pride, and fuck your identity, and fuck your symbols, and fuck you. There is only one symbol now--Planet Earth. A blue circle in the darkness. If you need a symbol, sew yourself new flags." Addy narrowed her eyes. "I hate this. And I hate you. But right now, I hate the marauders just a fraction more." She reached out her hand. "Do we have a deal?"

His face reddened. Fury filled his eyes. For a moment Addy thought he would strike her. But then he grabbed her hand and squeezed it--painfully, creaking her joints.

"We have a deal, Addy Linden."

He squeezed her hand, nearly crushing it, for long moments, staring into her eyes with a steely gaze. She refused to show her pain, to look away. Finally he released her hand, then walked back to his people, his leather coat billowing in the snowy wind.

I just shook the devil's hand, Addy thought. She lowered her head. She knew that Ben-Ari, Marco, Lailani, and Kemi--her dearest friends--would all be ashamed of her. She was ashamed of herself.

* * * * *

At noon, the combined forces of the Human Resistance feasted in the mess hall. Steve, who had grown up in a pub's kitchen, worked the stoves and ovens with several men to help him. The military base, once belonging to the HDF, was filled with canned and packaged goods--corn, tuna, ham, flour, sugar, and more. They found bottles of wine, and they drank until their voices and songs rose loudly. Addy drank with them. She drank until her head spun. She drank to drown the pain. And she sang-- loudly, hoarsely, old songs of Earth.

Her head was spinning when they met in the war room, a bunker below the base. Maps hung on the walls and spread across the tables, and monitors displayed data from sensors across the base and the wilderness. Hunt was here, along with two of his lieutenants. Addy had brought Jethro and Steve.

"This is what we know," Addy said, sharing the information she had gained in the Resistance--the location of webs, hives, and marauder spaceports where their ravagers idled. She spoke of the great slaughterhouse outside the ruins of Toronto, of the thousands who perished there, and of the aliens who had overrun the city.

But she did not speak of her friends' quest to find the Ghost Fleet. Some secrets she would not share. Not with Hunt.

The bald, beefy man pointed at maps, revealing his own information--both of marauder hives and other rebel holdouts.

"There are more of us," Hunt said. "Survivors. Rebels. We have no central leadership. Most are just pockets of ten or twenty fighters, mostly military guys, their officers killed, their units destroyed. Many are just farmers with their families, armed with shotguns and knives."

"We'll bring them here," Addy said. "We will unite them. And we will strike back. Here." She pointed at a spot on the map. "The slaughterhouse."

Hunt stared at her over the map, his fists on the table. "Waste of resources. It's not a military target."

"It's where thousands of humans are dying each day!" Addy blurted out. "It's where we can save the most people. The marauders have raised concrete and metal walls around the slaughterhouse, and many of them guard it, but if we can unite the rebels, we'll have enough force. We'll destroy the slaughterhouse. We'll liberate the humans who are still alive inside."

Hunt shook his head. "Our men and weapons are limited. There are more valuable targets to hit. The hive here, from which they launch assaults on the highways, or the ravager yard here, or--"

"Hunt." Addy pounded the table. "Listen to me. I was there. I was a prisoner in the slaughterhouse. I saw the horrors. I saw the marauders strip humans naked, shave off their hair, and torture them. I saw them rape little girls for sport. I saw them rip babies from the arms of their mothers, toss them into the air, and catch them in their jaws, then laugh as the mothers screamed. I saw them cut off the hands of humans who disobeyed. I saw them hang living humans from meat hooks, thousands of them, driving the metal into their flesh. I saw them slit the throats of screaming prisoners, then slice them into pieces while they were still bleeding out. You want to fight for humanity? That slaughterhouse is where humanity is raped, deformed, torn apart. That is our target. That slaughterhouse and any other we find on this weeping planet."

Hunt stared steadily into her eyes. Finally, not breaking eye contact, he lifted a model from the table--a metal bomber jet.

"We'll take Big Boy," he said.

Addy had seen the real jet outside in the yard. An old HDF bomber, the size of a bus, armed with enough bombs to

level a town. It was the greatest weapon the Resistance had,
putting even their three helicopters to shame.

"No." Addy shook her head. "That's insanity. That
bomber would blast holes in the slaughterhouse large enough for
a car to fall into. It would kill the human prisoners along with the
marauders."

Hunt nodded. "Exactly. We bomb the whole damn
installation from the air. Our helicopters will offer backup. We
drop hundreds of bombs. We wipe the place out."

She gasped. "Fuck this shit. Fuck it! I knew I couldn't trust
you. I--"

"Linden!" Hunt boomed. "Those prisoners in there are as
good as dead. You know it. Once you enter that place, you leave
piece by piece, nothing but packaged meat. Killing them would be
a mercy."

"So that's your idea of fighting for humanity?" Addy said.
"Killing humans?"

"Saving humans!" said Hunt. "Saving the next shipment of
humans that would be slaughtered there. We stop the cycle. We
kill the prisoners already in there, yes. By doing so, we stop the
next batch, and the batch after that, and thousands of other
shipments."

"We can destroy the slaughterhouse without butchering
every man, woman, and child inside," Addy said. "We storm the
gates. We have an armored truck, Humvees, motorcycles,
bulldozers. We have three assault helicopters for aerial cover. We
have nearly three hundred warriors, and we'll collect more from

the other bases. We even have a goddamn tank. We tear down the walls. We hit them with everything we've got--aside from those bombs."

Hunt stared at her across the table, eyes simmering. "Many warriors will die."

She nodded. "Yes, they will. But many thousands of civilians will be saved."

He was silent for a long moment, staring at her. "You make many demands, Linden."

For the first time, Steve stepped forward and spoke. "She's your commander, Hunt. Remember that. She's not asking for your opinion. She gives you orders. You obey. You Nazis love hierarchy, don't you? So respect ours."

The young hockey player's cheeks were flushed red, and his eyes blazed, and at that moment, Addy loved Steve more than she ever had.

Hunt stared at them, not bothering to mask the loathing in his eyes. But then he stiffened. He raised his chin. He saluted.

"I will not cower from a fight. All right, Linden. We will storm the gates with the glory of the warriors of old. We will sound the war horns, and the fury of Earth will rise."

Fire with fire, Addy thought, *and the whole world burns down.*

That night, even lying in Steve's arms could not soothe her. He slept, and she curled against him, her loins still tingling from his lovemaking. This was normally a time for comfort, warmth, and deep slumber. But this night, she kept thinking of iron crosses, flames, and falling bombs.

Daniel Arenson

CHAPTER TWENTY-EIGHT

The pod of starwhales swam through the cosmic ocean. They glided through darkness and starlight. They flowed toward the Cat's Eye Nebula and swam between its shimmering curtains of luminous starstuff. Through swirls of light in every color, the pod swam and sang. On the third day of their journey, with the nebula distant behind them, they reached their destination.

On the lead whale's back perched the *Marilyn*--scarred, broken, barely still flying. From the bridge, the crew stared out into the swirling lights of warped space.

"These are the coordinates," Lailani said. "We're here. After months of traveling, we're here. According to everything we studied in the Oort Cloud, the Ghost Fleet is right ahead."

Marco looked out the viewport. "I can't see anything."

"We're still traveling through warped spacetime," said Lailani. "We won't see objects as small as ships. But all my sensors are picking up something massive." Her eyes shone. "The Ghost Fleet is here."

Marco took a deep breath.

We're coming back soon, Addy. We're coming back with help.

Ben-Ari stood at the front of the bridge, hands behind her back, gazing out into space. She nodded and whispered something

Marco couldn't hear, perhaps a soft prayer. Then she nodded and looked over her shoulder back at the crew.

"Lieutenant Abasi, rise off the alien and fly out of its warp bubble."

"Yes, ma'am." Kemi worked at her controls. "Rising off the starwhale."

With a jolt, the ship rose. They ascended between the other starwhales, moving higher in the pod. The giant aliens gazed at the ship, singing their song. Marco brought the conch to his lips and played a last note--a sound of thank you and farewell.

"Reaching the edge of the warp bubble now," Kemi said. "About to pass into regular spacetime. Hold on. This might get bumpy."

They ascended higher, and Marco shuddered as they passed through the border. Bending and straightening spacetime always felt like having his organs sucked out, rearranged, and shoved back into him. He rubbed his temples, struggling to focus his eyes, and saw a streak of light as the starwhales vanished in the distance, moving faster than light.

Farewell, friends, he thought.

"Do you see it anywhere?" Marco asked, turning back to the others. "The Ghost Fleet?"

The rest of the crew stared ahead, silent. Marco frowned, his vision still blurry, and stared outside. His eyes widened.

"What . . ." he whispered.

He saw no great, ancient fleet. Instead he saw the starlight curve ahead, spinning in a whirlpool. Space dust formed a glowing ring. In the center--a massive black sphere, a floating orb of darkness.

"It's a black hole," Lailani said.

Kemi cringed. "And it's starting to tug us." She flipped some switches, and engines rumbled. "I'm pulling back to a safe distance. This sucker is more powerful than God's vacuum cleaner."

Like Addy when she sees hot dogs, Marco thought.

As the ship pulled back, they all stared at the wider view. A pair of binary stars shone nearby. The Cat's Eye nebula was a small splotch behind them. Ahead, looming, the black hole gaped open, a hungry mouth in the cosmos, ringed with luminous debris.

"I don't see any ghost ships," Marco said.

Ben-Ari turned toward Lailani. "Sergeant de la Rosa, run a scan. Send out a few probes to the rim of the black hole. The ships would be too small to see visually from here. They might be floating among that space dust, or they might just be dark. Scan everything."

Lailani nodded. "Yes, ma'am." She hit buttons in a fury, and numbers scrolled across her monitors. She chewed her lip. "There's a fuck-load of interference from that black hole. It's warping every goddamn signal around here. I'm not picking up anything that might be a fleet."

"Send out those probes, de la Rosa," Ben-Ari. "And mind your language on my bridge."

Lailani nodded. "Aye aye, Captain. Sorry, Captain. Sending out a probe."

The probe shot out from the ship. They watched it fly through space, growing dimmer, dimmer. Closer to the black hole, the probe seemed to stretch out, then vanish into the darkness.

Addy would say we're probing a giant space butt, Marco thought. But the crew aboard the ship was silent, just staring.

"Let me send another," Lailani finally said.

Another probe flew toward the black hole, then got sucked in.

Lailani sighed. "I'm picking up all that dust, rocks, radiation . . . nothing that might be a ship. At least, not a functional ship."

Ben-Ari nodded. "All right. If there's a fleet here, it might just be shut down. In sleep mode. It might still be ahead, just emitting no signals."

Lailani wrung her hands. "From the Oort Cloud, we clearly received signals denoting a massive armada. An alien intelligence was broadcasting those signals. But at that distance, the signals were thousands of years old. I'm picking up nothing now."

"Lieutenant Abasi, can you bring us closer?" Ben-Ari said. "Right to the event horizon? Let's orbit the black hole along with that space debris."

"That would be extraordinarily dangerous, ma'am," Kemi said. "A kilometer off, and we might get sucked in. Or the debris might hit us."

"Understood," said Ben-Ari. "I trust your abilities. Bring us closer, as close as you can. I want to get a clear visual of whatever's floating up there."

Kemi cringed, gulped, but nodded. "Aye aye, Captain."

The *Marilyn* flew closer. The black hole grew in the viewports, seeming to stare back at Marco. Unlike a wormhole, this hole in space emitted no light; its gravity was so intense it sucked in photons, sucked in spacetime itself. In fact, it didn't look like a hole at all. Holes, as Marco was used to thinking of them, were circular. This emptiness ahead was spherical, a three-dimensional void.

"If you gaze for long into an abyss, the abyss gazes also into you," he said softly. "Nietzsche."

Lailani shuddered. "Don't be a poet for once. That thing creeps me out."

Keewaji sat on the bridge, staring at the black hole. The alien was so frail he could no longer walk; they had made him a wheelchair. His white hair and beard flowed across his body, and his eyes peered from deep nests of wrinkles. He clutched his wheelchair's armrests.

"The Emptiness," the Nandaki whispered. "Our elders spoke of it. The portal to the underworld. Death in the darkness."

Lailani shuddered. "Great, another poet. Both of you, stop freaking me out."

Keewaji looked at the young woman. "There is no reason to fear death. Death is but a journey to another life. The Emptiness is a gateway to an afterlife. It is a journey I myself will soon take."

Marco approached, knelt, and placed his hand on the Nandaki's shoulder. "You will live for many more days, my friend."

The ship began to rattle. Controls flashed and alarms beeped. Keewaji's wheelchair rolled toward the wall, and books fell off a shelf.

Kemi winced. "We're as close as I can get. The gravity is stronger than any star I've seen." Her mug of coffee bounced, splashing the hot liquid. "Any closer and it'll tear us apart. I'll try to place us into orbit."

"Watch out for those asteroids," Ben-Ari said.

Kemi nodded, pulling on the joystick. "I see 'em. It's time for some fancy flying."

Thousands of rocks were orbiting the black hole, maybe millions. Some were massive, larger even than starwhales. Others seemed as small as grains of sand. Marco kept looking for alien starships. Nothing.

"Still scanning," Lailani said. "Definitely no radio signals. No unusual radiation, just what's coming off those binary stars. I'm running a scan on the shapes of the boulders. It'll take a while. So far, nothing but irregular, jagged rocks, nothing that's tripping the scanners." She bit her lip. "We're in either the wrong place or the wrong time. Damn it! Centuries ago there was something here, something ancient, something that had been floating here for a million years. Did somebody find it before us?"

They hovered for several hours, sending probe after probe, running scan after scan, examining asteroid after asteroid. Nothing. Not a signal.

They slept--an uneasy sleep, tossing and turning, waking every few hours to check the signals. In the morning, they gathered in the galley for a dour breakfast. The meatloaf was gone. They were down to eating crackers and jam, their last morsels.

They had to mush Keewaji's food into a paste, and he coughed and could only handle a few bites. The Nandaki bragged that he had already lived to prodigious age, longer than most of his kind, but Marco couldn't help but pity him, that he had grown from childhood to old age within only three months.

"Ideas," said Ben-Ari, sitting at the kitchen table with them. "Anything. No matter how stupid. Give me your ideas."

"Well," Lailani said, "we could fly into the black hole and hope we find a Taco Shack on the other side." Everybody groaned. "What? The captain said no matter how stupid!"

"Lailani, you obviously had the wrong coordinates," Kemi said. "Maybe if you recheck your notes, you can find the--"

"This is the right place." Lailani glared at the pilot. "I know what I'm doing here, *ma'am*." She tossed out that last word like an insult.

Kemi bristled. "I never demanded that you call me ma'am, *Sergeant*."

Lailani barked a bitter laugh. "And yet you just flaunted your higher rank right now."

"You started it!" said Kemi.

"Very mature." Lailani leaped to her feet. "Where were you, anyway, when we were fighting in the hive of Abaddon, princess?"

"I was battling scum in the sky!" Kemi shouted. "You know this."

"Oh, yes, you pilots always have some excuse. Even Ben-Ari, who's also an officer, fought with us on the ground, but you--"

"De la Rosa, enough!" Ben-Ari said. "Sit down!"

Lailani sat down, grumbling. "Sorry, Captain." She glanced at Kemi. "Sorry, Kemi. I'm antsy. I have cabin fever. And this fucking place . . ." She clutched her hair and groaned. "Ugh! It should be here! I'm sure this is the right place, but . . ." She sighed. "Somebody else must have found them first."

"The marauders," Marco whispered. "They got here first." He stood up. "Lailani! Maybe scan for marauder vessels around, maybe we can--"

"Way ahead of you, Poet," Lailani said. "I scanned as far as I could. If anyone was broadcasting signals here, even marauders, they're long gone. No vestige of them. No radio signals, no radiation, nothing. There are no ripples in the pond. As far as I can tell, we're the first starship to have flown here in centuries."

Marco rose from the table, unable to stomach the dry crackers any longer. Frustration welled in him. After all this--

fleeing the marauders on Haven, defeating them in the forests of Haven, flying through the wormholes and on the back of starwhales--only to find nothing? Had this been only a wild goose chase?

How can it end like this? he thought.

He left the galley, walked past the lounge, and entered the crew quarters. His fingers shook.

We failed you, Addy. We failed Earth. We failed everybody.

And he could feel it--that black hole watching him. Mocking him.

He turned toward the porthole. He gazed outside into space. The asteroids and dust were lazily orbiting the black hole, hovering just outside the event horizon. Marco focused his eyes on his reflection in the window. He saw a man who was still young, only twenty-six, yet had eyes that were much older. In many ways, like Keewaji, he had aged too quickly, already felt like an old man. Tired. So tired. His eyes were sunken. His brown hair was limp. Where was the eighteen-year-old boy who had made love to Lailani in the tent, who had laughed with his friends, who still believed in a future? That boy had died in the mines of Corpus. Since then, only a ghost had walked in his shoes.

And as Marco stared, it seemed to him that a ghost face rose in the darkness, overlaying his reflection, forming a pale mask like the kabuki mask the girl had worn in Haven. He blinked and narrowed his eyes, refocusing.

He took a step back.

"What the hell?"

An asteroid floated just outside, and a face was engraved onto its surface--right behind Marco's translucent reflection.

He rubbed his eyes and blinked. It was still there. A face carved into the asteroid. A human face. A face startlingly similar to his own. It must have been a kilometer wide.

Just a case of pareidolia, he told himself. The human instinct to see faces in things. Like the face on Mars people sometimes saw.

Yet this face ahead seemed different. Too well-defined. It had been carved by intelligence, not just a random formation.

"Why does it look like me?" he whispered.

The door banged open.

"Marco!" Lailani rushed in. "Marco, hurry! To the lounge!"

He spun around toward her. "Did you see the face too?"

"What face?" She reached toward him. "Hurry, there's something wrong with Keewaji!"

Marco ran.

They raced through the ship and back into the lounge. Keewaji lay on the floor by the jukebox. Captain Ben-Ari sat beside him, cradling his head in her lap, stroking the elderly alien's hair.

Marco approached slowly. He crouched by them. "How are you feeling, Keewaji?"

The old Nandaki blinked rheumy eyes. He clasped Marco's hand. He spoke through a mouth in one of his other four hands.

"I am ready, Master Marco," he whispered. "I am ready for my greatest adventure."

Ben-Ari stroked his hair. "Won't you stay with us longer, Keewaji?"

"My time has come," the alien said. "I have lived for many days. I am ready to sail into the great beyond, to join my ancestors."

Marco tightened his grip on Keewaji's hand. "You can't leave yet! Stay with us longer! Until we can take you home." His eyes dampened. "Don't die here in space. You deserve to be among your people, in your forest. Fight it! Live!"

Keewaji gazed at him, peace in his eyes. "Young Master Marco. Yes, you are young. You always seemed so ancient to me, but I realize now. How young you all are. Yet I am old, by the measure of my people, though I am only five months old to you. For my people, that is a ripe old age. I do not regret dying here, kind masters." Light filled his eyes. "I have lived to see great wonders! I fought the Night Hunters with heroes from Earth. I sailed in a great ship to the stars. I found the Tree of Light and traveled along its paths. I rode upon the mythical starwhales, and I gazed upon the great portal to the worlds beyond." His tears fell. "I am so blessed. So blessed to have seen such wonders. So blessed to die among such dear friends."

Kemi and Lailani approached, knelt, and each held one of Keewaji's hands. Ben-Ari kept cradling his head, stroking his long white hair.

"It has been an honor," the captain said. "*Shalom*, friend."

"*Paalam*," Lailani whispered, saying farewell in her own language.

"Goodbye," said Marco. "Goodbye, my dear friend."

Keewaji smiled, tears flowing. "My friends . . ."

His breath faded. His eyes closed.

They did not know his customs. They did not know much about his faith. But for most of his life, Keewaji had been a warrior. Perhaps he had worn no uniform, had carried no weapon, but he had fought against the marauders, those he had called the Night Hunters. They gave him a military funeral, and Ben-Ari spoke of his courage, his kindness, his wisdom. They sent his body out into the darkness, a burial in the cosmic ocean.

"I'm not a religious man," Marco said softly as they gathered in the airlock, watching the shrouded body float away. "But I've seen such wonders this year--ships and wormholes and creatures I would have thought impossible. So today, I will believe. That Keewaji found his way to his afterlife. That he's happy. I'll miss him."

After the funeral, Marco told his companions about the face on the asteroid. They managed to track it again, and they all agreed that it looked eerily unnatural--and eerily like Marco. That memory resurfaced, a nightmare from the mines of Corpus: finding a ball of flesh that had stolen his DNA, had grown his face. Yet this asteroid didn't seem menacing. The engraved face was serene.

"It might all just be a coincidence," Ben-Ari said. "We humans evolved to seek out faces, to recognize them on stones, landscapes, even grilled cheese sandwiches."

Lailani licked her lips. "Mmm, cheese . . . You're torturing me, Captain."

Kemi nodded. "Yet we all agree this face looks *too* good."

"Well, I am rather handsome," Marco said, incurring groans. He looked back outside at his likeness. "It's a sign."

"It's a sign that you have a massive head?" Lailani said.

"My head is perfectly normal!"

"Uh huh," Lailani said. "Is that why you could barely find any helmet to fit you?"

"We can't all be the size of a tadpole like you," he said. "But no, this isn't a sign that I have a large head with a very large brain. I think . . ." He gazed out the porthole again. "It's a sign from them. From whoever flew the Ghost Fleet. They knew we would come. They left it here for us."

"They should have carved Kemi's face," Lailani said. "She's the pretty one."

"I am not!" Kemi said, bristling, then bit her lip. "Oh. I mean--thank you."

Marco gazed out at the black hole. He spoke softly. "Through dangers untold and hardships unnumbered, I have fought my way here . . ."

"Shakespeare again?" Lailani asked. "Nietzsche?"

"Jones and Henson," Kemi answered, a soft smile on her lips. "*Labyrinth*. Our favorite movie."

Marco looked at her. Kemi smiled back. They both remembered those times in their youth.

Marco turned toward his captain. "Ma'am, I suggest the following course of action. We fly into the black hole."

They all started talking at once.

"You're crazy!" Lailani said.

"The forces would rip our ship apart!" said Kemi.

"Marco, no," said Ben-Ari. "That would be suicide."

Marco waited, listening as they kept objecting, until they all quieted down.

"Has anyone ever flown into a black hole?" he said.

"Well, no," Kemi confessed. "At least, not in any story I ever heard in flight school. But . . . Marco, this isn't like a wormhole. Wormholes are portals to other locations in the galaxy. A black hole is an immense funnel of gravity. It would crush us like a tin can."

"Except this isn't an ordinary black hole, is it?" Marco said. "It didn't exist when Lailani was studying this place. And it has a sign here. My face, carved like a celestial Mount Rushmore. That's an *invitation*. Remember what Keewaji said? In his people's stories, this is the great emptiness. A passageway to a world beyond. He was right about the Tree of Light and about the starwhales. I say we listen to him now too. We fly into the darkness. Maybe we'll find what we seek beyond."

"And if you're wrong?" Kemi said.

"Then we die painlessly," Marco said. "Better than starving to death here without a working warp drive."

"We could call the whales back," Kemi said. "We don't have to die here."

Marco took her hands in his. He looked into her eyes. "Kemi, the marauders have taken over the world. The world we love. And they have Addy. Sometimes we have to take a leap of faith. Sometimes we just have to believe."

She looked down, then back into his eyes. She nodded.

They all stepped onto the bridge. Kemi sat at the helm. The black hole loomed before them.

Captain Ben-Ari stood with her back to the viewport, and she spoke to them.

"Eight years ago, I was an ensign, fresh out of Officer Candidate School. I had never commanded soldiers in battle. You were all new to the military, frightened teenagers, homesick. And I tried to mold you into soldiers. I tried to teach you strength, dedication, and honor. But you were the ones who taught me these things, and for eight years, it has been my honor to serve with you. You followed me through fire at Fort Djemila, into the darkness in Corpus, and into the searing inferno on Abaddon. You followed me thousands of light-years away from home. And every step along the way, I've been more awed by your wisdom, your ability, and your human spirit. You make me proud to be human."

Marco stood up. He saluted his captain. His voice was hoarse. "It has been our honor, ma'am."

Lailani stood up too, and she too saluted. "An honor, ma'am. I came to you a broken girl, scars on my wrists, suicidal." Her voice cracked. "You saved my life, ma'am. You showed me what a strong woman looks like. I will follow you anywhere."

Kemi too rose and saluted. "Since I was but a youth, you have been my beacon, my lodestar. I will follow you always, my captain. To hell and back."

Ben-Ari smiled at them, blinking her damp eyes. "Kemi Abasi, my brave lieutenant, my swift pilot. Lailani de la Rosa, my fierce little warrior and my eyes in the darkness. Marco Emery, my conscience in a cosmos gone mad. You are all my soldiers. You are all my friends. You are all my brothers and sisters." She returned the salute. "It is likely that we fly now to our deaths. We must take our leap of faith. Will you follow me one more time?"

They all nodded.

"Now and always," Marco said, and Kemi and Lailani repeated his words. "Now and always."

Kemi returned to her seat and placed her hand on the accelerator. "Together?" she said.

Marco placed his hand over hers, and she smiled up at him. Lailani placed her hand atop his, and finally Ben-Ari added her hand too.

"Together," the captain said.

They pressed the accelerator.

The *Marilyn* shot forward, scattered luminous space dust, and flew into the black hole.

CHAPTER TWENTY-NINE

The Resistance rolled down the highway, heading to war.

The ruins of the world spread around them. Their drums boomed, echoing across the devastation.

They were survivors. They were haggard, wounded, roaring for triumph. They were rebels. They were humans.

This was their finest hour.

They did not bother to mask their arrival; their enemy's ears would hear their vehicles from afar. They announced their charge with howling throats, with roaring engines, with blasting stereos. Men stood atop armored vehicles, savage, shirtless even in the cold, beating mighty drums. Riders roared forth on motorcycles, crying out for war, firing into the air to herald their assault. Armored trucks rumbled, heavy metal thundering from their speakers, and the world trembled under their bass. Six tanks stormed along the flanks, warriors standing on their roofs, chanting and raising their fists. Above the force, loudest and fiercest, flew their three assault helicopters, loaded with missiles and bullets.

The Resistance. Seven hundred warriors collected from across the desolation. The pride of humanity.

You might be up there in space, Marco, gallivanting around, Addy thought. *But down here in the muck, this is true Earth might.*

She rode at the vanguard on her motorcycle. An assault rifle hung across her back, two pistols and several grenades hung from her hips, and her pouches were stuffed with ammunition. Each of her leather boots hid another pistol and knife.

Strapped to her thigh was her most precious weapon: the marauder tooth. She had knocked it out from Orcus's mouth. She had used it to slay her first marauder. She had used it to cut herself free from the web in the slaughterhouse. More than any rifle or gun, this tooth signified her might. She had fashioned it a hilt, and she bore this ivory sword like a knight of old.

And like a knight, she wore her armor. A helmet covered her head, painted with a snowy dragon. A bulletproof vest encircled her torso, and she had painted a blue circle in its center, symbol of Earth. From her motorcycle rose her flag: a blue circle in a black sky.

I am a knight, she thought. *This motorcycle is my horse. The marauder tooth is my sword. And my coat of arms is the blue circle of Earth.*

"For Earth!" she cried, fist raised.

Behind her, her army answered her cry. "For Earth!"

Addy reared on her bike, pushed down on her throttle, and roared forth. Behind her, the trucks, Jeeps, Humvees, and tanks followed, and above the choppers thundered. Clouds of dust rose around them and the earth itself shook.

I flew to battle with a hundred thousand starships, Addy thought. *I stormed to war with millions of soldiers. But here, this army, these seven hundred--this is my greatest battle. This is my army. This is my hour. This will be Earth's greatest victory.*

Ahead she saw it, spewing its foul smoke on the horizon.

The slaughterhouse.

It rose before a backdrop of Toronto's shattered, decaying skyscrapers. It rose from a field of ice and blood. It rose at the end of their path and the beginning of their war. It rose like it had risen a thousand times in Addy's nightmares, a place of death, of breaking apart, of man reduced to a beast, of humanity made into meat. There it was, behind those walls and barbed wire. The place of all her terror. The place where her courage would blaze like a thousand suns.

She raised a megaphone to her lips.

"Armored vehicles, flare out!"

At her sides, the armored Jeeps and Humvees rode off the road. They charged across the fields, raising dust and snow, a hundred machines of war, all topped with machine guns and grenade launchers and howling men.

"Tanks, stay right behind me!" Addy cried.

Behind her, she heard the war drums beat in approval.

"Motorcycles, with me!" Addy looked around her at her other riders. Fifty men and women. She recognized Steve by the tiger drawn on his leather jacket. He rode up toward her and stayed near.

"Stay strong, my friends!" Addy cried. "You are men and women of the Resistance. You are human. You will win! For war, for glory, for Earth!"

"For Earth!" they howled. "For Earth!"

"Earth rises!" Addy shouted, and they echoed her cry. "Earth rises! Earth rises!"

And ahead, from the slaughterhouse, the enemy stormed forth to meet them.

The creatures from the darkness. The apex predators from the shadows. The monsters from their deepest nightmares. Creatures of claws, of fangs, of eternal hunger. The marauders.

There were hundreds.

For an instant--an eternal instant that nearly shattered her--terror flowed over Addy.

We're going to die. We're all going to die.

She kept charging forth.

She narrowed her eyes.

She unslung her rifle from across her back and yanked back the cocking handle.

So I die fighting.

"This is Earth, bitches," she whispered and pulled her trigger.

Her bullet blasted out. Across the distance, hundreds of meters away, a marauder screamed and fell down dead, the bullet in his eye.

With deafening sound and furious fire, the wrath of humanity blazed forth.

The missiles from the choppers. The tanks with their cannons. The soldiers, screaming, firing their machine guns. The riders of steel, hot guns in hand. The shells and bullets stormed forth and slammed into the enemy.

The aliens screamed.

The aliens tore apart.

The aliens scattered their blood and organs and jagged limbs across the weeping land.

A missile slammed into a line of marauders, and a dozen of the creatures flew, limbs ripping off. A tank fired into their formation, pulverizing several marauders, burning others. Bullets slammed into the charging beasts, shattering the skulls on their backs, denting their hardened skin, finding eyes and sending the creatures careening across the road and fields.

We can do this, Addy thought. *We can win.*

"Onward!" She raised her rifle overhead, storming forth on her motorcycle. "To the gates! To the--"

With hundreds of shrieks, the marauders answered the assault.

Their webs shot out, the strands like steel cables. One strand caught a motorcycle at Addy's side, lifted it into the air, and hurled it at a Jeep. The vehicles slammed together, crushing rebels, and blood splattered before the machines exploded. Another web caught a helicopter, yanked it down, and the blades whirred, screeched, cracked, and the helicopter fell and men screamed. The helicopter tried to rise, belched out smoke, and another web pulled it down onto the road. Jeeps and a motorcycle slammed into the helicopter, and blades tore free and lopped the head off a rider and blasted open a truck. Missiles fell from the helicopter's hardpoints, skidded across the road, and one fired, and Addy screamed and ducked as it whizzed over her head. Another missile whizzed across the field, spraying fire, and slammed into a tank. The massive vehicle--all one hundred tons-- tore apart, and men crawled out from it, burning, screaming, falling to the road.

"Onward!" Addy cried. "To the gates!"

The marauders raced toward them, howling, casting forth more webs. A web shot toward her, and Addy yanked her handlebars, narrowly dodging it. She loaded another magazine, kept firing. Ahead, a hundred marauders or more rose from the road, flying with mechanical wings of metal, spewing webs and venom at the charging rebels.

Great, Addy thought. *So they can fly now.*

A web caught another motorcycle near Addy. The driver, a black-haired girl with sleeves of tattoos, screamed as her bike overturned, as her head cracked open on the pavement. Marauders leaped from above, shrieking, claws extended, fangs like swords.

One marauder crashed into a Jeep, shattering the windshield, and tore the driver apart. Another alien landed on a motorcycle, claws lashed, and the rider's limbs scattered on the road behind him, tripping another motorcycle.

Her motorcycle roaring, Addy wove around the creatures. They were everywhere now, racing across the road, leaping from the fields, descending from above. The bullets kept ringing out. Machine guns pounded the enemy, and searing metal flew everywhere. Flamethrowers blasted forth their fury. Another tank fired, and a hole opened on the road. The two remaining helicopters were raining down their vengeance. Corpses piled up on the roadsides, both of marauders and humans. Vehicles burned, another one falling every moment.

Steve never left her side, firing grenades from his launcher, tearing marauders apart. A Humvee shattered, flipped over, and slammed down ahead of Addy in a burning tangle of metal. She scooted around it, burning rubber.

"Keep going forward!" Addy shouted through her megaphone. "Charge to the gate!"

They were close now. Four kilometers away, maybe three. The barbed wire walls rose ahead, the gate between them, topped with skulls. She could smell it now, even through the gunpowder. The stench of it. The slaughter.

If Hell is a real place, we're riding toward it, Addy thought.

A marauder flew toward her on mechanical wings. She fired her rifle, ripping through its engines, and it came crashing down toward her, claws lashing, jaws snapping. Addy veered her motorcycle aside, let a grenade drop, and the marauder tore apart. She ducked and swerved, dodging the flying limbs. A hot piece of shrapnel kissed her leg, cutting and instantly cauterizing the wound. Another scar. Another memento of who she had become.

They were almost at the slaughterhouse. Moments away. The gate rose, and through its bars, Addy could see them. Thousands of them. Human prisoners, naked, beaten, dying. Calling out to her.

I'm coming.

Addy stormed forth, tears in her eyes.

I'm here.

And from beyond the barbed wire and concrete walls, they rose.

Addy stared, her hope vanishing like a candle in a storm.

Ravagers.

Ten ravagers, the fighting starships of the enemy, shaped like clawed hands with the fingertips touching. Slowly, as they hovered skyward, their claws bloomed open. Within, balls of plasma crackled.

"Scatter!" Addy shouted.

The inferno blazed forth.

Streams of fire blasted out from the ravagers.

Around Addy, her comrades burned.

Time seemed to slow as the hellfire spread.

Addy rode in a daze. She looked around. She saw them screaming, the men and women of her uprising. A boy. He couldn't have been old enough to shave. A boy running, the fire consuming him like a demon crawling across his back, finally pulling him down. A figure wandering, a girl, her hair aflame, burning, all burning, woven of fire, stumbling around, silent, almost confused as the fire peeled away her flesh. A man crawling, legless. A woman with no face, with no mouth to scream with, reaching out.

The ravagers hovered above, and it seemed to Addy that they grinned, that they were living creatures, goddesses of space, krakens of the dark seas, spreading out their flaming ink and tentacles. That they could see her. That they mocked her. And above them burned the stars.

Addy.

Their voices thrummed through her chest.

Burn with us.

Join us.

Become one with the fire.

She pushed down on the brakes.

Her motorcycle skidded to a halt.

Around her, the men and women ran, the fire engulfing them. Around her, the corpses and vehicles burned.

Addy stared up at them. They hovered in a ring above her head, ten of these demons of metal claws and flaming hearts.

And she spoke to them.

"No."

She stepped off her motorcycle. She shook her head.

"No."

She attached a grenade to the launcher on her rifle. She stared up at the deities of metal and starfire.

"No!"

And she sent up her answer with a trail of smoke and light.

The grenade flew into the flaming maw of one of the creatures, and the ravager tilted, almost graceful, almost beautiful. From inside the fire spread. The alien ship glided and shoved into one of her sisters. They fell together. And the world shook.

In this field of burning corpses, Addy turned back toward what remained of her army. A couple hundred warriors. A handful of vehicles. The greatest army in the world. The pride of humanity.

She stared at them, and she smiled, and she whispered, "Earth rises."

"Earth rises!" they shouted.

Motorcycles reared and roared and charged around her, leaving trails of fire. Helicopters stormed forth, firing their missiles into the maws of the ravagers. The great bomber dived from the clouds, shrieking, as large as the ravagers, and barreled into them in the sky. Three ravagers and the bomber fell together, and the explosions roared, and a mushroom cloud rose, and Addy covered her ears. Dust flew everywhere. She couldn't see. Only smoke, fire, a storm of earth and metal.

She climbed onto her motorcycle. Blindly, she rode through the inferno. She leaped through fire.

It rose ahead, three stories tall, crowned with skulls. The slaughterhouse gate.

Marauders crawled above the archway, the guard towers, the barbed wire walls. They squealed. They cast down their webs. A hundred men ran up to stand around Addy, raised flamethrowers, and blasted out a tidal wave of fire.

Webs burned.

Marauders shrieked and fell through the flames, crashing into men, ripping them apart.

A tank rolled up and stopped beside Addy on her motorcycle. She turned toward it, and she saw Hunt standing in the open gun turret. He still carried his riot shield, the white lion emblazoned upon it.

"A hand?" she said.

Hunt nodded and slapped the top of his tank. "You heard her, boys! Let's knock on the door!"

Addy covered her ears.

The tank fired.

The shell slammed into the slaughterhouse gate, shattering it.

Hunt gestured at the broken tangle of metal.

"After you, madam."

For a moment, Addy sat still on her bike, hesitating. The battle still raged around her, and yet . . .

"Addy, you ready?" Steve rode up to her side, straddling his own motorcycle.

She stared at the shattered gateway. She stared at the last rebels and marauders battling around her. She watched as a grenade launcher took out the last ravager, as the alien starship slammed down onto a field.

"This is too easy," Addy said. "They should have put up more of a resistance."

"Too easy?" Steve's eyes widened. "Addy! They butchered more than half our people! Hundreds died! And we killed hundreds of them." He tilted his motorcycle, reached out, and touched her arm. "Come on, Ads. Together. Let's roll in. Let's save these people."

She stared through the gateway. Smoke was rising ahead. She couldn't see much else. Even the prisoners were hidden from view.

Run, whispered a voice inside her. *Run far from here. Run now.*

She inhaled deeply.

No fear. Be strong. Leap of faith.

"Resistance!" she said. "Follow!"

With a deep breath, Addy rode into the slaughterhouse.

Smoke spread ahead. The place was so quiet. Where were the screams, the shrieks of the enemy? Where were the prisoners?

She slowed down. She rolled through the smoke, gun held before her.

She stopped.

She stared.

Her heart shattered.

Tears flowed down her cheeks.

I'm sorry. I'm sorry.

Hundreds of marauders were crawling forth. On their backs, instead of their ceremonial skulls, they wore living humans.

The human shields were bound with webs, slung across the marauders. Some of the aliens carried two, even three adults, the naked prisoners beaten and bleeding. Other marauders carried bound babies. The enemy approached from all sides, hissing, drooling, covered with their living armor.

At their lead walked a twisted marauder with three eyes and a crown of horns. A rotting, quivering wound gaped open on his side where once a parasitic twin had squealed; only a single twitching limb remained of the deformity. On his back, the alien carried three little girls and one man.

"Orcus," Addy whispered.

The marauder who had kidnapped her from Haven. Who had shoved a feeding tube down her throat. Who had tortured her.

She recognized, too, the bleeding man bound on Orcus's back.

Steve did as well.

"Stooge!" Steve cried.

"Wait!" Addy said.

"Stooge, I'm coming!" Steve shouted again.

"Wait!" Addy shouted.

She climbed off her motorcycle. She stood before the enemy. The hundreds of marauders spread before her in a semicircle. Behind them, she could see the rest of the slaughterhouse. The assembly lines were still moving, the meat hooks still carrying humans to be butchered and packaged.

"Hello, Addy," rumbled Orcus, his voice like bones grinding together. "Welcome home."

"Let them go!" she cried. Soldiers advanced behind her. She raised her hand, holding them back.

"Gladly!" said Orcus. "I can always find more meat. Such a lush planet, bountiful with prey." He laughed, revealing severed heads in his mouth. "I can always hunt more. I will release the livestock held in this facility. We will make a swap. Their lives . . . for yours."

"You son of a bitch!" Steve shouted. He leaped off his motorcycle and made to run forward, but Addy held him back.

She stared into Orcus's eyes.

He grinned at her.

She lowered her head, tears burning, fists clenched.

So here it is. I will not die in battle. But I will die in glory. I will die saving thousands.

She looked back up. Her tears flowed.

I'm sorry, Marco. I'm sorry. I wanted to hold you one last time.

"Release them first!" she said to Orcus. "Let them go, and then I'll come to you. My life for theirs."

Orcus barked a laugh. "No, Addy. No. You do not give us your terms. Come to me now. Come be mine. I will deliver you to Lord Malphas myself, as I vowed to him. Perhaps he will allow me to mate with you before he devours your brain. Once you are in my claws, the livestock will go free. You can trust dear Orcus. I always keep my word."

Addy turned toward Steve, eyes damp.

"No," Steve said. He grabbed her. Tears filled his eyes. "Addy, no."

She embraced him. She wept against his chest.

"Goodbye, Steve. I love you."

"Addy, no," he whispered. "No. We'll fight them together. We'll stop them."

She touched Steve's cheek. She gazed into his eyes.

"We can't," she whispered. "Goodbye. Fight on without me. Always fight. Always know that I lo--"

"Fire!" boomed a voice behind her, and engines roared.

Addy spun around to see Hunt charging forward on his tank, standing on its roof, firing a rifle.

"For Earth!" shouted his men, running forward, firing their guns.

Bullets slammed into the marauders ahead.

Bullets tore through the human shields.

Addy's heart shattered like the gate.

"No!" she shouted. "No! Hold your fire! No!"

But they didn't hear her. Their bullets kept flying. The tanks fired shells. The last helicopter rained down bullets and missiles. The Humvees and motorcycles roared forth, and machine guns blazed.

And they died.

Everywhere, the humans on the marauders' backs tore apart.

Elders. Mothers. Babies.

"Stooge!" Steve shouted.

The battle raged across the slaughterhouse. Grenades flew. A missile tore into an assembly line, scattering corpses. Another missile shattered a wall, and some prisoners fled into the countryside. The great webs burned, and hundreds of captives screamed in the holocaust.

Addy tightened her lips.

She walked through the devastation, humans and marauders dying around her.

She reached Hunt's tank.

She leaped onto the caterpillar track, climbed onto the roof, and approached the hatch. Hunt stood there, his legs inside the tank, his body exposed from the waist up.

"Hunt!" she shouted. "Stand down! I banish you from the Resistance. Leave this place now. You are cast out!"

He turned around in the hatch.

He stared at her. His lips were bloody. He licked them and grinned.

"I think I'll stay," Hunt said. He raised a gun and fired.

The bullet slammed into Addy's chest.

She fell.

She tumbled off the tank.

She hit the ground.

She couldn't breathe, could barely move. Her armor had stopped the bullet, but she was gasping for air. It felt like that bullet had cracked every rib in her chest.

The tank turned around slowly, then came rolling toward her.

A marauder leaped forth. Addy spun, fired bullets, hit its eyes. She spun back toward the tank.

She leaped aside. Hunt's tank nearly crushed her. She ran, and the tank followed. Hunt fired again, and she jumped aside, narrowly dodging the bullet.

She raised her assault rifle and fired in automatic, emptying a magazine at Hunt. He knelt in the turret until her gun clicked, then rose again, firing.

She rolled aside. A marauder leaped toward her. She had no more bullets in her gun. She grimaced, racing away, as bullets blazed from the tank. The marauder died but the bullets kept chasing Addy.

"It's over for you, Linden!" Hunt cried from the tank, rifle in hand. His overcoat blew in the wind, displaying Nazi runes stitched into the leather. "You've always been weak. This is my rebellion now."

The tank spun toward her. The cannon pointed her way.

Addy found herself staring into the massive muzzle.

The tank fired.

She flattened herself on the ground, and the shell flew above her. It exploded against a wall nearby, showering her with bricks. She screamed in pain.

The tank came charging toward her, prepared to crush her against the pile of bricks.

Addy ran. She saw her motorcycle in the dirt, lying on its side. She lobbed a grenade, knocking a marauder back, then leaped onto the bike.

The tank turned toward her.

Addy shoved down on the throttle. Her bike charged forth, raced up a fallen slab of concrete, and vaulted into the air.

Hunt fired his rifle from atop the tank. His bullets hit the motorcycle, not even slowing it.

As Addy flew, her front tire slammed into Hunt, crushing his face, shattering his skull, and knocking his head so far back his neck snapped.

Addy and her motorcycle tumbled.

The world spun.

All was metal, blood, smoke.

She fell off the airborne motorcycle and slammed into the mud.

A second later, the motorcycle landed on her leg, and she screamed.

She lay in the dirt, gazing up in a daze. She was hurt. Maybe badly. Her leg was twisted, and she could still barely breathe. She was bleeding. She wasn't sure from where. The battle still raged around her, marauders and humans dying every second. The world burned. Her vision grew hazy.

We should never have come here. She tried to push off the motorcycle pinning her down, could not. *We should never have gone into space. Never have awoken the terrors that lurk there.* She trembled. *I'm so afraid. Marco, I miss you, and I'm so afraid.*

Deep laughter sounded.

Claws scraped forth.

A shadow loomed, and she saw him there. On his back, Stooge and the three girls were dead.

Orcus licked his jaws, advancing toward her on six clawed legs.

"Now you are mine, Addy Linden."

She struggled, trying to push off the motorcycle. She yowled. She was stuck, her leg pinned beneath the heap of metal. The marauder stepped closer, grinning, and loomed above her. His saliva dripped onto her, sizzling hot, burning her. She screamed.

"So fair . . ." Orcus caressed her cheek with a claw. "You will make a fine mate . . . Once your brain is removed, that is." His jaws widened. "You took one of my eyes. You made me lose my beloved twin. You will pay for your sins, child of Eve. How you will scream!"

Addy stared up into those three black eyes. She saw her reflection in them. She barely recognized herself. Where was the girl she had been, happy, laughing, full of life? She was a wretch. Eyes sunken. Covered in filth and blood. A broken soul. Already dead.

And she thought of Marco, of fighting with him in the tunnels.

She thought of Corporal Diaz, the man who had taught her strength.

She thought of Captain Ben-Ari, the woman who had taught her courage.

"I am a Dragon," she whispered. "I am a soldier. I am a woman." She reached toward the handlebars of the motorcycle pinning her down. "I. Am. Human."

She pressed down on the throttle.

The wheel spun, ripping into her leg, tearing the skin.

The motorcycle roared forward, skidded off her, and crashed into Orcus.

The marauder squealed and fell back, and the motorcycle flew aside. The marauder sneered, three of his teeth shattered. The motorcycle's handlebar had taken another eye; it had snapped off, was still embedded into the socket.

Addy stood up. Her leg was bent, bleeding, a ruin. She stood nonetheless. She raised her assault rifle and loaded another magazine.

She stared into the creature's two remaining eyes.

Orcus screeched and leaped toward her.

Addy fired.

Bullets rang out, hitting another eye, and Orcus slammed into her. They fell together. He clawed madly, ripping at her, shredding her armor. She howled, her blood spilling. They rolled in the mud, and he snapped his jaws, several teeth missing.

"Addy, you will be mine! You will scream for me!"

Out of bullets, out of grenades, she grabbed the hilt of her sword.

She drew her ivory blade--his tooth. The tooth she had taken from him in his starship.

She stared into his last eye.

That eye widened, and at the end, it was full of fear.

With a hoarse cry, Addy thrust the severed tooth, driving it into Orcus's eye and deep into his skull.

The marauder fell, legs twitching.

Raspy words emerged from his jaws. "My beloved . . . my twin . . . I am sorry."

Orcus's head tilted sideways. The creature moved no more.

Addy tied a belt around her thigh, choking off the blood loss. She limped through the devastation, dragging her bad leg. All around her, they lay dead. Hundreds of humans. Hundreds of marauders. The last few claws swung. The last few bullets fired.

The last marauders fell dead.

Across the slaughterhouse they stood. A hundred human rebels, maybe less.

And hesitantly, moving closer, naked and bald--thousands of freed prisoners.

They gathered around Addy. Beaten, brutalized, their bodies pale, their shaved scalps bleeding. They reached out to her, tears in their eyes. Some knelt and raised the guns of fallen warriors. Others tore out the teeth from marauders and raised them as swords. Prisoners and rebels, they all stepped toward Addy. Their eyes shone.

Steve ran toward her. Blood and dirt covered him. He meant to scoop her into his arms, but he paused and paled.

"Your leg . . . Addy, are you all right?"

She looked into his eyes. "They cannot kill me. I am the Snow Dragon. I am human."

A rebel nearby, a young man with eager eyes, raised his gun overhead. "Addy Linden! The Snow Dragon!"

Another rebel raised her rifle. "The Snow Dragon!"

One by one, the others raised their weapons, and soon thousands of hands rose together. Some with guns. Others holding only rocks. Many hands empty. But all eyes gazed upon her. And all voices cried out for her.

"The Snow Dragon! The Snow Dragon!"

Her leg hurt, was fading to numbness. But she climbed onto the tank, and she stood above the crowd. Thousands of them, encircling her, spreading all across the devastated slaughterhouse. And through a hole in the wall, Addy could see it in the distance.

The ruins of Toronto.

The webs draped across the skyscrapers. Plumes of smoke rose.

She stared toward the distance, toward her old home. And she knew he was there. Gazing toward her. Waiting for her.

Lord Malphas.

We will meet soon, Addy thought. *But not today.*

She looked back at the crowd, and she raised her marauder tooth overhead.

"The enemy took our land!" she cried. "They took our children. They took the lives of so many. Today we say: No more!"

They shouted together. "No more!"

"We are the Human Resistance!" Addy said. "We will rise! We will cast off the enemy! Join me. Join me now. Join me here. Join me in rebellion, and together, we will fight them everywhere, and we will be free! For Earth!"

They chanted all around her, a sea of humanity, of courage, of nobility that no enemy could crush. Their voices rolled across the land, and Addy knew that in the distant city, he could hear.

"For Earth! For Earth!"

Addy chanted with them, tears on her cheeks, her weapon held high.

"For Earth!"

The story continues in . . .

Earth Valor (*Earthrise* Book 6)

DanielArenson.com/EarthValor

NOVELS BY DANIEL ARENSON

Earthrise:

Earth Alone

Earth Lost

Earth Rising

Earth Fire

Earth Shadows

Earth Valor

Earth Reborn

Earth Honor

Earth Eternal

Alien Hunters:

Alien Hunters

Alien Sky

Alien Shadows

The Moth Saga:

Moth

Empires of Moth

Secrets of Moth

Daughter of Moth

Shadows of Moth

Legacy of Moth

KEEP IN TOUCH

www.DanielArenson.com
Daniel@DanielArenson.com
Facebook.com/DanielArenson
Twitter.com/DanielArenson

Printed in Great Britain
by Amazon